"You have a very nice smile, Monsieur Kavanagh," Tally said.

"You have a very nice—" He looked pointedly at her chest. She'd bound her breasts, but he'd seen what lay underneath the wrappings. "You still have to pay a price for my saving your cow, Miss Bernard."

"She isn't my cow."

"Seems everything you touch ends up belonging to you." His grin vanished. "Why is that, Tally?"

She faltered under his stare. He put his hands on her hair, slid them down to cup her face.

Mon Dieu. It was truly happening. Not like before, when he'd stolen a kiss just to prove his indifference. There was no indifference in him now. And none in her.

"What will you give me, Tally?" he whispered.

She closed her eyes. "Everything."

SUSAN KRINARD

TO TAME a WOLF

HQN™

ISBN 0-373-77047-2

TO TAME A WOLF

This edition published by arrangement with Harlequin Books S.A.

® and TM are trademarks of the publisher. Trademarks indicated with ® are registered in the United States Patent and Trademark Office, the Canadian Trade Marks Office and in other countries.

www.HQNBooks.com

Printed in U.S.A.

PROLOGUE

Hat Rock, Texas, 1866

THE OLD DRUNK, Charlie, was the one who came to tell Sim his mother was dead.

Others would have known earlier, of course—the madam of the brothel, Evelyn's fellow soiled doves…and any number of clients, respectable and less so, who frequented the Rose of Texas. Gossip traveled fast in a whorehouse.

None of them bothered to pass the tragic news to Evelyn's only son. Charlie came not because he gave a damn about Sim, but because carrying the story made him feel important. More important than a worthless, troublemaking sixteen-year-old tramp.

Sim, standing in the dusty street in front of Hat Rock's pathetic excuse for a bank, heard Charlie's slurred speech without emotion. He'd learned to hide his feelings early on, when he figured out that Ma couldn't be trusted from one moment to the next. Sometimes she cuddled him and called him "my son," but more often she cursed him as the bane of her life, the burden who had ruined her for the better things she deserved.

Sim clenched his fists and walked out of the cloud of Charlie's whiskey-soaked breath. He strolled down the center of Main Street, making the carriages and buckboards and horsemen go around him.

Ma was dead. She'd been going at it a long time, riddled with some kind of wasting disease. But she'd kept working, even when only the lowest clients would take her. And Sim had visited the Rose every day to see if she needed anything from her only kin, if she would accept a little of the money he earned or stole in every petty way he had learned in his years on the street.

On his last visit she'd spat at him. He'd wiped the spittle from his cheek and left, though Madame Rose had tried to bribe him with promises of a hot meal and a free ride after. He'd sworn he wouldn't go back. He'd planned to break his oath this afternoon. He could have said goodbye.

She could have said she loved him.

He laughed, startling some fine lady's skittish horse. Her male escort, a rich rancher decked out like a pimp, spurred his long-legged eastern gelding in front of Sim and slashed the air with his quirt.

"Get out of the street, you savage," he snarled.

Sim tilted back the brim of his ragged hat and looked the man in the eye. The man yanked on the reins. "Filthy beggar," he muttered. "No better than a—"

His horse squealed as a length of heavy rawhide rope slapped down on the animal's well-bred rump. The beast took off like a shot, and the lady's mount plunged after it.

Caleb laughed the way he always did, loud and long. He beat the rawhide against his palm. *"Pelado,"* he scoffed. "Thinks he's too good for the likes of us."

His glance pulled Sim in like a brother's embrace. Besides Ma, he was the closest thing to real kin Sim had. Except Ma had known she was dying and finally told Sim that he had a pa. One even more important than Caleb's.

Caleb stopped laughing and gave Sim a hard stare. "What's wrong with you? Been eatin' leftovers out of Mowbray's rubbish heap again?"

Sim averted his face and headed for the nearest alley. He had a lump in his throat, and he was afraid he might start bawling. Bad enough to do it in front of Caleb, but if anyone else saw…

Caleb gripped his arm. "It's the bitch, ain't it? What'd she do to you this time?"

"Nothing." Sim yanked free and strode deep into the alley, where the shadows made him feel safe.

Caleb knocked Sim's hat off his head. "Liar." He squinted in Sim's face. "Your eyes are all red. She hit you?" Sim shook his head and snatched at his hat. Caleb held it just out of his reach. "I know damned well you'd never hit her back, no matter how much she deserves it."

Sim's heart balled up into a painful knot. "She don't deserve nothing anymore," he said. "She's dead."

Caleb whistled. "Damn." He set Sim's hat back on his head and gently pressed it in place. "Who told you?"

"Charlie."

"Figures." Caleb leaned on the wall and bent one knee, wedging his boot heel against the clapboard. "She didn't leave you anything, did she?"

Trust Caleb to ask that first. He was the one who usually planned their petty thieveries and moneymaking schemes; there was always some little trinket he coveted, some luxury he just had to have, and his father damned sure wouldn't give him the cash. Marshall Smith was as tightfisted as they came, at least with his own family. The whole town knew that Mrs. Smith and her son lived like the poorest Mexicans, while the marshall spent what he earned on himself and the pretty *puta* he kept in a house at the edge of town.

Sometimes Sim wondered if he was better off than Caleb. At least Evelyn hadn't lectured him about the devil and hellfire all day and night like Mrs. Smith. Sim didn't have his friend's big dreams for the future, so he wasn't disappointed.

The only thing he had ever really wanted was forever beyond his reach.

Unless he could find his father.

"You better get to the Rose and make sure your ma didn't leave anything, or one of the other girls'll steal it for sure," Caleb said, kicking the wall. "You have the right to take whatever she had."

A few rags of clothes too big for a wasted body, paint to hide sunken cheeks, a handful of cheap costume jewelry. Sim wanted none of it. But he would go anyway, to make sure Ma had a decent burial. If she hadn't saved enough, he would find the money somewhere.

His nose started to run from the effort of holding back the tears. He pulled out a handkerchief with the uneven initials stitched into the threadbare linen—S.W.K. Simeon Wartrace Kavanagh. Ma had sewn the cloth for him two Christmases ago, when she was feeling uncommonly charitable.

He shoved the handkerchief back in his waistcoat. Ma was better off dead than suffering. He'd wished her gone often enough. Hated her more than half the time. Hated what she was and what she could never be.

"Hey," Caleb said. "I'll make sure you get what's coming to you, don't worry. The ladies know me." He slapped Sim's shoulder. "Now you don't have her to drag you down, you're free. You can leave this stinking town. We can both get out of here and do all that stuff we talked about."

"Finding lost mines and buried treasure?" Sim said. The words cracked shamefully.

"Hell, that's only the beginning. We'll both be rich before we hit twenty. I swear to you, brother, they'll all remember our names."

Caleb would make sure they remembered his. If he couldn't force his father to pay attention to his misdemeanors around town—broken windows and pilfered store goods, mischief grudgingly permitted the marshall's son—then he would find some other way of getting the kind of life he wanted. He would never be like his ma, trying to ignore humiliation and poverty by believing worldly goods were the paving stones to hell.

No, Caleb would take everything he could beg, borrow or steal, and he'd never look back.

"C'mon," Caleb said, pulling at Sim's faded flannel shirt. "Let's go put the old bitch in her grave."

Sim stiffened. "Don't," he said softly. "Don't call her that again, Caleb."

"Or what?" Caleb laughed. "You remember when we met? You were bawling behind the livery stable because your ma beat you and called you her ruination. She said she'd wished she'd gotten rid of you before you were born."

"You think I don't remember?"

"I cried once, when I was six and Ma took a belt to my back to whup the demons out of me. I used it all up then. You still have a little left in you, Sim. Get rid of it. Now the War's over, there's fortunes to be made in New Mexico and Arizona Territory. We got to find them lost Spanish mines and Aztec gold before someone beats us to it." He slapped Sim's shoulder. "We're getting the hell out of this town, and we ain't coming back."

"There's something I got to do first."

"Go find your daddy?"

Sim acted without thinking, seizing the front of Caleb's shirt. "What do you know about him?"

"I told you, the ladies like me." Caleb shrugged him off. "Frank MacLean. One of the richest cattlemen in Palo Pinto county. I'm sure he's just rarin' to acknowledge his long-lost bastard son—if you really are his son."

Sim backed away, striking the wall behind him instead of

hitting Caleb. "Ma told me to find him. It was one of the last things she said to me. She wouldn't have lied."

"Then go. I ain't gonna stop you. Maybe I'll even wait around 'til you get some sense knocked into that hard head of yours."

"Don't do me any favors."

"Hey." Caleb grabbed Sim behind his neck and shook him like a newborn pup. He turned up Sim's palm to display the lumpy scar made six years ago with a dull knife and an oath meant to last for eternity. "We're blood brothers. Nothing can change that. So you do what you gotta do, and then we'll light out of this town so fast even the dust'll catch fire."

Sim almost smiled. Caleb was good at painting pictures with his words, making Sim believe anything was possible. Even a whore's son becoming one of the great MacLeans.

"I gotta go," Sim said. "If I don't come back, you'll know my pa took me in."

"Or you're dead," Caleb said, only half joking. "If they kill you, I'll avenge you right proper, don't worry about that."

Sim pulled his hat brim lower over his eyes. "Why would they kill me?"

But Caleb didn't have to answer. The MacLeans were rich, and also ruthless in protecting their property and their name. Frank MacLean had never come to see Evelyn after Sim was born. He could snuff out an inconvenient trespasser without attracting the slightest notice from anyone purporting to uphold the law.

Deliberately Sim rolled a cigarette, taking special care with the precious tobacco. Caleb lit it for him and rolled his own. They smoked together in silence. Sim crushed the butt under his boot and set off for the undertaker's. Caleb went his own way, but Sim knew all he had to do was whistle and Caleb would be there, right at his side.

If Frank MacLean accepted his bastard son, Sim would try

to bring Caleb in with him. Sim had never believed in fate, but he knew there were only two ways his life could go. If he didn't find a place with his father's family, Caleb would set the course for both of them.

Sim shivered in the afternoon heat and almost crossed himself the way his mother had taught him when he was very young. He didn't think there were saints or angels in heaven who listened to the prayers of people like him. He wouldn't try to pray for himself. But there was no one else to pray for her, and so he would go to the church and light a candle and pretend someone could hear him.

"Hey, kid!" Charlie shouted from the boardwalk of the Cock 'n' Bull Saloon across the street. "She used to be a good lay, your mama." He lifted the bottle in his hand. "Here's to all the whores in Texas. May they never—"

He broke off as Sim turned on his heel and strode toward the saloon. His hand slapped at his hip for the gun that wasn't there, but his expression was weapon enough. Charlie squealed and stumbled through the swinging doors.

Sim's fingers curled around the invisible butt of his imaginary pistol. He couldn't afford a gun. Caleb said he had something about him that worked just as well as a loaded six-shooter for scaring people off—when he chose to use it.

He went to the undertaker's and found that his mother's "friends" at the Rose had paid for her coffin and burial. He didn't go to the whorehouse. He had Evelyn's handkerchief, and that was the only memory of her he wanted to keep.

The next morning he set out for the MacLean spread, perched on a ewe-necked bit of crow bait Ethan Cowell had lent him in exchange for two days' work mucking out the livery stable stalls. The horse returned to town before he did. The doctor pronounced it a true miracle that Sim survived the beating, let alone made it back to Hat Rock on foot.

When Sim recovered enough to ride, he and Caleb stole horses and gear from the livery stable and rode out of Hat Rock so fast that the dust caught fire.

Sim laughed until even the wind was sated with his tears.

CHAPTER ONE

Cochise County, Arizona Territory, 1881

TALLY HATED TOMBSTONE. She hated its dusty streets lined
with saloons and brothels, its crowds of miners and gamblers
and cowboys out for a little "fun," its almost frantic attempts
at respectability.

Tombstone reminded Tally of herself. She was as dusty as
its streets, as false as the bright facades that lured the naive
and reckless into the gambling halls, where fortunes were lost
and won every hour of the day and night. She blended right
in with the more ordinary class of men, and that was exactly
the way she wanted it. No one looked twice at a figure clad
in baggy wool trousers and a loose flannel shirt, or a face
smudged with dirt under a sweat-stained hat.

Miriam, with her dark skin and simple cotton dress, attracted scarcely more attention, and neither did Federico.
People of all races came to the mines or passed through the
deserts and mountains of southern Arizona. Tombstone was
no longer the mining camp of a few years past but a fully in-
corporated city of seven thousand souls, with five newspapers,
its own railroad depot and a telegraph. There was a whole new
world to be won here, a new life to be made by those willing
to work—or risk everything for luck.

Tally was willing to work, but luck was definitely not going in her favor. She dodged a heavy wagon loaded with lumber for some new construction at the corner of Second and Fremont streets. The smell of cheap perfume drifted from the nearest cathouse, temporarily overwhelming the stench of horse droppings, whiskey and unwashed clothing.

If André was here, it might take her days to find him. But Tally didn't know where else to look. Her brother had made arrangements to buy fifty yearlings and two-year-old heifers from a rancher in northern Sulphur Spring Valley, but he should have been back at Cold Creek a week ago. She'd sent Elijah after him at the end of the first week, and now her foreman was missing, as well.

God knew the ranch couldn't afford to lose any hands in the middle of calving season, even if rustlers had run off with half their stock last winter. Bart and Pablito would make do as best they could, but an old man and a ten-year-old boy didn't have the time or strength to handle all that needed to be done.

There was a chance that André had met with some mishap. Apache renegades raided American settlements from time to time, and Arizona was an outlaws' haven. But Tally didn't believe André had run into that kind of trouble. Far more likely that he'd become distracted by the gambling halls and carnal temptations of Tombstone.

Tally sighed and surreptitiously pulled a handkerchief from her pocket, wiping the dust from her mouth. Miriam, whom Tally wouldn't think of sending into the saloons, was off buying supplies in the dry goods store while Federico investigated the establishments that catered to the Mexican traders and miners. That left Tally with dozens of saloons and bordellos to visit. She dreaded the brothels most of all.

For that reason as much as any other, she chose Hafford's Saloon, known for the hundreds of exotic birds painted on its walls rather than for its soiled doves. She walked up to the polished bar and leaned against it like any one of the men.

"What'll you have?" the bartender asked.

Tally considered her limited supply of coins and ordered the smallest drink she could get away with. "Maybe you can help me," she said as the barman slapped the shot of whiskey on the counter before her. "I'm looking for my brother— André Bernard. Blond hair, brown eyes, a few inches taller than me. Have you seen him?"

The bartender looked askance under his bushy gray browns. "You just described 'bout a hundred men who passed through here the past couple of days. I can't remember all of 'em."

"Then perhaps you've seen a black man, very tall…."

"Not as I recall." He scratched his unkempt beard. "Might ask the faro dealer. He always remembers a face."

Tally hid her disgust and downed the whiskey. It would affect her a little, but not too much. She'd learned to hold her liquor those first years in New Orleans.

"Listen, boy," the bartender said with a confidential air of one doing a great good service, "I'd hold off that stuff if I was you. Wait until you're a mite older. And stay out of Big Nose Kate's!" He laughed uproariously at his "joke" and slapped the counter so hard that Tally's empty glass bounced.

A shadow fell over Tally and the bartender. The newcomer seemed very tall in comparison to the stout barkeep—lean and taut with muscle, dressed in the wool pants and coat of a cowman rather than the duds of a miner. His black hat shaded his face, but something in his manner, the way he cocked a hip against the bar and dominated the space around him, alerted Tally's instinct for danger. She paid for her drink and turned to go.

"Hey," the bartender said, grabbing her shirtsleeve. "What name should I give if your brother comes looking for you?"

"Tal," she said, keeping her voice low. "Tal Bernard."

"Good luck."

Tally tipped her hat, but he was already serving the tall newcomer. The skin between Tally's shoulder blades quivered. She walked quickly to the gambling tables and searched out the faro dealer. He looked like a panther about to pounce as she approached, but he was pleasant enough when she explained her mission. A few of the gamblers took pity on the boy and speculated among themselves as the dealer laid the cards on the table.

"I think I seen him," a miner offered. "About so high, curly yeller hair? Saw him at the roulette wheel over at the Crystal Palace, oh, near ten days ago. You say he's your brother?"

Tally nodded, her heart sinking to the soles of her boots.

"Don't think he did too good. Lost a heap o' money. Heard him talk about buying gear and heading into the Chiricahuas to make his fortune." The miner chuckled. "Poor feller. Looked like he might know something about beeves, but mining…" He shook his head. "I'd ask over at the harness shops and livery stables. He'd'a needed a couple good mules, at the very least."

Tally thanked the miner and trudged out of the saloon. André must have gone crazy. He knew that money had to go for cattle or the ranch could fail. And he knew less about mining than she did. If he really had gone to the mountains, it was probably because he was too ashamed to face her and had thought up some cockeyed scheme to recoup his losses.

No, André wasn't crazy, just rash and sometimes thoughtless. She had hoped this time he would prove responsible. She had needed to trust him with the money she'd saved from her marriage, needed him to show that he cared as much about Cold Creek as she did.

She'd expected too much.

Still, reckless or not, André was her brother. He knew what she'd been, and he hadn't turned his back. He was the only family she had left. Even if all the money was gone, she had to find him and bring him home.

Tally began the wearisome rounds of Tombstone's numerous corrals, stables and supply stores. By late afternoon she knew that André had indeed bought a pair of mules and all the appropriate gear, and had set off from Tombstone over a week ago. His likely path would take him east, toward the Chiricahuas, but well north of Cold Creek's little side valley.

Tally muttered a curse she saved for only the worst situations and returned to the stable where she had left the wagon and horses. Miriam and Federico were waiting for her in the shade of the building. Federico looked as though he'd eaten a sour lemon, and Miriam was furiously knitting the shawl she'd begun on the ride to Tombstone. She stopped when she saw Tally.

"Bad news?" she asked softly.

"Bad enough. André gambled the money before he bought any cattle and went back to the mountains with mining gear."

"*Madre de Dios,*" Federico muttered.

"Elijah?" Miriam said.

The worry in her voice revealed far more than her dispassionate face. Tally knew how much she cared for Elijah, and he for her. God help the man if he ever made Miriam cry.

"I can't find any evidence that Elijah was ever in Tombstone," Tally said.

"He's been gone a week," Miriam said, crumpling the shawl between her graceful hands.

"He may be looking for André in the Valley. It's a big area to cover." Tally pushed back her hat and blotted the perspiration from her forehead. "We can't afford a hotel tonight. We'll sleep in the wagon and decide what to do in the morning—if you don't mind bedding with the horses, Rico."

The Mexican shrugged. "What will we do tomorrow, *señorita?*"

"I can find him for you."

Tally whirled to face the man from Hafford's—the one who had made the uncharacteristic shiver race down her spine. His back was to the sun, so she still couldn't make out his features. But his height was a dead giveaway, and his voice, deep and rough, made her think of dark alleys and smoking guns. He was what the girls at La Belle Hélène used to call a "long, tall drink of water." Tally's mouth had suddenly gone very dry indeed.

She held her ground, staring up into the shadows of his eyes under the black hat's brim. "Who are you?"

"Someone who has what you need." He angled his head so she could see that the slitted eyes were the palest gray tinted with green, nestled in a web of wrinkles carved by sun and wind. His hair was a brown so dark as to be almost black. No single element of his face could be called handsome, yet the overall effect was one of compelling strength and inner power. Few women would fail to look at him twice.

"You followed me here," Tally said.

"I heard you was looking for your brother," he said, glancing over her shoulder at her companions. Federico took a step forward, compelled against his mild nature to assume the role of gallant protector. "Call your man off. I mean you no harm."

"It's all right, Rico," she said, never taking her gaze from the stranger's. "Why do you think you can help us?"

The man drew closer, crowding Tally up against the wall of the livery. She dodged neatly, keeping her distance. He smelled of perspiration, as everyone did in the desert, but it was not an unpleasant odor. In fact, he smelled different from any man she'd met. He moved easily, smoothly, like a puma or a fox. But he didn't offer a threat, and if he wore a gun, it was well hidden under his coat.

"My name's Sim Kavanagh," the man said. "I heard your brother ran off to the mountains after losing big at the Crystal Palace. They say he's a tenderfoot who wouldn't know a pickax from a shovel, so I figured—"

"André's no tenderfoot. We have a ranch on the other side of Sulphur Spring Valley. He—" She wasn't about to confess André's irresponsibility to this man. "He has dreams, sometimes," she finished awkwardly.

Kavanagh narrowed his eyes. "He's your older brother? Sounds like you look after him. He gamble away all your money?"

Tally bristled. "What is your interest in my brother, Mr. Kavanagh?"

"I was a scout for the army. I know all the ranges—the Dragoons, Chiricahuas, the Mules. Tracking's what I do. And right now I need a job."

His confession startled Tally into silence. A man like this Sim Kavanagh wasn't the type to admit such a need any more than she was. She examined him more closely. His clothing, though of good quality, was much worn and patched at the seams. He'd been down on his luck for some time…or perhaps he was simply a scoundrel on the run. Surely even an outlaw wouldn't consider what they had worth stealing.

Federico appeared at her shoulder. "How do we know you are what you say you are, señor? How do we know you are good at what you do?"

Kavanagh shrugged. "I'm willing to take half pay before, half after your brother's found."

"I can't pay much," Tally said. "You'd do better to look elsewhere for employment."

"When your belly's empty," Kavanagh said, "even a few pesos look pretty damned good. You got supplies?"

This was moving much too fast for Tally. She didn't trust

men. That was the principle tenet of her life. "We can't be sure he went into the Chiricahuas," she said. "I sent my foreman to look for him, but he hasn't returned, either."

"Soon as I leave town, I'll be able to tell which direction your brother rode—and your range boss, too, if he was in Tombstone," Kavanagh said with an offhand conviction that brooked no argument. "Your brother'll be headed east on the road to Turquoise if he's making for the Valley. You pay me two dollars now and give me directions to your ranch, and I'll deliver your brother within the next two weeks."

Tally laughed. "Two dollars is your idea of half pay?" She turned her back on Kavanagh, and ice ran up and down her spine. Ice like the color of his eyes. "If I hire you, it's one dollar now and one when you bring André back. Alive."

Kavanagh also laughed, and the sound wasn't pretty. "He have a bounty on his head?"

"No. And I might as well tell you that he can't have much money left himself, so robbing him won't do you much good. As you said, he can't tell a shovel from a pickax. If he found anything worth mining, it would be a miracle."

Federico laid his hand on her arm in warning. Kavanagh barely shifted, but Tally was aware of the tracker's movement as if he had been the one to touch her.

"You don't think too highly of me, do you, boy?" he said with a faint smile. "What taught you to be so suspicious so damned young?"

Life, she wanted to answer. *And men like you.* She turned and met his cold eyes. "I don't know you," she said. "I don't know if anything you say is true. I could spend another day asking around town for references, but I don't want to lose any more time."

"I give my word that I'll do exactly as I say or forfeit the money."

His word. A man's word meant as little to her as a snap of her fingers, but Kavanagh's gaze held so steady that she began to believe him. Those eyes...

She shook her head to clear it. "There's only one way I'll hire you, Mr. Kavanagh, and that's if I go with you."

"I work alone."

She ignored him. "Federico, you take Miriam back to the ranch and wait. Maybe Elijah and André will turn up while I'm gone."

Federico's black brows furrowed above his brown eyes. "No, seño—no, Mr. Bernard. I will not leave you alone with this man."

"You don't think I'm afraid?" She smiled at Kavanagh. "What could Mr. Kavanagh do to me, Rico? Steal a few dollars and my horse?"

Kavanagh snorted. "You ain't coming with me, boy."

"I am, or the deal's off." She pulled a coin from her wallet and tossed it in the air, catching it in one hand. "One dollar now, one after, and I go with you. Take it or leave it."

She expected Kavanagh to leave it. She could see in his eyes how little he liked being ordered about, and there was a quiet menace simmering under the calm, cool air he affected. She was a little afraid. If he found out she was a woman— and he very well might, with them traveling together...

Zut. There wasn't a thing he could do to her that hadn't been done already. And she had her .44 hidden under her coat. She was prepared to shoot if any man touched her against her will, and the law would be on her side once they knew she was a woman. At least as long as they didn't know what kind of woman.

"You drive a tough bargain, kid," Kavanagh said gruffly.

"But I'm making one thing clear. If you can't keep up with me, if you fall behind, you're on your own, and I still get my money for delivering your brother."

Tally nodded. "I agree." She waited to see if he would offer his hand, and when he didn't, she bucked up her courage and offered hers. "My name's Tal Bernard."

He hesitated, then clasped her hand hard enough to squeeze the bones. The feel of his rough skin didn't repulse her as much as she expected. She pulled her hand away, flexing her fingers behind her back, and tossed him the coin. He caught it so fast that she didn't even see the gesture.

"We leave at dawn tomorrow," he said. "You can tell me more while we're riding."

"What about supplies?"

"I have my own. You have a bedroll and rations?"

"Enough for a few days."

"Don't bring too much. It'll weigh the horses down."

"I'll meet you at the south end of town tomorrow, Mr. Kavanagh. I have business of my own tonight."

His lip curled in a way that suggested he knew what business she'd be about. "Don't get too worn out, kid. I ride fast and hard."

"I'm overwhelmed by your concern," she said.

He leaned close, and she noted that his breath held not even the slightest taint of alcohol. "You talk mighty pretty, boy. Schooled nice and proper, I'll bet. But all the fancy education in the world won't help you out here."

You're wrong, she thought. *There are certain kinds of education that are invaluable in a place like this.* "Dawn. Tomorrow," she said, dismissing him. "Good night, Mr. Kavanagh."

He backed away, drawing his hat brim down over his eyes. A moment later he was gone. Tally let out her breath and met Miriam's gaze.

"What do you think?" she asked her friend.

"Dangerous, for sure, but I think he was telling at least some of the truth." Miriam looked down the street the way Kavanagh had gone. "You be real careful, Miss Tally. Real careful."

"It is not good," Federico put in.

"It has to be done. You know I won't take any chances."

"No chances," Federico grumbled. *"Ay, Dios!"*

"You just see that Miriam gets back to Cold Creek."

"I'll pray for you and Mr. André," Miriam said. And Elijah, but she didn't need to say it.

"Thank you, Miriam." Tally went to see the stable owner about staying the night and checked on the horses. She, Miriam and Federico shared fresh bread Miriam had bought at the bakery and a wedge of cheese, along with the jerky they'd brought from Cold Creek. Federico bedded down in a pile of clean straw, while Miriam and Tally lay rolled in blankets in the wagon bed.

At cockcrow the next morning, Federico harnessed the wagon horses. He and Miriam set out on the rough fifty-mile ride home, while Tally took Muérdago, her roan, and rode to the southern edge of town.

Kavanagh was waiting for her. He looked like Death himself, silhouetted against the lightening sky, the rolling, scrubby hills and mountains behind him. Tally hesitated only a moment and then urged Muérdago to join him.

She had a feeling that she would need every prayer Miriam could send her way.

CHAPTER TWO

SIM WATCHED THE SLENDER RIDER trot up the hill, admiring her graceful posture and firm seat. He didn't make a habit of admiring women—with one notable exception—but he had to give this one credit for the guts to pose as a man and the skill to pull it off.

Of course *he'd* known she was female the moment he stood beside her at Hafford's Saloon, and that was after he'd heard someone named Bernard was searching for a brother called André. He'd followed her at a distance through the streets of Tombstone, waiting for the right moment to get closer and hear the full story. It seemed too lucky that he'd located his prey so easily, but here she was, just where Caleb had told him to look.

Caleb had mentioned that André had a sister who'd lived with him in Texas, but nothing Caleb said had suggested she was vital to Sim's mission. What was her name…? Chantal. A handle as fancy as her speech. He rolled the name around his tongue, disliking the taste of it. He preferred the name she'd given herself: Tal.

He didn't trouble himself wondering why she disguised her sex. She gave off a powerful impression of fearlessness—even he had been hard pressed to sense her unease—but she must be pretty damned afraid of something. Afraid, and yet confident enough to keep anyone from looking too close at what lay beneath the mask.

He had a suspicion that she cleaned up a lot nicer than her outward appearance indicated. Her features under the grime were strong but just a little too delicate for a boy, her lips full, her eyes the color of coffee lightened with fresh cream and flecked with crystals of sugar. She must have a figure under those baggy clothes. But she was only a means to an end, unimportant to him except as a guide to André.

Likely she didn't know anything about the map or she would be a helluva lot more suspicious than she was. She didn't have any idea why André would have gone into the Chiricahuas outfitted for prospecting. But if André had told her about the treasure, Sim would learn soon enough. Meanwhile, he would let her keep pretending as long as it served his purpose.

He nodded to her as she drew her mount alongside Diablo. A wisp of blond hair had escaped from under her hat, the strand no longer than a boy's might be. She tucked it back with a gesture both artless and impatient. Her roan sidled, and Diablo snapped at the gelding's flank.

"Your horse has an unpleasant disposition," she remarked.

"Just like me," he said. "You ready?"

"Lead on."

He turned toward the east and broke Diablo into a gallop, racing down the slope of the dusty miners' road pointing toward the Dragoons. Diablo had something to prove and lit full out, leaving Tal and her gelding to choke on his dust. But she was game for the contest. In a few minutes her roan was neck and neck with Diablo. What Sim glimpsed of Tal's profile was grimly unamused. When Diablo had worked out a little of his spite, Sim reined him in and slowed to a steady lope.

Tal flashed him a smile edged with anger. "Trying to get rid of me already?" she said, breathing hard. "Or was that just a test?"

"That's up to you." He noticed that her hat had blown back a little ways. She caught his look and jammed it forward.

"Now tell me about your brother," he said.

She blinked at his sudden change of subject. "What else do you need to know?"

"How familiar is he with the mountains?"

"Our ranch is in the foothills near the south end of the range, in Cold Creek Valley, between the Chiricahuas and the Liebres."

Which meant she and her brother were squatters on land they hoped to claim once the southern Sulphur Spring Valley was surveyed and opened for homesteading under the U.S. land laws. Until they could claim it legally, they had to hold their spread against all comers, including the rustlers who swarmed over the Valley like lice in a miner's beard. Sim's respect for Tal increased.

"This is the first time your brother has shown any interest in looking for ore?" he asked.

"When we lived in Texas, he spoke of getting rich in Arizona Territory. I never—" She paused, darting Sim a wary glance. "I said he was a dreamer."

"And apt to go off half-cocked."

Her lips set in a straight line. "He's young."

"You ain't?"

She shrugged.

"What was he doing in Tombstone?"

"I don't know. He was supposed to be in the Valley, buying stock for the ranch."

"Doesn't sound like you should have trusted him."

She shot him a cold look. "You're not here to judge André, Mr. Kavanagh, only to find him."

Sim scratched the day's growth of new beard on his chin. Tal was defensive about her brother but still naive enough to lead a stranger right to him. She honestly didn't believe André had anything worth stealing. She valued him more highly than he deserved, and Sim couldn't figure out why.

"Your brother's a drinking man," he said.

"Isn't everyone?"

The disdain in her voice almost gave her away. "You talk like an abstainer," he said. "But I saw you take a drink in Hafford's."

"I think better when I'm sober."

"So do I. But from what they say in Tombstone, your brother talks when he drinks. That ain't a wise habit in this country. It's a good thing he don't have nothing to hide...except from you."

"He was ashamed to come home without the money. That's all."

"You sure he planned to come back?"

"I'm sure." But her voice had a little crack in it. She wasn't nearly as sure about anything as she let on. She would ride her heart out to prove herself Sim's equal, but under that tough skin was a weakness he intended to exploit.

He wondered how she would handle their first night together. They would have to make at least one camp between here and the Chiricahua foothills.

"What about this foreman of yours? He any good as a tracker?"

"Elijah was with the Tenth Cavalry, so he has the skill for it. He may very well still be looking in the Valley."

"But you want me to concentrate on your brother."

"Elijah can take care of himself."

Which meant André couldn't. That fit with everything Sim had heard so far.

Once they were well away from the overwhelming scents of Tombstone, Sim dismounted. "You got anything on you that belongs to your brother?" he asked.

She stared down at him, perplexed. "No. Why?"

"Never mind." Sim knelt close to the earth. A hundred horses, mules, oxen and men on foot had passed this way. He located a pair of mules' prints accompanied by the boot marks of a single man.

Sim gathered a pinch of dust and held it to his nostrils. The dirt was infused with a faint but distinct scent that linked this traveler with the woman riding beside him.

"What are you looking for?" Tal asked.

He didn't bother giving her an answer she wouldn't understand. "Your brother came this way," he said, mounting again. "He probably passed through Turquoise. We'll stop there next."

He rode a little ahead of Tal to get her smell out of his nose. The ground began to rise, and the trail turned south to loop around the tail end of the Dragoons. Seventeen miles without shade on a road with so many twists, hills and dips was hardly a pleasant jaunt, especially in the growing heat of the day, but Tal didn't complain. She drank sparingly from her canteen like an experienced desert traveler. Even Sim was glad to catch sight of the Chiricahuas when they finally reached Turquoise.

He knew that Indians had once dug the bright blue rock out of these mountains, but white men were far more interested in the lead, silver and copper they'd found a few years back. The hills were scarred with recent excavation and the discarded trash of human activity. The camp itself was no more than a series of tumbledown shacks, sufficient for the bachelor miners' stark way of life.

One of the shacks was a makeshift saloon of sorts, indicated by the crudely drawn sketch of a bottle on the door. Sim tied his horse to the hitching post and went inside.

The proprietress was a blowsy woman of early middle age and probably the only female within a ten mile radius—possibly the wife of one of the miners, more likely a willing companion to any who could pay. Her establishment was empty of clients. Flies buzzed lazily near the warped tin ceiling. Sim dropped a coin on the long, poorly fashioned table that served as a bar.

"How's business?" he asked.

The woman, whose rouged cheeks were the only bit of color in a face hard and gray as granite, looked him up and down. "Maybe better than it was," she said. She put a shot glass of whiskey down in front of him. The door creaked behind Sim, and Tal walked in.

"You boys lookin' to stake a claim? Ready Mary can help you get started, get you everything you need. Even a little fun." She leered at Sim, and he shoved the whiskey back at her. She drank it herself. "No, you ain't no miner. On your way to more important business, I'd say." She winked at Tal over Sim's shoulder. "Now *he* don't look as if he's done much riding at all. I'll give you a good price, cowboy. And half of that for his turn in the saddle." She laughed hoarsely until she realized that Sim wasn't smiling.

Sim glanced back at Tal. It was difficult to tell if she was blushing under the dust and the tan, but he couldn't mistake the pity in her eyes. Pity for this dried-up husk of a female, who was probably stuck out here because she couldn't compete with the younger whores in Tombstone.

"We're looking for someone," Tal said before Sim could reply. "Maybe he passed this way." She described her brother as she had before, but she wouldn't meet the older woman's avaricious gaze.

"Yeah, I saw someone fitting that description," Ready Mary said, leaning forward to display the sagging bounty of her bosom.

"Did he say anything?" Sim asked, ignoring the view she offered.

"Well, that depends. He did a bit of drinking—not that he

looked liked he'd gone thirsty too long." She wiped out the glass with a dirty towel and hummed under her breath.

Sim plopped down another coin. "What did he say?"

Ready Mary batted her eyelashes. "Well, it was some days back, and my place was crowded—when the miners come down they need their entertainment...."

Sim slapped his palm on the table. The woman jumped and nearly dropped the glass. She glanced at Sim's eyes. "Well, he…he wasn't making much sense. He was talking about someplace called Castillo Canyon, on the west side of the Cherrycows. He was all outfitted up, but everyone knows there ain't no mines there."

"Castillo Canyon?" Sim repeated, holding her with his stare.

"Y-yes." She swallowed, and the sagging flesh of her neck quivered. "What did he do to you, mister?"

"He's my brother," Tal said, grabbing Sim's arm. "Come on, Kavanagh."

Sim let himself be led more out of shock than cooperation. Once outside the saloon he pried her fingers from his arm and led his horse to the nearest trough, clearing away the scum with a sweep of his hand. Tal's horse dipped his nose in the opposite end of the trough, wary of Diablo.

"Never do that again," Sim said quietly.

"What?"

"Touch me like that. Drag me around."

"You didn't have to threaten that woman."

"That whore? She would've robbed you blind if she could." He pulled Diablo away from the water. "What made you think I was threatening her?"

Tal stroked her horse's neck. "Not with words. But she was terrified of you." Tal glanced at him sideways. "The way you looked at her… Do you dislike all women, or just a particular type?"

Sim snickered. "What d'you know about women, boy?"

Tal tightened the gelding's cinch and mounted. "I had a mother," she said softly. "I'll ask you to behave with courtesy and decency as long as you're in my employ. Even to whores."

Sim swung up to Diablo's back. So she expected decency, did she? Was the tough, capable shell a front as false as her male disguise? Let her put on some fancy frock and she'd probably want him to bow and scrape like some dandy from back East.

She would get quite a shock when she realized he saw right through her. He was looking forward to that moment.

"I thought you said you lived in Texas," he said.

"Is that important?"

"Most Texans I know ain't quite so delicate in their ways. But then, you had an *education*."

She chose to disregard his mockery. "You were born in Texas yourself, weren't you?"

"You wouldn't know the town. Whereabouts did you live?"

Immediately she became guarded. "We had a place in Palo Duro country."

She clearly didn't want to continue on that subject. Sim whistled a few introductory notes and then began to sing.

"Well I come from Alabama with my banjo on my knee, I'm goin' to Lou'siana, my true love for to see." He grinned at Tal's dubious expression. "Lou'siana."

"What?"

"That's where you were born."

She frowned. "You hear it in my speech."

"Like I said, I've been all over."

She considered that with a thoughtful tilt of her head. "You are too young to have fought in the war."

"So're you."

"I saw what it did to people on both sides."

"Is that why you left Texas?"

"My brother saw promise in this country," she said. "He imagined what it could become."

A dreamer, just like Caleb. Looking for something he couldn't see with his eyes, never content with what he had right in front of him. Always wanting more.

And exactly how are you different from either one of them?

Sim spurred ahead. Tal caught up, and they left Turquoise and the Dragoons behind them. To the east rose the Chiricahuas, a range of peaks extending north to south across the horizon. The grassy expanse of Sulphur Spring Valley spread almost unbroken for over twenty miles, but Castillo Canyon was nearly another twenty miles north once they'd crossed the plain. Sim didn't intend to push the horses too hard when they'd soon be facing much harsher terrain in the mountains.

Grass grew high where water collected in the draw down the center of the valley. A few hardy ranchers squatted on the richest land beside springs and creeks. Sim knew that the infamous McLaury gang had their own spread near Soldier's Hole, but he and Tal had no cause to pass that way.

"We'll make camp at Squaretop Hills," he said, indicating the cluster of buttes rising up from the valley some fifteen miles to the northeast. "There should be water there for the horses."

He watched Tal carefully, noting the slight stiffening of her shoulders and the jut of her chin. She didn't suggest that they stop at one of the squatter's holdings or the few more established ranches between here and the mountains.

"Do you know Castillo Canyon?" she asked.

"I know where it is," he said. "It's long and deep, cuts right into the high rocks. Hundreds of spires and pinnacles like towers on a castle. That's what gave the canyon its name."

Tal glanced at him with raised brows. "You have some poetry in you, Mr. Kavanagh."

He almost gave in to the urge to spit. "The whore—the *lady*—in Turquoise was right. Ain't no mining up there, at least not on the west slope. Anything else in the canyon that might interest your brother?"

"Not that I know of. I've heard there are settlers there—a family by the name of Bryson. I haven't met them."

"If your brother went that way, they might have seen him."

She nodded, lost in her own thoughts. They left the dwindling trail and rode across washes and gullies, past occasional beeves grazing on the yellowing grama, threeawn and bunchgrass that thrived in the valley. The dry season was on Arizona Territory, but Sim sensed rain coming in the days ahead. With any luck, it wouldn't fall until he had André Bernard right under his nose.

The shadows were growing long when they reached Squaretop Hills. Sim chose a campsite partially shielded by a thick growth of mesquite and unsaddled Diablo. Tal saw to her own horse while Sim sniffed out water running just under a dry creek bed.

He dug out a basin and let the horses drink. Once they'd been rubbed down and staked out for the night, Sim went hunting. He shot a brace of cottontails and brought them back to camp, where Tal had already gathered brush for a small fire. Once again he was grudgingly compelled to admire her practicality, no matter how schoolmarmish she could be when the notion struck her.

Damn all women. Most weren't worth the confusion they inevitably brought with their presence. But as he began to skin the rabbits, he remembered why he'd looked forward to this night.

He tossed the bloodied animals to Tal. They flopped into the dirt beside the new-made fire, and she gave a little jump. Sim smothered a grin of satisfaction.

"I got our supper," he said. "You cook 'em."

She picked up one of the carcasses and examined it with a critical eye. "Not much, is it?" she said. "Well, I'm not very hungry, myself."

Sim shot to his feet. "How many do you want?"

"I said I'm not hungry." She drew a knife and set to work without the slightest sign of squeamishness.

He went to stand over her, hands on hips. "Never heard of any boy who wasn't always hungry."

She wrinkled her nose, sniffed and waved at the air as if she'd smelled something distasteful, and after a moment he realized that her broad gestures were aimed in his direction. "Some things can spoil even the healthiest appetite."

"You ain't exactly a nosegay yourself," he snapped. "If you only knew how bad humans—" He broke off in consternation and quickly recovered. "Would you get your appetite back if I washed up, Bernard?" He yanked off his neckerchief, shed his buckskin jacket and unbuttoned his waistcoat. "I found a little water that ain't too muddy. You scrub my back, and I'll scrub yours."

The anticipated blush turned her face pink under its layer of dust. "That won't be necessary." She focused her attention on the rabbits. "You can make yourself useful by rigging a spit—that is, of course, if *you* have an appetite."

"A man on the trail takes what he can get—even if it ain't the sort of meat he prefers."

Her knife slipped, and he wondered if she'd guessed that he had seen through her masquerade. Sim rigged the spit as requested, letting her do the rest. He leaned back on his elbows a little way from the fire and studied her as night fell over the valley. The moon and stars had the peculiar effect of softening Tal's features, breaching her disguise more effectively than the brightest sunlight.

She knew he was watching her, but she pretended to be

oblivious. "Your supper is ready," she said, stepping back from the fire. "I'll be with the horses."

"You prefer their company to mine?"

She braced her hands on her hips and stared him down. "I don't have to explain myself to you, Kavanagh. Is that clear enough?"

Sim grinned, showing all his teeth. "Very clear, hombre." He crouched by the fire and tore into the meat with gusto. When he'd finished one of the rabbits, he took a tin plate and seldom-used fork from his saddlebags, rinsed them in a freshly dug water hole, and sliced off steaming chunks of meat from the second carcass. He piled them on the plate and went in search of Tal.

She never heard him approach. She'd laid her bedding next to the mesquite where the horses were picketed and now sat cross-legged on the blankets, her hat beside her, raking her fingers through her mass of tangled flaxen hair. It wasn't as short as Sim had imagined, for she wore it in tight braids that fit under the crown of her hat. She had a female's natural vanity after all.

Sim crouched and breathed in the woman-smell of her body. He'd lied when he suggested that she needed a bath. There was nothing unpleasant about her scent. Damn near the opposite. She smelled like a natural female—real and warm, like Esperanza, but different....

The memory of Esperanza cleared his head in a hurry. He set down the plate where even a human would find it and retreated as silently as he'd come. He walked around to the side of the hill, shucked his clothes and Changed.

Even after so many times, he still marveled at the miraculous novelty of the transformation from man to wolf. It was good to run free—free in a way he'd never understood before he accepted his MacLean blood, free as no human could comprehend. Stronger than either man or ordinary wolf, containing the best of both in one agile and powerful body.

He shook his thick brown coat and twitched his large, mobile ears. He raced across the valley floor, rattling the dry grasses and leaping waxy-leaved creosote and saltbush. Wind sang in his fur. Mice scurried under his broad feet, and a startled cow with a young calf stoutly turned to face him as if she could drive him away with her lowered horns and snorts of alarm.

He left her alone. He wasn't after prey this night, and when he hunted cattle it was for some gain other than the filling of his belly. Not that the wolf had ever brought him any profit but this…this shedding of human law, human conscience, human desire.

He opened his senses to their almost painful limits, heard the frantic heartbeats of quail in their nests and smelled the musk of an angry skunk. He sifted one scent from the next and found the place where André Bernard had made camp a few nights ago. The man's trail joined the wagon road that ran parallel to the Chiricahua foothills.

Sim circled back to Squaretop Hills and resumed his human shape and coverings. He washed his face at the water hole and spread his blankets under the open sky.

He was still wide awake when Tal approached, heavy-footed like all humans but more graceful than most. He heard her crouch several feet away, felt her study him as he'd watched her before, with a bewilderment he sensed like a hum behind his eyes.

"You're awake?" she asked.

He rolled over to face her, resting his chin on his folded arms. "I don't sleep much."

She nodded as if that fact were of little surprise to her. Her hat brim cast her face in shadow, but he could see the gleam of her eyes.

"You didn't have to do it," she said in a low voice. "The food, I mean. I can take care of myself."

"Not if you'll pass up a fresh meal on the trail," he said. He sat up, scraping hair out of his face. "You ate it?"

"Yes." She set his cleaned plate and fork in the grass, staying out of reach. "I just came…to thank you."

Those words came hard to her, just about as hard as they did to him. He'd thanked maybe half a dozen people in his life, if that. Never for something so small.

"Go to bed," he said. "I'll watch."

She retreated awkwardly. He heard her lie down and toss and turn on her blankets, trying to get comfortable. He didn't think it was because she was too delicate for the unyielding ground. Something about her scent had changed, and he knew instinctively what it was.

Until now, she'd regarded him as a temporary employee and treated him like one. She'd been aware he was a man about the same way any female would be, sizing him up without even realizing it, cool and objective. But somewhere between his banter about the bathing and her accepting the food he brought, she'd started looking at him different. Not so objective. Not anywhere near so cool.

His body stirred in spite of itself, and he cursed softly. So what if she was interested? She would never admit it. She had some stake in playing the boy, and no reason whatsoever to act on her impulses, given that he was a stranger and she wanted to keep her respectability.

André Bernard had been something less than respectable in Texas. Tal must have known that their ranch in the Palo Duro was a haven for rustlers, but she didn't seem the type to approve of such illegal activities. She made plenty of excuses for André Bernard, but she hadn't been running the Texas spread.

Sim flung his hand over his eyes. Why was he making excuses for her? He didn't give a damn one way or the other, and nothing would come of some fleeting attraction that was about as meaningful as a bull and heifer rutting in a field.

That was all it ever was to him—rutting. Drop your pants and thank you, ma'am. They were always whores, and he always hated himself when it was finished.

He'd only stop hating himself when he took Esperanza in proper marriage, touched that unsullied skin and knew she accepted him. Needed him. Loved him.

Tonight he would dream only of Esperanza. But as he slipped into that netherworld of shades and memories, he saw Esperanza dressed in a soiled dove's garish plumage, turning from Sim with disgust in her eyes. It was Tal Bernard, in robes of virgin white, who held out her arms to welcome him home.

CHAPTER THREE

TALLY BRACED HERSELF on the saddle horn like a raw-faced tenderfoot, trying to stay awake. She'd slept miserably last night, and not because of the meal Kavanagh had foisted on her. It wasn't the first time she'd eaten game roasted over an open fire, and once she'd decided to accept Kavanagh's "gift," she'd been glad for the hearty sustenance after a long day's ride.

It would be more accurate to say that the man himself was the source of her sleeplessness. God knew she hadn't expected him to go out of his way to feed her...and of course she'd wondered with every bite how much he'd seen when he'd left the plate at her bedside.

She sneaked a glance at him from under the brim of her hat. He hadn't shown any new awareness last night or this morning. He still treated her with an offhand indifference that sometimes bordered on contempt, just as she would expect a man like him to behave toward someone he clearly regarded as an overeducated, untried boy.

She'd been careful to pin up every stray lock of hair and powder her face with a fresh coating of dust when they broke camp early that morning. Kavanagh, on the other hand, had washed his face and combed out his dark hair, almost as if he'd taken to heart her rude comments about unpleasant odors.

Ever since she'd met him, Tally had been on the defensive. He hadn't threatened her in any way, but she felt the need to keep proving herself, striking before he struck. And that was absurd, especially when he scarcely bothered with conversation and seemed content to ignore her most of the time. He hadn't spoken after breakfast except to confirm that André had followed the road running north from Turkey Creek to Castillo Canyon.

Yet she knew he was watching her. Maybe he'd guessed her secret and was only waiting for a chance to expose it. But if he could sneak up on her as easily as he had last night, why wait? Perhaps he was simply not interested in the truth, one way or the other.

Dieu du ciel, she should be down on her knees in gratitude that he was so indifferent.

A meadowlark called from the grassland to the east. Tally cleared her throat. Kavanagh glanced at her and away again, turning his head toward the Chiricahua foothills. The mountains seemed an impenetrable wall from the valley, but Tally knew they were riddled with arroyos and streams that shrank to trickles in the spring, drawing abundant wildlife to the shallow pools left behind. Birds of brilliant plumage flashed like jewels in the darkness of the forest. Wolves and pumas roamed the highlands as once the Apaches had done. Miners might dig and scour the earth for precious metals, but the few settlers who'd made homes in the canyons had so far done little to alter the pristine world the Indians had been forced to abandon.

André wouldn't notice the beauty of this land. The promise he saw lay only in the profit to be had.

"*Petit fou,*" she muttered.

"That's French, ain't it?"

Tally welcomed the rough sound of his voice even when it drowned the lark's melodious song. "It is a common enough language in Louisiana."

"I hear it's useful for swearing."

She laughed in spite of herself. He cast her an unreadable look. She wondered if her voice had gone too high and quickly stifled her incongruous amusement.

"Teach me," he said.

"What?"

"We got another ten miles' ride to Castillo Creek," he said. "I figure that ought to be good for a few cuss words."

"I can't imagine that a man like you needs that kind of instruction."

"And what kind of instruction do I need, boy?" He snickered at her silence and flicked the ends of his reins across his muscular thighs. "You know, when we met in Tombstone, I thought maybe you had more experience than your looks suggested. But Ready Mary…like most whores, she has an eye for easy prey. You've never been with a woman, have you?"

He didn't know. Tally swallowed a sigh of relief. "What business is that of yours?"

He shrugged. "Let me give you a bit of advice, hombre. Stay out of saloons and whorehouses. When you find your brother, stick to that little rancho of yours and never trust anyone who offers you a free ride."

"Is that a warning drawn from personal experience?"

An ominous hush fell about him, like a calm before the storm. "Everything costs. You don't get nothin' without paying for it."

"What makes you dislike women so much, Mr. Kavanagh?"

"I only ever met one female who could be trusted as far as a man can spit, and…" His voice softened almost to a whisper. "She's more angel than woman."

"What is her name?"

"Esperanza."

Tally's throat tightened at the awe and tenderness in his words. "Is she the one you love?"

He jerked back on the reins, and his stallion snorted in protest. Kavanagh muttered an apology to the horse and glared at Tally. "I don't talk about her."

"You just did."

"*Ya basta.*"

"As you wish." She rode a little ahead and felt his stare burn into her back like a red-hot brand. She could hardly believe that a man like Kavanagh could love anyone. But there had been no mistaking the look in his eyes and the sound of his voice. She wondered what kind of paragon could win such devotion…and how an angel could love him in return.

Tally knew there were no angels on earth, male or female. In her two years of marriage to Nathan Meeker, she had met ambitious society ladies who aspired to perfection. They had all fallen prey to their very human weaknesses. No one understood such weaknesses better than Chantal Bernard.

She wondered how long it would take Kavanagh to realize that his angel had feet of clay instead of wings.

They rode on to the wide mouth of Castillo Canyon, where Castillo Creek had carved a wedge out of the hillside and opened up a lovely side valley dotted with oaks. Cattle lifted their heads to note the intruders and returned to their placid grazing. Grama grass gave way to sedges and rushes in the wet meadow near the creek bed and spring. Kavanagh made for the *ciénaga,* and the two horses picked up their feet in anticipation of sweet fresh water.

The welcome shade of sycamore, ash, walnut and cottonwood spilled over Tally's shoulders like a balm. Brightly colored birds flitted from tree to tree. Dragonflies skimmed across pools in the rocky bed.

Kavanagh dismounted, filled the canteens with the water bubbling up from the spring and briefly closed his eyes as if he felt the healing spirit of the place as much as Tally did. "Two mules stopped here in the past few days," he said.

"Then we can't be too far behind André," Tally said, joining Sim beside the spring. "The Brysons' cabin should be a little farther up the canyon."

Sim tossed Tally her canteen and drank from his own. He wiped his lips with the back of his hand. "We'll camp here tonight."

"We still have hours of daylight left."

"Better to get a fresh start in the morning. It's rough country up there, on horseback or afoot."

Tally gazed up at the wooded peaks of the mountains. They were much more imposing at the northern end of the range than near Cold Creek. "If you're worried about me, there is no need. I can keep up."

"Maybe." Kavanagh wet his neckerchief and scrubbed the sweat from his face. "You gonna take your bath now, or wait to see if these Brysons have a washtub?"

"Don't worry, Mr. Kavanagh. I'll be sure to stay downwind of you."

Without any warning, he dipped his hand in the pool, scooped water in his palm and sent it flying at Tally. She fell back on her rump with a cry of surprise, runnels of cool liquid sliding down the back of her collar and making mud of the dust on her face.

"There's a start," he said.

She recovered in an instant, ready to return fire. But he moved quick as a fox, jumping up from the bank and putting the pale trunk of a sycamore between him and her watery missiles.

Tally was too astonished to continue. Kavanagh was *playing*. It simply wasn't possible. He was laughing at her the way a boy would, treating her like a companion. A friend. And that didn't fit in any way with the Kavanagh she had begun to know.

As abruptly as he'd begun, Kavanagh ended the game. He stepped out from behind the sycamore, caught Diablo and swung into the saddle just as if the strange interlude had never happened. Tally knew that if she made anything of it, he would stare her down with that icy gaze and act as if she were the crazy one.

They left the magical sanctuary and rode on deeper into the canyon. The grassland oaks were dropping their leaves as they did every spring, conserving life for the hot days ahead. Mesquite trees on the hillsides hung heavy with yellow catkins. Turkey vultures circled lazily in a bright blue sky, portending death.

Tally shivered. André was not dead. She broke Muérdago into a trot and led the way between steeper slopes clothed with pines at their tops. The meadow narrowed, and soon Tally caught sight of a fence through the trees.

The Bryson cabin was small, built of logs hewn from the forest instead of the adobe often seen on the plain or nearer the border. A corral held a few calves, while a shedlike barn stood ready for weary horses. Chickens scratched beside a lopsided coop.

The first sign of human life was a slender girl of fifteen or sixteen hanging laundry to dry on a line. She gave a little cry of surprise when she saw the approaching riders, smoothed her calico skirt and raced inside the cabin. A few moments later a much older woman, stout and plain, came out the front door. The girl followed her.

Tally dismounted and led Muérdago the rest of the way, touching the brim of her hat in greeting. "Good afternoon," she said. "You would be Mrs. Bryson?"

"That I am." The woman shaded her eyes and looked toward Kavanagh. "Welcome. This is my daughter, Beth. Mr. Bryson is up in the canyon, but if you boys would care to take some refreshment…"

"Thank you, ma'am. That's most kind." Tally heard the faint brush of Sim's steps behind her and stood a little straighter. "My name is Bernard—Tal Bernard. This is Mr. Kavanagh. We've come from Tombstone, looking for my brother André. Have you by any chance seen a light-haired young man with two mules passing this way?"

"My goodness," the woman said, gathering her apron between her hands. "We do see a few miners and lumbermen, though most are on the other side of the mountains. Tombstone, you say? We usually go to Willcox for supplies."

"I saw him," Beth said. "Mother was in the barn tending Daisy when he rode by. Father invited him to stay, but he was in a hurry, like someone was chasing him." She regarded Tally and Sim with bright, curious blue eyes. "Why are you looking for him? Are you really his brother?"

"That's enough of that," Mrs. Bryson said. "Go inside, Beth, and make up a fresh pot of coffee. You boys will want to rest a bit and talk to Mr. Bryson. I expect him back any time now."

Tally glanced at Kavanagh, whose face was devoid of expression. "We're grateful, ma'am," she said.

"Then see to your mounts and come on in. If you'll excuse me, I have a pot on the stove." She bobbed her head and bustled back through the door.

"It's a good thing we ain't outlaws," Kavanagh muttered, passing Tally with Diablo in tow.

"Hospitality is the custom in the Territory," Tally said. "Most people welcome visitors."

"You better hope you don't get more hospitality than you bargained for."

He moved ahead before she could ask him what he meant. She followed him into the barn, empty of occupants save for a lone milk cow. Tally stripped Muérdago of his tack and

treated him to a measure of oats from her saddlebags. Sim did
the same with Diablo.

Beth arrived at the barn door, breathless and flushed.
"Mother wanted me to tell you…supper's almost ready. Father should be here any moment." Her gaze darted from Tally
to Kavanagh. "Mother also wanted…will you be…?" Her
flush deepened. "We can heat water if you want to wash up."

Kavanagh gave a bark of laughter. Tally imagined how
nice it would be to have a mule's hind leg for just long enough
to give him a good swift kick in the posterior.

"That's very generous of you, miss," Tally said. "But we
won't impose. We'd planned to keep riding until—"

"Mother wouldn't hear of it," the girl said with some spirit.
"Neither will Father. We have an extra room we keep for my
brother, George. He's in the army." Her pretty face took on a
wistful cast. "Will you tell me about Tombstone, Mr. Bernard?"

Tally's stomach chose that moment to rumble like a steam
engine. "Well, I…"

Beth turned toward the door and looked back expectantly.

Tally saw no way out. The Brysons clearly intended to
make the most of their unexpected guests. They wouldn't
only insist on providing a meal and a clean bed, but they
would also ask a hundred questions about the doings in Tombstone and throughout the Valley. Tally would have to maintain her disguise under the most trying of circumstances…and
then there was the problem of Sim Kavanagh. Beth had mentioned only one extra room.

In her heart, Tally knew she couldn't keep up the masquerade forever, nor could she continue to hide at Cold Creek,
avoiding contact with the other homesteaders. Safety was an
illusion. Sooner or later someone would discover that the
younger Bernard brother was female. Maybe it was time to
drop the pretense.

But not just yet. Not while she rode with Sim Kavanagh.

She followed Beth into the house, half listening for Kavanagh's panther-soft tread. Her own boot heels clicked on the smooth puncheon floor. The scent of simmering meat and vegetables filled the cabin's central room, which contained both the kitchen and a parlor with a fireplace. The parlor boasted an overstuffed sofa that must have been brought by train from the East, ruling grandly over the more humble homemade chairs and parlor table. A colorful quilt hung on one wall.

"I hope that venison stew suits you," Mrs. Bryson said from the stove, pushing damp hair from her forehead with the back of her hand. "Please, sit down."

Tally sat in one of the chairs at the dining table between the kitchen and parlor, admiring the braided rag rug that covered much of the floor. Kavanagh stalked in a slow circle like a beast in a cage.

Beth rushed into the room with a pitcher, spilling water on the kitchen floor. "Father's home," she announced. Kavanagh paused by the fireplace and lifted his head, nostrils flared.

"He always knows when supper's ready," Mrs. Bryson said with an indulgent laugh. She opened the stove's heavy door and pulled out a pan of biscuits, perfectly browned. "Get the butter, Beth."

The girl hurried to obey, and a few moments later a big man with salt-and-pepper hair strode into the cabin. His face was damp, and he wore much-patched but clean clothing, as if he'd made some effort to make himself presentable for his guests. Tally got to her feet and took his offered hand.

"Miles Bryson," he said, nearly crushing her fingers. "Glad to have you, Mr. Bernard." He looked over her shoulder. "Mr. Kavanagh."

Sim nodded without moving from his place by the hearth.

Tally smiled all the wider. "I hope we aren't putting you to too much trouble, Mr. Bryson."

"Not at all." He released Tally's aching hand, joined his wife by the stove and gave her a hug about the shoulders. "Mrs. Bryson loves to show off her cooking."

"Now, Miles." She feigned affront, but her eyes gleamed with pleasure. Beth arrived with the butter and began to set the table. The plates were china, chipped but lovingly preserved from some former, more genteel home. Soon the table was piled high with a crock of savory stew, a plate of biscuits and a steaming pot of coffee.

Kavanagh still hadn't moved, and Tally was about to risk calling him when he sat down next to her. Bryson took the head of the table, and once Beth and Mrs. Bryson had finished their serving duties, they sat in two of the three remaining chairs.

Bryson bowed his head, and his family did the same. Sim stared at the ceiling. Tally lowered her eyes to the table's painstakingly polished surface, reciting the prayer through stiff lips. If Mrs. Bryson had any notion of who was sitting next to her innocent daughter…

"Amen," Bryson murmured. Without another word he dug into the food, passing bowlfuls of stew to Tally and Kavanagh before serving his family. Mrs. Bryson watched Tally expectantly until she took a bite and made the appropriate noises of satisfaction. Kavanagh ate with single-minded attention and never once looked up from his plate.

Tally found it hard to swallow, though the food was as good as anything Miriam made at home. Beth's curious glances were more shrewd than those of her parents. Maybe she'd guessed something was not quite right about "Mr." Bernard. But Kavanagh earned her most fascinated stares, and it was all Tally could do not to shout a warning.

Stay away from men like that, ma bonne fille. *Wait and find a boy your own age. Don't throw away what good fortune has given you....*

She pushed her plate aside and patted her stomach. "Ma'am, I don't think I've tasted anything quite so fine in years. If he were more of a talker, I'm sure Mr. Kavanagh would say the same."

Kavanagh looked up from his cleaned plate. His pale eyes settled first on Tally, then quickly moved to Beth and Mr. Bryson. "Good," he said.

"Your friend does talk, Mr. Bernard," Bryson said with generous good humor.

"Tal," Tally said. Bryson offered her and Kavanagh a pair of pipes, which both declined. The homesteader lit his own and settled in one of the rawhide chairs in the parlor. Tally took the other, while Kavanagh crouched on his boot heels beside the fireplace.

Bryson smiled through his full beard. "Beth has told me something of why you gentleman are in the canyon. I did meet a man fitting the description you gave, Tal, but he was in a hurry to be on his way." He tamped the tobacco in his pipe. "You've been following him from Tombstone?"

Tally saw no harm in telling him at least part of the truth. "Our ranch is in Cold Creek Valley, in the southern Chiricahuas," she said. "My brother left to buy cattle from some ranchers in the north Valley two weeks ago, but he disappeared, and we learned that he'd come up here...supposedly to look for ore."

"You must be his younger brother, from the looks of you," Bryson said. "I'm sorry your kin has given you trouble."

"I'm worried that André...might have gotten lost up here. That's why I hired Mr. Kavanagh to track him in the mountains."

Kavanagh muttered something under his breath. Pans

clanged in the kitchen. Bryson puffed on his pipe. "Have you been with the army, Mr. Kavanagh?" he asked.

Kavanagh glanced at Bryson without interest. "From time to time." Bryson's eyes crinkled in amusement. "Army scouts are notoriously taciturn men, Tal. The best of them hardly ever make a sound, let alone indulge in idle conversation."

"So I've learned." She felt Kavanagh's stare and shifted in her seat. "Our foreman went looking for André a week ago," she said. "He's a former Buffalo Soldier with the Tenth Cavalry, very tall—"

"I'm afraid I didn't see such a man. I've heard good things about the Tenth, though. Formidable fighters."

They drifted onto the subjects of army movements, the Apaches and cattle prices. Tally let Bryson do most of the talking, while Kavanagh kept his thoughts to himself. Eventually Mrs. Bryson and Beth joined them, pulling chairs from the dining table.

"Will you tell us about Tombstone, Mr. Bernard?" Beth asked eagerly. "Is it as wicked as they say?"

"Now, Beth," Mrs. Bryson reproved.

Mr. Bryson chuckled. "You'll have to excuse our daughter, Tal. She's heard too many fantastic stories." He set down his pipe. "Willcox is wild enough for us. I'd like to hear more of your ranch, and how you find the south end of the Valley. There aren't too many of us here, but more will be coming every day now that the Apaches have cleared out. If not for the rustlers—" He glanced at Beth and thought better of that subject.

Tally asked Mrs. Bryson about the quilt on the wall, which led to an innocuous conversation about fabric and sewing. Tally listened with the polite incomprehension of any typical male. After Beth and Mrs. Bryson retired, Bryson asked Tally for general news of the Valley and its residents.

Tally had little to tell him. She'd spent most of her days deliberately sequestered at Cold Creek, working the cattle and letting André deal with the outside world. If Bryson found her ignorance strange, he didn't let on. He showed Tally and Kavanagh the plain, neat room they would share for the night.

"You've done Ida a heap of good by praising her cooking," Bryson said. "She gets a little lonely in the canyon with only Beth for company." He lit a kerosene lamp and set it on a table near the door. "You men are welcome here any time."

"As you are at Cold Creek," Tally said, glad that Bryson would have no cause for such a visit. She thanked him again and closed the door to the room, her heart beating unpleasantly fast in the heavy silence.

Kavanagh was sitting on the wood-frame bed, pulling off his boots and stockings. The moment of truth was at hand.

Tally turned and leaned against the door, folding her arms across her chest. "Can I ask you a question?"

Kavanagh arched his back in a bone-popping stretch. "When did you ever need my permission?"

"Why were you so rude to the Brysons? Is it because two of them are female?"

He looked at her with an expression of genuine surprise. "You still expecting pretty manners from me, boy? I thought you'd been disabused of such notions."

"I hired you to do a job, and I'm prepared to pay the price. The Brysons don't know us, but they've been generous hosts. The least they deserve is the respect due decent people."

He got up from the bed and strolled toward her with a lazy air of tolerant amusement. "You gonna fire me because I was disrespectful to them decent, proper folk out there?"

She edged away from the door. "Fortunately, I don't think they'll hold it against you. They trust instead of judge, and I admire them for it."

Kavanagh stopped in the middle of the room and cocked his head. "Took a liking to that little filly Beth, did you, boy?"

"Not the way you mean."

"She's wild for a little freedom, ain't she? How well d'you think she'd make out in Tombstone?"

Tally balled her fists. "Her parents take care of her. They love each other. You never had that kind of family, did you, Kavanagh? A sister, a brother to look after, or who looked after you."

"No." The denial cracked like a thick oak branch snapped in a storm. "I never had a family like that."

She met his stony gaze, swallowing the knot in her throat. She could see the pain he tried not to show, pain she saw only because she had become so accustomed to discerning the motives of men.

"I'm sorry," she said. "It's none of my business."

He seemed not to hear. "I had a mother and a father and half brothers. We never lived together."

Mon Dieu. Was he implying that he was a bastard? In the West that was not so terrible a thing as in the cultured East, but it would have marked him. She felt the compulsion to match his confession with one of her own…. Madness, just like the fact that they were here together, alone in this room.

"My father left my family when I was young," she said.

His gaze returned to hers. "That's a damned shame, boy," he said, only half-mocking. "Your ma raise you and André?"

"She worked hard." Tally stared longingly at the washstand, with its fresh water and clean towels. She was desperate to scrub the dirt from her face, remove her hat and let down her hair. That wouldn't happen tonight. "You go ahead and get some sleep, Kavanagh. I'm going to check on the horses."

She started for the door. Kavanagh was there first. "You're a lousy liar," he said conversationally. "Why are you so afraid of being in this room with me?"

"I'm not afraid." He was barely four inches away, nearly touching her chest to chest. "I just like my privacy."

He leaned closer. His breath stirred the fine hairs at her temples. "I'll just bet you do." His gaze dropped to her lips. "You ever been with a man, Tally-boy?"

She jumped straight up and scrambled sideways, clumsy with shock. It wasn't possible. She would have known. She'd met men like that before—the New Orleans brothels catered to every taste, no matter how eccentric. But Kavanagh had spoken of his angel Esperanza. He had known women. Yet there were all those comments about baths. Perhaps he was equally partial to both....

She didn't have time to think. She snatched the hat from her hair and pulled at the braids. Her hair tumbled loose about her shoulders.

"I'm not a boy, *cochon,* so keep your hands to yourself."

CHAPTER FOUR

KAVANAGH LAUGHED. He laughed so loud and hard that Tally was afraid he would wake the whole house. She charged, pushed him to the far wall beside the bed and pressed her hand over his mouth.

"Taisez-vous, dérangé!" she hissed.

He gripped her wrists and pried her hands from his face. His mouth came down on hers, lips barely open, as if he meant to bruise instead of caress. Just as suddenly, he released her. She scrubbed at her mouth while he withdrew to the bed and stretched out full-length, head pillowed on his wrists, bare feet crossed at the ankles.

"Now that's done," he said. "Unless you want more of the same."

Tally stared at him without comprehension. Good God, she had utterly failed with him in nearly every respect. And he was laughing at her. He was laughing.

She leaned on the wall and caught her breath, lungs straining against the bindings that held her breasts flat. "How long have you known?" she demanded.

"Since we met." He yawned and snapped his teeth like an animal. "I knew it'd have to come out sooner or later. Just a question of when."

She thought quickly back over every encounter she'd had with the folk in Tombstone, the woman in Turquoise and the Brysons. "How is it that you guessed when no one else has?"

"I see things that are hidden," he said. "I'm very good at it."

"So you've been playing with me." She smiled, picked up her hat and laid it on the table. "I'm sure it's been most amusing."

"You were playing games, not me," he said. "Are you afraid of men, or is it just that you wish you had a little more between your legs?"

Tally pronounced her most elegant curse. "I wouldn't be one of your sex for anything in the world. And as for being afraid…" She leaned over the foot of the bed. "I've known how to protect myself since I was fifteen."

He propped himself up on his elbows and stared pointedly at her chest. "Maybe it ain't fear. The devil knows what you're like under that getup. Maybe you're just scared no man would want you."

How she longed in that moment to prove just how much men had wanted her—still wanted her, whenever they saw her as she was, as she could be. But he was still playing like a cat with a mouse. He was testing her for weakness. Men did not make her weak.

"Maybe," she said, "I don't want them."

He wet his lips, and she shivered at the memory of his mouth on hers. *Cochon.* She should have hit him. And there was the .44 at her hip….

"How old are you—Tal?" he asked, interrupting her fantasies. "What's your real name?"

"A lady never reveals her age," she said. "And Tal is good enough for me. I don't need fancy things. Only my freedom."

"Freedom to ride around wild without any of the *proper* folk knowing about it?"

Heat rushed into her cheeks. "It harms no one. I work the

ranch like my brother, like our hands Bart and Federico. I have no children and no husband to tend."

He leaped up from the bed and crossed to the washstand, wetting one of the towels. Tally guessed his intent but refused to run. He bathed her face with surprising gentleness, wiping away the accumulated grime. He whistled softly.

"You clean up real nice," he said. "My guess is that ugliness ain't your problem."

She took the towel from his hand and returned to the washstand. Her own face, framed by golden hair, stared back at her from the oval mirror. "I have no problem," she said, "as long as people leave me alone."

Kavanagh's reflection joined hers. Solemn, not mocking, not cruel. "Why?" he asked. "You thought if I knew what you were, I'd hurt you. Did a man hurt you, Tal?"

The caressing note in his voice set her swaying like a willow in a high-desert wind. Oh, yes, he was very good at finding things that were hidden. But he had said she was a lousy liar, and that meant he, too, could make mistakes. She had become very good at lying with absolute sincerity.

"I've seen what men can do to women," she said, meeting his eyes in the mirror. "I prefer to keep myself unentangled."

He lifted a strand of her hair in his calloused fingers. "We're two of a kind, ain't we, Tal? I've got no use for women."

"Except Esperanza."

His eyes narrowed in anger and relaxed again. "You never loved a man?"

"Never."

"You were always safe from me."

"I couldn't be certain of that. If I dress as a man, it means I expect to live in a man's world. No special favors." *No being lusted after because of how I look. No lying under some smelly, sweating pig who can't or won't be true to a woman of his own. No more hypocrisy.*

"You told me never to touch you the way I did in Turquoise," she said. "Now I'm telling you the same thing. Never touch me again."

To her secret amazement, he backed away, hands raised as if to ward off attack. His mouth curled in a smile. "I don't plan to," he said. "That was just to prove that there ain't nothing between us but business."

Because he'd kissed her and felt nothing. He was a wonder, a marvel—true to his dream of one woman and not even tempted by such intimacy with another. Her opinion of him kept changing, and she wanted no more than to flee this house and breathe the sweet night air until her head was clear of this constant spinning.

"I believe you," she said slowly. "God knows why."

"You're a religious one, are you, Tally-girl?" he asked, heading for the door. "Say a few prayers for me."

"I doubt my prayers would do you any good."

"Maybe not." He pointed his chin toward the washstand. "Clean up. I'll be back in an hour, Tally-girl."

"Kavanagh! Don't call me Tally-gi—"

He walked out of the room and closed the door behind him. Tally felt her way to the bed and sat down with a thump. Perspiration prickled along the back of her neck, and she realized what she had denied every moment of the past ten minutes.

She'd been terrified. Only part of that fear had been of Kavanagh himself. The rest had come from her utter lack of control, her mistake in underestimating a man she should have known was more dangerous than she could imagine.

Moving with short, sharp jerks, she unbuttoned her waistcoat, unbelted her gun, pulled off her shirt and unwound the bandages underneath. Her breasts ached. She slipped off the men's britches and the suspenders that held them up around her waist. Layer by layer, she stripped down to her skin and stood naked before the washstand. She used two of the towels to bathe her body, combed out her hair until it was free of snarls and tangles, and unpacked her spare shirt from her saddlebags. She counted every minute she spent in the room.

When she was dressed again, she took the basin and refilled it from the pump between the cabin and the barn. Laundry flapped in the night breeze, but she caught no sight of Kavanagh.

She met him at the door of the bedroom. His hair was damp and his face clean. He looked her over and gave a short nod. "Good. I'll sleep in the barn tonight."

"No special favors, Kavanagh."

"Be a damned waste if that bed don't get some use."

Not a hint of innuendo shaded his words. Tally relaxed. "All right. You take it for three hours, and I'll take it after that."

"After I dirty up the sheets? I wouldn't wish that on anyone. You go first."

"You're a stubborn *tête de mule,* Kavanagh."

"Whatever that is, I'll take it as a compliment." He touched the brim of his hat and turned to go. She made a move to stop him. He froze.

"Why?" she asked. "You don't like women. You don't trust them. Now that you know what I am—"

He turned around, towering over her, though she wasn't small or in the least bit delicate—except in the minds of the men who'd wanted her to be so. "If you was a regular woman," he said, "I'd leave you here and forget about your brother."

"I suppose I should take *that* as a compliment."

"Take it how you like," he said. "You keep up with me the way you been doin', and we won't have no dustups between us."

She watched him stalk down the hall and out the front door. The bedroom seemed strangely empty. She took off everything but her shirt and lay down, stiffly at first, trying to catch Sim's scent on the sheets. It was almost too faint to be noticeable. She concentrated on the sounds of crickets and a whip-poor-will in the nearby meadow until exhaustion claimed her. Once she woke, briefly, to the sound of a distant wolf's howl.

Dawn sifted through the thin muslin curtains. Tally swung her legs over the side of the bed and pulled on her pants. Kavanagh's saddlebags were gone.

She finished dressing in haste, torn between annoyance with Sim and delight at the rich scent of frying bacon. There would be fresh eggs, perhaps flapjacks, as well, and she found herself ravenous.

With her saddlebags over her shoulders, she left the bedroom and entered the living area. Mrs. Bryson had the table set for breakfast. Beth brought a pail of fresh milk from the barn. She smiled at Tally.

"If you're looking for your friend, he's outside with my father," she said. She flushed a little, glancing aside at her mother.

"I hope you slept well," Mrs. Bryson said. She carried a frying pan of eggs to the table and slid them onto a platter.

"Wonderfully," Tally said. "Thank you, ma'am."

"Mr. Kavanagh said he wanted to let you rest up for the day ahead. He must have been out with the horses well before dawn; he's already helped Mr. Bryson repair the corral fence." She bustled back to the stove. "For a man who doesn't talk much, he can certainly make himself useful."

Indeed, Tally thought. "I'm afraid I haven't been."

"Never mind that. The men should be in shortly." As she'd predicted, Bryson and Kavanagh arrived a few moments later,

sharing the silent camaraderie of men who've labored together. Kavanagh hardly glanced in Tally's direction. Bryson
invited his guests to sit, said grace and served the meal.

Tally watched Kavanagh out of the corner of her eye. He
hadn't spent any part of the night in the bedroom, but the Brysons didn't realize it. Her secret was safe. When breakfast was
finished, Bryson saw her and Kavanagh out to the barn. The
horses stood saddled and ready.

"You be careful up there," Bryson said, passing Kavanagh
a bundle that Tally guessed must contain fresh food. "No
Apaches as far as I know, but still plenty of places to get into
trouble. I've been hearing wolves lately."

Kavanagh seemed to take the warning in the spirit it was
intended. He swung into the saddle. "We'll get by."

Bryson gazed up at the sky. "I'd swear it's going to rain.
Not that I'm complaining, mind you—rain in the dry season
is always welcome. But I hope it doesn't interfere with your
search."

Tally followed his gaze. She hadn't considered bad weather
to be a factor in finding André, but Bryson was right. Clouds
had gathered sometime in the night, and the look of them
boded a rare late-spring rain.

She concealed her worry and gripped Bryson's hand.
"Please thank your wife and daughter for their hospitality."

"That I will. You're welcome any time. Good luck."

She tipped her hat and mounted Muérdago. With a last
wave, she reined east along the canyon that curved deeper into
the mountains. She let the gelding pick his path, since there
was really only one way to go and her thoughts were otherwise occupied. Kavanagh rode beside her, easy in posture and
expression.

What had he said last night, after he'd kissed her? *Now
that's done.* A chore to be gotten out of the way, an irritating

distraction vanquished. Certainly nothing bad had come of it, except a little wounding of her pride.

So why couldn't she let it go, as he did? Was it anger she felt, that a man had bested her…or something else entirely?

"How did you sleep?" she asked casually.

"About as well as you."

"You left the bed to me all night. You're in danger of being mistaken for a gentleman, Kavanagh."

He cast her a grim, searching look. "I'm no gentleman, and you're no lady. That's the bargain."

She knew that he meant he had no expectations of her except that she do her part to find André. Kavanagh didn't know what a precious gift he'd given her—the gift of equality and respect.

She wondered if he would accord his Esperanza such a privilege.

Morning light cast long shadows in the canyon. The gain in elevation along the watercourse brought more pines interspersed with oaks. The forest closed in on either side of the path; red fox squirrels flashed bushy tails in warning. Clouds continued to gather in the southwest, thicker and darker than before.

The first notched pinnacles appeared just as the horses rounded a sharp bend in the arroyo. Red columns, many joined in wall-like ramparts, others standing alone, towered above the trees. Some were shaped like strange animals or birds or gesturing men. Deep joints, like miniature slot canyons, ran between them.

"We'll see a lot more of those," Kavanagh remarked, deftly guiding his stallion over a bulging mass of rocks. "This broken terrain was what made the Chiricahuas so good for the Apaches trying to escape the army. Wasn't easy for men to pursue on horseback." He glanced at the lowering sky. "Don't worry. I'll find him."

Kavanagh remained in the saddle for the next mile. Often he bent low over Diablo's barrel, supple as a cat, to examine the ground. When the main trail branched, Kavanagh chose the fainter course. But soon the way became rough and uneven, pushing between ocher turrets and thick stands of pine.

"We walk," he finally said. Tally dismounted and took Muérdago's lead. The air was rarer here than at Cold Creek, cooler and sharper. She saw traces of snow on the highest mountains. At noon they briefly stopped for Mrs. Bryson's sandwiches, made of that morning's fresh bread and leftover bacon. Kavanagh checked the horses' hooves for stones, and then continued along the track. He sifted dust between his fingers and paused to contemplate the very rocks as if they spoke to him.

"Your brother came this way," he said in answer to Tally's questioning look. "He moved slowly. One of his mules was lame." He gazed at the steep slope ahead. It was almost impossible to pick out any sort of trail amid the rubble, low shrubs and pinnacles. "I'm going on alone, on foot. The horses can't travel quick enough in this country. You'll have to stay here and watch them."

"I agree, Mr. Kavanagh," she said. "I'll make camp."

He blinked, as if he'd still expected her to argue in the way of a "normal" female. And then he smiled. The expression transformed him—for an instant, no more, just long enough for Tally to glimpse that playful boy who'd splashed her in Castillo Creek.

She smiled back at that boy like the thirteen-year-old girl from Prairie d'Or, the child who'd grown up with farm dirt between her toes and all the wild places as her sanctuaries. The girl who was so good at pretending.

Before she could regret what her own smile revealed, Kavanagh thrust Diablo's lead into her hand, sat on the nearest boulder and removed his boots and stockings. He sprang to his feet and sprinted lightly up the trail. Fast as he was, his bare feet didn't dislodge as much as a pebble. He rounded a curve out of Tally's sight.

Tally led the horses to the shade of a cliff. The strong afternoon sunlight hid behind heavy cloud cover, and she thought she smelled rain. The horses were restless, sensing both the change of weather and her unease.

She sat with her back to the cliff and closed her eyes, forcing her thoughts away from André. She wondered if Sim had learned his tracking from the Indians. She'd never heard of a white man running barefoot in the mountains. She'd never heard of anyone quite like Kavanagh.

A light rain began to fall within the first hour. Soon it became a downpour, and Tally moved Muérdago and Diablo to the shelter of a stand of pines. She paced restless circles around the horses, water dripping from the brim of her hat. Dusk fell quickly. Kavanagh returned just as the storm came to an abrupt end.

"I found André," he said.

TAL DIDN'T SWAY or swoon. Her gaze held Sim's as she waited for the worst.

"Dead?" she whispered.

"Alive. Barely." He took her arm and made her sit, though she flinched at the contact. He let her go as soon as he was sure she wouldn't fall. "He's only about a mile from here, but he was hidden in an arroyo. I didn't see any sign of the mules."

"Did he speak?"

Sim knew he couldn't give her anything but the truth, at least about her brother's condition. "There's not too much blood or deep wounds that I could see, but he's unconscious.

Looks like he fell and hit his head. Could have been lying there a couple of days."

"Oh, God."

"He's in one piece. Nothing got at him."

Tally scraped her palms across her face. "You left him alone."

He bristled, as if her accusation had the power to wound him. She couldn't know that he'd tracked most of the way as a wolf, hiding his clothes in a crevice until he was ready to return. The rain had made his hunt much more difficult. Even in wolf form, he'd been lucky to find André at all.

"I didn't want to risk carrying him," Sim said gruffly, "so I came for Diablo." He sniffed the air. "It won't rain anymore tonight. There's a pool on the other side of that low ridge. Find some dry wood, if you can, and get a fire going."

Her dazed eyes looked through him. "André needs me."

"You can help him best when I bring him back." He pulled a large empty can from one saddlebag and pressed it into her hands. "You can use this to heat some water."

She took the can and stood. "Go. I'll have everything ready."

He untied Diablo and left at once. The stallion was sure-footed and willing to follow where Sim led. Full night had fallen by the time man and beast stood on the ledge overlooking the deep but narrow gorge where André lay.

Sim scrambled down the rocky face to the bottom and crouched beside the fallen man. André hadn't moved since Sim left; he still breathed, and his heartbeat was steady, but his sandy hair was caked with dirt and blood, and one of his arms was broken inside.

The other hand grasped a torn fragment of paper, nearly disintegrated by the rain. Enough of it remained for Sim to recognize what he'd been searching for. Someone had been here with André—someone who'd taken the rest of the map and had made a clean getaway with the mules and gear.

Sim's first thought was that Caleb had done it, but Caleb was behind bars in Amarillo. That was why he'd sent Sim. All telltale tracks of the intruder and the mules had been washed away in the storm. André's clothing was too saturated to hold any scent but his own. Not even a wolf had much hope of hunting down the thief.

Sim crouched beside André and scooped the soggy scrap of paper out of the young man's hand. If it weren't for Tal, he would be off looking for the map no matter what his chances of finding it. But she was waiting, and he'd promised to find her brother.

"I found you," he said in disgust. "Not that you were worth the trouble. I'd as soon leave you here for the buzzards."

André didn't answer. The rise and fall of his chest was the only outward sign that he was alive. There was some risk in moving him, but André's odds of survival were nonexistent if he didn't get out of the mountains.

With a scowl, Sim gathered the young man's sprawled limbs and lifted him, trying not to move the broken arm more than necessary. He shifted André over his shoulder, made sure of his balance, and climbed back up the cliff face.

Diablo snorted and flared his nostrils, snuffling at André with frank disapproval. Sim quieted the horse, lifted André onto his back and secured the unwelcome burden with rope from the saddlebags. André was as limp as a sack of grain.

Darkness made for a treacherous descent, but Sim's keen vision picked out the easiest path. Firelight marked his destination for the last quarter mile. When they arrived, Tally ran up to Diablo and stopped to stare at her brother's pale face. She murmured French words in a voice broken with horror.

Sim fought the urge to dump André on his head and end

his troublemaking ways for good. "Your brother's still alive, and at least he ain't bleeding," he said as he untied the ropes. Tally helped Sim ease André to the ground, cradling the injured man's head in her hands. She'd made a bed of blankets and laid out scraps of cloth to bind any wounds, but Sim was pretty sure that the worst of André's injuries were inside, where she couldn't reach them.

Tal cut away her brother's shredded clothes, covered him with blankets and continued to speak to him in her melodious French, alternately scolding and pleading. The scolding was all an act to hold the tears at bay, but it seemed to work.

Sim gathered sturdy sticks to make a splint for André's arm, while Tally cleaned André's cuts and bathed his face and hairline with warm water, revealing the huge raised bump and ugly gash where he'd hit his head in the fall. Tal sucked in her breath and closed her eyes.

"He could have bled to death," Sim said awkwardly. "Head wounds are like that. He was lucky."

"Lucky." She shivered. "How did this happen?"

"Looks like he missed his footing," Sim said, which wasn't really a lie. "Easy to do up here."

"Mon pauvre." She rinsed the cloth in the can of hot water and dabbed at the wound. "You never saw the mules?"

"The rain washed away their tracks. They must have escaped when André fell. Could be on the other side of the mountains by now, if a panther didn't get them."

"No sign of Elijah?"

"He probably never picked up your brother's trail."

"He may even be back at the ranch by now." She brushed at the damp tangles of André's hair. "The important thing is that we saved André. He'll explain what happened when he…" She bit hard on her lower lip. "You don't have to tell me. Men who hit their heads and don't wake up—"

She was still fighting tears, and Sim couldn't bear it.

"Some recover," he said.

"Some," she echoed. She bent to kiss André's brow. "There isn't much more I can do for him here, but the Brysons must have a wagon we can borrow to carry him home."

"You should leave him with them until you can get a doctor."

"No. I want him home, where I—" She shook her head. "It will take days to a get a doctor, no matter where we are." She rose and searched her saddlebags. Coins jingled in a small leather pouch. She picked out three silver dollars and offered them on her open palm. "You've more than earned your fee, Mr. Kavanagh. I'll pay you the same again if you'll ride to Tombstone and send a doctor to Cold Creek."

Sim stared at the coins with sudden and overwhelming distaste. "What about getting your brother home?"

"It's less than forty miles from the mouth of Castillo Canyon. I can manage with a wagon."

Anger tightened Sim's chest until he could barely breathe. "Why should I bother to earn the money when I could take it from you right now?"

She closed her fist around the coins. "You could have done so at any time, Mr. Kavanagh."

"Don't call me that." Sim got up and stalked out of the firelight, turned on his heel and faced her again. "No one ever calls me *mister.*"

"What do you want to be called?"

"Sim. Just Sim."

"I usually go by Tally at home."

"When you're not a boy."

She nodded, staring into the fire. "I was christened Chantal."

Sim felt the anger evaporate as quickly as it had come. "Simeon," he muttered.

"It's a nice name."

"There's nothing nice about me. But I'll ride to Tomb-stone, and you don't need to pay me a cent."

"I thought you needed the money."

"I'll take two dollars."

Solemnly she passed him the coins, and he shoved them in his pocket. "Now you get some sleep," he ordered. "I'll watch."

"No more arguments? You permit me to trust you after all?"

He pointed toward her bedroll. "Sleep. I'll ride for Tomb-stone soon's we get a wagon from the Brysons and you're on your way home."

She smiled at him warmly, and he was afraid she was about to say something stupid and sentimental. But she went to her blankets and lay down on her side, gazing at her brother's ex-pressionless face.

Sim sank to his heels by the fire and waited her out. Even-tually the long day took its toll, and Tally slept. He tested the air for the scent of two- or four-legged intruders. Nothing stirred. He tossed pebbles into the fire until it burned down to ashes, considering how best to proceed with his plan.

The map was gone, and there was no telling how close André had been to his goal when he met with his "accident." Sim wasn't likely to find the treasure with a random search of every arroyo, mining camp and settlement in the Chirica-huas. But it was a sure bet that the thief would be looking for it. Sim had to stay in the area if he wanted to catch his prey.

There was only one other way to learn the contents of the map, and that was to wait and see if André recovered enough to talk.

Either possibility presented the same challenge. Sim had to find a legitimate excuse to remain in the Valley, close to Cold Creek. And he had an idea how to manage it, even though it would make his life a thousand times more complicated. Even though he would have to keep lying to Tally for as long as it took.

The problem was that he *liked* her. Hell and damnation, he liked and respected a female who hadn't enough sense to see him for what he was.

Esperanza knew. She'd seen into his deepest soul. Without her...

A wolf's howl echoed among the pinnacles. Tally woke with a start.

"Sim?"

"Here."

She rubbed her eyes and tossed her blankets aside. "I heard wolves."

"They won't do us any harm."

The howling came again. Tally crawled to André and touched his cheek. "Could they have attacked André and caused him to fall?"

"Ain't likely. Wolves are more afraid of men than men are of them."

"Most people would consider them dangerous."

"Most people don't know them."

She sighed, stroking André's hair. "All the wild creatures are leaving the mountains," she said with an aching, almost tangible sadness. "The Apaches lost their country, and soon the wolves will be gone."

"A few will survive."

"The strongest. The most ruthless."

"Do you blame them?"

"No. I don't blame anything for trying to stay alive."

"Then go back to sleep. I'll be here."

She tugged André's blankets higher around his shoulders and lay down again. "*Bonne nuit,* Simeon. Good night."

The wolves answered for him.

CHAPTER FIVE

"SHE'S BACK," Miriam said, pausing breathlessly in the doorway of the barn where Elijah was shoeing Federico's dun mare. "Miss Tally's back!"

Eli set down the mare's hoof and straightened to wipe the sweat from his forehead. His heart thumped several times like a blacksmith's hammer and then settled into its regular rhythm. "How does she look?"

"I can't tell yet. Pablito saw her coming down the road in a wagon. God grant she's found Mr. André."

Eli closed his eyes. "I'll ride out to meet her."

"How's that leg?"

"Fine. I told you it was nothing."

"You'd say that if it was cut off at the knee. You take care while you ride. I'm getting that poor child something to eat." She rushed off, full of purpose, as she always was when she had someone to care for. Especially Tally. They had a long history together, sisters in all but the color of their skins.

When he'd first met Tally and Miriam, Eli had envied that unique female intimacy. Miriam had been born into slavery, and Tally Bernard had endured her own brand of servitude, but she'd been free enough to make her own choices. Just as Eli had.

He led the dun mare out to the corral and saddled his own favorite, a big-boned *grullo* gelding he called Hierro for his iron coloring. Pablo, Federico's ten-year-old son, was in the yard, excitedly repeating his news to his little sister Dolores. Bart and Federico were combing the range for cows with newborn calves, but they would be back in time for supper.

Elijah rode out of the yard, past the outbuildings and the main house to the rutted dirt road that ran alongside Cold Creek. Road and creek emerged from a *bosque* of sycamores, ash and cottonwoods into a spare land of broken hills dotted with oak and piñon pine. On every side rose mountains—Liebres to the west, Chiricahuas to the northeast and Pedregosas to the south. A few cattle—pitifully few—stood out against the dried grasses like fat ticks on a yellow dog's hide.

A plume of dust marked the wagon's position, and Elijah spurred Hierro to meet it. He could just make out the bundled human shape in the bed of the wagon.

André. He wasn't moving, but Tally hadn't covered his face. His head was bound in heavy bandages, and his right arm had been splinted and strapped to his chest. Tally's features were strained and weary, yet she still summoned a smile for one of the few men she trusted.

"Elijah," she called as he pulled up beside the wagon. "Thank God you're here."

Eli touched the brim of his hat. "I'm sorry I gave you cause for worry, Miss Tally. I just got back last night. I rode over half the Valley looking for word of Mr. André, but—" He choked on his excuses and shook his head. "You found him."

"Two days ago, up in Castillo Canyon." She glanced over her shoulder at her brother, and Eli saw the fear she so seldom revealed. "He's alive, but badly hurt."

Eli stared into the wagon bed. André didn't look alive. Any man might mistake him for just the opposite. "When Miriam told me you'd gone on from Tombstone…"

"Don't blame yourself, Eli," Tally said. "I know you did what you could." She frowned. "What happened to your leg?"

He rubbed the stiff limb. "Hierro caught a prairie-dog hole and threw me. It's just a little sore."

"I'm glad you're all right."

His health was the last thing he wanted to discuss. "Miriam said you'd hired a tracker. She's been sick with worry herself."

"I know." Tally clucked to her footsore team. The horses had already smelled the water from the spring and increased their pace, ears pricked toward the green swath of trees. "The tracker rode straight for Tombstone to bring the doctor. I expect both of them any time."

"Miriam knows you're coming, Miss Tally. I'll tell her about Mr. André." Eli wheeled Hierro about and rode back to the house, grateful to escape the horrible sight of André's pale, staring face. Miriam came out as soon as he dismounted at the garden fence.

"She's found André," Eli said. "He's hurt bad, but a doctor's coming."

"Then we'll need an extra bed made up," Miriam said. "Miss Tally?"

"As well as you'd expect. Bone-weary and downhearted."

"Alone?"

"Someone patched André up, but she's by herself now. That tracker she hired is getting the doctor in Tombstone."

Miriam pursed her lips. "I didn't know back then if Miss Tally did the right thing in hiring him, but I was wrong to doubt her judgment." She peered up at Eli's face. "And why the sorrowful looks, Sergeant Patterson? The Lord's blessed us this day."

Eli pretended to adjust Hierro's bridle. Miriam always knew what he felt inside, even when he didn't show it. "I failed Miss Tally, Miriam."

She gripped his forearm with a strong, slender hand. "It was Mr. André who failed her first. Now go help Miss Tally and let me get back to my work."

She rushed inside, leaving the faint comforting scent of flour behind her. Pablito dashed up to Eli and tugged at his sleeve. "Can I ride Hierro, Eli?"

Now you hide behind a child, Eli thought as he scooped the boy up onto the saddle. But he was glad for Pablito's incessant chatter, especially when Tally made the last turn away from the creek and past the outermost corral. Eli met the wagon, letting Pablito stay on Hierro's back while he carried André into the house.

Miriam gave Tally a firm hug in the doorway and spoke softly to her friend. Tally answered, but Eli didn't hear her words. André felt like skin and bones in his arms. He didn't stir even when Eli laid him down on his bed.

"Thank you, Eli," Tally said. She touched his arm and knelt at her brother's bedside.

"Do you know how this happened?" Eli asked, sick in his belly.

"Don't you be bothering her with questions," Miriam said. She put a basin of steaming water on the side table. "You're just getting in the way, Elijah Patterson."

He knew she was right, but he lingered for a few moments, watching André's face for some sign of awareness. "I'm sorry, Miss Tally."

But she was lost in her own worries, and Miriam had no time for him. He left the room and the house, swung Pablito down from Hierro's back, and rode for a certain hill where a man could see most of the valley and the road along Cold Creek. At dusk he glimpsed a funnel of dust and then two riders approaching at a steady lope.

He met them half a mile from the homestead and quickly

took stock of the newcomers. The older man bowed low over his horse in exhaustion, but the younger sat erect in the saddle, and his stare was that of a born predator. This was the tracker Miriam had spoken of with such wariness.

Eli turned to the other man. "Doctor?"

"Johansen," the man coughed. "I hope the patient is still alive after…all this way."

"He's alive. Please follow me."

The doctor sighed and kicked his mount's sweat-streaked barrel. The tracker reined his seal-brown stallion alongside Hierro.

"I guess Tally made it back all right," he said.

Tally. Eli bristled at the informality but took care not to show his annoyance. "Mr. Bernard arrived with his brother a few hours ago," he said.

The tracker laughed. "You keep your secret from the doc, but don't bother with me. I already know the lady pretty well."

Eli clenched his fists on Hierro's reins. "I doubt that, Mr. Kavanagh."

"Tally talked about me."

"She mentioned hiring a tracker in Tombstone."

Kavanagh clucked his tongue. "Don't hardly do justice to what we've been through together. And who're you?"

"Elijah Patterson, range boss of Cold Creek."

Kavanagh's pale eyes glittered with the last of the day's light. "The man who disappeared looking for André. Tally said you'd probably be here."

Eli held his emotions in check. Neither Tally nor Kavanagh could know anything of what was in his heart unless he let them see. "I was looking in the Valley. Miss Bernard found her brother in the mountains."

"Good thing I was in Tombstone to help out," Kavanagh said, "or Mr. Bernard would be panther meat about now."

"I'm sure you lent your assistance with no thought of gain for yourself, Mr. Kavanagh."

Kavanagh laughed. "I reckon you're the one who runs off any varmints that trouble the Bernards."

"I have that privilege."

"And I look to you like one of them varmints." Kavanagh made no display or open threat, but Eli knew a man of his nature would pack at least one gun and probably a selection of knives for good measure.

"Miss Bernard hired you. I don't usually question her judgment."

"That's right loyal of you, Patterson."

"Are you of the opinion that Miss Bernard doesn't deserve loyalty, Mr. Kavanagh?"

The tracker scowled. "Tally asked me to deliver the doc to her door, and that's just what I'm doing."

"Then your services are no longer needed. You'll be paid what you're owed and put up for the night. I advise you not to bother Miss Bernard. Am I clear, Mr. Kavanagh?"

"I understood Tally's fancy talk, and I understand yours."

"Then we have no quarrel. I'll see you at the bunkhouse." He fell back to join Johansen, who was nearly falling off his horse. Eli guided the doctor toward the lanterns Miriam had put around the yard to light the travelers' way. Bart and Federico had come in from the range; they looked after the horses, while Pablo proudly carried the doctor's saddle-bags into the house. Miriam took the doctor in custody a moment later.

Kavanagh was almost to the door before Eli could stop him. Eli blocked the threshold and folded his arms across his chest. "You've got no business in the house," he said. "You'll bunk and eat with me and the men."

The tracker stood a few inches shorter than Eli, but his stare was as potent as a punch to the gut. "I don't take orders from you," he said.

"You take them or get on your horse and ride out now."

"No, Eli. It's all right."

Tally brushed past him from the doorway. She'd kept on her hat and dusty clothes so she could introduce herself to Johansen as André's brother, but it was obvious to Eli that she was desperately in need of rest.

"Mr. Kavanagh," she said, stepping between the two men, "thank you for your quick return with the doctor."

Kavanagh nodded brusquely. "You all right?"

"I'm fine. The doctor…he needs some time to examine André. There's not much more any of us can do but wait."

"I was telling him that he can get his grub with the men tonight," Eli said. "I'll pay him off, Miss Tally. No need for you to trouble yourself."

"It's no trouble, Eli. We'll all eat in the bunkhouse so that André can rest undisturbed." She turned to Kavanagh. "Is there anything else you need, Mr. Kavanagh?"

Eli looked with bemusement from Tally to the tracker. Kavanagh had scarcely moved since Tally had appeared, but his hard face bore the addled expression of an outlaw bronc who'd been saddled and ridden around the corral before he could even think of putting up a fight. Tally had done that to him with a few quiet words.

"I can see you're done in," Kavanagh said after a long hesitation. He fiddled with the brim of his hat and pulled it low over his brow. "I'll go see to Diablo."

"I'll ask Pablo to give him and the doctor's horse an extra ration of oats. Good night." She smiled at Kavanagh and returned to the house. Kavanagh didn't try to follow.

"Do you think you can find your way to the barn?" Eli asked pointedly.

"I found Tally's brother," Kavanagh said. "Don't *you* ever get yourself lost, Patterson."

"I won't, Mr. Kavanagh." Eli waited until Kavanagh turned on his boot heel and strode toward the barn. Miriam came to stand beside Eli, following his stare into the darkness.

"He did what he promised," she said.

"That may be. But he's no good, Miriam. When I was in the army…we hunted men like him. I know a killer when I see one."

"Then why didn't he hurt Tally when he had the chance?"

Hurt. Miriam had been "hurt" more than once, and no one had less reason to forgive than she did.

"I don't know," he said. "I don't know why Tally trusted him in the first place. But that man is not in this for a few dollars. He's got too much interest in Miss Tally. Or something else at Cold Creek."

Miriam rested her cheek against Eli's arm, and his heart gave a painful thump. "You don't have enough faith, Elijah. There's good in every man. And there's a reason this one was sent to Miss Tally."

Eli covered her hand with his. He couldn't deny Miriam the comfort of her faith. He, too, believed in certain supernatural powers that could neither be seen nor touched. "I'll be watching him until he leaves Cold Creek."

"Don't you ever stop being a soldier?"

"A man doesn't have to be a soldier to protect the folk he cares about."

They were silent for a time. Coyotes yipped in the hills, and voices whispered in the back of the house.

"Come and help me get supper to the bunkhouse," Miriam said at last. "I've got to make Miss Tally take some food and get a good rest tonight, or she'll fall apart."

"She won't leave André's side."

"I'll sit up with Mr. André so she can sleep."

Eli bowed to Miriam's superior will and helped her fill several plates with chicken and biscuits, a special meal she hoped would tempt Tally to eat before the long night was over. He spoke to Federico and Bart about what had happened, left them to their meals and took a lantern to the barn to look in on Kavanagh.

The tracker had laid out his bedroll in the box stall with his stallion, apparently unconcerned that the high-strung animal might trample him in his sleep. His eyes reflected red in the lantern light like those of a night-hunting animal.

"Are you comfortable, Mr. Kavanagh?" Eli asked.

"Very comfortable." Kavanagh stretched, cracking the joints of his knuckles. "Sweet dreams, Mr. Foreman."

He knew as well as Eli that no one at Cold Creek was likely to get much sleep. And that Eli's nights would be troubled for a long time to come.

SIM COULD HAVE GONE to Tally any time he chose. No one would hear him slip in the door to the main house or crawl through a window—no, not even Elijah Patterson, with his soldier's air and suspicious eyes.

But he had no reason to see her until morning. This peculiar need was like a small cholla spine lodged in the palm of his hand, barely more than annoying for one used to frequent discomfort. Yet he'd been gone only two days, and during those two days Tally had been a constant presence in his thoughts no matter how much he tried to be rid of her.

"Miss Tally." The way the black man spoke of her, a stranger might think she was some kind of princess from the other side of the world instead of a plainspoken, relatively sensible female who wore men's britches and a battered slouch hat.

"Ha," Sim muttered, and rolled a cigarette. He didn't

smoke them anymore, but he still liked to roll them. The habit was hard to break, and it gave his fingers something to do. The taste of tobacco hadn't set well with him ever since he started Changing and running as a wolf.

Diablo dropped his head and nibbled at Sim's hair. Sim gently pushed the big head away. "You're a little frisky after such a long ride," Sim said. "You smell mare, do you?"

Diablo blew sharply through his nose.

"I knew I should have had you gelded," Sim said. Diablo shook his head. "You think I should be, too? It don't work that way, pard." He kicked off his boots and lay back on his bedroll, the unlit cigarette clenched between his teeth. "The only cure I need is for André to wake up and talk about the treas—"

The faint crunch of feet on gravel silenced him instantly, and he sat up with his hand on his gun before he recognized the tread. He let go of the ivory grip and stood up to meet her.

Tally entered the barn slowly, as if she were afraid she might be intruding. Sim struck a match and held it near his face.

"I'm awake," he said.

"Elijah told me you refused his offer of a bunk with the other men," she said.

He blew out the match, leaving the barn in darkness. Sim didn't need the extra light. He saw her well enough, and what he saw made his voice rough with surprise.

"What else did Elijah tell you?" he asked.

Tally hopped up on the partition of the stall and sat there, perfectly balanced. "He told me he didn't trust you...but I think you know that already."

"He's quick to decide what he doesn't like."

"So am I. But when it comes to Cold Creek, I follow my own judgment."

Sim stared at her bare feet braced on the partition—strong feet, not in the least delicate but strangely fascinating. She still wore britches, but a woman's unbound breasts pushed against the cloth of her plain farmer's shirt. And she'd done something to her hair. He'd seen it loose before, as she wore it now, yet he hadn't imagined it could look so clean and shining, like a field of ripe wheat rippling in the wind. And her face... He didn't know what she'd changed, but no man in his right mind would ever mistake her for a boy.

Sim bit down so hard on the cigarette that he got a mouthful of tobacco. He spat it out and jammed a piece of straw in his mouth instead. "How's your brother?"

"The doctor examined him and put on fresh bandages, but there wasn't much more he could do. André...may or may not recover. He needs rest and quiet...and time."

Her matter-of-fact tone was meant to hide the grief she must be feeling, just as Sim disguised his own disappointment. Disappointment, hell—this was disaster, if the doc's worst prediction was right.

"I'm sorry," he said, amazed at how sincere the words sounded in the mouth of a man who'd seldom had occasion to use them.

"I believe you are."

He knelt and pretended to examine Diablo's near foreleg. "You'll be running the ranch yourself now," he said. "You'll be short-handed."

"Elijah's a very good range boss—not that we've ever had enough men to need one. We're not a big outfit. Not yet." Tally brushed her hair out of her face with a casually graceful gesture that pushed Sim's heart into his throat. "What are your plans after this, Sim? Where are you going? To Esperanza?"

The mention of the name hit Sim like a clenched fist. He hadn't forgotten about Esperanza. Not for a second. But she seemed very far away in that little town in Sonora, not even knowing he would be coming for her.

When? When are you finally going to do it?

He'd learned long ago that it was better to tell part of the truth than a packful of lies. "I ain't exactly a rich man," he said. "I planned on going to Esperanza when I had a little more money saved up, so we could get married."

"That's quite understandable. Where is she?"

"Mexico."

Sim watched Tally out of the corner of his eye, engrossed by the way she bit her lower lip. He remembered the feel of those lips under his. He'd kissed Esperanza only twice, and he had difficulty picturing those distant moments in his mind.

Kissing Tally was supposed to be a cure, an end to the temptation of straying from his dream. Tally must have seen it for what it was. Of course she had.

"I have a proposal for you, Sim," she said.

Sim snapped the straw in two. "And what would that be?"

"I'd like you to stay here and work for me. Considering the trouble we had with rustlers last winter, I can use a man to take André's place until he's well again. I can't promise you good pay—you could get better almost anywhere else—"

"This time of year?" Sim leaned against the opposite wall of the stall and chose a fresh bit of straw. "Even the big spreads lay off men in summer."

"That may be, but we scrape by at the best of times. Elijah's here by choice. So is Miriam. Federico lost his wife two years ago, and Miriam looks after his little girl while he's riding. Bart has a crippled hand that makes it more difficult for him to find work where the owners and foremen can afford to be more fussy about who they hire."

"And you can't."

"I've been very lucky."

"What makes you think an army tracker would make a tolerable cowhand?"

"You're good with horses. My guess is that you've worked cattle in your day, and done just about everything else that's required on a small place like ours."

"Just about everything else" was right. He'd even tried a few excruciating stretches of legitimate labor, but blacksmithing and bronc-busting hadn't panned out when he'd needed real money to begin a straight life with Esperanza. The kind of cattle working Sim knew best wouldn't meet with Tally's approval.

But here she was, offering him a way to stay near André and keep looking for the thief who'd taken the map. If her brother hadn't recovered by the end of the summer, he probably never would. A steady job at Cold Creek would give Sim food and shelter and time to think through what he would do if the map…or, worst case, the treasure…was gone for good.

He'd seen enough of Cold Creek to know that Tally wasn't being modest about either its size or prosperity. The land itself was promising, with a spring and a creek that flowed the better part of the year, but she couldn't lay legal claim to any of it until this part of Arizona was officially surveyed. The main adobe house was serviceable, as were the barn and the few other outbuildings, but they weren't the work of someone with lofty ambitions for wealth and status. Tally had admitted she'd lost cattle to rustlers, and she probably hadn't owned many to begin with.

Those very disadvantages made her stubborn courage all the more remarkable. She knew what she had and planned to make the best of it, no matter the odds against her. There was no doubt in Sim's mind that she'd always been the boss at Cold Creek.

Ay, muy loco. He was crazy to seriously consider staying anywhere near a woman who interested him the way Tally did. No good telling himself that he could look at Tally and not feel…not feel something that even Esperanza, with all her purity and goodness…

Damnation. Tally and Esperanza weren't alike. Not anything alike. As long as he remembered that, he was safe. As long as he remembered that he had to earn Esperanza the way a man earns his way into heaven.

If he began to feel trapped, the wolf gave him a way out.

"Patterson won't like it," he said.

"He'll accept my decision." Tally slid down from the partition. "Do you want the job?"

"I'll take it, at least through the summer."

She hesitated, then offered her hand. He took it, feeling the calluses on her palms and the steadfast strength of her grip.

"There's only one other thing," she said, holding his gaze as firmly as his hand. "Everyone at Cold Creek keeps my secret away from the ranch or around outsiders like the doctor. I'm Tal, André's brother. That's the way I started out here, and how I intend to continue."

He released her hand, flexing his fingers to relieve the tingle in them. "Call yourself whatever you choose. I've got no reason to care one way or another."

"I didn't think so." She smiled at him the same way she smiled at Elijah and Miriam and probably at everyone who worked for her. "I'll inform Elijah. Tomorrow night you can sleep in a bunk."

Sim nodded and stepped back out of range of her scent and her touch. "Are you going to get some sleep now, boss?"

"Yes," she said quietly. "I think I will."

She walked out of the barn. Sim leaned against Diablo and breathed in the familiar smell of horseflesh until the stallion's head drooped and Sim gave himself up to the merciless reckoning of dreams.

CHAPTER SIX

DOCTOR JOHANSEN LEFT Cold Creek early the next day. He offered no more hope for André than he had given when he arrived, but at least he admitted to Tally that recovery was possible.

She paid Johansen out of her very limited stock of cash and devised a schedule so that either she or Miriam remained with André at all times. He continued to lie quietly, sometimes opening his eyes without seeing, at others moaning disjointed syllables that made no sense. Miriam made up a thin gruel that he was able to eat much as a baby would, but Tally worried that his health would fail even more quickly on such a diet.

The everyday work of running the ranch kept Tally sane after she'd spent several hours at her brother's bedside. Elijah was well able to manage the spread without her help, but Tally couldn't have borne day after day inside the house the way Miriam did. She went back to riding the range, working with Federico and Bart as they branded stray and orphaned calves, doctored sickly cattle, and mucked out tanks and water holes.

Elijah had another task. He hadn't been pleased when Tally had told him about Sim, but it was his job to show a new hand the ropes. The two men had to accept each other sooner or later, and Tally intended that it be sooner.

Tally saw little of Sim or Eli for several days. On the third evening both of them appeared in time for supper and assumed their places without ceremony, Elijah in André's chair and Sim in the foreman's seat, next to Bart.

Federico, halfway between scolding his children for bad table manners and describing a recent encounter with a cantankerous cow, fell silent when Sim sat down at the table. Bart grabbed a biscuit and bit into it, risking Miriam's wrath for eating before grace had been said. Pablito and Dolores, seated at their own miniature table, stared with wide, fascinated eyes at the stranger.

Miriam behaved as if this were just another ordinary meal. She served up the frijoles, ham and potatoes, and took her chair at Tally's other side. Her dark eyes met those of every man and woman at the table, coming last to Sim.

"We will pray," she said.

Heads bent and eyes closed, but Sim stared at Tally. She stared back. Miriam said grace, perhaps a bit more loudly than usual. She had an unerring sense for detecting lost souls.

Tally wasn't surprised that Sim didn't pray. She also wasn't surprised to find that she'd missed him over the past few days, even his sarcasm and double-edged remarks. The night he'd come with the doctor, she'd felt herself driven to speak with him in the barn, and for no good reason except her own loneliness. She'd taken strange comfort from his stolid inability or unwillingness to offer the usual pretty words meant to ease her grief. When he did speak, he meant what he said.

Here, among the spare comforts of her own home, he looked just as out of place as he had at the Brysons'. His eyes seemed more vivid, his features sharper and somehow feral in the lamplight. She couldn't begin to read what lay behind his stare or guess what he saw in hers.

But she knew she hadn't made a mistake in offering him the job. Elijah had brought him to the table; that was as close a sign of acceptance as Sim was ever likely to get from the former soldier. At least they hadn't come to blows....

"Amen," Miriam said.

"Amen," the others echoed. Miriam gave Tally a reproachful glance. Elijah scooped up a spoonful of frijoles. Pablito and Dolores set to their own meals with enthusiasm.

Tally cleared her throat. "You have all noticed by now that we have a new hand at Cold Creek." She smiled, trying to ease the unmistakable air of discomfort that hung so thick in the room. "Of course we've never been much for formality here, so we won't start now. I would like you to meet Simeon Kavanagh. He'll be working with us for the summer, until André is on his feet again."

Heavy silence followed her last remark. She folded her hands on the table and took a deep breath.

"It may seem as if everything has changed overnight. No one could have…expected my brother to get lost and hurt, but if it weren't for Mr. Kavanagh, I never would have found him. I won't give up hope, and I ask you all to do your best to keep things going the way they always have. It's what André would want."

Federico looked up from his plate. "*Como tú digas,* Señorita Tally. We must go on as before." He nodded to Sim. "*Bienvenido,* Señor Kavanagh. I am Federico Rodriguez, and these are my children, Pablo and Dolores." He glanced with mock severity from son to daughter. "How do you greet the gentleman, *mis hijos?*"

"*Bienvenido,*" Pablo said obediently, and grinned past a mouthful of beans. Dolores stuck her finger in her nose. Sim's mouth twitched, but it was obvious to Tally that he didn't know how to speak to children.

Bart shifted nervously in his chair. "Bart Stanfield," the gray-haired cowman said to Sim, offering his hand. Sim met his gaze, and Bart withdrew his hand, rubbing his palm on the side of his pants.

Tally frowned at Sim. "Bart has been in the Territory longer than almost anyone. He's fought Apaches and lived to talk about it."

Bart ducked his head. "Everyone had to in those days," he said.

Sim leaned back in his chair until it creaked dangerously and balanced on two legs. "Stanfield," he said thoughtfully. "I've heard of you."

The older man's faded blue eyes peered up at Sim, bright with hope. He returned to his food with gusto.

"You've met Miriam," Tally said. "She runs the house and manages our food stores. Don't cross her unless you want a little too much chili in your frijoles."

Sim gave a startling smile, all white teeth and an edge of dark humor. "I like my chuck hot."

"I imagine Miriam could lay her hands on a little rat bait if she set her mind to it," Elijah said.

Bart choked on his biscuit. Miriam clapped a hand over her mouth, and Federico sighed. Pablito burst into giggles. Sim continued to smile.

"You know a rat 'round here needs killing?" he asked Elijah.

Eli smiled back at him. "Even rats can be useful from time to time."

Sim's chair crashed back to all four legs. "Elijah and me had a nice tour of your spread, Miss Tally," he said. "He's a mighty fine range boss, Mr. Patterson is."

"And you're satisfied with Mr. Kavanagh's work?" Tally asked Elijah.

She knew Eli well enough to expect him to tell the truth, even if it embarrassed both her and Sim. Eli took his time about answering. He slathered butter on a biscuit and ate it almost daintily.

"He'll do," he said at last. "Until Mr. Bernard is well again."

"I'm glad to hear it." Tally took a slice of ham. She would have to speak to Miriam about such lavish expenditures for everyday meals, even though she knew her friend was doing it for her sake. God knew she hadn't had much of an appetite. "Since we are speaking of rats, has there been any sign of the rustlers since I left for Tombstone?"

"None," Eli said. "They must figure we don't have much left worth stealing."

"We have a new crop of calves," Bart said. "Once they're weaned…"

"They won't succeed again," Eli said grimly. "We'll be ready for them."

"You have a strategy in mind, *mi amigo?*" Federico asked. He turned to Sim. "Señor Patterson fought with the Buffalo Soldiers, the Tenth Cavalry. I understand that you also served in the army, Señor Kavanagh."

Sim shrugged. Eli pinned Federico with an eloquent stare. He hated to talk about his past with the army. Tally knew only scraps of his history. Like her, he couldn't entirely escape the influence of his former profession. Discipline and skill were evidence of his training, just as his educated upbringing showed in his speech and manner.

"I'm more interested in Mr. Kavanagh's suggestions on how to deal with cattle thieves," Elijah said.

Sim regarded the other man through half-lidded eyes. "I didn't know you were interested in any opinion of mine."

"I gather you two didn't do much talking in the last few days," Tally said dryly. "Do you have a suggestion, Sim?"

A hunter's spark lit his eyes. "Do you know who they are? I've heard the name McLaury in this part of the Territory."

"We never got a good look at 'em," Bart offered. "But the McLaurys are said to be among the worst of the cowboys in the Valley."

"I like to know the name of my enemy," Sim said. He held Tally's gaze. "You don't need to worry about those cowboys, Miss Tally. They won't bother you again."

Elijah leaned over the table. "That's pretty big talk, Kavanagh. It makes me wonder if you know these kinds of men a little better than you've let on."

Tally stood up. All the men but Sim jumped to their feet out of habitual courtesy.

"Please sit down," she said firmly. "Elijah, I'd prefer that you don't make accusations without proof. I'm satisfied as to Mr. Kavanagh's background and abilities. At times like these, we can't afford to turn against each other."

Eli sat down, but his muscles were taut with strain. "If I owe you an apology, Mr. Kavanagh, you have it."

"If I ever need one," Sim said, "I'll take it."

Tally banged her hand on the table. *"Gentlemen,"* she said, deliberately implying that they didn't deserve the name, "I think that's enough of this discussion for tonight. Sim, are you set up in the bunkhouse?"

Sim nodded, but Tally could see that his thoughts were elsewhere. Miriam got up to clear the dishes, effectively ending the meal. Federico took his children away to wash up before bed, and Bart left so quietly that no one seemed to notice he was gone. Elijah spoke briefly to Miriam and walked out the front door.

Sim scraped back his chair and rose with an extravagant stretch. He stalked around the table, intercepting Miriam with her armful of dirty plates.

"Mighty good cooking," he said, taking the plates from her hands. He winked at Tally. "Better than Mrs. Bryson's, I'd say."

Miriam stared at him, openmouthed, and took a step back. "Why…thank you, Mr. Kavanagh."

"No one calls me that," he said. He set the plates down beside the washbasin. "It's Sim."

Miriam exchanged startled glances with Tally. "Sim," she repeated. "Simeon."

"No one calls me that, either," he said. Somehow he insinuated himself next to Tally without seeming to have moved across the room. He drew her out the door and onto the porch. A breeze had risen to drive away the day's heat, and Tally turned her face into the wind's caress.

Sim pulled a rolled cigarette from his waistcoat pocket and contemplated it as if it were a rival to be defeated. "I meant what I said in there," he said.

"About the rustlers? I never doubted it."

He cast her a sideways glance. "No questions? No suspicions?"

She leaned against the house's cool adobe wall. "Elijah may be right. I'm not ignorant, Sim. I never dismissed the possibility that you've walked on both sides of the law."

Sim dropped the cigarette and crushed it under his boot. "Some men might take offense at that implication."

"Do you?"

"Do I look angry?"

She wasn't about to admit how difficult it was to read the expressions on his face. "Then Elijah has reason for his concern."

"You still want me here?"

"Everyone deserves a chance to make a new life. A better life." She met his eyes. "Isn't that what you want, Sim?"

Slowly he lifted his hand, fingers spread. Tally forgot to breathe. She barely felt the brush of Sim's fingers on her cheek.

"I thought I did," he said. "It's easier to go the other way."

"It's always easier not to change."

He let his hand fall. "Maybe it's impossible."

"Alone, yes. You aren't alone at Cold Creek."

His eyes did something remarkable then, permitting her a glimpse of vulnerability, even fear. She saw a boy who had lost as much as she had but had turned in anger against the loss, crushing its power and even his memory of it.

But the memories were not dead. She had aroused them again. In a moment the child behind his eyes would become a man, enraged that his careful shields had been breached by a mere woman.

She turned away. "I'm grateful for what you said to Bart and Miriam. As for Elijah…"

The porch stair creaked. Sim was gone, lost in the dusk. A minute later Eli joined her.

"You still intend to keep him on?" he asked.

"You gave your approval," she said. "I assumed you meant it."

Eli gripped the porch railing. "He's a good worker, fast and strong. He knows cattle and horses. In fact, I'd say he has an almost uncanny way with them. But I don't like him, and I never will."

"You truly think he's a rustler?"

"I don't know. He wouldn't talk about his past, or about much of anything, really. He just did what I told him."

"At least he's not like a lot of the men in Texas."

"The ones who wouldn't take orders from a black man?" Eli smiled. "They're not the most dangerous. Not by half."

"I'm willing to take the risk, Eli."

He looked down at her. "This is about more than just finding a replacement for André, isn't it?"

"He helped me save André's life."

"It's more than that, too." Eli shook his head. "You and I— we're friends, Tally. Maybe it's strange to the world that a black man and a white woman could be friends. But we made a haven here that's safe for all of us…to be what we are."

She touched his arm. "I know, Eli. That's why we can't turn away someone who may need a place just like this."

"Pity for a man like Sim?"

"If it ever becomes more than that, I think you'll know." She gave him a little push toward the door. "Go inside. Miriam's waiting."

He went, reluctantly and with several backward glances. Tally lingered on the porch. Federico's voice, singing some Mexican lullaby, drifted from his little cabin behind the main house. Dishes clattered in the kitchen, while Eli and Miriam shared their own secret language.

Tally envied them. At first glance they seemed to have little in common. Elijah had been born to a prosperous family in the North and had fought for the Union during the war; when his father had lost his fortune, he'd continued on with the army to the western frontier. Miriam had been born a slave, freed as a girl when Union troops defeated the Confederacy. She took great comfort in her faith, while Eli professed to have none.

But each of them knew about suffering and facing the ignorant judgment of others. Eli had been treated badly in Texas after he left the army. Miriam had found work as a maid in a brothel, earning a tiny fraction of what the soiled doves made by selling their bodies. Once she'd been given her freedom, she'd never let it go.

Eli and Miriam might have left Texas and made lives for themselves apart from the memories that came with André and Chantal Bernard. Tally never asked them why they'd chosen as they had. They were family, and Eli had become more a brother to her than André had been.

What did that make Sim?

She wandered off the porch and walked aimlessly around the homestead. What did she feel for Sim Kavanagh? Certainly not pity. He wasn't a man to be pitied by anyone. If he was lonely, he'd chosen his own loneliness.

Nevertheless, she liked him—his skill, his gruff respect for her as a person, his unexpected and oddly timed spells of compassion and even playfulness. He wielded scorn as a weapon, but he didn't judge her for dressing and living as she did. She found him attractive as a normal woman might find a well-favored man.

Enfer, that shouldn't even be possible. She hadn't found a man attractive since she'd believed herself in love at the tender age of fourteen. "Mademoiselle Champagne" felt no physical desire for her lovers. Tally wasn't even sure of what such feelings consisted. Her marriage hadn't been built of love or passion, but convenience; she'd simply gone from one type of bondage to another. She had grown to loathe the touch of men's bodies or even the thought of submitting in that way again.

She had few illusions about Sim. Maybe she felt an attraction because he had declared himself unattainable, bound to another woman.

Tally sat on a stump near the chicken coop and looked up at the stars. Coyotes wailed in the distance, but their cry was cut off by the deeper howling of wolves, much nearer.

Wolves could decimate what remained of Cold Creek's herd, but until a week ago they'd stayed in the northern Chiricahuas. Tally dreaded the prospect of laying traps. Captivity of any kind turned her stomach. But if the very survival of Cold Creek was at stake…

She'd told Sim that she didn't blame anything for trying to stay alive, and it was true.

She got up and strode back into the house. Miriam had finished her cleaning and was sitting with André in his room. Tally paused in the doorway.

"You should have reminded me, Miriam. It's my turn now."

"I don't mind, Miss Tally," Miriam said, putting down her knitting.

"I thought you might like to spend a little time with Eli."

"Not when he's in such a mood."

"Over Sim Kavanagh."

Miriam sighed. "I don't rightly know what to think of that one."

"Neither do I. You go to bed, Miriam. I'll stay up for a while."

"Call me when you need me." Miriam took her knitting to her room down the hall and closed her door. Tally took the warm seat beside the bed.

"I don't know if you can hear me, André," she said. "I can hardly recognize you anymore." She pulled the chair closer and smoothed her brother's hair. His eyelids twitched, but no expression showed on his face. "What would you have said about Sim? You were always quick to trust people—at least the wrong sorts of people." She smiled sadly. "Why did you go to the mountains? Were you so afraid of facing me after you lost the money? Did I expect too much of you, *mon cher?*"

Of course you did, she told herself. *You wanted things to be different here. You wanted to make a whole new beginning. But André's heart never seemed to be in the ranch itself. There was something else calling him, and you weren't interested in his dreams....*

"Are you lying here because of me, André?"

He didn't answer. She wouldn't have dared to ask him if he could. He'd given her a home when Nathan died, even though he knew what she'd been. When that home proved less than ideal, he'd been willing to try to change. Her faults were far more damning than his weaknesses.

She leaned over the bed and touched her forehead to his. "We will survive this, André. You have to keep fighting. Promise me you'll keep fighting."

Her tears splashed his cheek, and she wiped them away with her thumb. No one had seen her weep since the terrible night of her "initiation" in New Orleans, and she'd sworn no one ever would again.

If you die, I'll have to break my oath. Live, André. Live for both of us.

SIM HEARD TALLY WEEPING, though the sound was so soft that human ears couldn't have detected it. He smelled her tears through the thick window glass of André's room. She wept for *him*, a milksop who didn't deserve her grief, and Sim hated André for turning her into another ordinary woman.

He strode away from the house, listening for the howling of wolves in the hills. His thoughts ran round and round in circles, like a dog chasing its tail. He had lied to himself when he called Tally ordinary. He'd lied because he'd given away too much tonight, and it was more comfortable to blame her than his own stupidity.

She'd asked him if he wanted a new life. A better life. For a moment, there on the porch, he'd completely forgotten Esperanza. Tally was all he saw, all he could imagine. He'd touched her. And with that touch he'd betrayed the only woman who could make it possible for him to change, to have that new life.

One touch and he knew how it would be to lie with Tally Bernard. He didn't know if she was a virgin. She used her brother's name, but that might be for protection and freedom, like the male disguise. She could be a widow, for all he knew. She was respectable, yes, but something—his wolf senses, perhaps—told him that she wasn't an innocent.

Esperanza was. When he imagined a life with Esperanza, he tried to picture them sharing a bed. He'd kissed her in New Mexico, out of anger more than passion, but those kisses gave him nothing to go on. He couldn't see himself holding her naked body in his arms, hearing her moans of pleasure as he took her. The image was almost obscene.

But with Tally, nothing interfered with his illusions. He could envision every line and curve of her body under the plain masculine clothes. Just being near her affected him. He hadn't had a woman in months, because he wouldn't sully his dream rutting between the legs of cheap whores and light-skirted barmaids.

It's easier to go the other way, he'd told Tally. He always took the easy path, the road to hell. It would be simple now to leave Cold Creek, forget about the map, forget Esperanza. Forget redemption.

Tally had said he wasn't alone, but she was wrong.

Halfway to the bunkhouse, Sim turned on his heel and went to the stable. Diablo had been turned out in the home pasture to graze and rest after carrying Sim all over the ranch; an elderly, placid gelding occupied the stall, and the old fellow had no interest in a man who shucked his outer coverings, hid them under the straw and ran naked into the night.

Sim knew the wolves were near. He'd listened to their calls every night since his arrival at Cold Creek, and he was certain they were the same pack he and Tally had heard in Castillo Canyon. He couldn't be sure that they'd followed him here. But now he needed them…needed their wildness, their freedom, their indifference to human joy and suffering.

He Changed and let his nose lead him to the east, skimming over the hills and arroyos of the valley, and climbing into the forested uplands of the mountains. The wolves were silent now. They knew he was coming. Sim smelled fear and curiosity and challenge. Then the wind shifted, and so did the pack.

They led him higher into the mountains. The pack leader left his scent on rock and tree, mocking and threatening one who might dare to steal his place. But even he grew weary. He brought his mates to rest in a rocky hollow framed by tall pines and waited for Sim, tail bristling and teeth bared for battle.

Sim was more than ready for a fight. He was bigger than the gray male who faced him, bigger than any wolf who had ever run in the Territory. But even if he'd been half the size, it would have made no difference. He'd lived through a hundred confrontations just as deadly.

In at least one way, wolves were like men: they bluffed. And if their enemy called their bluff and proved superior, they either backed down...or they died.

He advanced stiff-legged, staring the leader in his slanted yellow eyes. The gray bristled and snarled. Sim focused all his will on the beast, testing the power that some *hombres-lobos* were supposed to possess.

The pack leader lowered his head, ears pressed to the sides of his skull, and tucked his tail between his legs. Sim felt the wolf's defeat as if it were his own, and it gave him no satisfaction. There was no fairness in such a contest, for Sim had abilities these wolves did not, abilities he had hardly begun to discover.

He let instinct take hold, showing him how to use the fluid motions of his lupine body in a dance of recognition and acceptance, how to explain in the wolves' native tongue that he had not come to steal the leader's place. They gathered about him, wagging tails and licking his muzzle, welcoming him as one of their own.

He was not, but he pretended. He ran as they ran. He hunted as they did, driving game to them so that they and their pups fed well that night. For a while he forgot why he had fled to the mountains. But when the sun's creeping warmth tinged the air with the scent of a new morning, he remembered his purpose at Cold Creek and decided to test his abilities once more. He made the wolves understand what he sought.

The pack leader acknowledged Sim's request. The wolves would find it easy enough to watch for human intruders in the vicinity of Castillo Canyon. If the map thief spent any time in the mountains, they would report it. But they were not like the cattle and horses Sim controlled with little more than a thought. He had no desire to force the wolves' obedience, or determine the limits of his powers.

A young subordinate male bounced from the pack, squirmed like a pup at Sim's feet and set off for the north. Sim returned to Cold Creek. He dressed and slipped into the bunkhouse with no one the wiser, rising with the other hands at dawn.

FROM THAT NIGHT ON, Sim's life took on a simple rhythm, divided between two very different worlds. Each morning he rode out on the range to do a cowhand's work, sometimes with one of the other men, often alone. He never rode with Tally, and she didn't seek his company. He ate at the supper table every evening, learning how to make conversation that never touched on his past or his innermost thoughts.

And at night he ran with the wolves. There were times when he was tempted to remain with them beyond the sunrise, for he sensed that if he chose such a path, his humanity would gradually fade and leave him without memory of the life he had known as a man. The temptation came and went, but it never entirely left him.

Without his dream, he might have surrendered. He made a ritual of remembering, calling Esperanza's image into his mind and carrying it with him like a talisman. But all too often dark eyes and hair turned to gold and honey, gentle innocence to tough practicality, and he was lost again.

He wasn't a praying man. He didn't ask for help from some indifferent God in heaven. But every night he howled to the stars, seeking a peace he hadn't earned.

CHAPTER SEVEN

HEAT AND DUST.

Tally lifted the brim of her hat, wiped at the perspiration on her brow and settled the brim low over her eyes. The early July sun beat down on the range like a fist, loosening the dirt into endless clouds of fine dust that got into boots and clothing and eyes and mouths with equal abandon.

These were the summer doldrums, the long days of waiting for the heavy rains that fell in late July, August and often into September. The grass was dry and brown, though the tough Mexican cattle were happy enough to eat it; the creek had shrunk to a trickle, and the spring near the homestead attracted every bird and wild animal within several miles.

Tally knew that Cold Creek was fortunate. In addition to the spring, it had several water holes where cattle congregated after a day of grazing under a ferocious sun. None of Tally's beasts were dying of thirst or hunger. Animals still needed doctoring, and the tanks required frequent work to clear them after constant trampling by thirsty beeves, but even those unpleasant tasks were small enough price to pay.

This was freedom. It was all she'd ever wanted—honest hard work she could do with her hands, standing on her feet or with her legs around the barrel of a horse. Her nails were chipped and her fingers calloused; the muscles in her arms were firm and taut and her face was permanently brown. But she regretted nothing of what she'd given up, feared nothing of the future except losing what she'd found.

She rode to the top of her favorite ridge and looked out upon the valley and the wagon road winding along its center. Scattered oaks sheltered cattle enjoying their noon siestas. Jays chattered among the piñons, and a hawk soared in wide, sweeping arcs high overhead. The nearest neighboring homestead was ten miles away—not that Tally often left the ranch—but she never felt lonely in this austere land.

The hawk cried, calling her bluff. Never lonely? A year ago, six months, two…then it might have been true. But André still lay in his bed, little changed, and Tally's heart had developed a crack, kept raw and unhealed by a yearning she had no means to cure.

The weakness was her own. She'd left New Orleans convinced that she didn't need or want any man; that was a fact she had guarded like a precious treasure chest for which only she held the key. Finding André after so many years of separation had softened her resolve as nothing else could. Even though Eli had also become a friend and trusted partner, André remained the vital symbol of the peaceful, ordinary home life Tally had hoped to create at Cold Creek.

Now that cherished dream lay nearly in ruins. She'd learned to need André as well as love him. She'd wanted to depend on him, expecting him to be the strong elder brother, betraying herself with the desire for a protector who had no interest in her body.

She laughed and leaned her head against Muérdago's warm neck. She hadn't really given André a chance to protect her. The scars ran too deep. She became the protector, trying to save her brother from himself. And she'd failed him. Now, when he'd gone far away to a place she couldn't reach, she had merely looked for another to take his place.

Another man, nothing like André. A stranger. A dangerous man who could never be ruled or controlled. He rode beside her under the burning sun, but only in her mind. Eight weeks Sim had been at Cold Creek, but whether by choice or Eli's direction, he always found work at the opposite end of the range. She and Sim met at the supper table, as polite and distant as any boss and hired hand could be.

Tally longed for the end of every day—and dreaded it.

This day had just begun, and she was glad to be alone where Miriam couldn't look at her with too-knowing eyes and Eli didn't have to hide his scowl of disapproval. She clucked to Muérdago and had started down the side of the ridge when she saw the rider emerge from a plume of dust.

The rider was small and clung to his mount's neck as if he had ridden to the point of exhaustion. His horse was in little better state. Its coat was slick with sweat, and Tally guessed that it moved as quickly as it did only because it smelled water, hay and a place to rest.

Muérdago was every bit as curious as Tally and willingly galloped full out to meet the stranger. Tally slowed the gelding at the road to keep down the dust, but one look at the rider's face made her pull to a dead stop.

Beth Bryson. She rode astride, her skirt stretched over the saddle and rump of her mount. Riding boots covered most of her lower legs, but she still displayed much more limb than a proper girl ought to do. She was hatless, which was foolish as well as improper, and her hair was a tangled mess flying about her flushed face.

If she'd ridden from Castillo Canyon alone, her physical appearance was the least of her worries. Tally checked the angle of her hat and reined Muérdago alongside the girl's sorrel mare.

"Beth?"

The girl looked up from between hunched shoulders and stared at Tally. "Tal?" She croaked. "Am I here? Is this Cold Creek?"

"Yes." Beth swayed in the saddle. Tally caught her by the arm. "What are you doing here, Beth? Where are your parents?"

Beth tried to sit up straight and stifled a gasp of pain. "They didn't come." Her shadowed eyes welled with tears. "They don't want me to go anywhere. They keep me at home as if I were a…a—" She coughed, and Tally unhooked her canteen. The girl accepted it eagerly. She splashed water over her face and bodice as she drank, turning dust to mud.

"You and your horse both need rest," Tally said. "You can explain later."

Beth finished with the canteen and clutched it to her chest. "They don't think I can do anything. I had to show—" She sucked in her breath. "I feel sick."

Tally took the mare's reins. "Can you ride a little farther?"

"Yes."

"Then save your breath until we get to the house."

Beth thrust out her jaw as if she would argue, but fatigue got the better of her. She was drooping over the saddle horn by the time they reached the homestead. Tally pulled Beth from the mare's back and half carried her into the house.

"Miriam?" she called.

Miriam emerged from the back of the house, Dolores holding on to her skirts. "Tally? Oh, my Lord."

"I'm afraid I have another patient for you," Tally said. "This is Beth Bryson, from up in Castillo Canyon."

"Castillo…but isn't that—"

"A good forty miles, and she came alone."

Miriam's face crumpled with sympathy. "Poor child. Why would she do such a thing?"

Beth lifted her head. "I…it's because…"

"Don't you try to talk," Miriam scolded. "Put her in my bed, Miss Tally. Mr. André is sleeping."

Tally carried Beth to Miriam's room, while Miriam settled Dolores with her favorite doll. Once Beth was safely in Miriam's care, Tally went out to look after the girl's horse. She turned Muérdago out in the home pasture and changed from her riding gear to more comfortable house clothes, preserving her masculine appearance.

By then Beth was sipping tea, propped up on several pillows on Miriam's bed. She flushed when Tally entered the room.

"How is she?" Tally asked Miriam.

"Worn out, parched as a sack of bones and more than a little sore—" she pressed her skirts against her legs in illustration "—but she'll live."

"I'm sorry," Beth stammered, setting the china cup on the bed table. "I didn't mean to cause so much trouble."

Tally pulled up a seat beside Miriam. "What did you mean, riding all this way alone? Where did you spend the night?"

Beth buried her hands in the bedclothes, avoiding Tally's gaze. "I slept under a bush. I brought food and water, but it didn't last as long as I expected." Her lips pressed together in a show of defiance. "I had to get away. All Mother talks about is how I have to learn to be a lady. She says I might meet a man any day now, and I must win my husband with my fine cooking and pretty face. But that's not what I want."

"Not what you want?" Tally struggled to keep her voice under control. "Do you know what your parents must be thinking at this moment? They'll be terrified for you, not knowing where to look."

"I know. I said awful things to Mother. I just got on Brandy and started riding...and then I thought of you and Sim."

"How did you know where to find Cold Creek?"

"Your vaquero Federico told us when he returned the wagon. How is your brother?"

"We aren't discussing my brother, young lady. Do you have any idea how lucky you are to have a family who loves you and cares for you?"

"I'm not lucky." Beth hesitated, and then the words burst forth like a flash flood after a rainstorm. "You're the lucky one. You can do whatever you please, live in any way you choose—and all because everyone thinks you're a man."

Miriam started and glanced at Tally. "Miss Beth—"

Tally held up her hand. "I know you aren't trying to insult me with such talk," she said in her lowest voice. "Maybe I'd better leave you with Miriam."

She rose to go. Beth sat up, nearly knocking her china cup off the table. "I know you're a woman," she announced. "I knew it when you first came to our house."

Tally paused in the doorway and debated her answer. Beth might be guessing, but Tally saw a little too much of herself in this young woman. "What made you decide such a thing?" she asked in a neutral tone.

Beth sank back among the pillows. "I just figured it out. But I didn't tell anyone. I knew you were keeping it a secret."

"Your parents don't know?"

"It's a very good disguise," Beth said helpfully. "Do you use it all the time, even in town?"

Tally sighed. "I think you've had enough excitement for one day."

"You don't want to tell me," Beth said, bunching the coverlet into a ball against her chest. "But I know why you do it. People listen to men. They pay attention. A man can choose what he wants to do, not wait around for a husband to make all the rules. No one tells you how to behave."

Tally wanted to laugh. Beth had only guessed the half of

it. She didn't know Tally's other reasons, and Tally didn't intend to share them. Nor would she set an example of hypocrisy and deception.

"I'm a grown woman," she said sternly. "I've lived at least
ten years longer than you, and I've learned things I hope you
never have to."

"But I want to learn them. I want you to teach me."

"Teach you what, Beth? How to act like a man?"

"If that's what I have to do to be free." Beth pushed the covers away almost violently. "I want to ride and work cattle and
go into town whenever I feel like it. I want to choose whether
or not to get married, not have a husband picked out for me.
You're not married…are you?"

"No."

"But this ranch belongs to you and your brother. Men work
for you. Like Sim."

Tally had wondered when his name might come up. "Sim
works for me, yes."

"Is he…do you—" Beth flushed again. "You were in the
same bedroom all night. If Mother knew—"

"Sim spent that night in the stable," Tally said, too quickly.
"Sim is one of my hands, nothing more."

Beth's shoulders sagged as if in relief. "Then you're not—
he's not your…your—"

"Non, non."

"But he knows you're a woman."

Tally nodded reluctantly.

"If other people found out, they'd say terrible things about
you. I've heard Mother talking about fast women in the towns.
That's why she keeps me at home. She thinks a woman by herself has to be bad, but that isn't true."

Mon Dieu. "I was married once," Tally said. "Widows are
allowed more freedom than young girls. You could have been

hurt coming here, Beth. There are bad men in the Territory who don't care about a woman's honor."

"Men can defend their own honor," Beth said fiercely. "You have a gun."

"I never use it."

"But you could if you had to. That's what I want to learn."

Tally closed her eyes. She didn't even know how to begin to make Beth understand the consequences of her dream. She removed her hat and freed the pins that held her hair close to the crown of her head.

Beth gasped. "Your hair…it's beautiful."

"As yours would be if it weren't in tangles," Tally said. "We've talked enough for now. Miriam will make up a bath and help you wash your hair. Then you'll rest, and we'll decide…what to do."

"I won't go back."

Tally stood over the bed, hands on hips. "I'm bigger and stronger than you are, *ma fille*. Remember that."

Beth chose to change the subject. "Where is Sim now?"

"Working, with the other men."

"Will he come back later?"

Ah. Tally examined her short-clipped nails. "He'll be here for supper, but you'll take your meals in this room."

"But—"

"Sim would be shocked to see the young lady he met in Castillo Canyon looking as you do now," Tally said, falling on the ease of a fairly harmless white lie and hoping Beth would believe it. "Do as Miriam says."

"I have some bread and cold ham," Miriam suggested. "You keep quiet, Miss Beth, and I'll heat water for your bath."

Beth rolled her eyes like one much put upon. "Oh, very well," she said. She remembered her manners as Tally and Miriam reached the door. "Thank you."

"You're welcome," Tally said. She closed the door and clutched Miriam's arm, shaking with silent laughter.

"If you think this is funny, I'd like to know the joke," Miriam said.

"It's absurd," Tally said. "A sheltered girl of fifteen is the only one who sees through my disguise, and she wants to be just like me."

"What she thinks you are," Miriam said softly. "She believes freedom is simple."

Tally wiped her eyes. "Most freeborn people never question their fates, Miriam. The ones who do always suffer."

"It's suffering that brings wisdom."

"But that shouldn't be the only way to learn. How can I discourage her, Miriam? How do I tell her to be a good girl without crushing her spirit or turning her into...something she'd regret for the rest of her life?"

Miriam gave Tally a brief hug. "You'll find a way to talk to her, Tally. Your heart will tell you." She started briskly for the kitchen. "The child seems to have an interest in Mr. Kavanagh."

"She only met him once."

"Sometimes that's enough."

Miriam was right. Tally spent so little time around other women that she'd forgotten that conventional females found "dangerous" men attractive. A man like Sim would fascinate a girl who resisted the rules society decreed for her sex.

Sim had his own perfect "angel" waiting for him in Mexico. Beth hadn't tempted him in Castillo Canyon, but any man might respond to a young woman who found him irresistible. The last thing Beth needed was the kind of provocative company Sim would provide. He would only fan the flames of her rebellion, even if he didn't intend to.

And who do you worry for most, Beth or yourself?

Tally drove such thoughts from her mind and helped Miriam carry the hip bath down the hall. Then she looked in on André. He was sleeping, as he usually did for the better part of each day. She sat in the chair, listening to Miriam bustle around the kitchen. Beth must have cooperated with her bath. Tally dozed, waking to a tap at the door.

"Miss Tally?"

Tally stretched and glanced at the window. The angle of the sun suggested that it was just after noon. "How is Beth?" she asked.

"Sleeping. The hot water boiled away some of that vinegar running through her veins." Miriam glanced at André. "Have you decided what you're going to do?"

"Take her back to Castillo Canyon tomorrow morning. Try to make her see how much she has to be grateful for."

"Maybe you ought to put on a dress when you do the talking."

"To show her what a nice lady I am?"

"She looks up to you. You can show her there's nothing wrong with being a woman."

"You would be better at that than I, Miriam."

"Only because you still can't see the difference between what you are and the things you had to do to survive." Miriam rested her hand on Tally's shoulder. "I was a slave, but that isn't who I am."

"You didn't choose your captivity."

"Neither did you. Now come on out of this room. There's something I've been meaning to tell you." Much to Tally's astonishment, Miriam's brown cheeks took on a russet warmth of self-consciousness.

"What is it?" Tally asked. "I believe you're keeping secrets from me, *m'amie.*"

"I just found out last night, and…come into the parlor, or I won't say a word."

Mystified, Tally followed her friend and sat beside her on the worn sofa. Miriam squirmed as if she couldn't get comfortable. Tally trapped Miriam's restless hands between her own.

"Enough. What is this great revelation?"

Miriam broke into a broad grin. "Eli asked me to marry him."

Tally shrieked and then covered her mouth to muffle the cry. She embraced Miriam, unsure which one of them was shaking the most.

"It's about time," Tally said. "He's been in love with you for years, you know."

"I know." Miriam pulled back, sitting up very straight. "But I wanted to make sure it was all right with you before I said yes."

"All right with me?" Tally shook Miriam gently. "*Grande folle!* Why shouldn't it be? You can do whatever you choose." Her throat formed an icy knot. "You know that, don't you? You aren't beholden to me in any way. You are my dear friend."

"I know that." Miriam took Tally's hands. "I just didn't want you to feel alone."

All at once Tally saw why Miriam had been hesitant to share her joyful news: she feared that Tally would never know the kind of happiness she was experiencing. She had thought of Tally's feelings before her own. She was watching Tally's eyes for a spark of envy, resentment, sorrow—all the emotions Tally would most despise in herself.

"Are you—" Tally caught her breath and stared down at two pairs of clasped hands, pale and dark. "Are you and Eli planning to leave Cold Creek?"

Miriam tightened her grip. "No. When we came out here, you and Mr. André made Eli a partner, so that when this land is surveyed we can claim the whole valley. He believes in Cold Creek, and so do I. This is our home."

Tally shivered and bowed her head. "Even if you were to go, you would do so with my blessing. But I'm glad…very glad you're staying." She smiled. "When is the wedding to be?"

"I'd hoped we could have it here, maybe in January."

"Of course we will have it here. I'll arrange to bring in a clergyman from Tombstone, and—"

Miriam chuckled. "I know how much you'd like to make it a big affair, but we don't have any friends in the Territory except the people at Cold Creek. It should be simple, before God and those we love."

Tally knew that Miriam had other friends in New Orleans, but that was a long way to travel. "What about Eli?"

"You know he doesn't like to talk about his time in the army, but I'll ask him if he has any comrades he'd like to invite."

"Oh, *ma chérie*. I couldn't be more pleased."

"Only one thing would make me happier, and that is if you could find someone of your own."

"You know that…isn't likely."

"You think no one would have you."

"Look at me, Miriam. I choose to defy all the rules, and I've already lived in a way that most could not forgive."

"Even Sim Kavanagh?"

Tally gave a startled laugh. "Are you suggesting *he* would make a good husband?"

Miriam frowned. "I wouldn't have thought so before. But I've seen you look at him the way you've never looked at any man."

"You're imagining things."

"And he looks at you the same way."

"Elijah would be appalled at such a suggestion."

"You aren't."

"I no longer think of marriage. Sim has a woman waiting for him already."

"Then he'd better go back to her before he hurts you."

"My heart is not in danger, Miriam."

"You've got about the softest heart I know. You tried to make yourself hard, but it just never took. You don't think any man will ever accept what you had to do in New Orleans. But there'll come a day when some man is going to need your forgiveness as much as you need his." Miriam cupped Tally's hand between hers. "God has already forgiven you. When you forgive yourself, you won't need to be so scared of the world anymore."

Tally pulled her hand free and rose from the sofa. "Congratulations again, my friend. If you can look after Beth, I should check on the west tank before sunset."

Miriam stood and followed her to the door. "I'm sorry if I said what I shouldn't."

"I'm not upset, Miriam. Not with you." She smiled and kissed Miriam on the cheek, leaving quickly so that her friend wouldn't mistake her agitation for anger.

In the pasture, she saddled Muérdago and rode fast toward the west. A mass of iron-gray thunderclouds had gathered to the southwest, promising rain in the late afternoon. Hot wind whipped Tally's unbound hair. She galloped past the muddy water hole and into the foothills of the Liebres Mountains, urging Muérdago to climb until the house and the barn were hidden beneath blotches of green trees in a rolling sea of yellow and brown.

You aren't losing them, she told herself. *They aren't going away.* But the longing and sorrow remained lodged under her ribs, because she knew that, come winter, life at Cold Creek would never be the same again. Miriam and Eli would truly belong to each other. And Sim would very likely be gone. Back to his perfect woman.

Freedom isn't free.

Tally rode back down to the tank, unpacked the shovel and buried her thoughts in mud, dung and sweat.

ELI SET THE LAST of his traps and sank back on his heels. His mind was wandering again...wandering to the house and Miriam, pushing black hair away from her face with the back of her slender hand while she labored over the hot stove and sang a hymn in her low, pretty voice.

He smiled and hummed part of her favorite song, though his own voice was hoarse and rough. Maybe he could hire musicians to play it at their wedding. Winter seemed far away, with the air so hot and dry, but when he looked up he saw the massing clouds and knew change was coming.

He checked the trap again, just to be sure. Those damned wolves wouldn't get away this time. He'd been listening to them for weeks now—mocking him, just waiting for their chance to go after the smallest calves. The fact that they hadn't done it yet was pure luck. It was only a matter of time, and he didn't intend to lose one animal to those worthless vermin.

Mindful of his distraction, Eli mounted Hierro and rode back along the line of traps to make sure each was properly laid and hidden. He wouldn't reach the last one until dark, but that gave Miriam plenty of time to talk with Tally and reassure herself that she could accept his proposal with a clear conscience.

Eli continued his humming, experimenting with different keys to see which sounded best. He almost rode right past the man crouched over his second-to-last trap. Hierro snorted and twitched his ears in recognition.

The man stood up, the two halves of the broken trap in his hands.

It was Sim Kavanagh.

CHAPTER EIGHT

SIM TOSSED THE TRAP to the ground and kicked it away. He met Eli's eyes with casual hostility.

"What the hell do you think you're doing?" Eli slid from Hierro's back and went to examine a piece of the trap that had fetched up against a thick pine trunk. The springs had been smashed and the toothed jaws torn apart with deliberate intent. By human hands.

Eli spun on Sim. "You just wrecked my trap. What's wrong with you, man?"

Sim hooked his thumb in the waistband of his britches near the holster of his gun. "I want you to leave the wolves alone."

"Leave them alone?" Eli took a step toward Sim, and the tracker bared his teeth. Just like a wolf. "Do you know what they do to livestock once they've got it in their heads that calves are easier to kill than deer?" Eli shook his head in disgust. "I always knew there was something wrong with you, Kavanagh, but this—"

"You leave them be," Sim repeated. "They won't do your beeves any harm."

Laughter stuck in Eli's throat. "You guarantee that, do you? You been up here making friends with them?"

"You could say that."

"Good God. I'd say you're crazy, but it seems about right that you'd associate with the vermin you take after."

"Maybe they take after me."

Eli flattened the pile of pine duff and old leaves where the trap had lain. "I wouldn't be surprised if you had them trained like dogs."

"Nothing like dogs," Sim answered. "But you don't trap them, and they won't kill what belongs to Miss Tally."

Eli stared into the pale, unblinking eyes. Kavanagh was worse than a simple outlaw or rustler. He was gone in the head…or he had some scheme that rested on provoking Eli into a fight Sim expected to win.

Eli could let this go for now and get help from Federico and Bart, or he could handle it alone. Good sense had nothing to do with his choice.

"What do you want, Kavanagh?" he asked. "What are you doing at Cold Creek?"

"Working cattle and running with wolves," Sim answered, straight-faced.

"It's more than that. I *will* find out."

Sim seemed about to answer, then suddenly lifted his head, tilting it toward the south. His nostrils flared. "You want to save Miss Tally's property, Patterson?"

"If you think—"

"I think you'd better ride to the house and get the other men, if you can find them," Sim said. "You've got strangers on your land, and they ain't here for a picnic."

"How do you know?"

"Same way I know about the wolves."

"Why should I believe anything you say?"

Sim shrugged. "Follow me." He sprang from a standstill into a dead run in the space of a second, racing through trees and brush like no man ever born. Eli scrambled into the saddle and turned Hierro the way Sim had gone. He glimpsed flashes of movement, a patch of blue shirt among green leaves and brown branches. He rode into a clearing and found Sim waiting for him, yawning as if from boredom. Then the tracker leaped into motion again.

Eli's feelings had gone far beyond anger. This country was easier for a man afoot than on horseback, but Kavanagh stayed ahead of him with no effort at all.

Sim had said he went "running with wolves." Once Eli would have dismissed such a fairy tale outright, but he'd learned a hard lesson since his youthful days of strict rationality. He remembered stories of Indian witchcraft and skin-walkers, evil beings who'd traded their souls to hunt as beasts.

Hierro pulled up with a snort, and Eli found his horse perched on a granite bluff overlooking a nasty drop. Sim stood even closer to the edge, balanced precariously, as if he could sprout wings and fly.

"Look," he said.

The view to the south and west was unimpeded, the late afternoon sky clear as crystal save for the looming clouds. Light reflected on metal, a piece of tack or a concho decorating some fancy sombrero. Eli saw tiny mounted figures driving a bunch of cattle into Threefork Canyon. From there a reasonably low pass cut between the Pedregosas and the southern Chirica-huas, running into the San Bernardino Valley.

The rustlers were back. Eli knew he would have to ride fast to reach the other men and go after the thieves, but the cattle would slow the outlaws down once they started climbing into the pass. There were precious few hours of daylight left, for bad men or good.

He turned to Sim. "Listen, Kavanagh. You—"

But Sim was gone, not a pebble disturbed to mark his passage. Eli cursed in a way Miriam would surely disapprove of and urged Hierro toward home by the fastest route he could think of.

He was lucky enough to come across Federico driving an unthrifty cow and her half-starved calf toward the home pasture. The sky was nearly black over the southern horizon by the time they reached the house. Bart and Tally were out on the range. Miriam quickly explained about Beth, who was sleeping in her room.

Eli was glad that Tally wouldn't be part of this hunt, but even as he armed himself and Federico with every weapon at Cold Creek, she rode in. She and her horse were plastered with mud from head to foot. She took one look at Eli and touched the .44 at her hip.

"What is it?" she asked. "Where's Sim?"

Eli hid a scowl and unsaddled Hierro. "Kavanagh located rustlers driving our cattle into Threefork Canyon. He's still out there. Federico and I are riding after them."

"I'm coming with you." She dismounted and accepted a rifle from Eli, leaving the shotgun for Federico. "How many?"

"Half a dozen rustlers and about twenty cattle, near as I could tell." He met her gaze. "You stay here, Miss Tally."

She scraped dry mud from her forehead. "You'll need more than three men."

"Someone should stay here to look after Miss Beth—and Miriam—in case any of those thieves come this way."

"It sounds to me as if they've already got what they came for. Miriam, you keep your rifle handy and stay inside."

"I'm not afraid, Miss Tally."

"I know. Any sign of Bart?"

"He went to the north range this morning," Eli said.

"If he comes by, I'll send him after you," Miriam said.

The commotion brought Pablo and Dolores running out of Federico's cabin. Pablo's darting gaze fixed on the firearms, and he did a little dance of excitement. *"Que pasa, Papá? Puedo ir?"*

"You stay here with Miriam," Federico said sternly. *"Quedarse, me entiendes?"*

Pablo's shoulders drooped. *"Sí, Papá."* He brightened. "Don't worry. I'll protect the ladies."

"I know you will." His worried brown eyes scanned the sky. "It will rain very soon."

"A good rain will hinder the rustlers more than it will us," Tally said. "Pablo, run as fast as you can and bring the spare horses from the pasture. Then you can rub down these three and give them their grain."

"Sí, Señorita Tally." Pablo bolted toward the pasture. He returned quickly with three fresh mounts and took charge of the others while Tally, Federico and Eli saddled up and made ready for a hard ride.

Eli barely had a moment to spare for Miriam, who watched with carefully hidden anxiety. He was itching to get his hands on at least one of the thieves for spoiling a day he'd hoped would end in Miriam's promise to marry him. Sim Kavanagh had better show up to help with the rustlers, or he might end up dangling at the end of a rope himself.

Tally drew her mount alongside his. "You said Sim discovered the rustlers," she said. "He's probably gone ahead to track them, maybe even delay them from getting into the pass."

"I hope you're right." But Eli avoided her eyes as he settled his rifle into his saddle scabbard. "Let's ride."

They set off at a gallop, maintaining that pace as long as the ground remained relatively level. They slowed once they reached Lower Threefork Canyon. Cattle droppings and the prints of many hooves marked the dry streambed. The rustlers had made no attempt to hide their trail.

The rain began when they were halfway up the canyon. The drops were heavy and full, scattering dust as they struck the earth. Thunder rumbled, and lightning split the sky only a few miles to the south. Then the storm broke, drenching riders and horses alike.

"We have to get out of the arroyo," Eli shouted. He didn't have to explain about the danger of flash floods sweeping down from the mountains. The rustlers faced the same danger. Even if they'd climbed high enough to avoid the inevitable floods, they would still have a bunch of nervous, balky cattle on their hands.

Tally and Federico spurred their mounts up the steep bank to one side of the arroyo, while Eli took the other. The horses' hooves slipped on the fresh skin of mud, so the riders dismounted and picked their way among the pines on foot. Water dripped continually from the brim of Eli's hat, blinding him. The center of the storm swept closer. Lightning struck just over a nearby ridge. Thunder drummed a deafening tattoo.

Eli searched for Tally. She and Federico were no longer visible, and he took dubious refuge under a stand of pines that reduced the downpour to a liquid veil.

No further progress could be made under such conditions. Tally and Federico would seek their own shelter until the rain let up. Eli consoled his nervous horse with a pat and soft words. The sky grew darker as the sun began its descent. After a while Eli heard the telltale rumble in the high canyon, and a few minutes later a wall of foaming water swept down the arroyo, carrying everything before it.

That was the crescendo of nature's mad symphony. The dense ceiling of black clouds broke up, showing their red and orange underbellies. The torrent gave way to rain and then showers. Glistening drops hung on every surface. Sunlight struck the tops of the eastern peaks.

Tally emerged from the woods on the other side of the arroyo. Eli waved, and she returned his signal. There wasn't a chance in hell that they would catch up with the rustlers before dark, but the thieves couldn't go far until morning. Eli reckoned the odds at about fifty-fifty that the cattle would ever be recovered. And if they weren't…

Cold Creek couldn't afford the loss of even twenty cattle after last winter's theft. André had taken the money meant for the buying of new cows, a fund to which Eli had contributed most of what he had saved from his wages in Texas. Tally might have a little left, but she'd also put the better part of her former marriage's meager inheritance and savings into building Cold Creek's foundations.

Without the ranch and the promise of a legal homestead, Eli had nothing to give Miriam. Tally would lose her hard-won freedom from the past. Bart, Federico and the children would find themselves deprived of a home where they were treated more like family than employees.

Eli mounted and rode out into the fading sunlight. The flood in the arroyo had subsided to an easily forded stream. Tally and Federico crossed over to join him, and the three of them stared up the canyon.

"We'll stay here tonight," Tally said. It would be a cold, miserable camp on wet ground with damp bedrolls, but no one suggested an alternative. Eli studied Tally's grim profile. She was thinking the same as he was—that Sim had never shown up. He'd deserted, maybe even gone over to the rustlers….

Suddenly a low, miserable bawling echoed down the canyon, accompanied by a chorus of bovine voices. A longhorn cow burst out of the brush on the rim of the arroyo, and a calf splashed along the shallow stream bed. More cattle poured down the hillside.

Tally swore. Cows and their calves crashed through the undergrowth, eager to get back to their home territory. Every beast bore the double-C Cold Creek brand. Behind them trotted a foursome of unfamiliar horses, two without saddles.

Sim followed, mounted on a handsome pinto. He whistled and called out to the herd, keeping them together as if by magic. Federico and Tally rode to help. Eli set his jaw, turned his horse in a wide circle to skirt the herd and traced Sim's back trail.

The dirt had been churned to a soup of mud and pulverized branches, but the cattle had made a road out of a once-narrow trail. A few hundred yards up, where the ground leveled out into a meadow, Eli found a saddle, a pair of trampled hats and a gun buried up to its butt. Two halves of a rifle lay at opposite ends of the meadow. Of the rustlers there was no sign.

Eli caught up with the others at the foot of the canyon. Sim still rode alone, his concentration fixed on the cattle. But Tally perched in her saddle with her head high and a smile on her face. All her faith in Sim had been justified.

And all Eli's doubts had been tripled.

Sim had accomplished something no solitary man should be capable of. He'd driven off the rustlers—without killing any of them, it seemed—and returned with the stolen beeves. He hadn't even had a horse when Eli saw him with the wolf traps.

A clever man in league with the rustlers could easily paint himself a hero by making a show of running them off. But what would he or the other thieves have to gain by throwing away what they'd almost obtained? It would only make sense if they had something far bigger in mind, bigger than anything Cold Creek had to offer.

Miriam had lit all the lamps at the house, hoping against hope that the riders might return that night. She was at the door to greet Eli after he, Tally, Federico and Sim hazed the wayward cattle into the corral to await a more thorough examination in the morning.

"I prayed," Miriam said, embracing Eli with her warm, round arms. "You're all right?"

"We never met the rustlers." He threw his hat on a chair by the kitchen table. "Sim did it for us."

"Sim?"

Tally walked in, followed by Federico and Bart. The older man listened to Federico's rapid Spanish with a half-open mouth and many a head-shake. Pablito bounced up and down at his father's heels.

"Sim saved the cattle!" he crowed.

Miriam shushed them with a finger to her lips. "Quiet, you all. You'll wake the girl." She winced at the mud flaking off the riders' boots and cast a pleading look at Eli.

"We'll clean up for supper," he announced. "Then I'd like a word with you, Miss Tally."

"Of course, Eli." Even a layer of dust-covered mud couldn't dim the brightness of her face. "I'll wash in the barn, Miriam."

"You'll do no such thing. I've hot water on the stove, and you'll have a bath."

Tally nodded absently, looking toward the door. For Sim. Eli swept up his hat and strode outside. The other men followed. Sim was not at the bunkhouse, nor did he show up at the main house when the considerably cleaner hands returned for the evening meal.

Federico, Bart and Pablito waited in the parlor, still talking with enthusiasm about the day's adventure. But when Tally joined them, all conversation ceased.

Eli had seen Tally wearing a dress once or twice in the past year, somewhat more often in Texas. Her gowns were always simple calico or muslin, plain as could be, generally without the frills, petticoats or tight corsets decreed by good taste and propriety.

Tonight's ensemble was something different. Little as Eli knew about women's fashion, he recognized fine cloth when

he saw it. The bodice was snug like a sheathe and reached down
past Tally's hips, and the skirt was equally tight about the legs
with numerous flounces and ruffles at the hem. There was a
sort of bow at the base of the rump that reminded Eli of a
horse's tail. The most stylish ladies in Tombstone wore getups
like that, but they were lucky if they could walk faster than a
hobble. To see Tally so confined was an unpleasant revelation.

And yet…she was beautiful. Miriam stood in the kitchen
doorway admiring her openly, while Bart gaped like a fish.
This must have been what she'd looked like in New Orleans,
when men had paid so generously for her favors. Why would
she want to bring those bad days back?

Eli knew the answer. He stepped up to Tally, nodded his
head in a half bow and offered his arm. She took it and accompanied him across the room to a private corner.

"Well, Eli," Tally said, patting nervously at her drawn-up
hair. "Where did all this formality come from?"

"Where did that come from?" he asked, indicating her
outfit.

She brushed her palms over the shiny cloth at her waist and
plucked at a bit of ribbon. "I bought it in Tombstone early this
year. I don't know why." She laughed. "Are you so shocked,
my friend?"

"Just a little surprised. The man you wore it for hasn't
shown up to appreciate it."

Tally lifted her chin. "You make an inaccurate assumption,
Eli. What is it you wished to speak to me about?"

"Don't you find it a little convenient that Sim got those
cows back so easily?"

"Extremely convenient, and admirably efficient."

"Not the least bit suspicious?"

"Because he managed not to kill any of the thieves and did
it all alone?"

"Something like that."

"You're a very intelligent man, Eli, but not so good at hiding your thoughts. You think Sim was in with these rustlers, though his behavior, and theirs, would seem to forestall any gain to them. Why would Sim concoct such an elaborate hoax?"

"I don't know. Not yet."

"You've disliked him from the beginning, but he's more than proved his skill and loyalty. Until you have more than wild speculation—"

"He destroyed my wolf traps."

She blinked, caught off guard. "What?"

"I set traps to catch those wolves before they start killing our livestock. I caught him breaking them. He told me to leave the wolves alone."

Tally hesitated, lightly running her hands over the back of the rocking chair André used to occupy in the evenings. "That is peculiar, yes, but hardly a condemnation. Unless you suggest that the wolves are also in league with Sim and the rustlers."

"I wouldn't put anything past—"

"Elijah Ezekial Patterson," Miriam said, coming up beside him, "you are about to upset Miss Tally's digestion. Leave her be."

"Miriam—" Tally began.

"Miss Tally, I'm the first to admit I didn't like Mr. Kavanagh when I first met him. But now I agree with you. Eli, come away."

"This is none of your business, Miriam."

Her dark eyes flashed. "The welfare of the folk on this ranch is my business. Or do you hold that no woman but Miss Tally has a lick of sense?"

Eli clenched his jaw. "This house is your kingdom, Miriam. I don't dispute that. But outside—"

"What goes on outside reaches inside. No one thinks the less of you because of what Mr. Kavanagh did. But when you start pouting like a jealous child, the way you are now…" She threw up her hands and charged back into the kitchen. "You all who want your supper, come and eat."

Eli's face heated near to boiling. Tally didn't help him with her sympathetic glances. He and Miriam almost never quarreled, but for her to start a fight here, in front of everyone…

Sim. He was the cause of all this trouble. But until Eli had proof that Kavanagh wasn't what he seemed, Tally wouldn't listen.

"Eli," Tally said softly. "I'll speak to Miriam."

"No." He lowered his voice. "No need. I—"

Sim walked into the parlor. He took one look at Tally and went absolutely still. Eli enjoyed his astonishment for as long as it lasted. But then Sim's eyes went cold and calculating, and Eli knew the tracker had reckoned just why his boss had dressed up in all her finery and was standing around blushing like a virgin schoolgirl.

"Miss…Bernard," Sim said.

"You've arrived just in time for supper," Tally said casually. She started for the kitchen, measuring her steps to the confinement of her narrow skirts. Sim and Eli reached the door at the same time. Sim waved Eli ahead of him with an edged smile that made it clear that he knew just how deep Eli's suspicions ran…and just how little he cared.

Fitful conversation resumed soon after the food was served, but no one would meet Eli's gaze. Miriam had just sat down when a young girl walked into the room, dressed in a pair of Tally's britches and an oversize shirt.

"Tally?" the girl said, glancing around the faces at the table. "I heard—" Her gaze came to rest on Sim, and she beamed. "You're here."

Tally cleared her throat. "Bart, please bring a chair for the young lady." She beckoned the girl toward her. "Gentlemen, this is Miss Beth Bryson, from Castillo Canyon. She and her parents assisted us in our search for André. Miss Bryson, you remember Sim Kavanagh. This is our range boss, Elijah Patterson. And these men are Bart Stanfield and Federico Rodriguez, and his children Pablo and Dolores."

"Good evening," Beth said, trying for adult dignity in spite of her coltish awkwardness. She glanced again at Sim and blushed. Bart set one of the parlor chairs between Tally's and Eli's. Beth took her seat and turned to gaze at Tally's gown.

"It's beautiful," she said. "You look so different."

"She looks like a lady," Miriam said.

Sim took a bite of potato and pointedly ignored all three females. He hadn't known about Beth's arrival, having been out smashing Eli's traps, but he was keenly aware of the feminine intrigues thick in the warm kitchen air. Seeing Tally in the fancy gown had been shock enough.

Sim had first assumed that Tally had put the gown on for him. He'd thought they'd come to an understanding when he'd uncovered her disguise at the Brysons', even if sometimes that understanding suffered a certain strain. And though plenty of women dressed up to win a man's regard, he couldn't believe Tally would try that trick even if she'd suddenly decided she wanted him.

The girl's presence made things a little more complicated. She hadn't known Tally was a woman at Castillo Canyon, but she sure as hell did now. That must have been deliberate on Tally's part. Beth's presence at Cold Creek without her parents was peculiar in itself, and the way she looked at Sim made the hackles rise on the back of his neck.

No explanations were given during the meal. Federico, full of talk under any circumstances, was happy to regale the visitor with the story of the rustlers and Sim's return with the stolen cattle. He didn't seem to notice Tally's warning glances or Eli's stony face. Several times he paused and looked at Sim as if he expected the great hero to tell his part, but Sim kept his eyes on his plate.

He'd had enough long before the meal was over. He didn't recognize Tally the way she was now, and Beth Bryson's stare held too much admiration. Whatever pleasure he'd taken in getting the best of Eli was long gone, and he was desperate for the freedom of the high hills.

He got up the moment he sensed all attention had shifted to something other than himself, but his ploy failed miserably. Miriam had taken Beth safely out of sight, but Tally fixed him with a stare that pinned him to the floor.

"I'd like a word with you, Sim. In the parlor."

The other men drifted away, even Eli. Tally followed Sim's longing gaze toward the door.

"You aren't comfortable with praise, are you?" she asked.

"I just did my job."

"A job few others could have done. There'll be a bonus for you, Sim, though it's not as much as you deserve."

He searched her eyes for any trace of double meaning in the words, but her face was as open as always. The same face, same golden hair, but they seemed to belong in a different world.

She motioned him into the parlor, and he let her go ahead of him the way a proper gentleman would. His lip curled with disdain.

"You don't care for my dress," Tally said.

He wiped all expression from his face. "I'm not used to... seeing you like that."

"Neither am I." She took a seat in one of the fancy parlor chairs, barely able to bend her body. "I wore it for a reason, Sim. I wore it for Beth."

Sim glanced at the fragile-looking chairs and decided to remain standing. "The girl?"

"She showed up this morning, exhausted and frightened. She'd ridden all this way alone, without her parents' knowledge or consent."

"I figured that much."

"Do you know why she came?" Tally's eyes had that rare quality of being serious and amused at the same moment. "She realized that I was a woman when we were at Castillo Canyon. She decided that she wanted to be free like me, and that I should teach her how to live like a man."

Sim laughed. "That little filly?"

"That little filly has a great deal of spirit, and she doesn't like the fate her parents have in mind for her."

"What fate?"

"To become a wife to some steady rancher or merchant, and raise a family."

Sim crossed his arms. "Isn't that what she should do? Become respectable?"

Tally stood up again and paced around the room, somehow managing not to trip in the ridiculously tight skirt. "I am concerned for Beth. She's strong-willed and hotheaded. I put on this dress to show her that even I can be a lady—" she tossed Sim a wry smile "—and in the hope that I might tempt her with a bit of female finery."

"I didn't know farmwives dressed so fancy."

"They don't." Her smile faded, and she looked away. "I won't lie to her. But...I have seen something of the world, Sim. So have you. Perhaps you've never lived a settled life in a town or city, yet you must know what becomes of young women who stray too far outside the boundaries of propriety."

Sim stiffened. What she'd said wasn't personal. Only a few people knew about his mother, and they wouldn't have any reason for talking.

"I know," he said heavily.

"Most men use such unfortunate women without ever thinking of where they came from, or what drove them to such terrible circumstances."

Heat surged up in Sim's face. Was she trying to remind him about his treatment of Ready Mary so many weeks ago?

"That wouldn't happen to a kid like Beth," he said.

"Are you so sure?" She ran her hands over the tiny buttons of her long bodice as if she feared they would come undone and leave her standing naked before him. "I was married. I didn't tell you, because it wouldn't affect your work here—"

"Married?"

She nodded without meeting his eyes. "I've explained to Beth that my status as a widow gives me more freedom than she should expect at her age. I do not wish to underestimate the danger Beth faces if she flouts the expectations of society, even in a place as 'uncivilized' as Arizona Territory."

Sim hardly heard her final words. His mind was filled with pictures of Tally wed—Tally as a bride, a virgin lying in her marriage bed, taken again and again by the man who called himself her husband....

CHAPTER NINE

"WHO WAS HE?"

"Who?"

"The man. Your…?" The word stuck in his throat. "Husband."

"It isn't important. He died several years ago."

Sim clenched his fists behind his back. "You weren't happy," he said.

The faint line of concern between her brows deepened into a crease. "And how would you know that?"

"I know." He paced across the room, turned, strode back. "If you were happy, you'd tell Beth how much she has to look forward to. But you aren't going to tell her that, are you?"

"Many women find great joy in marriage."

"Women like you?" He ground his teeth, no longer sure what he was saying or meant to say. Nothing was coming out the way he intended. "You'd never let yourself be ruled by a man."

Tally sat down and smoothed her skirt over her knees again and again. "I believe you meant that as a compliment. But it's not an argument I can use with Beth. That is why I want you to speak to her."

"Me?"

"It may seem strange, but our Beth has become 'sweet on you,' as they say."

If she'd laughed, he would have walked out of the room. But she didn't laugh. She was serious. And very worried.

"I didn't talk to her at Castillo," he protested. "I hardly even looked at her."

"You didn't have to do anything," Tally said softly. "Beth's imagination was sufficient. In you she saw a legend, a knight of the range, a mystery. Your silence only made you more fascinating."

"She's only a kid."

"She's old enough. Women have found you attractive before."

Tally wasn't talking about herself. Sim thought of Esperanza. "I'd never touch a child."

"I know."

"I can't talk to her."

She looked down at her hands, rough and chapped against the silk. "You told me once that you didn't have a family like the Brysons. If you had—"

"It wouldn't make no difference." He sucked in a breath as if the evening air could cool the burning in his gut.

"Neither one of us had the advantage of two loving parents to take care of us. Beth has something wonderful. And I'm certain—" She looked up, holding his gaze. "I'm sure of one thing. You'd do whatever you could to prevent a girl like Beth from ruining her life."

"How can you be so sure of me?" he snapped.

"Because of the way you speak of your Esperanza," she said. "Go to Beth. Tell her to return home and listen to her family."

"You're asking too much."

"I don't think so." Tally's eyes were so still, so level and unafraid. Sim's knees felt like willow saplings. "I believe in you, Sim."

Hell and damnation. He was slowly going crazy in this

room with her, wanting to strangle and kiss her at the same time. Unless he did what she wanted, he would never have a moment's peace. And if he could keep Beth Bryson from ending up like Evelyn Kavanagh…

"Send her here," he said. "And you stand right outside the door."

Tally rose and left the room, elegant and alien. A few minutes later Beth crept into the parlor. She stared at Sim, her mouth trembling on the verge of a smile. She sat down when he told her to. And she listened, even when he scolded her like some older brother ready to bend her over his knee for a good thrashing.

When he finished, Beth was weeping. She didn't make a sound; the tears ran down her cheeks, tears of humiliation Sim felt in his own belly. Her face was white as bone.

Miriam came and got her. Tally blocked the way as Sim charged for the front door.

"I heard," she said. "You did well, Sim. It's a pity you never had a sister."

Tally's scent made it hard for him to focus on the clean air outside the walls of this trap she called a home. "It's a blessing for that sister that she was never born."

She brushed a strand of hair out of his eyes. "Ah, Sim. You're a harsher judge of yourself than Eli could ever be."

He jerked away, breathing fast. "Eli's not harsh enough." He pushed past her like the ill-bred scoundrel he was. "Don't ask me to take Beth back to Castillo."

"I wasn't planning on it. Miriam and I will escort her. As long as Beth keeps my secret, I'll still be Tal Bernard—and Beth's escapade won't appear quite so serious if Miriam travels with her."

"And if she spills your secret to her ma and pa?"

"I'll survive."

He continued down the steps. A lone howl drifted from the mountains.

"What secrets do they hold, I wonder?" Tally said behind him. "I think I know why you destroyed Eli's traps, Sim. You can't bear for anything to be held against its will."

Sim stopped. "The wolves are my only brothers," he said, knowing she would never take his words for the literal truth.

"Then send them my best wishes," she said. "And ask them not to eat our cows."

The laugh inside him got all tangled up around his heart. He left Tally at last, but he didn't go to the wolves. Tonight he was too human. Tonight they would growl and slink and avoid him, because he stank of human passion.

He visited Diablo in the corral, where the stallion was kept apart from Cold Creek's mares. Sim found a brush in the barn and curried the dark brown coat, letting the long, sweeping motions carry him into a state of calm detachment. Diablo stamped and snorted.

"You and I have something in common, my friend," Sim said. "We both want something we can't have. But a strong fence divides you from your prize. Only a dream stands in my way."

TALLY AND MIRIAM RETURNED from the Brysons' two evenings later. Tally was glad to be home; her deception as Tal Bernard had seemed more of a trial when Beth knew the truth. The girl had cast her reproachful and pleading looks during most of the trip north to Castillo, withdrawing into sullen silence as the spring wagon approached the Bryson homestead.

Beth's parents had been overjoyed to see their daughter, but Tally suspected the girl was in for an unpleasant reckoning. Tally had slept in the barn that night, while Miriam took the extra room, and they had left early the next morning. Tally felt as if she'd condemned Beth to a life of unhappiness.

If a woman were very rich or very brave, she might find a way to live at the edge of propriety and still find acceptance among her peers. Beth had courage but neither the sense nor experience. She'd be extraordinarily lucky to find a man who respected her spirit.

"You did the right thing," Miriam said when Federico and Pablo had come to unhitch the team. "She'll be safe."

Will she? But Tally didn't speak the question aloud as she followed Miriam into the house. The kitchen was cooler than normal, because Miriam hadn't been at the stove since dawn. Eli had done a little makeshift cooking in the bunkhouse, but the men had mostly subsisted on warmed-over frijoles, baking-powder biscuits and jerky. Supper that night would be equally frugal.

Tally went to her room to wash and change, her thoughts torn between André and Sim. She clung to the unlikely hope that André had shown some improvement during the brief time she'd been away from the house. But she also wanted to see Sim, because there was always a chance that he would be gone one day. And he wouldn't say goodbye.

André was sitting up in bed, looking toward the door when she entered his room. She stopped cold. Surely it wasn't her imagination that his face had changed, that it held a light of intelligence, awareness…recognition.

"Tal…" he croaked. "Ta-"

She rushed to his bedside and knelt beside him, clasping his thin hands. "André, it's Tally. It's me."

"Tal-ly." The corners of his lips moved in what was clearly meant to be a smile. His fingers twitched. "Home."

"Yes, *mon cher.* I'm home." She kissed the back of his hand and pressed her cheek to his chest. His heartbeat felt strong and steady. "Can you speak, André? Have you come back to us?"

"Tally." He patted her hand clumsily. "Good...glad."

"He still doesn't say much," Eli's deep voice said from the doorway. "But it's more than he's done since the accident."

Tally closed her eyes. "Thank God."

Eli dropped into a soldier's crouch beside her, studying André's face. "It's too soon to tell. Don't...hope too much."

She glanced at her friend, catching an expression of agony and sorrow she'd never seen before. "I know it's been difficult for you, too, Eli," she said.

He wouldn't meet her gaze. "I'd like to speak to Miriam," he said. "Are you all right?"

"Fine." She refused to ask about Sim. "When you've properly welcomed Miriam home, come to the parlor. I think we deserve a little celebration."

Eli arched his brow but didn't ask her meaning. He hurried off to find his love. Tally sat with André until, exhausted by his efforts to speak, he fell into a deep sleep.

Though Tally's stomach was grumbling for real food, she had no appetite. She went directly into the parlor and the grand oak sideboard she and André had brought from Texas. In the sideboard were André's bottles of whiskey, untouched since his accident, some port and fine bourbon. She pushed them aside. She was after the excellent red wine she had brought when she'd come to live with André.

Neither bottle had been opened. But Tally was giddy with hope, and she was tired of saving the vintage for distinguished guests who would never come. One bottle she would reserve for Miriam's wedding; the other she would share with her friends tonight.

She located the corkscrew, brought out the set of stemmed crystal glasses and arranged them on a silver tray. With an ease born of practice and experience, she opened the bottle. One sip was sheer heaven.

Miriam's and Eli's voices preceded them down the hall. Tally quickly poured two more glasses and stood ready when her friends joined her in the parlor.

Eli's big fingers folded gingerly around the fragile stem of his glass. He sniffed. "I thought you'd been saving this for a special occasion," he said.

"This *is* a special occasion." She gave a reluctant Miriam the other glass. "Try it. It's wonderful."

Miriam wrinkled her nose. "You know I never—"

"I promise that a few sips won't do you any harm." Tally gladly finished off her glass and poured a little more. Eli sampled the wine, licked his lips and made short work of his portion, though he refused Tally's offer of a refill. Miriam was equally cautious, yet she drained her glass and giggled when she put it down.

"I feel a bit dizzy," she complained, swaying against Eli. "I don't think…this was a very good idea."

"Enjoy the feeling, Miriam. It won't last."

Miriam made a face halfway between disgust and amusement. "I remember those fancy French cooks who poured wine and spirits in just about everything they made. It's a wonder they didn't drown in their own gumbo."

"None of them could touch your cooking," Eli said, steadying her with gentle arms. "Do you need to sit down?"

"Certainly not." She pushed him away, but playfully. "Now, if we're done celebrating, I have work to do."

"Not tonight, Miriam," Tally said. "Eli, why don't you take her for a walk in the moonlight? I hear it does wonders to clear the head."

"I think that's a very good idea," Eli said. He nuzzled the back of Miriam's neck. She muffled a shriek.

"Men," she huffed. "It would be so much simpler if we could do without them."

Tally gazed at the remnants of burgundy in her glass. "Yet there are a few we would miss."

Miriam touched her arm. "You know I didn't mean…Mr. André—"

"So he's talking again."

Sim sauntered into the parlor, stopping at the sideboard. Eli pulled Miriam close and steered her toward the kitchen. Sim watched them go with lazy, cynical eyes. "Does he think I'd hurt her?" he asked.

Tally had learned to listen for the subtle underlying notes in Sim's gruff voice. She heard them now. "He's very protective of Miriam. They're to be married."

"Well." Sim picked up an empty glass and turned it in his fingers. "Elijah don't look too happy about it."

"We were celebrating my brother's progress," she said with deliberate good cheer. "Would you care for some wine?"

He set the glass down. "Never touch it."

"I do have whiskey, if you prefer."

"Not tonight."

"Admirable." She smiled, unwilling to continue his game of constant challenge. "Will you at least share a little of my joy in André's recovery?"

"He spoke to you."

"He said my name." She blinked back the moisture in her eyes. "I know he's getting better."

"I hope you're right."

He spoke as if he meant the sentiment. She poured herself another glass of wine. One more after that and the bottle would be empty. "You might like to know that Beth arrived safely at Castillo Canyon, and her parents were very glad to see her."

"You think what I told her will do any good?"

"She was angry with me, but I think she took your advice to heart."

"She wanted to be like you. She never could."

Tally tossed back her wine like a miner. "Oh, yes. I'm unique."

"You look like yourself again," he said, gesturing at her clothes.

"You mean not really like a woman at all?"

"No." He took a step toward her and came to a halt as if the floor had opened up between them. "You look plenty… real."

Streaks of heat raced up and down Tally's legs. She emptied the bottle into her glass and sat in the nearest chair. "What does Esperanza wear?"

He looked as though she'd brought up a subject as unexpected and foreign as ancient Greek philosophy. "Esperanza?"

"Does she also dress in trousers?"

"No." She expected annoyance, but he scraped his hand through his dark hair and frowned in concentration. "She wears…skirts. The Mexican style."

"You like the way she looks."

"She's beautiful. But she's—" He made a dismissive gesture. "I never paid any mind to her clothes."

Tally was too relaxed to care if she provoked him. "How does she arrange her hair?"

"Down. She wears it down."

"She must be young."

"Not like Beth." He reddened under his tan. "She's old enough."

Tally sipped her wine. "What are her dreams, Sim? What are yours, besides marrying her? What life do you want for the two of you?"

He looked more than a little unsteady on his feet. "I'll see that she never knows want. She'll have a home, and nice things…."

"She never had nice things before?"

"She came from a small village in New Mexico."

"Where you met her?"

His jaw flexed. "Why do you care?"

"Because I've wanted to understand her since you first mentioned her name. How any woman could so completely capture your heart."

He turned away and leaned against the wall, arms braced above his head. "She's good," he said. "Good like no one else. And she has…she sees what people are inside."

"What do you mean?"

"She knows what other folks feel. Sometimes what they think."

"Do you mean she is a clairvoyant?"

"I don't know that word."

"'More angel than woman,'" she quoted him softly.

"You think I'm not good enough for a lady like that?"

She gazed regretfully into her empty glass. "I wouldn't want to be an angel—or live with one." She managed to set her glass on the side table after only three tries. "Is she still a virgin?"

Dead silence. Tally muffled a small hiccup. "I'm sorry," she said. "I shouldn't have…asked that."

He walked to her chair and knelt before her. "You're right," he said. "You shouldn't have." His breath dried the moisture on her lips. "I answered your questions. Now you answer mine. How did you meet your husband?"

Intemperate laughter gurgled from Tally's throat. "His name was Nathan Meeker. We met in San Antonio. He was nearly twice my age and very rich. He liked the way I looked and dressed. He thought I'd make a nice addition to his big, fancy ranch in eastern Texas. And I…I'd been separated from André for many years. *Maman* was dead. I needed…I wanted a real home."

"He didn't see you the way you are now."

"*Mais non.* I wore dresses in those days."

"And what were you doing when you met him? You weren't no schoolmarm."

She pressed a finger to her lips. "I've worked since I was fourteen. I had to, because of *Maman.* She got sick, and André—"

"André wasn't much use to anyone."

She shrugged. It was strange, but she wasn't afraid of Sim asking her how she'd earned her living. She wasn't even sure if she would lie or tell the truth. The wine in her blood gave Sim's face a benevolent, kindly glow that made him seem almost like an angel himself. Someone who would understand.

But Sim had other things on his mind. "Did you love your husband?" he asked.

"You asked me before if I'd ever loved a man, or don't you remember?" She tipped her glass idly, back and forth, back and forth. "Nathan and I didn't marry for love. I was his hostess and ran his house, and he liked to show me off to his guests. He was a big man in the county. We had an…understanding."

"You shared his bed."

"We were married. Don't you expect to share Esperanza's?"

For a moment she had the sense of teetering on the brink of a yawning chasm, seconds from falling into oblivion. Sim caught her wrists and held her. His face came very close. "Did you like it?"

"Nathan was not an overly demanding husband."

"You had no children."

Her chest began to ache. "None."

Abruptly he released her. "Were there other men…after him?"

He didn't ask about before. "After Nathan died? No others."

Sim turned his head and gripped the arms of the chair. "Do you wish there was?"

"Didn't we discuss this in Castillo Canyon? You said I wasn't the kind to let myself be ruled by a man. I have Cold Creek now. If I marry again, I risk losing my freedom."

He got up and walked away. "You dress like a man so you can do a man's work. But you don't want to be troubled by men. I think you're afraid if you didn't disguise yourself, men would want you the way your husband did."

The chair seemed to shrink around her. She flailed out, caught the glass with her elbow and sent it crashing to the floor. She stared at the crystal shards, seething with laughter.

"How funny you are, Sim. When you first learned I was a woman, you said I was afraid that no man would want me."

He shoved at the broken glass with the scuffed toe of his boot. "Not much scares you, but you're afraid of something."

"You paint such a lovely picture, *mon cher.* All I need do is put on a gown and walk down Allen Street, and every man in Tombstone will fall at my feet."

"Maybe they wouldn't fall. But they'd look." Crystal crunched under his heel. "It isn't your reputation you worry about. You just don't want to lie with a man ever again."

She sputtered a giggle. "Thank God Miriam isn't listening. Do you think because I don't throw myself at any hand who comes to work at Cold Creek—"

"Meeker did something to you. He hurt you."

He was so wrong, so completely wrong. But he had broached this very possibility before, that "some man" must have hurt her. Why not let him believe? It was so much simpler.

"Men and women are not the same," she said. "Men need certain…comforts…that women can live without. If you want that kind of company, Sim, go into town. You've earned a few days off."

He hit the wall so hard that flakes of whitewash showered down from the adobe. "I'm not talking about me. You told me you'd seen what men could do to women. You couldn't lie to Beth and tell her that being married to any man was better than risking her reputation. You knew it might be bad for her, like it was for you."

Tally found her feet and got up, swaying a little. "There are always women who break the rules and pay the price. Until Beth understands that price…" She took a step. "I'm feeling…I think I'll lie down."

Sim blocked her path. "I thought you protected André too much. I haven't seen any evidence that he did much around this ranch. But a woman can live respectably with her brother. If he's gone, and folks find out you're a lady, living alone here—"

"I have Miriam."

He dismissed her argument with a wave of his hand. "What will you do if André never gets better?"

"But he is. He—"

"What will you do, Tally?"

She met his gaze. He wasn't mocking her. He was concerned, worried about her future. And—*Dieu du ciel!*—he was jealous of any man who'd ever been near her. Even André.

"I will survive," she said firmly. "But it won't happen that way. You'll see." She started for the hall once again. Sim let her go. She half stumbled to her bedroom and collapsed onto the bed. Weariness overwhelmed her. It couldn't be the wine, surely. But she'd so seldom indulged since leaving New Orleans….

She stared at the chair by the window, where she'd flung her skirts and bodice and petticoat and corset in a heap, heedless of the expensive fabric. Foolish. She would have to wear the whole assemblage again at Miriam's wedding. And if the world discovered that Tal Bernard was a woman, she would be buying more dresses in Tombstone.

The thought was too troubling to hold in her mind. She stretched out on the bedclothes and listened for footsteps.

Sim didn't come. Tally muffled a laugh in her pillow. She thought she'd seen lust in enough men's eyes to recognize it in Sim's, and she'd had an idea that he saw through her just as easily. But maybe the past had blurred her vision. Sim hadn't been jealous of her dead husband after all. All those questions about her future, her safety on the ranch—maybe that had been his way of letting her know he was getting ready to leave.

He remained true to his Esperanza, and Tally held fast in her fortress of fear and memory. They had both passed the test she hadn't even known she'd set.

The worst of it was, a part of her wished they'd failed.

SIM STOOD in the doorway of Tally's bedroom and watched her sleep, half of him listening for intruders while the other half was lost in imagining what might have been.

If he'd met Tally before Esperanza, he wouldn't have seen how extraordinary she was. Esperanza had taught him that all women weren't alike. She'd forgiven his mistreatment of her, even the blackness in his heart. It wasn't until after she'd left New Mexico on a quest of her own that he'd realized only she could save him. And that he could protect her delicate soul from all the harshness of the world.

Tally didn't need protection. That was what she claimed, what Sim wanted to believe. Sooner or later he had to leave this place, abandon Tally to whatever fate lay in store for her. And he couldn't bear the thought of never seeing her again.

He breathed in slowly, absorbing the scent that permeated the room, underlain with the bouquet of wine. He walked silently to the bed and skimmed his hand over the golden strands of her hair. His body throbbed with wanting. She slept deeply; it would be easy to lie down beside her and touch her body, cup the round breasts beneath her shirt.

His imagination carried him beyond simple touching. She would wake to his caresses, and her eyes would warm with desire. She would welcome him with kisses, a little uncertain at first, because she'd be remembering her husband and how he'd treated her. She would know she was breaking the rules, her own and the ones society made to keep people in their place. But her body wasn't dead. She was in her prime, hot-blooded and overflowing with life. She would recognize Sim as her true match.

"Only you," she would whisper as he felt her wet and ready for him. The man from before was forgotten, and there would never be another afterward. "Only you. Forever."

In his fantasy, Sim took her in her widow's bed, as if she were a virgin and he a boy who believed in love. Moving inside her, he felt joy that he'd never known in any mere joining of bodies with a thousand forgotten women.

Then he remembered his promise, and that he was standing beside Tally's bed in the darkness. He turned away from temptation and called Esperanza's face into his mind like a shield.

Esperanza hadn't heard his promise. He'd made it only to himself, but he'd lived almost as chaste as a monk since that day. He knew where Esperanza lived, and that she remained unwed. She waited for him to find her and lay his heart at her feet.

Two rooms down the hall, a man named André Bernard waited to be relieved of his secrets. The time had come to learn if Tally had reason for her celebration. Sim closed her door halfway, as she'd left it, and went to André's chamber.

As always, Tally's brother lay propped among a fortress of pillows, his thin hands resting on his stomach. He looked no different than he had during the weeks since his accident, yet his breathing quickened when Sim entered the room. His eyes moved under sunken lids.

"Who?" he croaked.

Moonlight sifted through the muslin curtains, painting a white bar across André's immobile legs. Sim crouched in the shadows at the foot of the bed.

"André," he said. "Where is the map?"

The air caught in André's lungs and rattled like a snake in dry grass. "Map?"

"You know, André. You had it in the mountains."

André sighed. "I...had it."

"Do you remember what happened to you?"

"Fell."

"That's right." Sim rose to his feet. "Tally saved you. But now she needs the map."

Bloodshot eyes struggled to find the source of the voice. "Who...are you?"

"A friend."

"Eli?"

André was still far gone if he could make that kind of mistake. "I want to help you and your sister. But you have to help me."

André moved his hands back and forth across his lap, fingers spread and twitching. "Don't...don't hurt me."

"I don't want to hurt you." Sim slipped to the side of the bed, still keeping to the shadows. "But someone else did. You fought with a man in the mountains. That man took the map. He almost killed you."

"*Oui.*" André grimaced and batted at the air with aimless fists. "He said...*C'est impossible.*" He rolled his eyes. "Bastard."

Good. André was angry, and anger was better than fear. "Who did it, André? Tell me his name, what he looks like."

"I...I don't—" André closed his eyes. A vein pulsed in his

temple. "Doesn't matter. *C'est assez.*" He seemed to fall into a fitful sleep, and Sim was about to wake him when he shot up with a look of utter terror on his face.

"I didn't mean it," he said in a thready whine. "I didn't."

Sim was rapidly losing his patience. "You stole the map from Caleb," he said harshly. "Who took it from you?"

"She doesn't know," he wheezed. "Don't tell her."

"Tell her what?"

André opened his mouth. Voices, one masculine, hummed from the direction of the kitchen. André shrank deep into his covers.

Sim grabbed the shoulder of André's nightshirt, but the voices were too close. Sim retreated from the room, turned the hall corner and slipped from the house.

He leaned against the wall just outside Tally's window. There would be other chances to question André, but he must be careful. André was only half-sane, unreliable. He needed to be rational to describe what had happened on the cliff, but Sim didn't want him telling Tally about the interrogations. It could take days or weeks to get enough information from André's ravaged mind.

Whoever had fought with André on the cliff must have the map, but the thief wasn't using his prize. The wolves had yet to report the appearance of unfamiliar visitors to Castillo Canyon, and Sim's nightly runs hadn't flushed out any strangers lurking in the mountains. The mystery remained, but by the end of summer, Sim expected to be gone from Cold Creek.

And Tally.

Her scent floated out to him through the open window of her bedroom. Days or weeks, it made no difference. The damage was done. Tally didn't deserve to be punished for Sim's weakness.

I will survive, she'd said. Sim believed it. And he could go on living with himself, knowing nothing he did could ever take that away from her.

CHAPTER TEN

CALEB SMITH RODE into Cold Creek Valley from the south, through the pass that wound its steep, narrow way between the rocky peak locals called Cap Rock and the Liebres Mountains. His first glimpse of the ranch was a *bosque* of tall cottonwoods marking the spring and the creek at the head of the valley. Splashes of adobe red bloomed amid the green, a modest house, outbuildings and a shed or barn for livestock.

From here the place looked easy enough to take. A few of his men had wanted to come; he'd accepted a calculated risk in telling the most trusted among his gang about the map, the ones he could expect to be patient.

But he himself was growing impatient with Sim. He'd had no word in the months since his partner had ridden to Arizona Territory in search of the map, no message waiting for him when he'd broken out of the Amarillo jail. That bothered him, because Sim Kavanagh had his own brand of honor. He wouldn't double-cross his blood brother.

Caleb smiled and stopped his horse on the last hill above the homestead. He lifted his hat, slicked back his hair and touched the ivory-gripped revolver at his hip. The chestnut stamped, smelling water. Caleb held the animal to a walk. He didn't want to announce his presence too early.

A few cows and calves bunched near the spring, part of which had been walled off to keep livestock away. Caleb let the chestnut drink just enough and jerked its head back toward the road. He examined the buildings and fences with a practiced eye. The spread was well kept, but hardly the dwelling of a wealthy man.

André hadn't found the treasure. He'd had over a year to look for it, all the time Caleb had been in various cells awaiting trial as a rustler and murderer. But the Bernards were still in residence, and Sim would have found them easily enough. Anyone could. André had to know that. He was clever, but he'd made two very bad mistakes.

He'd stolen from Caleb Smith, and he'd left his enemy alive.

Caleb whistled cheerfully as he approached the house. Chickens scattered beneath the chestnut's hooves. A dark-skinned woman came out the front door, wiping her flour-coated hands on an oversize apron. She squinted at Caleb. Her hands went still.

Caleb touched the brim of his hat. "Hello, Miriam," he said. "Pretty as ever, I see."

Miriam turned without a word and vanished inside the house. Caleb dismounted, stretching his legs and making a bet with himself about who would come next. André didn't much care for work, so chances were good he wasn't out on the range with the other men. Once Miriam warned him, he would probably go running out the back door. He wouldn't get far.

"Caleb Smith."

The voice was a woman's, low and firm, but the figure in the doorway wore men's britches and a slouch hat. She stepped out of the house's shadow and tilted up her face.

André's sister was still beautiful. Caleb hadn't known her well at Peñasco Rojo; she'd kept mostly to herself, away from her brother's associates. Caleb had never doubted that she disapproved of their activities. Such a pretty woman dressed in black widow's weeds had been something of a temptation, but André—with a rare display of cojones—had warned Caleb off. And Caleb had women enough to let her go.

"Mrs. Meeker," Caleb said. "How you've changed."

She looked him up and down. If she'd been a man, he would have expected her to spit. "*You* haven't, Mr. Smith," she said. "Why are you here?"

It wasn't a question she would have asked if she knew the truth. André was *cabrón y estúpido,* but not stupid enough to confide in his sister.

Caleb sighed. "Now, Mrs. Meeker, that ain't the way to welcome an old friend."

"The name is Bernard," she said. "And you were never our friend."

A thin Mexican boy ran around the corner of the house and skidded to a halt. "*Qué es esto,* Señorita Bernard?"

"Señorita," Caleb repeated, rolling the word on his tongue. "Not the grieving widow after all, Miss Bernard. Wish I'd known that in Texas." He snapped his fingers at the boy. "Take care of my horse, *hijo.* And don't be stingy with the grain."

The boy looked to Chantal Bernard. She nodded, tight-lipped. "It's all right, Pablo," she said. "The gentleman won't be staying long."

"Maybe your brother'll have something to stay about that." Caleb slapped the chestnut's sweaty rump as Pablo led it away. "It's been a long time, hasn't it?" He made a sweeping gesture with his left hand, encompassing the house and the outbuildings and the bedraggled garden. "André was so fired up to sell the old ranch and start over in Arizona, but it don't look as though he's done as well as he hoped."

Tally shifted her weight, and Caleb figured she had a gun tucked in her britches at the small of her back. "We don't need your sympathy, Mr. Smith. I—"

"Caleb." He grinned, working the charm that so seldom failed him.

"I don't know why you came so far," she continued, "but André paid off all his debts. I'm sure he made it clear that he wanted nothing more to do with you or your associates. What we have here was built with honest work."

"Whose work? Your brother was never one for hard labor. Where are your men, Chantal?"

"Close." She looked past him. "Where are yours?"

Caleb grew alert, watching her eyes. Maybe she could use that gun, and maybe she couldn't. Didn't matter. He would cut her down before she touched it. But killing a woman would bring attention he didn't want.

He raised his hands, palms out. "Wouldn't have been very neighborly of me to bring you so many mouths to feed," he said.

"My brother's free of the old business, Mr. Smith. We intend to keep it that way."

Miriam's face bobbed behind Tally's shoulder. She whispered in her mistress's ear.

"Speak a little louder, Miriam," Caleb said. "This ain't the time for secrets. Be a good girl and fetch me some water."

Tally stiffened, but the black woman went inside and returned with a pail and dipper. Tally took the pail from her and banged it down halfway between Caleb and the door. Dust turned to mud on the tips of Caleb's boots.

"Help yourself," she said. "And then you'd better go."

Caleb crouched and drank, never taking his eyes from Tally. "Much as I enjoy your company, *Miss* Bernard, I came to speak to your brother. Where is he?"

"Away."

"You sure didn't learn how to lie from André."

"I don't know what you're talking about."

Caleb wiped his mouth with the back of his hand. "That's between him and me. You'd best fetch him, señorita."

"I told you he's not here."

"Then you won't mind showing me around this nice little farm of yours."

"You aren't setting foot inside this house."

They stared at each other. Caleb kicked the pail over and hurled the dipper against the wall of the house, inches from Tally's head. Before she recovered, he was striding for the barn, and by the time she caught up with him, he had Pablo by one scrawny arm. "Where's your boss, Pablo? *El jefe?*"

"Let him go," Tally demanded, breathing fast. "If you have a quarrel with my brother—"

"A quarrel? What makes you think that?" He tousled Pablo's hair. The boy strained to break free, and Caleb tightened his hold. Pablo whimpered.

"Cochon," Tally snarled. Miriam joined her, clutching a broom in her brown hands. "What do you want?"

"Like I said, it's between me and André. You don't want nothing to do with it."

"I'm sure she doesn't."

Caleb spun on his heel. A man in grimy work clothes stood a few feet away as if he'd popped into being like a ghost. The Remington 1875 in his hand was very real and aimed at Caleb's heart.

"Let the boy go," Sim Kavanagh said.

Tally's face flushed with color, and she pulled Pablo out of Caleb's grip. She and Miriam all but squashed the kid between them. Sim holstered the Remington and pushed his hat off his forehead.

"I'll be damned," he said. "Caleb Smith. I never thought I'd see you again outside of a jail cell."

"You know this man?" Tally asked Sim.

Sim met Caleb's gaze. The moment of shock passed, and Caleb saw the cold mockery in Sim's pale eyes.

"I know him," Sim said. "We grew up in the same town. He been giving you trouble, Miss Bernard?"

ASTONISHMENT AND RELIEF robbed Tally of a ready answer. She snatched a moment to gather her thoughts and nodded to Miriam. "Take Pablo inside, please," she said. "Everything will be all right."

Miriam glared at Caleb and backed away, holding Pablo with one hand and the broom in the other. It would have made a good joke to say that Caleb got off lightly after facing such a weapon in the hands of an angry woman, but Tally knew it wasn't a laughing matter.

She had no idea why Caleb Smith had come to Cold Creek. She'd heard that the Texas Rangers had caught up with him and his gang shortly after André had sold his part of the ranch. André had gotten out just in time. If he'd some unfinished business with his former partner, he hadn't thought it important enough to share with his own sister.

Unfinished business with Caleb Smith. She held back a shiver and moved closer to Sim. "If this man is your friend," she said, "you might advise him that visitors who threaten our people are not welcome here."

Sim cocked a brow at Smith. "Is that what you been doing, Caleb? Threatening these folks?" He shook his head. "I can't let you do that." He pulled papers and tobacco from his pocket, deftly rolled a cigarette and offered it to the other man. "You'd better tell me why you're here."

Smith took the cigarette, produced a match and lit it, blowing a long stream of smoke into Sim's face. "Never figured you for a bucket-man," he remarked. "Not in your usual line, is it?"

Sim glanced at Tally, and she could have sworn she saw a

hint of shame in his eyes. "I ain't proud of the sins of my youth." He flicked the butt of his gun with his fingertips. "Was it your men who came for our cattle a few days back?"

The earth gave a sudden spin, and Tally locked her knees to keep them steady. "You know Smith is a rustler?"

Sim returned her sharp look with one of his own. "Seems I'm not the only one."

"Didn't she tell you, Sim?" Smith said. "Mrs....Miss Bernard and I are old friends, too." He sucked on his cigarette with almost obscene delight. "That's why I came by...to pay my respects to my former partner."

Tally walked away, unable to meet Sim's curious stare. In her heart, she'd always realized there was much she didn't know about Sim Kavanagh's past, and now he was beginning to recognize how little he knew of hers.

"It's true," she admitted. She faced him again, hot under the skin. "I told you we had a ranch in Texas. What I didn't tell you is that my brother provided a haven for certain outlaw elements in the Palo Duro—men like Caleb Smith. And André profited by it."

Caleb laughed. "Only André never got his hands dirty rounding up the cattle and changing the brands. He was the respectable one, the front for our operation."

"He isn't proud of what he did," Tally said.

"He didn't quit until two years after you showed up."

"But he did stop. That's why we came here...to make a fresh start."

"Ain't that sweet."

"That's enough, Caleb," Sim said in his laziest, most dangerous voice. "Where did you ride in from?"

"South."

"I think you'd better head on back to the pass, old friend."

"Without seeing André? Now that would be a shame." He

dropped the cigarette and crushed it under his heel. "I've been looking over the Territory, and I think a place like this would be a perfect base for a new operation."

"Never," Tally snapped.

"I don't think the local cowboys would appreciate you invading their hunting grounds," Sim said.

"I've heard of these McLaurys and Clantons. Amateurs, all of 'em. Now you and I, Sim—"

"The lady doesn't want to hear any more about it, and neither do I. Ride on, Caleb."

The two men stared at each other for so long that Tally was certain one or both of them would draw at any instant. She would do anything, give anything, to avoid the spilling of a man's blood on this untainted ground. Anything but take up the old life again.

"I'll give you whatever provisions you need," she said, stepping between Sim and Caleb. "You can have one of our horses if you need a fresh mount. But don't come back."

Caleb leaned forward and plucked her hat from her head, dropping it on the ground. He twisted a strand of her hair between his fingers. "If you're gonna bribe me, Miss Bernard, there's something I'd like even better."

Sim lifted his friend by the collar and deposited him several feet away, not gently. "Ride out now," he said between his teeth. "I'll bring you your provisions so you won't have no need to bother other decent folk."

"Sim—" Tally began.

He grinned at her. "You think I can't handle my good old friend? Don't worry. We understand each other." He pointed toward the barn. "Go get your horse, Caleb."

To Tally's surprise, Smith obeyed. He sauntered toward the barn, taking his time about it, and returned with his chestnut saddled and bridled. He mounted with the same deliberation and aimed a wad of spittle between Sim's feet.

"I'm sorely disappointed in you, Sim Kavanagh," he said. "You've gotten soft."

"Someday you might get a chance to find out if that's true," Sim said. He whistled sharply, and the chestnut broke into a trot. Caleb caught his balance like the expert horseman he was and didn't look back.

Tally released her breath. "It shouldn't be so easy," she muttered.

Sim picked up Tally's hat, dusted it off and set it back on her head. "How well did you know Caleb in Texas?"

"Not well. I avoided his company."

"That's good. He blows a mighty blast of wind, but he ain't much to worry about."

"Did you ride with him?"

"Once." He rubbed the two-day beard on his chin. "I'd better go after Caleb, make sure he leaves the area."

"I promised him provisions. Wait until I have them ready."

The cool darkness of the house was a welcome sanctuary after the blazing tension outside. Miriam waited in the kitchen, her bread forgotten in the oven.

"He's gone," Tally said.

Miriam whispered a prayer. "Thank God Eli wasn't here. I don't know what he would have done."

Tally fervently agreed. Caleb had treated Eli with undisguised contempt at Peñasco Rojo. There was no love lost between the two men. Miriam didn't realize that Eli had ridden to Tombstone early that morning to buy her a ring for their engagement; he'd made some other public excuse about the need for the trip.

At the time, Tally had considered it a good sign that Eli trusted Sim enough to leave Cold Creek overnight. She didn't intend to tell Eli that Sim and Caleb had been friends, destroying that fragile trust.

She explained to Miriam about the provisions, and the two women put together a package that would last a frugal man almost a week. Sim was mounted and waiting in the yard. Tally passed the sack up to him, touching his hand in the transfer. Her fingers trembled as she withdrew them.

"Be careful," she said.

"I told you not to worry. How's Pablo?"

"He isn't hurt."

"Good." He clucked to Diablo, and the horse started down the road. Once he was out of sight, Tally sat on the porch and dropped her head into her hands.

Mon Dieu. Sim had admitted that he'd ridden with a known cattle rustler and likely murderer. But Tally saw a world of difference between Sim and Caleb, a difference she couldn't begin to put into words.

If Caleb wanted something at Cold Creek, he wasn't likely to disappear. Sim had handled the situation perfectly, just as he'd dealt with the rustlers. If he were to stay on permanently…if she could somehow convince him…

And steal him from another woman? What would that make you, Chantal?

She pulled the gun from the back of her pants and rubbed the dull metal with her thumb. If she was to become a true defender of the ranch, like Eli, she must be prepared to use this thing of death. Elijah had taught her how to protect herself. He hadn't taught her how to kill.

She opened her hands and let the gun fall to the earth.

"WHAT THE HELL are you doing here?"

Caleb leaned against the trunk of a blasted cottonwood near the mouth of the pass, paring his nails with the blade of his knife. He barely looked up as Sim dismounted.

"Why are you so surprised, Sim? I ain't heard nothing

from you in four months. Did you think I'd wait around and let you walk off with the treasure?"

"Hell." Sim strode toward Caleb, who shifted his knife into a defensive hold. "You never was any damned good at waiting. I thought you were in jail."

"Didn't care for it much." Caleb sheathed his knife and studied his fingers. "I thought I'd ride out here and see how you were doing, partner."

"I was fine until you showed up." Sim kicked the base of the tree. "Tally Bernard trusts me—or at least she did."

"I can see that." Caleb smiled, implying a passel of nasty thoughts with the curl of his lip. "She's a fine piece. How long have you been riding her?"

"Leave her out of it," Sim snapped.

"She's André's sister."

"She doesn't know about the map."

"I 'spect she don't know how her brother set me up with the Rangers, either."

Sim paced a tight circle. "If she did, I'd know it. And there's something you'd better understand right away. André is at the ranch, but he might as well not be. He hurt his head in a fall. He can barely talk, and I've been waiting for him to get better. That's why you haven't heard from me."

Caleb's eyes narrowed. "You don't know where the map is?"

"I told you. André ain't talking. I tracked him into the mountains when I got here in spring, but I found him after he'd fallen, and he didn't have the map on him. My guess is that he destroyed it. I figured once he recovered he could tell me what was in it—since you never could read the goddamned thing."

Caleb got red in the face. "You came to me, Sim. You needed money, and I offered you a partnership. Half the treasure I always knew I'd find…the one you never believed in."

"If it's real."

"Oh, it's real. André risked his life for it."

"And now he babbles like a child—when he talks at all. We have no choice but to wait, Caleb. As long as it takes."

"Have you tried persuasion, Sim, or don't you have the stomach for it?"

"'Persuasion' only works if a man has all his mind to be afraid."

Caleb uttered an extremely foul curse, drew his knife again and jabbed it into the cottonwood. "You sure his sister don't know anything?"

"I'm sure." He pulled Caleb's knife from the tree and tested its edge against this thumb. A thin line of red welled up from the cut. "You have to stay away, Caleb. You'll wreck what I've done here, and Bernard's range boss is already suspicious."

"Elijah Patterson? I heard he came with them to Arizona. He was always panting after that pretty little Miriam." He held out his hand, and Sim returned the knife. The cut on his thumb was nearly healed, but Caleb didn't notice.

"You know something else about Patterson?" Caleb said, hacking leaves from the lowest branches. "He deserted from the Tenth Cavalry before he came to Peñasco Rojo."

"Deserted? How would you know that?"

"He must have told André, because one night, when André was drinking, he told me. He felt sorry for that black bastard." Caleb snorted. "Patterson had a whole bunch of them commendations before he ran off. Awards for courage. But I know for a fact he's a coward."

Sim digested these new facts in silence. That kind of information might serve him well if Elijah ever made too much trouble. "Does anyone else know about this?"

"He'd keep it quiet. He's uppity-proud for one of his kind."

His kind. Sim had heard words like that before, referring

to his mother. Decent people had whispered about "her kind." They'd gossiped about the sort of boy who had a whore for a mother and lived by any means he could.

"Some of us can't help the way we're born," Sim said quietly.

"You still so touchy about your mama, Simeon?"

The revolver at Sim's hip could be aimed at Caleb's chest in a second, and Caleb knew it. Sim kept his fingers hooked in his belt.

"It must be quite a trial for you to take orders from Chantal Bernard," Caleb added. "Much as you despise the ladies."

"She's better than most."

"Not bad, but a little too well-seasoned. I like mine young." Caleb licked his lips. "Like that little filly I saw riding out with *Miss* Bernard a couple of days ago."

Sim suffered an unpleasant shock. If Caleb had been nearby for several days, he should have sensed it. "Where did you see them?"

"In Sulphur Spring Valley. I wanted to know every way in and out of this canyon before I came a'callin'."

Then maybe he hadn't been so close. Sim still didn't relax. "That filly's name is Beth, and you leave her alone."

"Beth. Reminds me of a nice little light skirt I knew in Abilene."

Sim clenched his fists. "Caleb—"

Caleb grinned. "You got a personal interest?"

"I don't want no complications until this is over."

"So I'm supposed to cool my heels and trust you to finish it?"

"You've trusted me before." He lifted his palm to show the ancient scar. "When did I ever double-cross *you*, Caleb?"

His friend looked away, though shame wasn't a feeling he had much acquaintance with. "I'll trust you, Sim. Anyway, I got my boys waiting for me in San Bernardino Valley. Still lots of good hunting on both sides of the border."

"As long as you keep away from Cold Creek." Sim stepped forward and stood toe to toe with Caleb. "Swear you'll keep out of Cochise County."

"Should I swear on the Good Book or the Virgin Mary?"

Sim backed away. "You've got enough grub here to get you to your men. I suggest you try the beeves in New Mexico. I hear they're sweeter than anything you'll catch in this part of the Territory. I'll find you when I have what we need." He mounted and turned Diablo, deliberately leaving his back exposed. Caleb didn't move from the tree.

There wasn't any more to be said. It was the things Sim hadn't told his "old friend" that weighed on his mind as he retraced his path to the homestead. He'd led Caleb to believe that André had memorized and destroyed the map; it seemed likely that Caleb would return to his men and rustling cattle, at least for a while. He understood the risk in confronting Sim directly.

But Caleb was also unpredictable. If he found out that some unknown thief had stolen his ill-gotten "property" from André, he would never leave the Territory until he found the latest owner. Sim didn't want to think about what he would have to do if Caleb threatened Tally again.

Don't make me choose, amigo. *Either I go to Esperanza without fresh blood on my hands, or I'm already damned.*

THE CHESTNUT WAS SHAKING with exhaustion by the time Caleb descended to level ground south of the pass, but he forced the animal to continue until they'd rounded the end of the Liebres and were headed north into Sulphur Spring Valley. Only then did he dismount and lead the horse to a water hole recently filled by summer rains.

The clouds were darkening over Caleb's head, fit to match his mood. So Sim wanted him out of the Territory, did he? He demanded this and that like he was some kind of big hacendado lording it over his campesinos. He would take care of everything, Sim would…if that female Bernard didn't get in the way.

Caleb smiled sourly and dragged the chestnut from the water hole. Sim didn't think much of his old friend's brains. He assumed that Caleb couldn't see how much he hankered after André's golden-haired sister—Sim, of all the bastards this side of the Rio Grande.

Years ago, when they'd ridden together, Sim could be counted on to curse anything in skirts. But when he'd come to Texas looking for Caleb and a chance to get back into the business, he'd talked of some pretty señorita across the border. What was her name? *Esperanza*. He'd wanted money for her, for some future he imagined they had together.

Caleb hadn't paid much attention to the conversation. He'd been in jail awaiting trial, and he'd been thinking about the map and how Sim could track André Bernard and get it back. He'd agreed to split the treasure once they found it. And Sim was desperate enough not to laugh at his old friend's dream. He'd wanted that Mexican gold as much as Caleb did.

A few fat drops of rain spattered on Caleb's shoulders, and he slammed his hat lower over his eyes. He mounted again and continued north as the clouds piled up and dropped their afternoon load. The valley seemed deserted, even of wandering beeves searching out the season's fresh new grass.

Stupid as they were, they had the sense to get out of the storm. It looked like Sim had walked right into one. Sure, he'd played a clever hand pretending to chase Caleb off the ranch. If André was touched in the head—and Caleb had only Sim's word for that—it made sense to get Tally's confidence, and obviously she didn't know much about Sim's past. But Sim had defended the "reputations" of Tally Bernard and the girl Beth when he had nothing to gain by that kind of talk.

Be good, Caleb. Don't bother those nice people, Caleb. Don't make trouble, Caleb. Sim sounded just like Ma, telling him what he should and shouldn't do, what he should and shouldn't want. Don't be hungry, don't be thirsty, don't covet thy neighbor's ass, don't lust after thy neighbor's wife. The meek shall inherit the earth, Caleb. You must be patient, or you'll surely burn in hell.

Patient. Caleb jabbed his spurs into the chestnut's flanks, and the animal half reared. Caleb whipped it into submission.

He'd been patient. He'd been locked up in that cell for months, wondering what Sim was doing with the information Caleb had given him. Well, Sim seemed to have stuck to his part of the bargain, as far as it went. He wanted Caleb to trust him, but that cut both ways. Sim had to trust that Caleb would head south to meet his men and take up rustling again until the map or its secrets were recovered. He was counting on boyhood loyalty, just like Caleb.

Loyalty was worthless if it couldn't stand a good test once in a while. It would be interesting to see how much Sim let his new respect for the ladies affect his good sense. And Caleb was more than ready for a bit of fun.

Caleb shucked his hat and let the rain wash over his face and drench his hair. His bad mood was passing like the clouds, and pretty soon he would be coming to a nice little ranch where the folks would be happy to give him a bed for the night. He would play the gentleman, and the garrulous old man who lived with his two sons would gladly tell the polite young visitor everything he wanted to know about the local girl called Beth.

CHAPTER ELEVEN

ELI HEARD THE WOMEN'S LAUGHTER as soon as he walked into the house. He was still sweaty and hot after the hard ride back from Tombstone; the afternoon thunderstorms were late today, leaving the world in a dark and breathless hush.

He walked quickly through the kitchen and paused out of sight beside the parlor door.

"Look at this one," Miriam said.

Eli peeked around the corner into the parlor. Tally and Miriam were sitting on the sofa with a magazine spread open across their laps. The pages were yellowed with age, but Eli could make out the drawings, some in color, of elegant ladies in figure-hugging gowns.

"It *is* lovely," Tally said, her finger brushing the picture.

"And expensive." Miriam sighed and shook her head. "I shouldn't be looking at this. Even the patterns are too dear, let alone the material."

"If you think I'm going to let you get married in your calico dress, you are quite mad," Tally said firmly. "We'll go to Tombstone and find something suitable for a bride."

"And what will you use for money?" Miriam asked with her usual practicality.

Eli smiled and touched the package tucked inside his shirt over his heart. She wouldn't swoon when she saw the ring.

He would bet fifty dollars that she would demand he take it back. This time she wasn't getting her way.

"…that I've kept since Nathan died," Tally was saying. "They're worth quite a bit, and there are several jewelers in Tombstone who'll give me a fair price."

"I can't let you sell your things—"

Tally chuckled. "Don't worry. I won't spend all of it on you, dear friend though you may be."

"I wish you'd do something for yourself once in a while."

"But I do, Miriam. Every day at Cold Creek, when I ride out and breathe the clean air and know that all this is ours. Our home."

Miriam was silent a long moment. "Will you still feel that way when Sim Kavanagh is gone?"

Tally closed the magazine and clasped her hands on the cover. "What makes you think he's leaving us?"

"Because things can't stay the way they are now, with the two of you dancing around each other like leaves in the wind. You aren't giving him any encouragement, and without it—" She covered Tally's hands with hers. "A man like that needs something—or someone—to hold him."

"Ah." Tally smiled. "You did have such high hopes for him, didn't you? I tried to explain before why such a thing couldn't be."

"You were trying to convince yourself, not me."

"Perhaps that's true. But you see, Miriam, I never told you that he already has a woman."

Miriam bit her lip. "No, you didn't."

"I'm sorry, *ma chérie*. I never found the right time to mention it."

"No one said it was any of my business." Miriam sniffed, abandoned her indignation and leaned closer. "Who is she?"

"I don't know much about her, except that he is devoted to her. She isn't…she isn't his wife. Not yet."

"How long have you known?"

"Since Sim first came. But I didn't think it would matter."

"You didn't think you'd come to care for him?"

"I had no reason to. I still don't know what I feel. I don't understand—"

"How you could want a man again?"

Tally nodded. "Mademoiselle Champagne never *wanted* any man. She only played the game. It isn't a game with Sim. He was honest about his plans, Miriam. He never intended to stay…permanently."

Eli clenched his teeth and turned his back to the wall. That filthy son of a bitch, toying with Tally when he had another woman.

"I think he's only stayed this long because he wanted to help us," Tally said. "He worries how we'll manage without him."

Eli nearly choked. Good God, the arrogance. His fists ached with the desire to cast Sim Kavanagh down into the dirt where he belonged.

"He is a good man," Miriam said, "though he doesn't want anyone else to know it. Not everyone can be as simple and honest as my Eli."

The knot in Eli's throat expanded to the size of a boulder. *Oh, my Miriam. How can you be so blind and so wise at the same time?*

"After what happened yesterday," Miriam said, "I wouldn't be surprised if he stayed on. He seemed mighty eager to protect you from Caleb."

"Not just me, Miriam."

"Well, it's hard to believe he ever knew Caleb, let alone rode with him."

"He said it was a long time ago."

"'The sins of youth.' No one is free of those. But Caleb Smith is just plain—"

Eli stepped around the corner into the parlor. "Caleb Smith?"

Miriam and Tally stared at him. "Elijah Ezekial Patterson," Miriam said, rising to her feet, "how long have you been eavesdropping?"

"Caleb Smith was here?" Eli demanded, ignoring Miriam's question. "What did he want?"

"He's gone now, Eli," Tally said. "You've just returned?"

"That's clear as day," Miriam said, waving her hand in front of her face. "Once you've washed up, maybe Miss Tally will be able to stand your company."

Eli took a step back. "My apologies, ladies. But you'll understand why I was concerned—"

"Completely," Tally said. She gave Eli a long, knowing look. "Caleb did us no harm. He wanted to speak to André, but he didn't get the chance."

"Sim drove him away," Miriam said with some satisfaction.

Eli was careful not to let them see his disgust. "Last I heard, Smith was in jail and likely to remain so. I'm sorry I wasn't here to deal with him myself."

"Was your trip successful?" Tally asked pointedly.

"Yes." Thunder boomed overhead, seeming to shake the house. "If you ladies will excuse me, I'll make myself more presentable, and then I'd like to hear more about Caleb's visit."

He went down the hall to André's room as he did every day, driven by pity, guilt and old habits of loyalty. André, lost somewhere inside his injured mind, didn't hear him enter or leave again. At the bunkhouse, Eli made a place for his treasure in the cigar box by his bedside. Then he washed and changed into fresh clothing as the thunderstorm gave way to the cool of evening.

He was eager to see Miriam's face when he presented his gift. But there was another task to be completed first, and Eli had never been one to put off a difficult job in favor of a pleasant one.

He knelt beside his bunk and reached underneath for the holster tied to the frame. His palm brushed cool, polished wood. The Colt army revolver fit his hand so perfectly, yet he'd hoped never to hold it again. He buckled on the gun belt with nerveless fingers.

Then he went to find Sim Kavanagh.

"I KNOW WHAT you are."

Sim didn't turn right away. He took his time with the last strokes of the brush over Diablo's sleek coat and listened to the straw crackle under Elijah Patterson's boots.

"We have a visitor, Diablo," he said. "I think he wants a word with me, but I don't think he'll mind if you listen in."

"Diablo," Eli said. "A good name for a horse that belongs to a man like you—if he ever was yours."

Sim turned, leaning against the stallion's firm shoulder. "He's mine, all right—bought and paid for. And I don't want you shooting him by accident."

Eli's hand stayed well away from his holster. "I don't shoot anything by accident, Kavanagh."

"Just the same…" Sim gave Diablo a final pat and strolled past Eli out of the barn. The earth was damp underfoot, and every tree and shrub sparkled with the aftermath of the storm. Eli smelled of fear, but his face was hard with determination. He kept to the driest ground and held his body ready for immediate action.

Sim sat down on an old cottonwood stump and folded his arms across his chest. "Well," he said, "go on, Patterson. Just what am I?"

Eli planted himself opposite Sim, hands loose at his sides. "Caleb Smith was here."

"Been and gone."

"And you know him. You rode with him. Is that why you're at Cold Creek, riding point for a murdering outlaw—setting us up by winning Miss Tally's trust?"

Sim stretched his arms, and Eli's hand jerked nearer his gun. "You almost sound surprised, Patterson. You made it pretty plain that you think I'm an outlaw myself."

"I know you are. Just like I know you're not a normal man."

"Now that could be taken as an insult."

"And men like you don't take insults."

"I thought you just said I wasn't a man." Sim cocked his head. "You hate Caleb."

"I hate all cold-blooded killers."

"Even though your boss worked with him in Texas?"

"Did Caleb tell you that before you came here?"

"I just found out today. Haven't seen Caleb in years."

"You're a liar, Kavanagh. You got Caleb to leave. A man like him doesn't just go away on command. It was all an act, wasn't it? You're the fox guarding the henhouse. Either you're in on some scheme with Caleb, or you've got plans for evil of your own."

"I rode with Caleb when we were young. That's all."

"I don't believe you."

"That's a damned shame."

"I want you gone from Cold Creek."

Sim stood up, paying no attention to Eli's weapon. "You the superstitious type, Patterson?"

The former soldier's eyes took on a haunted expression. "I know there are things in this world that can't always be explained."

"And you figure I'm one of those…things."

"I saw you run faster than a horse and smash a trap with your bare hands. You act more like a wolf than a human being."

"So that makes me…what, Patterson? A monster? You think I'd creep into the house one night and tear open those pretty throats with my teeth?"

Eli shuddered. "If you are what you seem—"

"I could have killed everyone here the first night I rode in. And if you thought I could do that, why did you leave me alone with the ladies while you rode to Tombstone?"

"Because I still had doubts. Not anymore."

"You have too many doubts, Patterson. Even now."

The muscles in Eli's jaw flexed tight. "There's one thing I'm sure of. You're leaving tonight."

Sim eyed the gun. "Army issue, ain't it? How long's it been since you used it?"

For a moment Eli seemed taken aback, as if Sim had touched a subject he didn't want to think about. Sim smiled. "Why did you leave the cavalry, Patterson? I heard you won commendations for courage."

"Who told you that?"

"They don't know—Tally, Miriam, the other men? Why hide it, Patterson?"

"That's enough. If you're not a wanted man in more than one state, I'm whiter than a daisy. I could call the law on you any time, Kavanagh—and I would, if it wasn't for Tally. But you're riding out of here tonight. If you come back, I'll shoot you where you stand."

Sim yawned. "Why wait? Monster or outlaw, I deserve to die."

"At the end of a rope."

"No one's managed that yet. You could be a hero, Patterson. Or are you really the coward Caleb says you are?"

Eli's hand trembled. In one gesture Sim could have him disarmed and on the ground, but he bided his time. Eli didn't move.

"It seems Caleb don't like you any more than you like him," Sim said. "When he heard you worked here, he was downright eager to tell me about you deserting from the cavalry. That's something Miriam doesn't know about you, isn't it?"

"You bring my woman into this—"

"Miriam and Tally think you're a brave soldier who can do no wrong. I'll bet you killed plenty of men in your day."

"You think it's a proud thing to take lives, Kavanagh? You enjoy it, like any wild animal?"

"No." Sim sat down again, finding his legs suddenly weak. "I never killed no women or children or any man who was innocent. You think you know me, Patterson. That's your mistake. You could shoot me if you got up the nerve, but that's your problem, ain't it? You can't kill. You've had a bellyful of death."

Eli's skin was too dark to change color with shock, but the desperation was in his eyes. "I'll do what I have to."

"I see the truth, Patterson. I'll make it easier for you. Even if you shot me, I'd probably survive. That's the sort of thing that goes along with running fast as a horse and breaking traps with my bare hands. I'd live, and your gentle Miriam would eventually find out that the man she loves is a deserter and a coward who'd try to kill an unarmed man."

"Miriam wouldn't—"

"You don't want her to know." Sim sighed. "You and me both done things we ain't proud of, but no one else has to find out. Not Tally or Miriam, not the law or the army, who'd surely like to hear where you've run off to."

"Caleb could report me any time."

"He's got his own concerns right now. I figure you have two choices—kill me or let me be. I ain't leaving Cold Creek without a fight."

Eli ran his hand through his short-cropped black hair. "Why? Tally said you have a woman waiting for you somewhere. You never planned to stay at Cold Creek. What do we have that a man like you could want?"

There was a tone in Eli's voice that Sim couldn't quite interpret, a hint of deception, as if the former soldier had asked the question only for Sim's benefit. "You think you know what I want, Patterson?" he asked.

"You don't care about Miss Tally," Eli said. "You don't have it in you."

"You understand only what you see," Sim said quietly. "And it ain't half of what's really there. I wouldn't hurt Tally to save my own life."

"I'd never trust any promise of yours."

"I ain't making any promises. It's your call, Patterson."

Eli held Sim's gaze as he lowered his arm and pointed the Colt toward the inoffensive earth. "I stopped praying a long time ago," he said. "But tonight I'll beg God to give you the fate you deserve."

"You do that. It'll be interesting to see if he answers your prayers or gives me another shot at salvation."

"Salvation?" Eli holstered his gun. "You'll never find peace, Kavanagh. Not in this life or the next." He walked away, skirting the barn and the corral beyond.

Sim rested his hands on his knees and stared at the ground between his boots. His stomach churned with nausea. Eli had been stupid to provoke a confrontation where Tally could have witnessed it. He was hotheaded for all his discipline, determined to do what he thought was right even at the cost of his reputation and honor. He didn't realize how close he'd come to death.

Would I have killed him?

"Sim?"

Tally's voice woke him as if from a dream. He sat up and smiled at her with the air of a guilty man caught in the act.

"I thought I heard shouting," she said. She stood just out of touching range, hands crossed over her breasts. The setting sun turned the gold of her hair to bronze fire. "Is everything all right?"

"Eli had a few questions about Caleb Smith," Sim said.

"They have a bad history between them," she said. "There were many men in Texas who hated the Buffalo Soldiers. Caleb was the worst." She hesitated. "I know he was your friend—"

"Not anymore." Sim listened to his own words and heard the truth in them, and an unfamiliar sadness. "Not like when we were kids."

But some old loyalties remained. The partnership wasn't broken yet.

"When are you planning to leave Cold Creek?" Tally asked abruptly.

The question stole his breath, though there was nothing startling in it. "I thought maybe the end of summer," he said.

"September?"

He clenched his hands between his knees. "I hadn't reckoned the exact date."

"Of course. It's just that—" She drew a deep breath. "I've been thinking of replenishing the stock that was stolen last winter. André was to have bought cattle in the spring, but…" She shrugged eloquently. "Federico knows of a hacendado in Sonora who often has surplus beeves to sell in autumn and might have what I wish to buy. Sonoran cattle are less expensive than those raised on this side of the border, and my resources are somewhat limited." She smiled wryly. "I'll be writing to Don Miguel this week, inquiring if we might make the journey to his ranch in September."

Sim knew what was coming. There was no reason to make Tally ask. "You want to know if I can go with you."

"Only if your plans permit it. I've heard you speak fluent Spanish to Federico and Pablo, and you've shown your knowledge of cattle. And there are bandits and Apaches to contend with in Sonora."

"Why not take Elijah?"

"I need him to watch the ranch, in case our rustlers return." She didn't mention Caleb Smith, but Sim knew she was thinking of him.

He stood. "You figure I'm more ruthless than Eli when it comes to a fight?" he asked.

"I didn't mean—"

"You're right. I can handle *bandidos* and Apaches."

"Not alone, of course. I'll take Federico, and hire men in Mexico to help get the cattle back to Cold Creek. I know this would keep you away from Esperanza longer than perhaps you anticipated, but I'd pay you well for your trouble."

He looked her in the eye. "Where are you getting the money for this, Tally?"

"I have a few valuables from my marriage that I saved for unforeseen necessities," she said. "The price they bring in Tombstone should be just enough to purchase the stock we need to get started again."

The hope in her gaze was too much for Sim. The hair on his neck rose, and his heart beat just a little too fast for comfort. He could imagine traveling with Tally, chaperoned only by the amiable Federico. Such a journey would bring them very close. Dangerously so.

Of course, Caleb was still waiting for news of the treasure, and Sim had yet to obtain it. He might get what he needed out of André tonight…or tomorrow, or two months from now. That was the problem. "Where's this hacienda?" he asked.

"Near San Lucas. I would allow eight weeks to make the journey there and return, with the expectation of delays should we meet with trouble or bad weather."

Sim consulted his memory and realized what Tally had just given him. One possible route to San Lucas passed very near a certain small village named Dos Ríos.

Esperanza lived in Dos Ríos. She'd moved in with distant relatives a year after leaving New Mexico. Sim had tracked her to the village, keeping himself hidden while he made sure she would be safe and settled until he gained the means of properly courting her.

If he went with Tally, he could see Esperanza again. Once more she would be real to him, flesh and blood, filling him with the inspiration to remain true to her and to his dream.

But September was weeks away. If André talked before then, Sim would get his share of the treasure. He wouldn't have to creep into Dos Ríos like a thief just to remember his purpose.

"I can't give you an answer right now," he said. "Send your letter. If I can't go with you, I'll find men who can do the job in my place."

Tally tried to smile. "If your other acquaintances are anything like Caleb, I'd as soon do without them." She hesitated, flushing. "Until you've decided, you're welcome to stay on as you have been." She turned to go.

Sim touched her arm. She flinched as if he'd stabbed her. His mouth went inexplicably dry.

"I'm sorry about Caleb," he said.

"It was hardly your fault." Her smile was crooked and all the more endearing for its imperfection. "Once more you came to our rescue." She swallowed and looked down. "We'll miss you, Sim."

"I'm not gone yet." He let her go before he could pull her into his arms. "Tally…"

"*Bon soir,* Sim," she whispered. "That's French for good night. When the time comes, I'll teach you how to say good-bye."

THE NIGHT WAS ANYTHING but good.

Sim went to the hills, met the wolves, ran with them for hours, and then continued running long after they'd tired and returned to their dens. He tried to follow Caleb's scent trail through the pass, but the rains had washed it away.

Over the next few days he took every opportunity to speak with André. Each attempt proved frustrating and fruitless. André had slipped back into a half-conscious state, and when he woke, he was more agitated than lucid. Tally was upset, though she made the best of André's relapse. Sim was sorely tempted to comfort her, though he knew he was the last man who had any right to do so.

In late July he ran as a wolf over the Pedregosa Mountains to the San Bernardino Valley and found evidence of an abandoned encampment that had all the earmarks of rustlers' temporary headquarters. As lazy August succeeded July, he visited the farthest borders of the range, skimming swift as an eagle over the Chiricahua passes. Once on the other side, he "borrowed" clothing and horses and rode into New Mexico, inquiring about a man fitting Caleb's description.

By such means he learned that Caleb had finally gone to New Mexico with his men and was harassing homesteaders up and down the Rio Grande. He'd decided to trust Sim after all. Sim found no evidence that the map thief had returned to the area where André had met with his "accident." Eli kept his suspicions and hostility to himself, and things were as peaceful as anyone had a right to expect.

But Sim had no excuse to stay at Cold Creek through the autumn unless he agreed to accompany Tally to Sonora for the cattle purchase. Truth to tell, he didn't want Tally traveling with only Federico and possibly a couple of hired men for company.

As August drew to a close and the larger outfits were hiring for their autumn roundups, Sim quietly began helping Tally prepare for the journey. He suggested crossing into Mexico through Nogales and following the Río del Halcón to San Lucas, a route that would take them within ten miles of Dos Ríos. He could easily cover such a distance in a single night if he ran as a wolf.

Tally had no objections to his taking the lead. Her solemn mood lightened, and she rode into Tombstone to sell her jewelry, returning well pleased with the deals she'd made.

Miriam had laid by a large supply of jerky and provided the fixings for baking-soda biscuits as well as beans and other staple foods to supplement any hunting the travelers managed along the way. Eli bought pack mules, and Federico selected a remuda of the ranch's best horses, five mounts each for himself, Tally and Sim.

The first week of September was warm and fresh, with a rich new growth of grass and wildflowers brought from the earth by the summer rains. The cows and weaned calves were enjoying the bounty, but on the morning of departure Sim was disturbingly aware of only one thing: Tally, sitting easy on her roan gelding, her scent more enticing than any that called from the wilderness.

Elijah, Miriam, Bart, Pablo and Dolores had gathered to say adios as the sun broke over the Chiricahuas. Diablo was restless, sensing adventure ahead; the mules looked disinclined to go anywhere, but Federico had proven to be a natural mule skinner as well as horse wrangler. The vaquero hugged his children one last time and leaped nimbly into his horse's saddle with cheerful bravado.

"Please remember what we discussed," Tally said to Elijah. "If you catch any sign of rustlers, don't fight them alone. A few cattle aren't worth your lives."

"I won't let him forget," Miriam said. She slipped her hand through the crook of Eli's elbow. Sunlight caught the precious stone on her left ring finger. "And don't you worry about Mr. André. I'll take good care of him. And the children, too," she added to Federico.

"Why can't I come?" Pablo complained. "I'm old enough. I can trail cattle, and—"

"Not this time," Tally said. "I need you here to help Bart and Elijah—and Miriam needs a strong young man around the house."

Pablo scowled, but he found little sympathy. Sim tried to remember when he'd been that young and naive. At Pablo's age he could have gone wherever he chose and no one would have cared enough to stop him.

Federico, ever the softhearted one, promised his children gifts from Mexico and turned away quickly, clucking to the mules. Sim fell in behind him. Tally hung back to share a few last farewells with her friends, and then she caught up with Sim. They started through the southern pass side by side.

"I'm glad you could come," Tally said, tilting her hat to shade her face against the piercing shafts of morning light. Perhaps it was only coincidence that she hid her face from Sim, as well, but he smelled her excitement.

"You've been looking forward to this," he said, "and not just because you're getting the ranch started up again."

"Yes. It's been a while since I've made such a journey."

"I thought you liked to stay in one place, make it into a home."

"I do." She looked at him, vivid eyes in shadow. "But I enjoy getting away from time to time. Home isn't supposed to be a prison."

"Like your last one?"

She turned the question back on him. "Where was your last home, Sim?"

"I've lived in lots of places."

"But you met Esperanza in New Mexico."

If he'd had it in his mind that she wanted to be alone with him on this journey, she'd just made short work of that notion. "I lived in New Mexico for a few years. I had a friend there—"

"A friend like Caleb Smith?"

"Nothing like Caleb. Tomás is a decent man. The things he did…he had good reasons for them."

"You mean he was an outlaw, too?"

"He married a fine, upstanding English lady. Or at least she was that way until she met Tomás. He taught her a few new tricks."

"Why did you leave New Mexico? Why didn't you and Esperanza settle there?"

"Esperanza didn't want to stay."

"Too many memories," Tally murmured.

"What?"

"Nothing. I was thinking of myself. I could never live in Texas or Louisiana again."

Sim looked straight ahead at the climbing path and the mules' broad, swaying rumps. "Esperanza had a rough time in her village. She was different, and they couldn't accept her."

"You said she could see into people's hearts."

He nodded. "Later she…needed to look for something. I…" He paused, frustrated by his inability to explain. He'd never understood it completely himself. "She needed to go alone."

"You let her look for her own dream."

It hadn't been like that. He'd let her go because he knew

she would never accept him otherwise…after he'd realized she was the one woman he might be able to love who could love him in return.

Tally was very quiet as they turned a narrow curve along the cliffside, leaving Cold Creek Valley out of sight behind them. "I'm glad you'll have a home of your own," she said. "A real home. A family." She smiled. "You'll make a good father, Sim."

The conversation disturbed him more than he dared let on. Why was it that he'd never imagined Esperanza great with his child, or holding his son in her arms?

"Raising kids is a woman's business," he said gruffly.

"You think so? Look at Federico. Miriam cares for his children, it's true, but he's a most devoted parent. Pablito and Dolores will never lack for love."

"What makes you think I'd make a good father?"

He hadn't meant to ask such a question, and now it was too late. Tally didn't laugh at him. She weighed her answer seriously, and when she spoke, her voice was choked with emotion.

"I saw you with Beth, and when Caleb had Pablo. You'd defend any child with your life. And you know what it's like not to have a father to look after you."

"I never told you that."

"You said your family didn't live together. They were separated, like mine."

He didn't want to talk about things that made his stomach knot and his eyes ache. "Right now you're glad to be away from André," he said harshly. "Isn't that the main reason you wanted to go on this trip? So you wouldn't have to look at his empty face and feel guilty for what he brought on himself?"

She stared at him out of stunned, hurt eyes and kicked her gelding into a swift trot, leaving Sim in the dust. He was glad to be alone. But the journey had just begun, and he knew there were going to be a lot more dangerous and disturbing conversations between him and Tally before it was over.

CHAPTER TWELVE

THE EARLY DAYS of the expedition covered familiar territory, and Tally was grateful that there was little necessity for talk. She, the men and the animals spent the first night just outside Tombstone. Over the next week they crossed the San Pedro River with its cottonwood *bosque* and ascended through the pass between the Santa Rita and Patagonia mountains. Though there were many ranches along the way whose owners would have been glad to offer a night's hospitality, Tally chose to camp in the open, where she didn't need to disguise her sex so diligently.

The modest trading post town of Nogales straddled the Mexican border in a valley thick with walnut trees. Tally insisted that her party spend the day resting in the shade, for the heat would only grow more intense as they traveled south. There would be many hills and arroyos to negotiate, and the constant possibility of encountering bandits or renegade Apaches.

Sim gave her no arguments. He kept his distance, silently going about necessary tasks such as gathering firewood without waiting to be asked. Several times he hunted and returned with small game for the pot. Federico took charge of cooking and joked with Tally when Sim was absent. The rest of the time he kept out of Sim's way.

That evening, stretched in her bedroll under the walnut

trees, Tally wondered what she had expected. Certainly she hadn't believed that Sim would suddenly reveal his innermost heart to her just because their circumstances compelled a certain intimacy. She'd been the one to mention Esperanza again, and he hadn't avoided the subject.

But she remained hungry—hungry to understand him, to learn more of his mysterious past, to discover what drove him to be the complex man he was. This trip might be her last opportunity. Once she truly understood him, perhaps she could forget that he'd ever been a part of her life.

She rode into Mexico the next morning with the memory of troubled dreams perched on the saddle behind her. From Nogales, she, Federico and Sim briefly followed the valley of a branch of the Río Magdalena and then crossed the Sierra Arizona. The landscape changed as they descended to the Río del Halcón. The scrubby desert Tally had known in Arizona changed to one occupied by tall, stately saguaros and countless chollas with needle-sharp spines. Cactus wrens chugged monotonously from cactus branches, and quail sobbed like mourning widows.

The road along the river was hardly more than a narrow, rocky trail. The jacals of poor farmers clung to the banks or the lower hillsides, where men and women in worn clothing eked out an existence from their little plots of soil and raised small livestock. Most waved and greeted the travelers with smiles, some with offers of food and drink. Tally accepted warm, freshly made tortillas for her party, but Federico firmly told her not to leave payment. The Mexican campesinos were poor, but their generous hospitality was a source of pride throughout their country.

Sometimes Tally's group passed villages where curious children peppered them with questions in rapid-fire Spanish. Federico answered as he watered the mules in the communal troughs, but on occasion Sim surprised Tally by speaking to the children with lazy amusement, almost as if he remembered the conversation about his potential fitness as a father.

Gradually the Río del Halcón curved east toward Tally's destination. The days were hot, the nights pleasant by comparison, but each was very much like the one before until they found the cow in the mud hole.

How the skinny, long-horned animal had managed such a feat was all too clear. It had apparently waded into a sluggish pool that had caught the river's overflow during the rainy season, unaware that the depression was more mud than water. Already weakened with the effort of nursing its large and unweaned calf, it had floundered itself into a state of exhaustion and now lay buried up to its belly while the calf bawled from the bank.

Tally reined in and studied the situation. There was no telling who owned the miserable beast; it might belong to a minor ranchero in the area, or it could be one of the many wild cattle that had learned to live off the land after Apache raids had driven farmers from the Sonoran wilderness.

Tally dismounted and approached the water hole. The calf skittered away, but its mother rolled a bloodshot eye at Tally and moaned pitifully.

"We have to get her out," Tally said.

Federico slid from his saddle and stood beside her. "It will be much work, señorita."

"We've both done the same job plenty of times at Cold Creek. I won't leave her and her calf to die because she made a foolish mistake."

Sim rode past them into the shade of a stately sycamore. "It's a foolish mistake to waste your strength on something that won't appreciate your efforts," he said.

His comment was the first thing he had said to her in days.

Tally held on to her temper. "Do you choose whether or not to assist someone based on how grateful they will be?"

He dismounted and leaned against the tree's pale trunk, letting Diablo find his way to a patch of weedy grass. "My apologies to Doña Vaca. I didn't realize her importance."

Tally whipped off her hat and slapped it on her thigh. "I don't expect you to help."

"That's good." He sat down and stretched his legs out before him. "But I'll be glad to give you advice if you get yourself stuck in there."

Federico met Tally's eyes and shrugged. She gave him her brightest smile. Tally untied several lengths of rope from one of the mules' packs. Federico fetched his riata and made a few practice swings. By unspoken agreement, he and Tally removed their boots and stockings, rolled up their pants and perched at the edge of solid ground. The cow bobbed her head in warning.

Federico let loose with his rope, catching the cow about her scrawny neck on the first try. She gave a halfhearted toss of her horns. Tally waded in cautiously, mud sucking at every step, and positioned herself at the cow's hindquarters. While Federico pulled, she pushed. The cow didn't budge. Tally tugged on the cow's tail, and she moaned.

Nothing could get her to move, no matter how often Federico and Tally changed angles or experimented with various configurations of rope around every part of the animal they could reach. Finally Federico climbed out of the mud, saddled his strongest horse and tied his rope around the saddle horn, but even the big gelding's best efforts were of no use whatsoever.

Sim laughed. The sound seemed to bounce off the hills and beat down on Tally's head like the pitiless sun. She pulled more furiously on her rope, which slipped from her hands yet again. She sat down in the mud. The cow grunted and closed her long-lashed eyes in resignation.

Federico's shoulders sagged. "This will not work, señorita," he said with regret. "She is too—"

"Give me that." Sim snatched the rope from Federico's hands and waded into the hole. "You two get out."

"You think you can do it a—" Tally broke off, meeting Sim's eyes. They twinkled with mischief and mockery. If he fell on his rump and made an idiot of himself, it was no more than he deserved.

She backed out, dragging each leg free of the sucking ooze. She and Federico collapsed on the bank to catch their breaths and watch Sim's operation.

There was nothing to see…nothing that Tally could later remember. One moment Sim was up to his waist in mire, leaning against the cow's heaving side, and the next the beast was clambering out of the hole with much snorting and rolling of eyes.

Sim climbed out after her, shaking himself like a wet dog. A blob of mud slapped Tally's cheek. The cow was too tired to do anything but stand still on trembling legs, but her calf rushed to her side and began probing for its long-delayed meal.

Sim shook his head in disgust and knelt on the riverbank. Tally walked up behind him, hands on hips.

"You're very proud of yourself, aren't you, Mr. Kavanagh?"

He scraped his hand across his face. "I'm very muddy."

"That is a condition, unlike your natural state of arrogance, that can easily be mended." She bent and gave him a firm push. He tumbled headfirst into the shallow water.

He came up spitting and grabbed her before she could take a single step away from the bank. Somehow he managed to pull her into the river without letting her fall, and she landed gently on her rump.

"Is that better?" Sim asked, his face very close to hers.

She scrambled out of his reach and looked toward Federico. He stood on the bank, unscathed, his eyes crinkled with laughter. Suddenly, inexplicably, Tally was filled with a happiness almost akin to joy.

"It's wonderful," she said, and rolled onto her back. Cool water sluiced over her body. Sim opened his mouth to speak, and she flicked a handful of droplets at his face. It was like that day at the *bosque* in Castillo Canyon, but they weren't strangers anymore.

Sim snarled and advanced on her, ready to pounce. She tried to slide out of his path, but he struck, fast as a rattlesnake, and caught her foot. She shrieked, feigning terror. Sim crouched and bit her toes lightly, growling all the while. A charge of erotic sensation shot up Tally's leg and into the pit of her belly.

She began to laugh, spilling emotion before it could explode inside her. Sim pretended to gnaw on her ankle. She twisted up and pulled hard on Sim's bedraggled hair. He yelled in mock pain and grabbed her wrists. A moment later they were sitting in the river, staring at each other, grinning like great fools or innocent children.

"You have a very nice smile, Monsieur Kavanagh," she said.

"You have a very nice—" He looked pointedly at her chest. She'd bound her breasts, but he'd seen what lay underneath the wrappings. "Very nice feet."

"Unfortunately, you are not permitted to devour them, even if you were raised by cannibals."

He pressed his hand over his heart. "My secret is out. But you still have to pay a price for my saving your cow, Miss Bernard."

"She isn't my cow."

"Seems everything you touch ends up belonging to you." His grin vanished. "Why is that, Tally?"

She faltered under his stare. He put his hands on her hair, slid them down to cup her face.

Mon Dieu. It was truly happening. Not like before, when he'd stolen a kiss just to prove his indifference. There was no indifference in him now. And none in her.

"What will you give me, Tally?" he whispered.

She closed her eyes. "Everything."

That was when she realized she was in love with Sim Kavanagh.

She tilted her face. He bent his. Breath mingled. Lips touched.

The cow gave a great bellow of protest. Sim sprang up. Tally covered her mouth with her hands. They both looked toward the bank, where Federico stood with the calf neatly hog-tied at his feet, out of reach of its worried mother.

The vaquero turned slightly red and bent to release the calf. "I was…practicing," he said.

Tally waded out of the river, wringing water from her loosened hair.

Sim remained where he was a moment longer. Federico and the cow had saved him from plunging into far more dangerous waters with Tally, but he wasn't sure how he was going to repay the debt. His present physical state wasn't any good for making serious decisions.

The afternoon was too far gone to allow much more travel before nightfall, so Tally and Federico set up camp in a nearby *bosque.* That suited Sim just fine. Esperanza's village was less than twenty miles away, southeast of the juncture where the Río del Halcón met the Río Magdalena. There would never be a better or more appropriate time to remind himself what he truly wanted.

He left before sunset, mumbling some excuse about taking a walk. He went on foot, carrying a special leather pack just large enough to hold his clothing, boots and gun. Once he'd left the camp well behind, he stripped, stuffed his belongings into the pack and Changed. Wolf's jaws seized the strap.

Sim reached the village of Dos Ríos in a little over an hour. The village was of decent size for a rural Sonoran town, complete with a tiny adobe church and many fields in the level areas beside the river. A single rutted road ran between the huts and houses. Light streamed from the windows of the larger dwellings, silhouetting the figures of men socializing in the cool of evening.

Sim Changed, donned his clothing and hid his gun under his coat. He crept into the village from the hills, staying out of sight. These villagers had seen every kind of outsider imaginable—miners, outlaws, Indians, wanderers. They weren't easily frightened. But Sim wanted to learn of Esperanza without revealing his presence to her. He wasn't ready for them to meet again just yet.

Hugging the shadows, he slipped past the outlying houses. He knew exactly which one belonged to Esperanza's relatives, and he approached with great care. A single lamp burned in one of the two rooms. Sim smelled recent cooking, frijoles and tortillas and squash from the evening meal.

He paused at the front door, listened, then entered the main room. A few simple pieces of handmade furniture were its only adornments save for the garish painting of a saint hung in a prominent place on one whitewashed wall.

The light came from the second room, where a woman's voice was reciting a prayer in a low monotone. Sim edged up to the adjoining doorway. The woman knelt beside a sleeping pallet, telling her rosary as she prayed.

She wasn't Esperanza. Sim recognized her as the female relative, Carlotta Sanchez, who had welcomed Esperanza so warmly two years before. The fact that she was alone at such an hour made no sense. Esperanza should be here, unless she had moved to another house….

The thought alarmed Sim into unwary motion. His boot scraped the floor. A dog barked from the street, and its warning was taken up by several others. Carlotta ceased her prayers and looked toward the door.

"Who's there?" she asked, more curious than afraid. "Jorge?" She rose stiffly from her knees. "Esperanza? Is it you?"

Sim retreated from the house and slumped against the outer wall in relief. Carlotta clearly expected Esperanza, which meant she still lived with her relatives. The other possibility—that Esperanza had married some local campesino—had frozen Sim's heart with dread and rage.

She wouldn't do such a thing. In all his secret visits, Sim had never seen her with a young man, nor had she shown any interest in marriage. She was saving herself. She knew Sim was coming for her….

Even though you never told her?

Maybe he'd waited too long. He'd been so sure that Esperanza was destined only for him, that somehow she would always be there when he was ready. Now he could see what a fool he'd been.

It had to be tonight. After what had happened with Tally—almost happened a dozen times before—he couldn't wait any longer. He would find Esperanza and declare himself once and for all. He would make her understand that he needed a little more time to make a home for them, a life she could be proud of. And when he looked into her eyes again, he would know he'd chosen the right path.

But first he had to find her.

Most of the village huts and houses were as quiet as the Sanchez home, and the few voices Sim heard didn't match Esperanza's. He visited the church, but it was empty. The walls and paint and altar wood smelled new, as if the sanctuary had been recently built to celebrate some extraordinary event.

Sim followed the sounds of music to the plain adobe structure that passed for Dos Ríos's saloon. Someone was playing the guitar with considerable skill. Slurred voices suggested that the men inside were enjoying the night's measure of pulque, the native agave liquor. There would be no women in such a place—no decent women—but drunken men talked just as freely as any female.

Sim crouched beside the nearest window. His keen hearing could easily separate one conversation from another, filtering each for the words he wanted to hear.

"No, no. I tell you Lopez's rooster is twice the fighter—"

"—was filled with worms. I—"

"—grant that she returns tomorrow. We cannot prosper without our little saint."

"That is dangerous talk, Bernardo. The priests—"

"Bah. When do they ever come here? We all know holiness when we see it. She is our sacred flower, who has brought great good fortune to us all. Now she is on a mission of healing as befits her generous heart, but soon she will return and bless us again."

Sim stretched to peer over the window ledge. The two men sat at a small, uneven table with earthenware cups of pulque, far from the guitar and off-key singing. One man was young and black-haired, the other old, with an air of caution about him.

"Admit it, Vincente," the young man said. "You have not seen a *curandera* such as Esperanza in all your long years."

Vincente stroked his white beard. "I admit it. How can I do otherwise? But I still say the priests—"

"Let them come. She has been chosen by God. Let the Holy Father himself test her and find her worthy."

"If others do not come first and steal her from us. When the world learns of her power…"

"We will stop anyone who tries."

The old man sighed. "Ah, *hijo,* you have not seen very much of the world."

"I know it is filled with evil. Such evil will never touch us here."

Vincente made a silencing motion with his hand and glanced toward the window. Sim dropped down. The men continued to talk of other things, and Sim heard no more of Esperanza.

Little saint. Sacred flower. Sim shook his head and cursed under his breath. The last time he had come to Dos Ríos, there had been no such talk of her. Her name was not so uncommon. But Sim knew that they had spoken of his Esperanza in the same hushed and respectful tones they would use in discussing a high cleric of their own church.

Sim had called her an angel. Was it any wonder others would think the same? Bernardo had said she was soon to return from some mysterious mission, perhaps even tomorrow. Too late for Sim.

A man staggered out of the *taberna,* reeling and reeking of pulque. Sim grabbed him as he passed the window on his drunken way home. He dragged the villager around the corner and pressed him to the wall.

"What is your name?" Sim asked.

The man blinked. "Gil…Gilberto. What d'you want?"

"Only answers to a few questions."

Gilberto considered resistance and decided against it. "Who are you?"

"That doesn't matter. Where is Esperanza?"

"Esper…anza?"

"She's left the village. Where has she gone?"

Gilberto belched. Sim stepped back and turned his head from the stench. The villager swayed dangerously to one side.

"La santita," he said at last, pronouncing each syllable with great deliberation. "She's...not here."

Sim growled. Gilberto's Adam's apple worked up and down, but suddenly he straightened and pushed Sim away.

"You...wanna steal her," he accused. "You can't have her. She belongs to us."

"She belongs to me."

"Who are you?" Gilberto leaned forward and took a swing at Sim's jaw. Sim sidestepped easily. Gilberto lost his balance and toppled to his knees. A moment later he was lying on his side, insensible. Sim nudged the villager with his boot and left him snoring where he lay.

Sim strode away from the *taberna*. He knew he could find another, more cooperative informant to tell him Esperanza's whereabouts, but he had no heart for the effort.

She belongs to us, Gilberto had said. Drunk though he was, his words had been sincere. Esperanza hadn't only found a home in Dos Ríos, she'd become important to these people—important enough that at least two men were willing to fight for her. They probably weren't alone. Once these villagers got some superstition into their heads, they would stick to it until death.

And what did Esperanza think of all this? She would never seek out such worship. The girl he knew would shun it. The expectations of these people would be a burden on her slender shoulders, the kind of burden Sim had wanted to take away forever.

But she could have run. She'd done it before. She could have returned to New Mexico, where she would always be welcome with Tomás and his aristocratic bride. Or she could have looked for Sim.

YOUR PARTICIPATION IS REQUESTED!

Dear Reader,

Since you are a lover of fiction – we would like to get to know you!

Inside you will find a short Reader's Survey. Sharing your answers with us will help our editorial staff understand who you are and what activities you enjoy.

To thank you for your participation, we would like to send you 2 books and a gift – **ABSOLUTELY FREE!**

Enjoy your gifts with our appreciation,

Pam Powers

**SEE INSIDE
FOR READER'S
SURVEY**

HOW TO VALIDATE YOUR
EDITOR'S FREE THANK YOU GIFTS!

1. Complete the survey on the right.

2. Send back the completed card and you'll get 2 brand-new Romance novels and a gift. These books have a combined cover price of $11.98 or more in the U.S. and $13.98 or more in Canada, but they are yours to keep absolutely FREE!

3. There's no catch. You're under no obligation to buy anything. We charge nothing—ZERO—for your first shipment. And you don't have to make any minimum number of purchases—not even one!

4. The fact is, thousands of readers enjoy receiving their books by mail from The Reader Service. They enjoy the convenience of home delivery…they like getting the best new novels at discount prices BEFORE they're available in stores…and they love their *Heart to Heart* subscriber newsletter featuring author news, special book offers, book reviews and much more!

5. We hope that after receiving your free books you'll want to remain a subscriber. But the choice is yours—to continue or cancel, anytime at all! So why not take us up on our invitation, with no risk of any kind. You'll be glad you did!

YOURS FREE!
We'll send you a fabulous surprise gift absolutely FREE, simply for accepting our no-risk offer!

YOUR READER'S SURVEY "THANK YOU" FREE GIFTS INCLUDE:

▶ Two BRAND-NEW Romance Novels
▶ A lovely surprise gift

The Reader Service — Here's How It Works:

Accepting your 2 free books and gift places you under no obligation to buy anything. You may keep the books and gift and return the shipping statement marked "cancel." If you do not cancel, about a month later we'll send you 3 additional books and bill you just $4.99 each in the U.S., or $5.49 each in Canada, plus 25¢ shipping & handling per book and applicable taxes if any.* That's the complete price and — compared to cover prices starting from $5.99 each in the U.S. and $6.99 each in Canada — it's quite a bargain! You may cancel at any time, but if you choose to continue, every month we'll send you 3 more books, which you may either purchase at the discount price or return to us and cancel your subscription.

*Terms and prices subject to change without notice. Sales tax applicable in N.Y. Canadian residents will be charged applicable provincial taxes and GST.

The possibilities rang like dissonant church bells in Sim's head. He silenced them with the Change. He barely remembered his return to the camp, but when he'd dressed and went searching for his bedroll, he found Tally sitting beside the ashes of the fire, wide awake.

"You shouldn't have waited up for me," he said.

"I wasn't tired."

He made a low sound of disbelief and sank into a crouch, elbows resting on his knees. "I told you I might be out late."

She met his gaze and knew it was the wrong time to push him. He was upset and angry—she could read it in his posture, in his eyes and his voice. She knew he wasn't happy that he'd come so close to kissing her in the river, and that was why he'd wanted time to himself. But something else had fed his anger during the hours he'd been gone, and she could think of nothing in this wilderness that could provoke it.

"What's troubling you, Sim?" she asked softly.

He looked sharply at her and then away. "Nothing."

"If it's what happened this afternoon…" She poked at the ashes of the fire. "I was only playing, but—I'm sorry."

"Playing." He picked up a handful of dust and let it blow away on the breeze. "Do you think you need to protect me?"

Sim hardly seemed to require any kind of protection, and yet part of Tally still feared she might unwittingly seduce him from his vows to Esperanza. She'd been so sure she had left the old habits behind her, but Sim brought them out again in a new way, bound to feelings she had never truly known before. It wasn't his fault. Men could be so weak when it came to their sexual needs.

"You think I can't control myself," Sim said, as if she'd spoken aloud. "Maybe you're right."

Tally shivered and prodded more furiously at the ashes. "We should both get some sleep."

"You've never been afraid of me."

"I never had any reason to be."

"I'll give you one." He stared at some point over her head. "I'm not a good man, Tally. I've done a lot of bad things in my life. Things I can never make up for."

Tally stood and paced back and forth on her side of the fire. "We've all made mistakes."

"I didn't think they were mistakes at the time," he said dryly. He wasn't smiling. "Eli was right about me."

"You've rustled cattle."

"And worse."

She squeezed her eyes shut. "Tell me."

He got to his feet. "I've robbed trains and stages…a few of them with Caleb, years ago."

"Did you kill people?"

He was quiet a long time, pacing parallel to her, as if the circle of ashes were an impenetrable barrier. "Not then. But later I worked as a hired gun for men who had plenty of enemies." He hesitated. "I could say the men I hunted were bad, like me. But then I'd be making excuses like a damned coward."

His confession seemed strangely unreal in the moonlight, as if it might vanish in the brightness of day. "And innocents?" she asked, driven to hear the worst. "Women and children?"

"Never." He turned on her, and his eyes glowed eerily red like a wild animal's. "Never anyone who couldn't fight back."

The stale air burst from Tally's lungs. "And did you…did you ever take a woman against her will?"

He grunted a painful laugh. "I've stolen a few kisses," he said. "But I never took an unwilling woman. Most of the ones I've known…they were professionals."

He almost spat the word. Tally hugged herself and pressed her chin to her chest. "I've done things I'm not proud of," she said. "You and I aren't so different, Sim."

"Have you stolen? Have you killed?"

There are other sins, she thought. But unlike Sim, she was a coward. She wasn't ready to match his confession with one of her own.

"You regret what you did," she said.

"Yes. But I can't change what I was. I can't make it go away, Tally." He held up his hands. "These will always be stained with blood."

As she, too, would always bear the stains of her past. "Why have you told me this now, Sim? Why tonight?"

"You asked."

"No. It's more than that. You had to talk about it…to someone."

How well she'd learned to read the subtle changes of his face. "You think I should have looked for a priest?" he asked harshly.

"You trusted me," she said.

"I knew you wouldn't turn me in."

"If I thought you were a cold-blooded murderer…"

"If I were, you wouldn't get the chance." He sighed and rubbed his forehead with the back of his hand. "I couldn't hurt you."

Such a simple statement. Tally felt that if she unwrapped her arms from around her ribs, her body would shatter into a million pieces.

"You said you can't change what you were," she said, "but you can change what you *are.*"

"I don't know if that's possible."

"I do. You have a dream of a better life. You can have it, Sim. You can become whatever you want to be."

"How can I do that when you're gone, Tally?"

"I'm not the one who's leaving."

"What if there was no Esperanza?"

Deliberately, she turned her back on him, fixing her stare on the bulky shapes of the mules and horses picketed under a tall cottonwood. "What has happened, Sim? What's changed?"

He was silent so long she thought he'd walked away. "Nothing," he said at last. "Nothing at all."

He was lying. He'd said all he was going to say, enough to unburden himself and give her good reason to stay away from him. The problem was that he hadn't succeeded in the second goal. He hadn't extinguished the love he didn't know she felt.

Tally doubted he ever would.

TALLY'S FIRST SIGHT of the Hacienda del Gavilán was of miles and miles of grass and scrubland cradled between hills not unlike those at Cold Creek. Long-horned Mexican cattle wandered at liberty to graze where they would—thin, tough beasts who could survive under the very worst of conditions.

Closer to the river, now a mile from the main road, campesinos or tenants worked plots of land devoted to corn, beans and other crops. Tally guessed that the hacienda was largely self-sufficient and must employ many of the local villagers on a seasonal basis. The Apaches had clearly not been a regular threat for some time.

Vaqueros wearing colorful sashes and kerchiefs whooped greetings to the strangers, sending one of their number ahead to alert the hacendado of his guests' approach. Tally knew Don Miguel Torres only by reputation, but like most Mexican nationals he would treat even the newest business associates like old friends. Such was the way in a land where Indian attacks, disease and drought had long been constant companions.

Federico, after several wary glances at Sim, asked permission to join his countrymen on the range. Tally waved him on. She was more than grateful to have arrived at their destination, for Sim had maintained a grim and prickly silence ever since he'd bared his soul to her over the ashes of a dead campfire.

Tally expected to be far too busy to think much about Sim and their troubling conversation. Since she would continue to pose as a man and the head of her party, she would be handling the final negotiations and inspection of the mixed herd Don Miguel had set aside for her purchase. It was her first time taking on such responsibility, but she relished the chance to prove her competence, especially to herself.

The hacienda road passed a fenced vegetable garden and ended at a heavy wooden gate slung between thick adobe walls built in the days when such isolated ranches were compelled to fend off Indian raids. The gate stood open, revealing a flagstoned courtyard. The horses' hooves clattered on the uneven surface as Tally led men and mounts up before the columned archway of the main residence.

Well-dressed members of Don Miguel's staff waited at the foot of the steps that led to carved double doors. A portly gentleman introduced himself as Señor Gonzalez, *mayordomo* of the hacienda, and directed a maid to deliver cool fruit drinks to the riders as soon as they had dismounted.

"Greetings, Señor Bernard," Gonzalez said in careful English. "Don Miguel will be here to greet you in a few moments. Then you will have time to bathe and prepare for the evening meal. All you desire is yours in this house."

Tally inclined her head. "*Gracias,* señor. I trust that Don Miguel is well?"

"*Sí, Sí.* It is a very happy time for us, señor. You see, Don Miguel's daughter was very sick, but now she is well again."

"That is happy news."

"Indeed. Our great good fortune is all due to the efforts of the precious *curandera.* Perhaps you have heard of her?"

"All the world will soon know her name." The new voice

belonged to a tall, handsome man of middle age whose hair was nearly black, though his mustache was as white as snow. His clothing was fine and close-fitting, proclaiming his station.

"Don Miguel Torres," Tally said. "I'm honored to meet you."

"And I you, Señor Bernard." He offered his hand, and Tally shook it firmly. She introduced Sim as her partner.

Don Miguel shook Sim's hand with hearty delight. "It is indeed a time for celebration, my friends. A miracle has brought my daughter back from the dead. Only one in the world carries God's grace so purely." He smiled with unmitigated joy. "I hear in her own village they call her *Santa* Esperanza."

CHAPTER THIRTEEN

ESPERANZA.

A maid in a full skirt and peasant blouse darted close to catch Sim's glass before he could drop it, bringing him out of his shock.

Esperanza was here. This was the place she had gone to on her mysterious mission, and Sim couldn't think of worse circumstances for meeting her again.

He avoided Tally's glance, barely hearing the hacendado's effusive words of welcome. He followed Tally from the colonnaded entrance to a tiled patio with a whispering fountain, and through carved wooden doors into the *casa principal*. The *sala*, or main parlor, was furnished with tufted velvet couches, silk damask chairs and brocade drapes. Whitewashed walls were lavishly decorated with paintings of landscapes and holy images, and Sim's boots trod fine imported carpets.

Such details didn't interest him at the moment. He considered how best to make a swift escape as Tally and Don Miguel settled in the *sala* to make desultory conversation about the trip and the weather. Maids offered a choice of coffee, tea or tequila, along with biscuits, to tide the guests over until dinner.

Sim all but gulped his tequila. It hardly affected him. He sank back in his overpadded chair and closed his eyes.

"Are you well, Señor Kavanagh?" Don Miguel asked.

"Sim?" Tally said.

Sim squeezed the bridge of his nose. "I don't know."

"Perhaps it is the heat," Don Miguel suggested. "Not even *Americanos* from the South are used to it. The best cure is rest, much drink and quiet, but I can send for the *curandera*—"

"That…isn't necessary," Sim said. "I can rest wherever your vaqueros bunk, if it's not too much trouble."

"*Tonterías*. You will rest in the house. We have rooms enough for all our guests." He motioned to a white-clad male servant of Indian descent. "Show Señor Kavanagh to *la habitación de las aguas danzante* and see that he has everything he requires."

"*Sí*, Don Miguel." The servant approached Sim's chair and gave a slight bow. "Señor?"

Sim stood, staggering for effect. Tally got to her feet. "I think you should stay in the casa this afternoon, Sim," she said in her deepest voice. "I'll ride out with Don Miguel after dinner."

"*Ciertamente,*" Don Miguel said. "A light repast will be brought to your room, Señor Kavanagh."

"*Gracias.*" Sim briefly met Tally's eyes. She recognized that he was faking his illness, and she probably had a good idea of the reason. Sim quickly followed the servant from the *sala*. Once he had been delivered to his room—a pleasant chamber with a doorway looking out on yet another patio and fountain—he sat on the iron-framed bed and collected his chaotic thoughts.

Santa Esperanza. Hell and damnation. He had to go to her, but not until after supper, when the don would take Tally out to inspect her purchase. He didn't want any witnesses to this meeting.

Sim lay back on the bed and tried to sleep. An hour later a maid brought him a silver tray of fruits, broth and thinly sliced meat. He picked at the food, set it aside, and listened to the voices and scuffle of feet in the hall, bedrooms and *sala*.

He recognized Tally's tread as she entered the room next to his. She remained to rest during the traditional late afternoon siesta, and then left again with Don Miguel. The house fell into a drowsy silence.

Sim slipped from his room, led by his senses. The patio was all in shadow. Brilliant flowers cascaded from terra-cotta pots along the perimeter of the open, colonnaded *galería*. Warm evening air hummed with the constant droning of hungry bees. The servants were either in the separate kitchen area or had gone to join their families who lived on the hacienda grounds. Sim easily found the scent he recognized.

The door to the chamber was closed, but Sim entered without knocking. He saw at once that this was a sanctuary meant for a member of the family, fitted with an elaborate brass bedstead and furniture painted in bright colors suitable for a young girl.

On the bed lay a dark-haired child, and beside her, on a stool, sat a young woman in a simple cotton dress. Her black hair cascaded down her back and over her shoulders, obscuring her face.

Sim had no need to see it. His legs trembled, and he had to lean against the door frame. The girl on the bed slept on undisturbed, but Esperanza turned and looked at Sim without a trace of surprise on her lovely, tranquil features.

"Sim," she said.

"Esperanza."

She turned back to the girl and kissed the child's forehead. Then she rose, gracefully freeing her skirts from the stool, and walked toward Sim. He backed away through the door. She followed and closed it behind her, leaving them alone in the *galería*.

She searched his eyes and his face, his clothing down to his boots, taking him in as if he were a ghost suddenly restored to life. Sim saw no joy in her eyes, no delight, only the same serene acceptance as when she'd first noticed him standing in the doorway.

"You have been on a long journey, Sim," she said. "A journey that has not yet ended."

He stared at her, paralyzed by his emotions. She was still the woman he remembered—young, innocent, fragile, and yet hiding a core of strength he had learned to recognize and admire in New Mexico. He could swear no man had taken her. She wasn't afraid of him, nor would she flinch from his touch.

But something was wrong. This wasn't what he'd imagined when they came together again.

"My journey has ended," he said roughly. "I've found you."

She bowed her head. "Have you been looking so long?"

"I've known where you were since you settled in Dos Ríos," he said. "But I didn't mean to come to you before…" He stopped, tongue-tied as a boy with his first woman. "I wanted to bring you a new life, Esperanza."

"A new life." She hesitated and slowly took his hand. "There is a place where we can talk."

Her hand was soft and warm, small-boned and fine. But her grip was strong, and he let her lead him to another turn in the corridor, a cool and narrow passage that opened to a tiny yard and the pink adobe walls of a chapel.

Sim balked. She tugged. "The priest is with a dying man in the village. You need fear nothing."

She thought he was afraid of a church. He pulled his hand free and walked ahead of her, through the open doors and into the coolness of the nave. Two rows of wooden pews led the eye to the altar and the crucifix above it.

Esperanza sat in the pew nearest the door and slid down its length to make room for Sim. He stood stiffly beside the bench.

"You have come so far," she said, "and yet you will not speak to me."

Sim looked from the altar to Esperanza's face. The crucifix was only a painted piece of wood, but Esperanza was alive, shining with some inner vision of peace Sim couldn't share. Nothing in her features revealed a desire for what he had come to offer.

Angel, he'd called her. Angels and saints didn't love like men and women. They didn't hate, or feel greed or desire.

"You know why I've come," he said.

"Yes. You wish me to be your wife."

Even her gentle voice gave the blunt words an edge of unreality. Sim gripped the carved back of the pew.

"Did you know I'd been following you?" he asked.

"I suspected only." She smiled. "Sometimes I sensed your presence. But there were so many others who needed me."

"They call you a *curandera*," he said. "You heal people? Cure their sicknesses?"

"I do what I can."

"Don Miguel said you worked a miracle in saving his daughter."

She let out a breath. "It was God's will."

"*La Santita*," he said. "You weren't so religious in New Mexico."

"I have learned much since those days, Sim."

"They built that church in Dos Ríos for you."

"Not for me." Her voice grew uncertain for the first time, as if she would ward off the honors others wished to do her. "For God's glory. He has given me a gift. I did not understand it in New Mexico. I sensed so many things, so many feelings in the souls and hearts of others, but I could not truly help. I was filled with my own selfish fears. I asked God to show me what I must do."

"You mean how to live your life for everyone else? How to give up...all your own dreams?"

"My dreams." She looked down at her hands. "I never knew what I wanted, Simeon. But I wandered alone in the desert for many months, and it came to me. Now all is clear."

He sat beside her and gripped her arm. "It's not clear to me, *chiquita.* You were a girl in New Mexico. Now you're a woman, and I'm going to make a place for you—a place where you can be yourself—"

"But I *am* myself, *mi amigo,*" she said, touching the back of his hand. "For the first time in my life, I am all I was meant to be."

Sim felt the stirrings of violence and let her go. She took both his hands in hers. "I was blind in New Mexico. I felt your sadness and your desire, but not the deep affection you held for me. I am honored, my friend, more than I can say."

"Honored," he spat.

"Yes. But I am hurting you, and I do not wish to, Simeon." She closed her eyes and gasped. "Your pain is very great. I cannot see how to ease it."

"You know how to ease it, Esperanza. Marry me."

Her shoulders began to shake, and tears spilled from her eyes. "You believe I can save your soul. But I am no saint, Sim, whatever some may say."

"You're everything that's decent and good, the opposite of me. But you can make me better. I can change...for you." He tried to calm the pitiful eagerness of his voice. "I have it all planned. A ranch of our own—a good place, fertile, safe—"

"Safe. You would protect me." She squeezed his hands. "You would not wish me to weary myself aiding those who come to me for healing."

"The people in Dos Ríos already think you belong to them."

"Do you not see, Simeon? When I find sickness, of the body or the soul, I must act. If I were forbidden…"

As I would forbid her, Sim thought. *I'd never share her with the likes of Bernardo or Don Miguel.…*

"*Sí,*" Esperanza said. "Perhaps I would heal you, Sim, from all your sorrows. Or perhaps I would fail, and you would come to hate me, as you hate so many of my sex."

"Hate you?" He deserted the pew and stood hunched in the aisle. "Is that what you think of me?"

A tear splashed on the polished wood of the bench. "It is not my place to judge." She blotted up the drop with her finger. "Do you love me?"

He should have expected the question. He should have been ready to answer it instantly, honestly, without hesitation.

He could not. His throat closed, as if an invisible hand were choking him from behind. He reached up to pull the curling fingers away and clutched at empty air.

"I…" He coughed. "I feel more for you than any woman in the world."

"Yes. But in your thoughts is another."

"No."

"A marriage such as you wish cannot be built on lies, Simeon."

A roar built up in his chest and burst from him like a storm. He grabbed Esperanza by the shoulders, lifted her from the bench and set his mouth to hers.

He got no further. One touch of her cool lips and he felt as though he were raping a nun in a convent. She didn't struggle, didn't respond even as much as she'd done in New Mexico when she'd tried to save her friends. She simply waited. And when he released her, all he saw in her eyes was forgiveness.

She didn't love him. She didn't desire him. She pitied him.

"You are my dear brother, Sim," she said. Her hand lifted to touch his face. "If you would let me try to help you, here in this holy place…"

He spun away, banging his hip into the pew so hard that he limped the few steps to the church doors. The setting sun cast every detail of the house and landscape in sharp relief. Sim ran to his room and stripped out of his clothing, tearing his shirt in two places. In wolf shape he kicked the door shut with a powerful blow of one hind paw. He dashed across the patio and down the corridor to the church.

Esperanza was leaving the chapel. She saw him, crossed herself and watched as he ran toward the hills. Sim laughed with a snap of sharp white teeth.

He returned to the hacienda well after dusk. Lantern light beat against the profound darkness of the surrounding countryside, but the humans had retired behind their adobe walls. The moment Sim Changed, all the emotions he had avoided crashed in upon him like the crumbling ramparts of a long-besieged fortress.

He sank against the closed hacienda gates and stared unseeing at the campesinos' huts clustered outside the walls. His dreams were dead. He'd known it when he'd met Esperanza's sweet, distant gaze, though he had tried to fool himself just a little longer. It would have been better if he'd died before he understood how stupid he had been to dream at all.

Esperanza had never loved him, couldn't love him. Yet there was no man he could challenge to win her. Her womb would remain barren, because she would carry the world's sorrow in her body for the rest of her life. The Esperanza he'd known in New Mexico was just as much a figment of his imagination as the image of the little ranch, the gentle wife and his own salvation.

Without Esperanza, he had no reason to return to Cold

Creek and find the treasure, no reason to go straight or become the kind of man she might have wanted.

Sim laughed. Now he had no constraints to bind him. No future but that he chose from moment to moment. And what would he choose?

He climbed to his feet and scaled the wall in a single jump. No one saw him glide like a shadow along the gallery or enter his room. He found his torn clothes laid out on the bed, snatched up the shirt and held it to his face.

Tally. She'd been here, touching his things, wondering where he'd gone and why. He flung the shirt aside. After a moment, chest heaving with each breath, he put on his britches and stretched out on the bed.

Tally was in the very next room. She wouldn't be asleep. Esperanza might be on her knees in the church, praying for Sim's soul, but Tally's concern was far more earthly. She cared. She cared too much.

Sim closed his eyes. He didn't want to know what Tally was thinking or feeling. Esperanza had held his heart in her keeping, and now it lay shattered on the floor of the church. The icy fragment that thumped inside his ribs held only one emotion: rage. And only a single wish: that Tally would stay far away from him tonight.

THE DAY HAD BEEN BOTH arduous and satisfying. Don Miguel demanded much of himself and his fine Arab stallion; he gave Tally an equally fine mount and led her on a tour of the ranch that began immediately after a brief afternoon siesta and continued until the traditional late supper at ten.

Tally had been impressed. Don Miguel had done well for himself despite Apache incursions and past economic troubles, and he seemed to treat his workers with generosity and fairness. The cattle he showed Tally were in good condition, with very few cutbacks to be separated out from among those she had purchased.

All throughout the ride, in any small moment of silence or stillness, Tally's thoughts turned to Sim. And Esperanza. She'd seen the shock on Sim's face when he'd learned a woman by that name was residing at the hacienda; she had guessed that his "illness" was a ruse so he could be alone...or seek out his future bride without having to reveal his intentions.

Sim's agitation hadn't come only from simple surprise, though. He had reacted to something else the don had said, something he hadn't expected to hear.

Determined not to lose control of her own emotions, Tally completed her business with the hacendádo and joined him in the *sala* for a glass of fine imported whiskey. She drank very little, courteously turned down Don Miguel's offer of an expensive Cuban cigar, and bade her host good-night as soon as she could politely make her escape.

Knocking on Sim's door brought no answer. She found his torn shirt and other clothing scattered across the floor, almost as if he'd ripped them off in a fury. Suddenly terrified, Tally roamed the hacienda in search of she knew not what.

She found the church and strode through the doors, drawn to enter in spite of her certainty that Sim would not be there. She paused to cross herself, brought back to the habits of childhood by the trappings of sanctity she had abandoned long ago. She kept her hat in place to hide her braids.

A lone woman knelt before the altar. Her hair was black and her figure slender. She turned before Tally had taken three steps.

"Buenas noches," the woman said with a smile. "You must be Don Miguel's other guest. I am sorry I was not present to greet you tonight." She inclined her head. "My name is Esperanza."

Though Tally had already known who she must be, hearing the name provoked a sickening twist inside her stomach. This was the woman Sim loved. It was easy to see why. Esperanza—so young, hardly more than a girl—wore purity and goodness like the rebozo draped over her head. Her face was smooth and radiant, and her eyes held profound depths of both pain and compassion.

A *curandera,* Don Miguel had called her. Tally could believe this woman worked miracles. She'd worked the miracle of opening Sim's heart to love, kept his devotion and loyalty as few women could hope to do with any man. Perhaps she was everything he claimed.

"I've heard of you, señorita," Tally said, keeping her voice even, though the pounding of her heart seemed to shake her entire body. "You cured Don Miguel's daughter."

"With God's aid," Esperanza said humbly.

Tally surrendered all prudence. "Have you seen my partner, Sim Kavanagh? He seems to have left the hacienda." She forced a chuckle. "He does that sometimes...wanders off to be alone."

Esperanza clasped her hands as if in prayer. "I have seen him," she said. "He left some time ago. I wish I could be of more assistance."

What did he say to you? How did you answer? "Don't concern yourself, señorita," Tally said, touching the brim of her hat. "He'll come back when he's ready." She hesitated. "Was he all right?"

"Why do you ask?"

"Sim spoke of a woman with your name. I thought perhaps—" She broke off, unable to ask the questions that burned in her throat. "I'm sorry to have disturbed your prayers, señorita."

"God was not disturbed, and neither was I." Esperanza reached out her hand and let it fall. "You are troubled. May I help?"

Tally had the most peculiar urge to take the woman's hand and confess all her fears. She did not. "I wouldn't add to your burdens," she said. "Good night, señorita."

She left to the sound of Esperanza's whispered farewell. But she felt the healer's gaze boring into her back, stripping her bare as only Sim could do. Tally wouldn't have been surprised if Esperanza realized that Sim's "partner" was a woman. And if she'd guessed that much, it might not be such a leap to figure out the rest.

What had passed between them? Had Sim declared his love and asked her to marry him? Had she agreed? And if she had, why had he run off?

Tally fled to her room and firmly closed the door, leaning against it as the tears came. She knew she was foolish and weak, beyond ridiculous to be jealous of a woman like Esperanza. Sim hadn't lied. He hadn't exaggerated. Esperanza was perfect, as perfect as any expertly carved angel hovering above the chapel's altar.

No wonder he saw in her the promise of his own redemption.

After a time, the tears ran out and Tally's body felt the toll of the demands she'd made of it. She undressed, bathed at the washstand and put on a voluminous nightshirt that hid her shape as effectively as the loose men's clothing she wore by day. She lay in bed, listening to the crickets and coyotes in the hills.

She was still awake when Sim returned. He was very quiet, but she knew his tread as she knew the shape of her own hand. Her mattress felt as hard as a slab of granite. She couldn't breathe for trying to hear any sound from Sim's room.

At last she sat up and tossed the light covers aside. She had to know—now, tonight—what had passed between Sim and Esperanza, even at the risk of losing the remnants of her tattered pride.

Loose shirt and trousers replaced the nightshirt. She stepped barefoot into the hall. All the lanterns had been put out, but moonlight sparkled in the patio's fountain. A perfect night for lovers.

She tapped on Sim's door and waited. One minute, two, five. She was lifting her hand again when the door swung open.

Sim loomed on the threshold, shirtless and hollow-eyed. He looked her up and down as if she were a stranger.

"What do you want?" he demanded.

Common sense suggested that Tally walk away and leave Sim to his foul mood. But his harshness spoke for itself; his meeting with Esperanza hadn't gone as he'd hoped.

"May I come in?" she asked.

"Why?"

"Because I think you need to talk to a friend." She met his glare. "We are friends, aren't we, Sim?"

"You shouldn't be here tonight, Tally."

His use of her name melted some of the tension from her body. "I know something went wrong…with Esperanza," she ventured.

"There's nothing you can do."

"You talked to her?"

He gave an exasperated sigh and stepped back into his room, letting her pass. She remained close to the wall as he wandered about the room, touching this or that decorative object with restless dissatisfaction. The muscles in his back and shoulders rippled with fascinating grace and strength. His every movement was feral, almost feline, like a cougar pacing in its lair before a kill.

"You didn't expect to find her here," Tally said. "I could see it was a shock to you."

"I didn't expect her at this hacienda," Sim said, coming to a halt beside the bed. "We passed near her village on the way here."

Suddenly Tally remembered the night he'd been away from camp so long. "You went there to see her."

"She'd already left, but I didn't know where she'd gone." He curled his hand around the brass bedpost. "I only wanted to make sure…she was all right."

"I spoke to her in the church," Tally said cautiously. "She seems very well, happy."

"Yes." His mouth twisted in a bitter smile. "She seems to have stronger gifts than when I knew her. She's a great healer now. They call her a saint in Dos Ríos." He squeezed the bedpost until his knuckles turned white. "What did you think of her?"

What did he want to hear? She couldn't be other than honest with him—as honest as she'd always tried to be except on the subject of her past. Even when such honesty was excruciatingly difficult.

"She is *très belle*—beautiful. She radiates goodness." Tally managed a smile. "You were right, Sim. She is an angel. It would be very easy to love her."

The brass pole of the bedpost bent in Sim's grip. He flexed his fingers as if they pained him. Tally rushed to his side and took his hand between hers.

"I'm all right." He snatched his hand free, and Tally realized he was trembling. So was she.

"You are not all right," she said. "This meeting didn't turn out the way you expected, did it?"

He snarled at her like a ravening beast, body coiled for attack. "What did she tell you?"

Tally looked up into his eyes, gray swallowed in black. "Only that she'd seen you. I didn't pry. I was worried for you. I still am." She reached for him, and he flinched. "Talk to me. Let me be your friend."

"You ask too much."

"Only because you won't let anyone in," she said. "Not even Esperanza."

Her accusation had the anticipated effect. He turned on her again, fierce and dangerous, with a light in his eye that should have sent her running for the door. "I asked her," he said hoarsely. "She refused me."

Tally closed her eyes. "Oh, Sim. I am sorry."

"You're a liar. You dreaded the day when I'd go to her."

Her skin went hot from head to toe. "Do you think I couldn't replace you at Cold Creek?"

"I'm not talking about the ranch. It's you, Tally. You've wanted me from the beginning."

The fire of humiliation scalded Tally's cheeks. "If you're so irresistible to women, why did Esperanza reject you?"

"She… She—" He shook his head violently. "She can't love any man."

"Do you love her, Sim? Enough to let her go?"

He smiled the way he always did when he mocked himself most cruelly. "Look at me, Tally. Do you see a man capable of love?"

"Yes." She could barely hold his stare. "I do."

"But did I really love Esperanza? Isn't that what you want to know?"

"I think you did, because she gave you a dream. I think you want what is best for her. That's why you're so angry, because you've been forced to choose…her happiness—or yours. You have made a great sacrifice for her sake." She bent her head. "That is what I call love."

"Then it'll never happen again." He grabbed Tally's arms. "I'm through with noble sacrifices. I'm through with dreams." He raised his hands to Tally's cheeks, lifted her face and kissed her.

CHAPTER FOURTEEN

TALLY KNEW THE TIME had come. She let him have his almost brutal kiss, and when he was finished, she wrapped her arms around his shoulders and returned passion for passion, yearning for desire.

She understood him all too well. So often males buried their pain in the pleasures of the flesh, no matter how fleeting such pleasures might be. Men didn't look beyond the moment. For Sim, a hasty, savage coupling might be relief for the ache in his heart, Tally a convenient substitute for the woman he really wanted. By surrendering her body, Tally could give him the comfort she'd offered.

But it would be no sacrifice. Because he'd been right—she wanted him. She had denied it, afraid of breaking the contract with herself she'd so carefully constructed when Nathan had died. She hadn't believed it possible that she could desire a man enough to lie with one, not under any circumstances. Such sensations were dead in her forever…if they had ever existed.

She'd mistaken sleep for death, the mechanics of sex for the need that came of love. The years of willing abstinence, of ignoring even the smallest hint of physical hunger—they vanished as if she'd never sworn to keep apart from men and their carnal appetites for the rest of her life.

She'd never expected to meet a man like Sim.

He lifted her to his chest, holding her by the waist and grinding his hips into hers. His member was hard and very large. For a moment she wondered if it would hurt after so long. Her own private parts ached and swelled in a way she scarcely recognized.

"Tally," he whispered against her mouth. He pushed his tongue inside, and she touched it with her own. He jerked away, holding her apart from him.

"Go," he said. "Go while you still can."

"No."

"You've been married. You've had a man before. But it shouldn't be this way for a decent woman. Not the way I'll take you in this room."

He was worried for her virtue. She nearly laughed, but he was deadly serious. There was no need for anyone in the hacienda to discover what happened tonight, not if she and Sim were careful, but Sim understood what a woman risked to lie with a man who was not her husband. He knew such a woman might blame herself afterward, and that the world would condemn her if her indiscretion were discovered.

Such a woman would never be the same again.

She cupped his cheek in her palm. "Sim, Sim. I would never have come to you if I were afraid."

He searched her eyes. "You expected—"

"I am not ignorant." *Or innocent.* "You can't ruin me, Sim. Not if I want this as you do."

His teeth snapped together. "It ain't right. I won't have you hating me, Tally. Get out now. Please."

She ran her fingers across his lips. "I ask nothing, *mon cher.* Nothing but what we give each other tonight. There will never be another man for me."

"God, Tally." He rubbed his thumbs along the edge of her jaw. "I can't promise...I might not be—"

She took his hand and placed it on her breast. Without the bindings, the shirt hid very little of what lay beneath it. Sim cupped her breasts, swore under his breath and abruptly swept her into his arms. He reached the bed in three steps.

Panic paralyzed Tally as soon as her back touched the cool sheets. She was in New Orleans again, and the room was permeated with the overripe scent of perfume and sweat. The men always stank…of pomade, perspiration, alcohol. They left their mark on her night after night, until she knew she could never make herself clean again.

Sim's weight came down beside her. He saw her fear, or sensed it. He began to recoil, and she pulled him on top of her, kissing him desperately. He resisted for all of a second. Then his fingers were working at the buttons of her shirt, opening the placket, baring her breasts.

In her old life, she knew exactly what to do to make men feel powerful, in control, able to arouse them to heights of ecstasy previously unknown. It was all a game, an act. Survival. Her expertise evaporated when Sim kissed her nipples. She was a virgin giving herself for the very first time.

He groaned. She echoed his cry. He suckled her hungrily as if he feared to lose her before he'd had his fill.

"*Oui,*" Tally murmured, stroking his hair. "*Oui, mon amour, je suis à toi. Fais comme il te plait.*"

Do what you will with me. No empty words, no sterile invitation. So often she'd taken men and felt nothing, either physical or emotional. Always the feigned pleasure, the compliments, the sweet, lying promises.

No more lies. She arched her back, begging him with her entire body. He obliged. He pulled the shirt over her head, tossed it aside and buried his face between her breasts.

Tenderness and arousal waged fevered war in Tally's heart. Sim was holding himself back for her sake, waiting to make sure she was ready. She loved him all the more for his patience, his desire to give pleasure as well as take it.

"Don't be afraid," she whispered, lacing her fingers in his hair. "You cannot hurt me. I want you, Sim…I want you inside me."

His face rested beside hers on the pillow. "Tell me," he said in a strained, muffled voice. "Tell me you never wanted another man."

"I have never wanted another man."

He fumbled for the buttons of her trousers. She slipped out of them easily. His hand stroked down her thigh. Her body wept with anticipation of what was to come. She helped him out of his own pants, felt the full length and weight of him fit perfectly into her curves and hollows like a part of herself she hadn't even known was missing.

She opened to him. He hesitated. His firm, full hardness slid along the inside of her thigh. Never had that sensation felt so welcome, so exciting. He teased her with his body, coming near and then withdrawing again, kissing her face as his taut belly rubbed hers.

Now, she thought. He was deaf to her silent pleas. She tugged him and arched her back, inviting him to take what he wanted.

"Vite," she gasped. *"Prend-moi maintenant, mon amour."*

He shivered once and plunged into her. He wasn't gentle; she didn't wish him to be. His heat drove deep, touching a part of her no man had done before. She locked her legs around his hips as he pulled back for another thrust. She couldn't bear the seconds when he was outside, not a part of her.

This was pleasure, not duty, not work. Sim made it so. He raised her hips so he could reach even farther and then supported her back with his effortless strength, suckling her breasts in time to his rhythm. Tally bit her lip to muffle her cries. His tongue branded her nipples like fire.

She could not imagine that it could be better than this. She could barely think at all. But Sim wasn't nearly finished. He lifted her, holding her impaled upon him, and moved from the bed. He carried her to the wall, where a woven hanging covered the adobe surface. Then he took her there, his powerful arms cradling her hips and thighs, his cheek pressed to hers. The eroticism of being held so easily, of surrendering all control, was beyond anything Tally had experienced in years of sexual dalliance.

It was too much. It would never be enough. When he slowed, she drew him in more deeply with her heels at the small of his back, begging and demanding at the same time. Coarsely woven wool grazed her back as he pushed her against the wall, again and again and again.

She would not let him stop until it was finished and he had his full measure of satisfaction. She felt it building in him, the hoarse rasp of his breathing as he approached the climax of pleasure.

"Oui," she urged. *"Remplis-moi. Laisse-toi aller—"*

Then the miracle happened. Other women had spoken of it, sometimes with ribald vulgarity and sometimes in whispers. Some even said this one thing made the burden of sex worthwhile.

Tally finally understood. A wave burst from the place of her joining with Sim, deep inside, hot and cold at once, radiating through her belly and her chest and her limbs like an electric current. She gasped and jerked. A moment later Sim thrust hard and fast, finishing as men always did. But it wasn't the same. She clutched the iron muscles in his back, murmuring endearments in a language invented for exactly this purest, most perfect joy.

"Je t'aimes, Simeon Kavanagh."

SIM DIDN'T UNDERSTAND her words. He didn't need to. Everything Tally could have said to him was contained in her enfolding arms, the grip of her thighs, the throbbing where their bodies joined.

A few times in his life he'd felt a woman come as Tally had, but even then he'd never been sure if the whores were faking their pleasure. That was their job, after all. He'd never tried to give. He'd taken, and he'd paid well for the privilege.

Tally wasn't deceiving him. Her climax was real, and his had been more powerful than any he could remember. Astonishing, overwhelming. So moving that he felt his eyes begin to water like a puling infant's.

But Tally wouldn't let him go, even when he carried her back to the bed. She rocked him, half singing in that fancy, lilting language she'd never gotten around to teaching him. She held him, and even after desire was gone, she continued to hold him as no woman had ever done.

Part of him felt trapped, desperate to escape those smooth, work-hardened arms. Part of him wanted to stay there forever. He didn't know this other Sim Kavanagh. The one he understood had been born when a gang of older boys in Hat Rock had beaten him up and told him what his ma did for a living. When he'd understood why he didn't have a father, why Evelyn had had so many male friends who didn't want anything to do with her little brat.

He stiffened his arms and pushed away from Tally. She let him go. He rolled over to his side of the bed, grabbed his britches and pulled them on.

"Are you all right?" she asked.

The world was upside down when *she* wanted to know if *he* was all right. He hadn't been gentle with her. "Are you?" he countered.

"Wonderful." The bed creaked as she stretched. Her fingers grazed his back. "You gave me great pleasure."

Sim flushed, keeping his face averted. He was used to Tally being blunt and honest about everything else, but not in this. Not this talking afterward, as if they were some old couple who took sharing a bed for granted—and stayed together after the sex was over.

He should have kept his mouth shut. He couldn't. "I wasn't…too rough?"

"Not for me."

"You like it that way."

"Not with anyone but you."

It was meant as a compliment, but the way she said it made Sim very uncomfortable. "You said there wouldn't be any other men."

"Never."

Even when I'm gone? But he didn't speak aloud, because he didn't know where he would be in an hour, in a day, in a year. All his plans were dust, the world reduced to this single room.

But he had to think of Tally's future, even if he couldn't imagine his own. Caleb wasn't gone for good. The secret of the treasure remained unsolved, and only that would buy Caleb off once and for all.

Slowly he turned, leaning on his arm to face Tally. "Do you want me to come back to Cold Creek?"

Her face suffused with happiness, fully as blinding as Esperanza's in all its sanctity. "Yes, Sim. I want you back. I want you to stay with me."

Stay. The word alone terrified him. He stared at the twisted sheets, permeated with the scent of their loving. "I can't promise anything, do you understand?"

"I understand." Her voice was solemn, serious. Tally

wouldn't make meaningless noises like other women, pretending to agree when she was already set on her own way.

"Have you finished your business with Don Miguel?"

"Yes. I see no reason why we couldn't leave—" She glanced at the door, where a sliver of light betrayed the dawn. "Tomorrow. I'll have to hire men and a cook with a chuck wagon to trail the cattle to Arizona."

"Then you'd better get back to your own room." He picked up Tally's shirt and britches, and held them out to her like some kind of gentleman. She slipped from the bed and stood naked, unashamed, gloriously beautiful. Hell and damnation, he was ready to take her again—on the floor, against the wall, any time and any place.

With an effort, he controlled himself and watched her dress, admiring every graceful motion, the uniquely female strength she was so good at hiding. She smiled at him when she was done, and he could hardly breathe past the knot in his throat.

"No one will know," she said. She went to him, stood on her bare toes and kissed him, stepping away before he could turn the kiss into another tumble on the bed. "Make peace with Esperanza if you can, Sim." She blew another kiss at him, cracked open the door, peered out, then darted into the gallery. Sim heard the door to her room close behind her.

Make peace with Esperanza. He laughed and flung himself down on the bed, pressing his face to the sheets. What kind of woman would suggest that her lover go to her rival for any reason? But that was Tally...trusting him, sure this one night bound them beyond all breaking.

He wouldn't see Esperanza again. There wasn't any point. Tally didn't have to worry that he would waste his time hating or pining after a female who didn't have any use for men. Esperanza would forget about him in a few days, and he would forget about her.

An hour after sunrise, Sim finished dressing and found his way to the *sala,* where Tally had joined Don Miguel for a cup of chocolate and sweet pastries. Esperanza wasn't with them. The don welcomed Sim with complete unconcern.

"I trust you slept well, Señor Kavanagh?" he asked jovially.

"Very well." Out of the corner of his eye, Sim caught Tally dipping her nose into her cup as if to hide laughter. "Your beds are the most comfortable I've ever enjoyed."

"Excelente." Don Miguel glanced toward the hall and the bedchambers. "I wish that my daughter could have visited with us this morning, but the *curandera* feels she needs a few days' more rest."

"I met Señorita Esperanza last night," Tally said. "I see why many regard her as something of a saint."

"Indeed. She is unfortunately very retiring, but her goodness is beyond all doubt." He looked more keenly at Tally. "I know you wish to hire local vaqueros to help you trail the cattle to your rancho. I would be more than happy to provide such men—without charge, of course—if you would escort the señorita back to her village."

Sim glanced sharply at the don, who noticed his stare. "It is true that I could send my men alone to take her back, but I prefer that *forasteros,* if you will forgive the word—those who live outside this region—take charge of the *curandera.* In this way there will be no rivalries or misunderstandings regarding her destination."

In other words, Sim thought, he worried that someone might "steal" such a precious commodity. Sim scowled into his rapidly cooling cup.

"That's most generous of you, Don Miguel," Tally said. "We'd be happy to accept such an agreement."

The don smiled approval. A maid appeared to clear away the morning appetizer. "Since our business is concluded,"

Don Miguel said, "I will arrange to provide you with vaqueros, a cook and chuck wagon, and see that your cattle are ready as soon as you wish to depart. But I hope you will join me in a proper breakfast later."

Tally indicated her pleasure at the invitation, and she and Sim left the *sala*. Their horses were saddled and well rested, so they rode out to inspect the new herd again, companionably silent except when Tally asked for Sim's opinion on one of the two-year-old heifers. Sim couldn't fault Tally's judgment. These animals would tempt any rustler, but no outlaw was going to get a chance at them—neither in Mexico nor at Cold Creek.

After a very large breakfast of roasted meats, eggs, frijoles and fruit, Tally politely refused Don Miguel's offer of another night's stay and gathered her borrowed vaqueros around the herd. Federico had already made friends among the Mexicans, and Sim didn't anticipate any trouble.

Except from his own treacherous heart. At the last minute before the *Americanos'* departure, Esperanza walked through the arches of the hacienda doorway. The vaqueros fawned like whipped curs, making certain that she was comfortably settled on her burro and well supplied with food and drink for the journey. She glanced once in Sim's direction, a faint frown between her brows, and was led to a place beside Tally at the head of the column, where the dust would not sully her saintly perfection.

Sim fell back to ride drag. The presence of even one of the women would have been difficult to bear, but both—that was beyond his toleration. He was safest where heat and dust were the worst inconveniences he would have to suffer.

The herd began to move forward with much lowing and bellowing. Sim and one of Don Miguel's vaqueros, working instinctively as a team, chased and bullied the stragglers into

line. Other men took positions on the flanks of the herd. The
trip back to Cold Creek would take several more days than
the journey to Hacienda del Gavilán, but Sim needed the time
to think. Working cattle was mindless labor for him. He
caught only occasional glimpses of Tally through the constant
haze of dust, and none of Esperanza.

At first Tally was kept busy riding up and down the length
of the herd while the vaqueros fell into the routine of the
drive. She made sure the men understood that she was in
charge, and that she was aware of everything that went on
from point to drag. She knew perfectly well why Sim had chosen the rear, and she respected his decision.

That left her alone with Esperanza. Tally's masquerade
made her feel at ease around the girl; Esperanza seemed
content to sit on her fat little burro and look at the passing
scenery. At the first night's camp, after the cattle had been
settled on the bedding-ground and the remuda was staked
out, the men contended over the right to wait on Esperanza
hand and foot. The cook Don Miguel had sent along took
special care with his beans and biscuits. Sim stood guard
somewhere near the edge of the drowsy herd, far beyond the
firelight's reach.

"He will not sleep tonight," Esperanza said. The vaqueros
had finally left her alone and sought their bedrolls; only Tally
and Esperanza—and the night guards—remained awake.

Tally jerked from her thoughts and glanced toward the
young woman, who sat on her Indian blanket with such peaceful dignity.

Esperanza smoothed her skirts about her knees and smiled
at Tally. "Did I disturb you?"

"No." Tally sat up and stared toward the small, restless
sounds that marked the herd's position in the darkness. "I
wasn't sleeping, either."

"It is a beautiful night." Esperanza closed her eyes. "Yet I know Sim has suffered. I feel his confusion."

Tally feigned fascination with the swathe of glittering stars overhead. "He's not an easy man to understand."

"Yet you know him well. Are you not his partner?"

"Sim's been working for me for a few months," Tally said. "He's good at what he does."

"But he is more to you than a simple vaquero."

Tally met Esperanza's gaze across the fire. "Look, señorita, I know that he asked you to be his wife and you refused him. He hasn't told me much more than that. It's none of my business."

"Not even though you love him?"

Tally felt for her hat. It was still in place. She assumed her deepest voice. "If you're suggesting—"

"Please do not be offended. I know you are not what you pretend to be."

First Beth, and now Esperanza. It was a miracle that Tally's disguise had survived so long. "What gave me away?" she asked calmly.

"Nothing in your manner. You are safe—"

"You aren't just a healer, are you, Esperanza? You have what some call the second sight."

"God aids me to see."

"So you look inside people whether or not they wish to be examined?"

"I try…" Esperanza began in a whisper. "I try not to see too much. To do so is like—" She twisted her fingers together. "It strips away the dignity and leaves the soul naked."

Tally felt as though she'd been stripped naked just like that first night in New Orleans. "If you know better," she said, "why are you telling me what I feel?"

Esperanza's eyes were warm and dark and full of compassion. "Your love shines from you, and I cannot help but see it. You should not suffer because Sim does not yet understand."

Tally stood and paced a circle around her bedroll. "Understand what?"

"That his destiny is not what he believed. That he and I once briefly walked the same path, but that time is past, and all the answers he seeks lie within himself."

Tally kicked a stone into the fire. Sparks danced and faded. "He knows he can't have you," she said. "As for the rest—"

"He hides secrets, Señorita Bernard. So do you. All secrets must be revealed."

"Why?"

"So that you can be together."

Tally shivered and wrapped her arms around her chest. "You are very generous with your advice, señorita. Saints must find it useful. But I am no saint. Neither is Sim, though he still loves you. I do not have your gifts, but I can see that much."

Esperanza sighed. "A man can love a dream. But a dream alone is not real. It does not bring happiness."

Tally didn't need to be told about dreams and happiness. She'd known true happiness for the first time in years when she'd lain in Sim's arms, content to accept the pleasure they gave each other. Every word Esperanza spoke nibbled away at that happiness. It was as if Esperanza demanded too much of her, too much of Sim. And demands of any kind would drive Sim away forever.

"Sometimes dreams are better than reality," Tally said. "I'll take whatever happiness I can find in this moment."

"For some, that is enough," Esperanza said. "But you are due more, Tally Bernard. The trials of your youth have ended. What you desire is within your grasp."

Tally almost asked Esperanza to explain, almost spilled her confession of pain and memory as she'd done to only one other living soul. But she clamped her lips together and refused the offer Esperanza held out to her like a priest conferring the holy host.

"Nothing is due to me that I haven't earned," she said. "You'd best get some sleep, señorita, or—"

Some noise, inexplicably out of place, snapped Tally's attention from the conversation. Without pausing to think, she snatched up a bridle and ran for the picket line.

Federico stirred in his bedroll. *"Qué esta pasando?"* He sat up, scratching his hair. "What has happened, Señor Bernard?"

"I'm not sure." Tally bridled Muérdago, grabbed a rifle and clambered onto the horse's bare back. "I'm going to check on the herd."

"I will come with you." Federico threw off his blankets and gathered up his own gear. Tally didn't wait. She rode out of camp and around the perimeter the men had established for the herd. The cattle were on their feet, rolling eyes at a disturbance Tally couldn't see by the waning moonlight.

Sim must be aware of the problem. "Find Diablo, boy," she murmured to Muérdago.

The gelding snorted, but not in agreement. He shied and planted his feet, twitching his ears toward the darkness ahead. A rider emerged from the dappled shadows. Like Tally, he rode bareback, but there the resemblance ended.

Tally reined Muérdago about, but it was far too late. Other Apache warriors joined the first, dressed like him in breechcloths, leggings and moccasins. Tally didn't need light to know that their faces were hard and merciless from years of fighting American and Mexican soldiers, for these were the men who had defied the government and lived by raiding in Sonora, Arizona and New Mexico.

They were here for the cattle, and they would find the odds very much in their favor. Their leader held his rifle casually across his pony's withers, well knowing that Tally couldn't use hers before she was struck down herself.

Where in hell was Sim?

Tally cleared her throat and sat very straight. *"Buenas noches."*

The leader stared at Tally with obvious surprise. He asked her a question in his own language.

"I don't know your tongue," she said slowly. "Do you speak *Inglés? Español?"*

One of the Apache made a sharp comment, and the others laughed. The leader held up his hand. *"Español,"* he said.

Tally gathered her halting command of Spanish. *"Si vienen por el ganado, llévense algunos. Son un regalo."*

"Our cattle sure as hell ain't no gift."

Sim rode lazily into the middle of the group, his feet bare in the stirrups, reining Diablo between Tally and the Apaches. He glanced at the Indian leader as if he were of no consequence and turned to Tally. "We're not giving any of these beeves away."

The Apache leader lifted his rifle and barked a question. Sim answered in the Indians' tongue, smiling all the while. He was deliberately provoking men who had no reason not to kill to take what they wanted. Tally knew from stories Eli had told that the Indians had cause for their hatred of Yanqui and Mexicano alike. She felt violence simmering in the air, waiting to erupt.

"No," she said. "No killing, Sim. If—"

She never finished her plea. Sim jumped to the ground. He planted himself in front of the Indian leader and unbuttoned his waistcoat, each movement exaggerated. One of the Apaches laughed, but the leader only watched in puzzled silence. Sim threw his waistcoat to the ground and pulled his shirt from his britches.

An Apache in a stained cavalry coat made a pointed comment that Tally had little difficulty interpreting. Sim was crazy. The Indians knew it. Tally had heard somewhere that certain tribes left the mad alone. Was that Sim's strategy?

She felt oddly calm as Sim finished undressing. He left his clothes in a pile and kicked them aside. He flung out his arms. The Apache leader's horse shied, and the Indian brought his rifle to bear on Sim's chest.

Sim vanished. In his place grew a cloud of dark smoke, blending with the night, and when it cleared, a wolf stood where the smoke had been.

CHAPTER FIFTEEN

TALLY KNEW AFTERWARD that the Apaches must have reacted to the trick, perhaps with shouts or cries of fear. She heard nothing. Her gaze was locked on the huge beast with its bristling brown mane and bared teeth, and all her senses had frozen.

Sim wouldn't have deserted her. But she'd never seen him with the wolf; it wasn't of the breed that roamed the Mexican highlands. She was still trying to make sense of the ruse when she realized the Apaches were gone. Diablo had likewise vanished.

There had been no battle, no deaths. The cattle hadn't stampeded. The wolf loped a few yards after the retreating Indians, tail held high, and then turned back to Tally. It sat on its haunches and stared up at her with frighteningly intelligent gray-green eyes. Muérdago held as still as a mouse transfixed by a snake.

What was that old saying about frying pans and fires? One wolf couldn't do much damage to an entire herd of cattle, but it was large enough to bring down a lone horse and rider. Tally shifted her rifle across her lap and carefully cocked the hammer.

The wolf lunged. Muérdago bucked, and Tally lost her grip on the rifle. She clung to the gelding's back as he wheeled about and raced for camp, the wolf hot on his heels. Federico and his horse lay directly in their path. Muérdago half reared to avoid them.

"The wolf!" Tally gasped. "Shoot it, Rico!"

The vaquero drew up alongside her trembling mount. "What wolf, señorita?"

She glanced about. The animal was gone, as swiftly and silently as the Indians. "Did you see the Apaches?"

Federico crossed himself. "No, *a Dios gracias*. Did you?"

"They're gone now." Thanks to the wolf. "How are the cattle?"

"Restless but unharmed." Federico cocked his head. "I've sent the other men to quiet them. The Apaches did not attack?"

"They...decided against it." She felt suddenly faint and bent over Muérdago's withers.

"You do not look well, Tally," Federico said. "I will take you back to camp."

"I can make it by myself. See to the cattle, Rico."

He nodded reluctantly and rode ahead of her. As she followed the glow of firelight to the camp, she considered and reconsidered everything she'd seen since the Apaches' arrival. That had been ominous enough, but the wolf's appearance was far more disturbing.

She could have sworn she'd seen Sim...*become* the wolf, which was nonsense. But if it *had* been a trick, where had he gone?

She nearly dropped from Muérdago's back when she reached the picket. She stumbled to her bedroll. Federico already had most of the men ahorse and riding out. A few cast curious glances Tally's way.

Esperanza knelt by her side. "You are not well," she said, setting her cool hand on Tally's forehead.

"I'm all right. Has Sim returned?"

"No. But something strange has happened, has it not?"

"Yes." She met Esperanza's gaze. "Did you see a wolf?"

"Not tonight," Sim said. He walked into camp, half-dressed

in trousers and waistcoat. A torn shirt hung like a rag over his arm. "But she probably knew what I was all along. Didn't you, Esperanza?"

The *curandera* raised her hand as if to cross herself and stopped. "I was not sure," she whispered. "You are like Don Tomás—"

"*Sí.*"

"What are you talking about?" Tally demanded, looking from one to the other. "Where did you go, Sim? That wolf—"

"Haven't you guessed?" He tossed the shirt to the ground beside his bedroll and stared down at the women. Fire bronzed the skin of his chest, shoulders and arms, and his dark brown hair was long and unkempt. He might have been Apache himself.

But he wasn't. The idea that lodged in Tally's mind was so preposterous, so incredible, that she didn't dare speak it aloud.

"Let me make it easier for you," Sim said. "You thought you saw me Change into a wolf and scare the Apaches away. You don't believe what your eyes told you. But there's nothing wrong with your eyes, Tally." His teeth flashed in a smile. "I *am* the wolf."

Tally burst out laughing. Esperanza touched her arm, and somehow that simple contact brought Tally firmly back to earth. She could see that Sim was pretending to be amused, but he wasn't. He was desperately afraid. Only truth could create such fear in a man like Sim.

The truth was that Sim had never been like ordinary men. Tally had recognized that almost at the beginning. He tracked like a hunting dog and saw in darkness like a cat. His speed and agility were remarkable. And he had wrecked Eli's traps....

He was the wolf.

"*Loup-garou,*" Tally murmured. She rubbed her eyes with the heels of her palms. "*Dieu du ciel.*"

"Hombres-lobos," Esperanza said. "I have met them before. They are not all evil."

"Some are," Sim said. He sank into a crouch. "But most of 'em are just like men, good and bad. Which am I, Esperanza?"

"Never evil." She bit her lip. "Sim…"

He ignored her and continued to stare at Tally. Waiting for her judgment. Rejection—or acceptance.

Tally struggled to drag reassurance from a chasm of shock. "We…have legends in Louisiana about such creatures," she said. "My papa used to tell the stories before he went away. I believed them then. I think he did, too." She heard the echo of her own words and shook her head. "No. I didn't mean—I know you're not a creature, Sim. But I don't completely understand."

"Neither do I." He cupped his hand over the back of his neck and kneaded the muscles with his fingers. "I've only started to learn. I didn't…accept what I was until a couple of years ago."

"You…you were born—"

"My father was what I am," he interrupted harshly, "but I didn't find out until I was grown. And then I didn't want anything to do with his family or what they gave me."

He spoke as if such an astonishing gift were like a terrible deformity passed from generation to generation. "Were you ashamed?" she asked.

"After a while I decided it was foolish not to use what I'd been born with. It isn't a curse. I'm stronger than normal men. My wounds heal fast. It takes a lot to kill me, like a bullet to the heart or brain."

"You said to me once that the wolves were your only brothers. Can you…control them?"

"They understand me, and I understand them. Sometimes they do what I ask."

"Like leaving Cold Creek's stock alone. But you're not really a wolf, either."

He snorted. "Last I heard, wolves couldn't talk."

"There are many others like you?"

"I don't know. I guess most keep it hidden—"

Like you did, Tally finished for him, but he hurried on.

"I knew of one other—a good man, a friend—and I hear there are some in Europe." He clamped his jaw tight, as if he didn't want to pursue the subject. "Are you afraid, Tally?"

She opened her mouth, then closed it again. *No secrets.* "Yes," she admitted. "And no. Because you are still Sim. You saved both my life and the cattle. I'm grateful."

He looked away. "You would have shot me."

"But I didn't know it was you." She got up, poised on unsteady legs. "Do you think I could hurt you, Sim?"

"You don't think I'm a monster?"

"Do you want me to run away?" She took a step toward him. "If I were afraid, then you could leave me without a moment's hesitation. It would be a fine excuse. You would have a reason for moving from place to place, never settling down, because people would be afraid if they ever learned the truth."

"They should be afraid. I was very good at killing, Tally. Now you know why."

"Yet the wolves in the mountains leave our livestock alone," she said. "Ranchers believe wolves are vermin. Is that all they are, Sim?"

"No."

"Then if you're like them, you would kill to survive, not for the pleasure of it."

"It's men who kill for pleasure."

"Wolf or man, I know what you are. In here." She thumped her chest. "You can't get rid of me so easily."

He cursed, glanced at Esperanza and stopped. "I knew the Apaches would run if they saw me change," he said quietly. "They have some sense."

"But we women maintain the privilege of being unpredictable," Tally said. "Isn't that so, Esperanza?"

The *curandera* nodded solemnly. *"Ciertamente."*

"Hell." Sim sorted through his belongings and pulled out a spare shirt. "You ladies won't be offended if I dress?"

"Don't forget your boots," Tally suggested.

Esperanza giggled. Tally and Sim turned to stare at the same instant, and all at once Sim grinned—a warm, uninhibited smile without a trace of mockery, cynicism or bitterness.

Sim had changed indeed. If Tally's acceptance of his little "peculiarity" had wrought such a miracle—if he could look at Esperanza without resentment and longing for what could never be—then Tally wouldn't have cared if he'd changed into a javelina or horned toad instead of a magnificent wolf.

All secrets must be revealed, Esperanza had said. Compared to Sim's revelation, what Tally was concealing seemed like a common, tawdry confession.

Tally felt Esperanza's gaze and busied herself smoothing out her bedroll. Dawn was in the air; soon Federico or one of the vaqueros would return with a report on the condition of the cattle, and the cook would prepare a simple but hearty breakfast to get the men started on the next leg of the journey home. Tally had a few minutes of relative privacy to show Sim that she trusted him as much as he'd trusted her.

Get it over with. Tell him. Then you'll finally know.

She let the minutes pass. The sun slipped over the horizon. Esperanza withdrew her rosary and went off by herself to pray.

Sim knelt beside Tally. "You won't tell anyone," he said.

"Of course not. You honored me with your confidence, and I will never break it."

"Even when you get mad at me?"

Something in his tone, some fragile intimacy, made her suddenly shy. "When would I ever be angry with you?" she joked.

"I don't know." He sidled closer, taking her hand in his. "Sometimes I rub people the wrong way."

"Not me." She rested her head on his shoulder. "You rub me exactly the right way, *mon loup*."

He closed his eyes. "I swore I wouldn't accept anymore dreams. Damn it, Tally—"

The drum of hoofbeats saved them from further argument. The vaquero-cook rode in and went straight to work with his pots and pans. Federico arrived to cheerfully report that no cattle had been stolen in the night. Breakfast was served while the men chatted in rapid Spanish about the near-attack by Apaches. No one mentioned a wolf. Several, however, spoke of miracles.

Tally was almost ready to believe.

THE PEOPLE of Esperanza's village knew she had returned long before she rode her burro down the dusty main street. Men had been watching from the hills; they sent boys running ahead to alert their fellow villagers, and by the time Sim, Tally and Esperanza entered Dos Ríos, every house had its cluster of observers waiting to greet the young woman as if she were a long-lost holy icon.

Sim had originally intended to leave the final escort to Tally, Federico and a few of the vaqueros. He saw no point in lingering farewells. But in the end he rode with the others into the village, openly and in daylight, listening to the cries of delight and welcome. Tally stayed close by his side.

Without confiding her intentions, Esperanza passed by her house with a brief smile for her eager relatives and continued on to the newly built church. There she dismounted, gave her donkey into the hands of a grinning boy and entered the open church doors.

Tally, Federico and Don Miguel's vaquero, Juan, also dismounted and were quickly offered water, pulque and tortillas by one of the women who'd followed in Esperanza's wake. None of the villagers accompanied their little saint into the church…as if, Sim thought, they didn't dare disturb one so hallowed in her communion with God.

Once he'd been as superstitious and gullible as these simple people, believing that Esperanza had the power to save him. If the villagers had any notion of what he was—what he could become—they would consider him damned to hell. But it wasn't his wolf blood that damned him. And he wasn't afraid of interrupting Esperanza's holy meditations.

He slid from Diablo's back and tossed the reins over a nearby rail. Tally caught up with him as he was about to enter the church's carved wooden portal.

"You're not going in to pray," she said with a touch of irony.

He smiled. "You afraid I'll be struck down soon as I'm inside?"

"No more afraid than I would be for myself. We both survived our last visit."

She meant the chapel at Hacienda del Gavilán. But she'd asked him to make peace with Esperanza. This was his last chance, and he didn't even know if he wanted it.

Tally searched his face and stepped back. She understood now, more than ever, that she couldn't hold him against his will. Not here or anywhere.

Sim strode into the cool, dim interior of the church. Esperanza was kneeling before the altar, her rebozo drawn over her head. Sim walked down the aisle between the backless pews. Halfway to the altar, he shucked his hat and clutched it awkwardly in his hands.

"You are welcome here," Esperanza said without turning.

"You speaking for God?" he asked.

She bent her head. "Will you pray with me?"

He nearly crushed the brim of his hat. "That ain't my way of doing things, *chiquita.* You know that."

"Yet God hears." She rose and faced him. "Let me pray for you."

"I can't stop you."

She smiled, a brief upward curve of full lips that would never know a man's touch again. "Do you forgive me, Sim?"

"For what?"

"For taking another path."

"I reckon...you need to forgive me. For New Mexico."

Her eyes shone so brightly that he was almost tempted to make an obeisance like some fool campesino. "I forgive you, Sim," she said. "Now you must forgive yourself."

He turned away. "Adios, Esperanza."

"Espérate!"

He paused. His breathing was harsh and loud in the silence.

"She waits for you," Esperanza said behind him. "Accept the happiness you have been given."

"Even if I don't deserve it?"

"There are many paths to salvation, Simeon."

"Not for a man like me. Not after the things I've done."

"Once you did not regret. That Simeon is gone."

He wanted to yell denials in this most tranquil of sanctuaries, assault Esperanza with cruel words and imprecations that would make her blanch and retreat in fear. But she was right. The Sim who might have done those things was gone.

Still, his ghost remained. Sim remembered hearing a story about a man who had done so many evil things in life that he'd unknowingly forged himself a chain he had to pack around with him in the world beyond, powerless to atone for his misdeeds. Sim reckoned that his own chain was about as long as the Rio Grande. He didn't want Tally helping him drag it back to Cold Creek.

He clenched his fists and spun on his heel. Illumination from the precious stained-glass window behind the altar painted a brilliant halo about Esperanza's head and shoulders. He returned to her slowly, counting each step. He bowed his head and knelt at her feet.

"Give me your blessing," he asked.

"I am no priest."

He swallowed hard. *"Por favor."*

Her hand rested on his hair as lightly as an angel's wing. She murmured over him, prayers and invocations he made no effort to interpret. He didn't want to know what she said to her God, or how he might answer.

He came out of a dream dazed and confused. Esperanza no longer stood above him. Colored light splayed across the packed-earth floor. He picked up his hat, brushed it off absently and got to his feet.

Tally waited just outside, though she pretended not to notice him when he walked into the glare of afternoon sunlight. She glanced toward him and smiled.

That was all he needed. He went for her like a charging bull, grabbed her arm and rushed her around the corner of the nearest casa. He took her face between his hands and kissed her as tenderly as he knew how.

"Sim," she protested, pushing him away. "What if someone sees us?"

"What if they do?" He grinned. "They'll think we're both unnatural sons of bitches." And he kissed her again until she gasped for breath.

"Now," he said, "we can go home."

THE REST OF THE JOURNEY, though slow and tedious, presented no insurmountable challenges to Tally, Sim or the vaqueros. A heifer or two needed doctoring for sore feet, or extra watching because of a tendency to stray, but the party passed into Arizona and reached the border of Cold Creek without incident.

Tally was supremely happy. Exhaustion drained her body but didn't touch her joy. During the trip she saw Sim only at meals and at the evening campfire, but each meeting confirmed what she'd known since leaving Dos Ríos.

Sim was hers. Oh, not her property. She wasn't fool enough to believe that he could be tied down by commonplace obligations or some preacher's blessing.

He trusted her. He desired her. Above all, he respected her, and that she cherished more than all the conventional promises in a month of Sundays.

He rode forward to join her as the men hazed the cattle down from the pass and along the road toward the spring. There would be plenty of work to do once the beeves were bedded down in the home pasture. Tally hoped to keep the vaqueros employed for the branding before they returned to Hacienda del Gavilán. After that, when the animals were put to pasture, and the older heifers were introduced to Cold Creek's bulls, she wouldn't need extra men until calving time in the spring. And Sim could do the work of four.

For the first time in her life, Tally considered herself a lucky woman.

Miriam waved from the doorway of the house, while the cattle streamed by in a cloud of dust. She drove the buckboard to the corral an hour after Tally and the men had secured the footsore herd inside the fence. Dispensing food and drink with welcome efficiency, Miriam fussed over everyone as if she'd never expected to see any of them again. Dolores did her best to help, much to the amusement of the vaqueros. Pablo had already ridden off to look for Eli.

Tally, mindful of her dirt, kept her distance from Miriam until her friend insisted on a firm hug.

"It's so good to see you," Tally said, enveloped by the comforting scents of yeast dough and clean cotton. "Is everything all right at Cold Creek? How are you and the children?"

"All fine. Bart hurt his knee, but he's up and riding again. Eli can tell you the rest."

Tally grinned slyly. "I hope that Eli has been behaving himself, what with you in the house all alone."

"I'll have you know that he has been the perfect gentleman." Miriam set Tally back and eyed her with a thoughtful frown. "And what about you?"

"I'm very well."

"You're too thin," Miriam announced. "But that's not the only thing that's changed about you, child."

"I haven't had a bath in three days."

"You don't have to tell me. I'll take care of that right enough." She shook her head. "There wasn't a day gone by that I didn't worry about you and Federico. I should have known you were always in God's good hands."

Tally thought it best not to tell Miriam about the Apaches, and certainly not about the wolf. She didn't like keeping secrets from Miriam, but this particular secret wasn't hers to share. Perhaps, in time, Sim would come to trust the others, as well.

"How is André?" she asked.

Miriam sighed. "About the same. He has his times of clarity, but they don't come often."

Tally wiped her forehead with the back of her hand. "I think it's too late for miracles, Miriam."

"It's never too late for miracles. There are just some things we don't understand."

"But it isn't fair that André should be suffering, while I—" Suddenly she couldn't think of the right words.

Miriam subjected her to an even more thorough scrutiny.

"He's still with you," she said. Her eyes widened at the sight of Tally's blush. "My, my. Something has changed." She craned her neck to look over Tally's shoulder. "'Course I'll know for sure once I get a good look at him."

"Miriam—"

"None of this comes as a surprise to me, mind you." She took Tally's hands. "As long as you're happy."

"I am, Miriam." She found it unaccountably difficult to look her friend in the eye. "I can't explain. It's not anything I thought would happen. Not to me."

"Being in love? Wanting a man like any woman?"

"If it was just that… Miriam, I—"

"Never mind. We'll talk about it when you're washed up and rested, and look like something better than a coyote's breakfast." She cupped Tally's cheek in her palm. "Eli will be glad to see you."

She didn't say what they both were thinking: that Eli wouldn't be so glad to see Sim.

Miriam gathered up the remains of the meal, while Tally spoke to Don Miguel's vaqueros about staying on a few more days to help with the branding. All were agreeable, especially after they'd tasted Miriam's cooking. Federico and Sim had made a final inspection of the cattle. The animals had an untouched spread of good grass and fresh water in the home pasture, and they would spend one peaceful night of rest before tomorrow's unpleasant but necessary work commenced.

Tally left Federico to get the vaqueros settled in the bunkhouse and accompanied Miriam back to the homestead. Sim rode some way behind them. Eli, Pablo and Bart waited at the main house, each wearing a very different expression.

"Did you see any Indians or *bandidos?*" Pablo demanded. "We had rustlers again!"

Tally hopped down from the wagon. "*Buenas tardes, Pablito.*"

"Welcome home," Eli said, unsmiling.

"What's this about rustlers?" Tally asked. "Miriam told me everything was all right."

"We didn't have any real trouble. The outlaws were poorly organized and weak. We dealt with them in short order."

"Did you recognize any of them?"

"All local cowboys. They aren't likely to bother us again."

"You didn't have to shoot them?"

"I guess you didn't hear. There was a gunfight in Tombstone. The Earps and Doc Holliday had it out with the Clantons and McLaurys. Several of the cowboys were killed. The ones who're left are busy burying their kin."

Tally shivered. "Then our new cattle will be safe over the winter." She faced Bart. "I hope you've been giving that leg proper rest."

"Now don't you worry, Miss Tally," Bart said, standing firmly on both feet. "I can keep up my end of the work."

"I'm worried about you, not the chores. You always have a home here, Bart, no matter what happens."

The old man swallowed and stared at the tips of his boots. "Thank you, Miss Tally."

Eli listened to the exchange with an unrelentingly grim expression. His gaze was fixed on a point beyond Tally's shoulder; Sim had dismounted and was leading Diablo to the stable.

Tally refused to let Eli's prejudice discourage her. She refused to let these people—her family—turn against each other when there was so much hope for the future.

"Is there anything else I should know?" she asked Eli.

"Nothing worth mentioning." He sighed, and some of the stiffness went out of his body. "It's good to have you back safe, Miss Tally. You got what you wanted in Sonora?"

"Better than I expected." *In more ways than one.* "This will be a new beginning for all of us, Eli."

Except for André. Once again Tally berated herself for celebrating, when her brother had paid such a high and unreasonable price for his own dreams. Without him, her happiness now would not have been possible.

"We'll begin branding in the morning," Tally said. "The men we brought from Hacienda del Gavilán will stay on to help—I can pay them with the money I saved on the purchase." She took off her hat and rubbed the back of her damp neck. "I'm going to see André, and then I plan to have a hot bath and a good night's sleep. You and Bart should do the same. It will be a long day tomorrow."

"I never did much care for branding." Eli's glance strayed toward the kitchen window. "I was thinking—if it's all right with you—that I might add a bit to the house in spring. Since Miriam and I—" He broke off, as uncomfortable as most men were with any talk of marriage.

Tally spared him the effort. "That's an excellent idea, Eli. You and Miriam will want a bit of extra room. And eventually your own house, of course."

"Maybe once we have a profit coming in again."

"That might not take as long as you expect. Wait until you see the cattle, Eli. We'll have a fat crop of calves in the spring."

Eli met her gaze. "I hope you're right. It's time we had our share of good fortune."

Tally touched his arm briefly, nodded to Bart and went into the house. She visited André, who was thinner but otherwise little changed. He didn't seem to hear her voice. She talked to him anyway, telling him of the journey and its success.

"You don't have to worry about me, André," she said. "I'll be all right. Cold Creek will prosper."

His breathing hitched as though he were about to answer,

but then he subsided back into a restless sleep. Tally kissed his forehead and left him to his unbreachable solitude.

Miriam was heating water for the bath, but Tally didn't wait for the tub to be full. She sank into the few inches of water with a groan and scrubbed vigorously until Miriam brought in another pail and poured it over her head and shoulders. After the last pail, Miriam pulled up a stool and unbraided Tally's hair, talking of this and that inconsequential matter in a way that made Tally forget all the things she couldn't change.

Tally dressed in the soft shirt and worn pants she reserved for wear around the house and sat on the porch watching the sun go down behind the mountains. Miriam brought out her knitting. Cattle lowed from the pasture, and a cheerful vaquero's ballad floated on the cool night air. Federico's bright tenor was not among the voices; he'd retired to his little cabin to enjoy the company of his children, and the songs he sang to them would be of a very different nature.

When it was time to retire, Miriam gave Tally a secret smile, picked up her knitting basket and slipped away. Tally went to her own room as she'd done a thousand times before, but her heart fluttered like a bride's on her wedding night. She shed her clothes and crawled naked between the sheets.

CHAPTER SIXTEEN

SIM CAME JUST after the moon rose. He didn't speak but undressed quietly and efficiently, laying his clothing over the corner chair. Tally held the covers up, and he slid into the bed beside her.

She expected, even wanted, him to begin immediately. Her body was ready the instant his hand brushed her hip. But he only took her in his arms and held her from behind, their bodies cupped like a pair of spoons as he nuzzled her loose hair.

It was foolish of her to weep over something so small. She sucked in her breath so Sim wouldn't hear, but he knew. He wiped the tears away with his thumbs.

"Why?" he asked. "Do you want me to go?"

She snatched his hand and held on for dear life. "It isn't you. It's only that…no one has ever done this before."

"Done what?" he asked, going very still.

"Just held me, without…" She couldn't finish the sentence. Sim rested his cheek against her shoulder and sighed, shuddering with some emotion he wasn't able to express.

"I guess it's the first time for both of us," he said.

Tally treasured that precious admission like the great gift it was. She could imagine what it had cost him. And what it meant that he was able to understand, without anyone telling him, how to hold a woman with such tender unselfishness.

She rolled to face him, tucking her arms into his chest. Their faces nearly touched on the pillow. She pushed brown hair away from his forehead, and he held her hand to his temple.

"We don't have to do anything," he said. "You need to sleep."

Tally sniffed inelegantly. "You could probably go weeks without sleep, couldn't you?"

"I don't know. I never tried it." He kissed her palm. "Never slept through the night in a woman's bed, either."

She closed her eyes. "I don't usually cry so much."

"You worked hard on the drive. You did well, Tally."

"So did you."

He stroked his hand down her back from shoulders to the base of her spine. "No doubts? You're sure about this?"

"Ah, *mais oui*," she whispered. "I'm sure." She kissed him. He hesitated, as if even he didn't want to trade such rare contentment for the turmoil of passion. And then he returned her kiss so lightly that she had to seize him around the neck and prove how much she wanted him.

She knew of one way to show it beyond all doubt. He might be shocked at first by her boldness, but she was prepared to take the risk. Without giving him a chance to protest, she wriggled free, pushed him onto his back and mounted him, thighs spread to either side of his hips. His erection stood proudly against her belly.

Instinctively, his hands went to her waist to steady her. "Tally," he said, a note of surprise in his voice. "Do you—"

She rose up on her knees and plunged down onto him. His eyes opened wide and then closed tightly as he expelled his breath in a long groan. To her immense gratification, he let her take the lead. She rode him, watching every slight shift of his expression from tense acquiescence to relaxation to the acceptance of pleasure. She gently squeezed his nipples between her fingers, brushing his chest with sweeps of her unbound hair. And always she kept the rhythm, matching it to his.

She tried to make it last, but soon she felt the signs that she would lose control and rediscover that wonderful paradise Sim had shown her at the Hacienda. Before she could consider how to slow her pace, Sim lifted her by the waist and rolled her to her side. A moment later he had her on her back and was kneeling between her thighs.

The touch of his lips and tongue in her most sensitive place startled her into a cry loud enough to wake the household. Sim was doing things that one or two of her former clients had enjoyed, but she had hated...hated because those men expected her to take pleasure from their great generosity and she had to pretend she did.

With Sim it was wonderful. He seemed to know exactly where and how to use his tongue to tickle and tease, drawing out each caress with rapid flicks and long strokes. Then he traced circles around the part of her that needed him inside, filling her up as only he could do.

She grabbed blindly at his hair, entangling her fingers in it in the ferocity of her need. He slid up along her body and covered her mouth with his as he gave her what she desired. He thrust with slow, regular motions that grew faster and harder until both of them trembled on the brink of the precipice.

Tally let herself go. Sim fell with her. They shivered in each other's arms, gasping, and then Tally began to laugh.

Sim pulled her face against his damp chest. "What's so funny?" he asked.

"Nothing. I'm happy. I'm so very happy."

SIM WOKE BEFORE DAWN. Tally slept sprawled like a wanton over the bed, her hair splashed across the pillow and her lips parted in unwitting invitation. He knew she would welcome him with a smile and open arms if he let his lust take him again, but he couldn't disturb such a breathtaking vision.

She looked like an angel. An angel who had chosen earthly love over the perfection of heaven.

Love. Sim rejected the word as soon as it came into his mind. He and Tally didn't need such fancy excuses for what they shared.

He swung his legs over the bed and walked to the window. The coolness of November seemed to sharpen his senses of smell and hearing, bringing him news of the mountains and their denizens. The wolves waited for him. It would be good to run with them again, and he had a very practical reason for doing so.

Caleb Smith might be dead by now, or back in jail, but he could just as easily be robbing trains or rustling cattle within a hundred miles of Cold Creek. He'd taken Sim's warnings seriously enough to stay away from the ranch, but Sim wasn't stupid enough to think Caleb had given up on the treasure. He never would, not as long as he lived. And that meant he would be back sooner or later.

Sim glanced at Tally. His woman. He wasn't about to let Caleb get near enough to ruin her peace. That left him with two choices: either find the treasure and let Caleb have it, or kill his one-time friend and blood brother.

He pressed his hand to the window, feeling the cold seep into his skin. If he killed Caleb, Esperanza's blessing meant nothing. The changes he felt inside meant nothing. Regret and remorse meant less than nothing. He would be killing his own crippled soul.

There wasn't much chance of getting anything useful out of André, but he had to make one more effort. Working the new cattle would keep everyone at Cold Creek busy for a good week or more. Without direct knowledge of the treasure's location, Sim would have to leave the ranch and thoroughly search the mountains where he and Tally had found André.

He could find it if anyone could. But he didn't want to leave Tally for a day, let alone the weeks it might take.

He dressed and left the room, closing the door silently behind him. It was past the hour when he would expect Miriam to be up cooking breakfast for the men who would begin their workday soon after the sun rose, but she wasn't in the kitchen or in the hall. Sim entered André's room and crouched at the young man's bedside.

André was awake. He was staring at the ceiling as if it held some fascination for him, his eyes following invisible patterns.

"I can see it," André said suddenly, his voice clear and strong.

Sim held very still. "See what, André?"

"The writing, of course." He lowered his head and gazed in Sim's direction. "I can't see you. Come closer."

Sim moved a single step. "Tell me about the writing, André."

"I've seen you before," André murmured. "I didn't hire you."

"Your sister did," Sim said. "She sent me to make sure you're all right."

André coughed and passed his hands over his mouth. "I remember now."

"What do you remember?"

"Everything." André choked on his own laughter. "Didn't he find it yet?"

Careful. "I don't know who you mean."

André looked at Sim with sly amusement. "He hasn't found it, has he? And he thinks he has the only copy."

"You were too smart for him," Sim said, playing along.

"Too smart for everyone." He returned his attention to the ceiling, tracing lines and circles on the coverlet stretched over his legs. "Tally doesn't know. She should have it, in case something happens...." He clutched handfuls of cloth in his fists. "The copy is in the house."

Sim set aside caution and moved closer to the bed. "Tell me where, André. I'll keep it safe for her, so no one else can take it."

"They all thought I was stupid. They used me. But not anymore."

"Mr. Kavanagh?"

Sim turned at Miriam's voice in the doorway. From the corner of his eye he saw André stiffen and then go limp, as if he'd fallen into a dead faint.

Either André was suffering some new fit, or he was a lot less sick than everyone believed. Sim wasn't in a position to figure out which.

"I thought I heard André talking," he said. "So I came to look in on him."

Miriam glanced toward the bed. "Talking, you say? He did little enough of that while you and Miss Tally were gone."

There was no suspicion in her voice, only curiosity. Sim relaxed. "He must have been dreaming. He said something about Tally, but I couldn't understand."

"After what he did to her, leaving her to run this place alone—" She shook her head. "I wouldn't be at all surprised if he has some awful tormenting dreams."

Sim stood and walked casually toward the door. "I'd like to see him get better, for Tally's sake. But I think he's probably more trouble than he's worth."

Miriam sighed. "We're supposed to love our neighbors, but the Lord doesn't always make it easy."

"Easier for some than others." Sim edged past her, but she stopped him with a touch.

"Tally loves you," Miriam said, her dark eyes somber. "Don't hurt her, Simeon. She's had enough of that in her life."

For a moment Sim felt as if he were standing in the presence of a stern but loving mother, the kind he'd never had. He was surprised to realize he wasn't angry at the touch or the warning. Miriam was worthy of his respect. And his honesty.

"I hear you," he said simply.

"I guess that's all I can ask." She nodded and started down the hall for the kitchen.

Sim gave André one last appraising look. His sleep was genuine now, even if it hadn't been before. Sim planned to look for the copy of the map before he tried questioning André again. Nothing the man said could be trusted, but there might be a few grains of truth in his madness.

And if it wasn't madness—if André was deceiving his friends and making Tally suffer for some twisted reason of his own—Sim would expose him for the liar and fraud he was.

Tally was pulling on her work clothes when Sim returned to her room. She greeted him with a dazzling smile, but he stayed outside the door.

"I'd better go join the men," he said. "Wouldn't do to have them see me come out of the house so early."

She straightened in her half-buttoned shirt and pushed golden hair from her face. "You think they don't know?" she asked. "If they don't now, they will by tomorrow. There's no sense in hiding it."

He went cold and hot at the same time. She told him what he already knew: that he was welcome in her bed any time, every night if he wanted, and she wasn't ashamed to have him there. She was the one woman in the world who could give herself freely and not become tainted like all the other females he'd lain with.

Because she was Tally. Because she loved him.

"The men will accept…this?" he asked.

"For my sake, yes. We are a family."

"If anyone insults you—ever," Sim said, "he'll answer to me."

She came to the door and leaned toward him, not quite touching, and it was as if they were back in bed again. "Don't you know by now that I can take care of myself?"

"I know." He backed away before his heart could jump out of his body and right into her hands. "I'll see you outside."

"Don't forget about breakfast!" she called after him.

But he wasn't hungry for food. He passed Bart and a couple of the vaqueros soon after he left the house. They greeted him in the normal way. While the men enjoyed their morning meal, Sim Changed and went for a quick run in the hills. The wolves played a little game with him, staying just out of his sight. He let them have their fun. He could find them whenever he needed to.

Just now he had other things on his mind. He returned to the homestead in time to join the others at the corral, where fires had been laid and the irons prepared for branding the new cattle. Two vaqueros served as flankers to pull and hold the cattle down, while Eli worked as the iron man and Tally recorded each animal in her record book. Miriam and the children brought food at noon and again in the early evening.

Sim had no opportunity to slip away and no privacy to look for the map after the day's work was done. On the second day he was forced to employ a ruse he despised; he let one of the angry cows kick him in the leg. He fell, rolled out of the way of stomping hooves and grimaced in very real pain.

Federico helped him limp to the fence, where Tally eyed him with worry and Miriam clucked about splints, poultices and ointments.

"It ain't broke," Sim said through his teeth, "or I couldn't walk at all. I just don't want it to stiffen up."

"Let Miriam look at it," Tally said. "You can ride the wagon back to the house."

"I know what needs to be done." He pushed past the well-meaning onlookers and walked slowly back to the house. Once he was out of sight, he ran the rest of the way. He knew from experience that his leg would throb for a while and then heal up quickly without any treatment. Even Tally didn't know all the peculiarities that came with being more than human.

At the house he paused to make sure that André was asleep and then stood in the hall, letting his senses take command of his body. His nose sorted out and separated all the smells he'd begun to take for granted: fresh bread, spices, soap, cotton, polished wood...and the unique signatures of the people who lived in the house or left their trace coming and going for meals in the kitchen.

He started his search in Miriam's room, quickly overcoming his discomfort at the trespass. He sniffed the air from one corner to the other, felt along the walls and floor and examined the contents of her clothes chest. Nothing of André lingered in the room, though Eli's scent was strong.

The parlor presented a greater challenge. Like the kitchen, it collected and distilled every odor in the house. Sim conducted another painstaking inspection, removing each book from the shelf and riffling the pages. Aware that his time was limited, he moved on to the kitchen and opened every container in the pantry.

He realized then that his human shape didn't have the skill he needed for such a hunt. As a wolf, he could smell a hundred times more keenly. He chose Tally's room to make the transformation. Immediately he was drowned in her essence, and he found himself rolling on the floor with all four paws in the air, wrapped in an ecstasy of sensual joy. An angel's chorus of aroma washed through his fur.

Only one note rang sour in the symphony of intoxicating fragrance. He hopped to his feet and lifted his head, the hair standing stiff along his spine. André's presence was faint, aged as a forgotten lullaby, and it didn't come from his room.

Sim put his nose to the floor. He joined human mind to wolf instinct, pushing all awareness of Tally behind a wall of concentration.

A wooden chest, redolent of camphor, stood at the foot of Tally's bedstead. André's hand had left its mark on the polished cedar. Sim Changed and knelt before the trunk. Could it be as easy as this?

He opened the lid. A natural perfume rose up to envelop him—Tally's, mingled with that of her brother and another female. Fabric lay carefully folded inside the chest. Sim recognized delicately embroidered linen handkerchiefs, a woman's lacy unmentionables…and a garment more substantial, heavy silk and satin that could only be a gown of some kind. It was all shades of white, from old ivory to the pure color of virgin snow.

The cloth was stiff and soft at the same time, catching on the calluses of Sim's hands. He laid the gown over the chest almost reverently and spread the full skirts. Little as he knew of women's fashions, he guessed that the style was some twenty years out of date, meant to be worn with many petticoats to stand away from the body. Perhaps it had belonged to Tally's mother. Sim wondered if Tally had worn it to her own wedding.

Sim hated the thought of that other man. He hated the stink of André's touch on something that belonged to Tally, something that she treasured. He would have no reason to handle his sister's clothing under ordinary circumstances.

Carefully Sim felt over the gown, not sure what he was looking for. The garment, bodice and skirt, had no pockets and far too many ties and buttons. He shook out the bell-shaped sleeves, then ran his fingers between the countless ruffles and gathers of the skirt. The stitching was even and delicate. But in one place along the hem of the lace-edged skirt he found a thickness that didn't belong.

He turned the hem to expose the seam. The neat original stitches had been undone and the opening awkwardly closed again by a far more clumsy tailor. A piece of paper, folded many times, was tucked inside the makeshift pocket.

Sim got his boot knife and cut the newer stitches. He pried the paper from the hem. One side was covered with mechanical type that looked as if it came from one of the books in the parlor. But the other side was marked with a sketch done in pencil and surrounded by cramped handwriting, most of it in Spanish.

André had copied the map. Sim studied it intently, memorizing the picture and the directions. He crumpled the map, went to the kitchen, and stirred up the ashes in the stove. He planted the ball of paper on the end of the poker and pushed it into the embers. Once the paper had been completely consumed, Sim returned to Tally's room, folded and replaced her dress, and put on his own clothes.

His inner sense of time told him that he'd been gone from the branding two hours, about as long as he could risk without someone coming to look for him. This had been the easy part. Now he had to think of some excuse for leaving the ranch to look for the treasure.

He was chewing on that thought and headed back for the corral when a rider came tearing into the yard. He flung himself from his sweating horse's back and stumbled up to Sim.

"Is Beth here?" he croaked.

Sim caught Miles Bryson before he fell to his knees from sheer exhaustion. "Take it easy," Sim said, guiding Bryson to the porch. "Everyone's at the corral. I'll see to your horse, and you can tell me what's wrong."

Bryson gasped and nodded. He leaned heavily on Sim's shoulder. "Much...much obliged, Mr. Kavanagh."

Sim left the older man sitting on the porch and led Bryson's horse to the trough, letting the animal drink sparingly. The gelding showed some signs of lameness, but not anything rest wouldn't cure. Sim got fresh drinking water from the pump and pressed the dented tin cup into Bryson's hands.

"All right," Sim said. "What's happened to your daughter?"

"She's gone, along with her horse." Bryson wiped his mouth with his sleeve and set the cup down with shaking hands. "She ran off before and came here. That's why I figured...I hoped—" He shook his head and bowed over his knees. "You haven't seen her?"

"A few of us, including Mr. Bernard, have been in Sonora buying cattle, but Mr. Patterson would have told us if she'd turned up at Cold Creek." He crouched in front of Bryson. "How long's she been missing?"

"Four days, including today. I was in Willcox on business, and while I was away, Ida had one of her headaches. She didn't even know Beth was gone until—" He closed his eyes. "Beth...she's had a habit lately of going off alone and staying out most of the night. She's that age when young people do a lot of changing, and she knows how to look after herself. I figured there wasn't any harm she could come to right in our canyon. I was too indulgent, I know that now. I didn't watch her carefully enough."

His voice cracked as if he were about to weep. Sim weighed the scanty facts with cold practicality. Bryson would have searched Castillo Canyon thoroughly before he rode elsewhere to look for his daughter. Plenty of things could have happened to Beth right there in the mountains—a fall like André had taken, an attack by a big cat or a stray Apache. Even if Bryson wasn't much of a tracker, he would have found evidence of the last two, and most of the Indians were pretty far north or south of the Chiricahuas.

Sim remembered what Tally had said about Beth: *That little filly has a great deal of spirit, and she doesn't like the fate her parents have in mind for her.* If the girl had stayed rebellious after Tally took her home, she could have ridden off just about anywhere, and she wouldn't look for sympathy at Cold Creek.

"You did the best you could," Sim said, realizing that he meant it. "You can't blame yourself."

"I can, and I do." Bryson met Sim's gaze. "I have a friend riding to Willcox, but if Beth has taken the train—"

"Do you have kin she might have gone to?"

"Not that she'd know well enough. And she couldn't have taken much with her." He caught his breath. "She doesn't have any girlfriends her age in the Valley."

"Did she have any men come courting her?"

Bryson started. "Men? No, no. Ida wouldn't have let her see any men for another year or two, and then she was going to pick out just the right one—start socializing with the other ranchers so that she could show off our Beth and what a fine wife she'd be." He pinched the bridge of his nose. "We had visitors, like you and Mr. Bernard, but none of them were anything but gentlemen with my daughter."

Maybe that was part of the problem. Beth wanted the free life she imagined she could have if her parents didn't get in the way. She'd had romantic notions about Sim, and he'd ignored her. She could have fixed her attention on some other wandering stranger.

Sim went over his two meetings with Beth, considering the things she'd said. More than once she'd asked about Tombstone. For a girl like her, it would seem like a grand and exciting place, all the more so if her folks considered it a den of iniquity.

Which, for a girl like Beth, it would be. Without money or prospects, young as she was, she would end up exactly the way Tally had feared.

"Have you sent anyone to Tombstone?" he asked Bryson.

"No." An expression of hope flashed across Bryson's tight features. "Could she have gone there? Why?"

Sim got to his feet. "You can ask her when we find her."

Bryson also stood, facing Sim with the look of a man just spared the gallows. "You'll help, Mr. Kavanagh? I know you're a fine tracker—"

"I'll have to talk to Mr. Bernard, but I can be ready to leave within the hour."

"If I can borrow a horse, I'll ride with you."

"Better if you get on home and wait there in case she comes back. You might hear something useful, and it won't take two of us to fetch your daughter."

Bryson worked his big hands as if he didn't know what to do with them. "I'd rather stay here, if you don't mind, Mr. Kavanagh. You're closer to Tombstone than we are at Castillo, and Ida will be there with neighbors."

Sim shrugged. "Do as you see fit, then."

"I don't know how to thank you, Mr. Kavanagh."

Sim was spared the need to answer. A buckboard came rattling around the corner of the road, Tally at the ribbons and Miriam by her side. Pablo and Dolores rode in the back. Tally stopped the wagon, passed the ribbons to Miriam, and strode toward Sim and Bryson.

"Mr. Bryson!" she said. "What's wrong?"

Bryson explained, his words much more level and under control as he repeated what he'd told Sim. Tally nodded when he spoke of Sim's offer.

"I would have suggested the same," she said. She met Sim's gaze with a mingling of pride and concern. "Are you up to riding with your injury?"

Heat spread under Sim's collar. "It's nothing much, Mr. Bernard. Looked a lot worse than it feels."

"I'm glad to hear it. Still, you shouldn't ride alone. I'll go with you."

An argument with Tally in public was out of the question, and in private it would be useless. Sim didn't want her along in case the girl did turn up in Tombstone and had suffered some harm; Tally would take it too hard. But a woman's presence might be useful, especially if a man had been involved.

Tally returned to the wagon and talked with Miriam for several minutes, asking her to carry instructions back to Eli and the vaqueros. Sim took Bryson inside the house and found him some grub while he put together rations for the ride to Tombstone.

Bryson clenched and unclenched his hands on the kitchen table. "Mr. Kavanagh…I have another favor to ask you."

Sim tied a knot in the cloth packet of jerky and day-old bread. "And what would that be, Mr. Bryson?"

"Don't tell anyone what's happened to Beth. If decent folk learn she's been riding out on her own, God knows where—" He broke off, dropping his head into his hands.

"Your daughter's reputation is safe with us," Tally said, entering the kitchen. She rested her hand on Bryson's shoulder—a slender hand dwarfed by the homesteader's heavy build. Sim reckoned the only reason anyone took Tally for a man was because she had a man's strength and determination.

But those qualities belonged to Tally herself.

Bryson turned in his chair and gazed up at her. "You're young yet, Mr. Bernard. You don't know how it is being a father. It's like nothing else in the world. You worry… Oh, God, if she's been hurt—"

"I had a sister," Tally said quietly. "She gave me and André plenty of worry. I think I understand."

"Bless you."

Sim almost felt embarrassed for the man's sentimental gratitude. "We'd better get going if you're ready, Tal."

"Yes. Let's go."

She released Bryson and headed for the door. Sim gathered up his parcels and followed, Bryson at his heels. Pablo waited proudly beside Muérdago, Diablo and a third horse, having saddled them all himself.

"Can I come?" he asked, already braced for disappointment.

"Not this time, Pablo." Tally ruffled his hair. "You're old enough to help your father in the corral. He'll need you with Sim and me gone."

Pablo sighed, accepting his fate, and joined Miriam on the wagon with Dolores.

"You be careful!" Miriam called.

Tally tipped her hat, nodded to Bryson and kicked Muérdago into a lope toward the north road, leading the spare mount. Sim caught up with her once they were outside the *bosque*.

"Sister?" he asked. "You never mentioned that before."

"I wanted to give Bryson some words of comfort," she said. "I could tell how alone he felt."

"I'd say you were talking about yourself, except André wouldn't have wasted much worry on anything but his own wants."

Tally's fists tightened on the reins. "How can you say that about a man you never knew?"

Sim couldn't explain. He'd heard Eli's talk and listened to his own feelings. That was enough for him.

"Maybe it was your ma who worried," he said, thinking of the old-fashioned white dress in Tally's trunk.

"Most mothers do."

She wasn't eager to discuss the subject. Neither was he. They rode in silence through the valley and around the north end of the Liebres Mountains. Alternating between a walk and a lope, they made twenty miles before it got too dark to continue. They camped near Whitewater Draw, hobbled the horses and lay side by side, not touching, until dawn.

Sim figured that Tally didn't sleep much, worried as she must be over Beth; he didn't even close his eyes. He was still thinking about the map and what he had to do as soon as they got back to Cold Creek. And he kept remembering the feel of Tally's white gown, sliding and rustling through his fingers. It felt as if that dress was a barrier between him and the woman at his side.

She didn't expect marriage. She'd made it clear that she hadn't enjoyed the one she'd had. She cherished her freedom. So why did that damned wedding gown make him afraid to touch her?

You would have married Esperanza, because that was the only way to have her. Is Tally so cheap in your eyes?

He brooded on such thoughts as he readied the horses, but it wasn't any use. He'd never been able to think his way out of a problem. Tally respected his mood and did her part without unnecessary conversation, reminding him what a rare and precious female she was.

They arrived in Tombstone a little before noon. Tally took the horses to a reputable livery stable, while Sim began making the rounds of the Allen Street saloons. At the third stop he heard a rumor about some rough-looking young cowboy riding into town with a pretty girl trailing after him.

Sim hunted down a better description of the cowboy, and his heart started galloping in his chest like a band of spooked mustangs. The gambler, who went on to describe the girl in lascivious and disrespectful terms, found himself lying on the floor with a broken nose while Sim charged out the swinging doors.

He forgot he was supposed to meet Tally at the Oriental Saloon. He forgot everything except that he was the one who'd told Caleb Beth's name and aroused the outlaw's interest by warning him away from the girl. Caleb might have gone after Beth Bryson because he was curious or bored, or because he wanted to spit in Sim's eye. Or he could mean to use her in his bid to get the map, as insurance for Sim's honesty.

The reasons didn't matter. Sim let his wolf senses out to track, focusing on Beth but ready for Caleb if he turned up first. The scent trail led Sim to a small and not very grand saloon off the main street. Whores with painted faces and barely concealed tits hung over the rickety balcony, shouting crude invitations. Sim walked through a cloud of cheap perfume and into another of thick cigar and cigarette smoke.

He banged his hand on the pitted bar counter. The bartender answered his summons with unconcealed indifference.

"What'll it be?" he asked.

"There's a girl here. She's young, dark-haired, a few inches over five feet—"

"You askin' about one of our soiled doves?" the bartender asked. "Got 'em for every taste, and cheap, too. You like 'em young—"

Sim grabbed him by the collar. "Listen to me carefully. I want to know where this girl is. She arrived in the last few days, maybe even last night. The man who brought her here is named Caleb Smith."

The bartender swallowed against Sim's grip. "Don't reckon I know—"

Sim flipped his coat away from his gun. "Six feet, wheaten hair, a man the ladies would take a second look at." He leaned in a little closer, not bothering to raise his voice. "You wouldn't want to get on his bad side, but he's a sweet young thing compared to me."

"I…I seen that man. He took a room for several days. I'll have to check the register."

Sim released the bartender, pushing him into the row of bottles behind him. By now he and his friend had an audience, a crowd of gamblers and drunks watching the exchange with growing curiosity.

"You don't need no register in a place like this," Sim said. "Where is the girl?"

The bartender rubbed his neck. "Upstairs. Third room to the left." He tried to smile. "You'll need a key—"

"No, I won't." Sim turned and made for the stairs. Men scrambled out of his way. He reached the landing and approached the third door to the left.

Caleb and Beth were inside. He smelled their natural scents, more of the cheap perfume, sweat and fear and arousal.

He drew back his boot and kicked in the door.

Caleb sprang up from the bed, gun in hand. Beth cowered against the headboard. She was dressed in a tart's abbreviated gown, one breast bare and dark hair disheveled. Her skirts were up around her knees, revealing silk stockings and bright red garters. She was scared to death.

"Sim," she whispered.

"Sim," Caleb said. He twirled his gun, grinning broadly. "You do have a way of making an entrance."

Sim didn't bother to uncover his pistol. He kicked the door closed behind him. "You shouldn't have done this, Caleb."

"Why not?" He smirked. "Just because you warned me off her? You know me better than that."

"I ain't interested in your reasons. There's only one thing I want to know."

"And what would that be, old friend?"

"Whether or not you've ruined Miss Bryson. Because if you've touched her, amigo, I'll have to kill you."

CHAPTER SEVENTEEN

CALEB WATCHED Sim's eyes. He'd known since he was a kid that you always watched the eyes to know what a man would do next.

Sim wasn't bluffing. He was as mad as Caleb had ever seen him, and that meant Beth Bryson meant a lot more to him than he'd let on before. Just like Caleb had hoped.

Caleb held up his free hand and slowly holstered his gun. "Easy, boy," he said. "This filly ain't broke yet." He glanced at Beth. "I don't reckon that condition will last too much longer."

Sim bared his teeth. "Move to the other side of the room, Caleb. Now."

Caleb obeyed, taking his time about it. Sim approached the bed. Beth shrank from him.

"It's all right now, missy," Sim said with something like gentleness in his voice. "Are you hurt?"

"No." She looked at Caleb and closed her eyes. "I'm all right."

"Good."

"What'd you think I'd do to her?" Caleb complained. "I never hated women the way you did."

"And I never killed one," Sim said.

"Now why would I do anything like that to such a pretty thing?"

Sim leaned against the bedstead, close enough to grab Beth if he had a mind to. Caleb let him think he had the upper hand.

"How long have you been back in Arizona?" Sim asked.

"A week or so. Long enough to renew my acquaintance with this pretty señorita."

"You met her before."

"Right after we talked about her, remember? I rode up north and asked around, went out to the Bryson place and made introductions all right and proper. Mrs. Bryson liked me, especially since I was the son of a well-off rancher in the north Valley." He smacked his lips. "Mighty hospitable people, them Brysons."

Sim's eyes gleamed in the room's dim light. "Why, Caleb?"

"You seemed eager that I stay away from her as well as your folks at Cold Creek. You aroused my curiosity, old friend. And I thought maybe someone like her would come in handy if you ever decided to go back on our agreement."

"You mean you'd use her as a hostage if I didn't come up with the map."

Caleb laughed. "You didn't give me too much confidence, putting me off the way you did. I trusted you, and what do I hear but that you go help Mrs.…'Miss' Bernard round up some Mexican cattle. I couldn't help but wonder where that map was, and why you hadn't been in contact with me."

Sim was good at hiding his thoughts, but Caleb had ridden with him too long not to know what he was thinking right now. "If you were so suspicious of me," Sim said, "why didn't you go to Cold Creek while I was away?"

"And miss seeing my good old compañero again?" He flicked a speck of dirt off his waistcoat. "I wanted to give you—what do they call it?—the benefit of the doubt one more time. I figured if you didn't find out I was back and come looking for me, I'd pay Cold Creek another visit very soon. But you saved me the trouble."

"Now I'm here, what in hell makes you think you can keep this girl?"

"But she wants to stay with me…don't you, sweetheart?" He gave Beth the long, caressing gaze that had won her over at their first meeting two months ago. "She fell in love with me first time we laid eyes on each other. She was eager to get away from her mama and papa, and when I came back through—why, I gave her just the chance she wanted."

Sim didn't look at Beth. "You convinced her to run off with you. What did you promise, Caleb? Marriage?"

"Hell, no. She didn't ask. She talked all about freedom and doing as she pleased, just like a man. She couldn't wait to get here to the big city. You think she didn't agree to put on those nice clothes I bought her?"

"You dressed her like a whore."

"What d'you call a woman who gives herself to a man without the bonds of holy wedlock?"

One minute Caleb was leaning on the soiled wallpaper and the next he was crashing to the floor at the end of Sim's fist. He snapped out his gun and aimed at Sim's heart. Sim barely paused in his advance. Caleb turned the gun on Beth.

Sim stopped. Caleb scrambled to his feet.

"That's right. You just think on what you're going to do next, amigo." He kept the gun pointed at Beth and sat on the nearest chair, rubbing his throbbing jaw. He wasn't amused any longer.

"You tell him the truth now, little girl," he said to Beth. "You came willing, didn't you?"

"Yes," she whispered.

"She'd say anything now," Sim said.

"It's true," Beth said, her voice trembling oh-so-pitifully. "I did want to get away. I thought Caleb… I thought I loved him. I thought I—" A tear spilled over her cheek. "It was different. It was exciting, to be with him."

"Did you want to lie with him?"

Caleb regained some of his good humor when he heard the weakness in Sim's question. Hell, Kavanagh actually had some stake in this girl's "honor." He was afraid what she would say, that she would prove to be no better than his mother. Caleb waited curiously to see if Beth would answer.

The girl surprised him. "I thought I did," she said. "But I changed my mind." She dared to look at Caleb, and her stare burned with futile defiance. "I said no. He didn't listen."

Sim's shoulders sagged, betraying his relief. "She ain't no whore, Caleb. She's got spirit. She deserves a lot better than you."

Caleb put his hand to his heart. "You wound me, brother." But it was strange how his heart was hard just like they said in stories, a thing made out of stone instead of living flesh. "Don't matter now what she deserves or what she wants. She's staying with me until you turn the map over."

"And if there is no map?"

Caleb felt a little sick even though the room was cool and he'd hardly drunk at all that morning. "You saying there isn't?"

"I have information, but you ain't getting it until the girl's out of this place and safe."

"You think I'm a fool, amigo? Course you do." He took a step toward the bed. "I think you've got the map, or you know where to find the treasure. You wouldn't have told me as much as you have if you thought you could get rid of me instead."

Sim looked tempted to spit. He didn't. "I don't give a damn about the treasure."

Caleb had no compunctions about spitting. "Sure you don't. You'll build that nice little ranch for your Esperanza out of thin air—"

"I'm through with Esperanza. I don't need the money."

"Hell, Sim, when we ran together, I was always sure you were the soul of honesty—"

"I ain't lying." Sim's gray stare was direct, unflinching. "I broke it off with her."

"You broke it off…or *she* did?"

"She has her own life now."

"And you have—" He grinned at Beth. "Which is it, the girl or Tally Bernard? Or both?"

"I don't need that money no more. That's all you need to know."

Caleb's fingers trembled on the gun. He wanted to shoot something—someone—to get rid of this sick feeling in his gut. "There ain't a man in the world who don't want to be rich, and that includes you. You chose to live by cheatin' and thievin' rather than honest labor, just like me. Esperanza was only an excuse."

"You're wrong, Caleb. You can have whatever we find, and I won't take a red cent."

"What is this?" Caleb banged his fist against the wall, scuffing the wallpaper. "You think you're ready to settle down and reform? You think you're better than me?"

Sim's silence answered for him. Suddenly Caleb was remembering all the good times they'd shared, when they were both kids with nothing to lose. Nothing stood in the way of what they wanted then—not women, not the law, not stupid sentimental crap about honor and compassion.

"We could go back," he said, holding out his free hand. "We could go back and take up where we left off. You and me, Sim."

Sim sighed and shook his head. "That's over, Caleb. You know why."

Caleb knew, and he hated Sim for reminding him. "You would have done the same," he spat. "They had you staked out in the desert, and you was as good as dead." His voice rose out of his control. "I thought you *was* dead, Sim. It wouldn't have done you no good for me to die, too."

"Your fancy talk scared Josie, and that's why she betrayed us. But you got away. And I didn't die."

Caleb pressed his hand to his temple. "You should have died. Any normal man would've. And I got revenge for you, Sim. I hunted that bitch down and killed her."

Sim half closed his eyes. "Do you want me to thank you, Caleb?"

"I would have killed all of them if I could've found 'em."

"You didn't have to." Stark pain burned in Sim's eyes, melting the steel into sorrow. "I ain't the man I was. That's why I'm telling you I know where to find the treasure, and I'll give it to you if you leave the Territory for good."

"Where is it?"

"I got the information from André. I'll have to take you there."

"So you can get me alone and kill me?"

"You can have my guns and knives and tie me up if you have to. But we ain't leaving this room until the girl goes free."

"And I told you, she's staying with me."

"No." Sim started around the bed, walking directly into the muzzle of Caleb's gun. "You won't shoot me, Caleb. You won't do it because you lose the treasure if I'm dead."

"I can get André to talk—"

"It took me months, and you wouldn't last a day before you killed him. Give me the gun, Caleb."

Caleb swung the gun back toward Beth, but Sim was in the way. He'd done it on purpose. He thought Caleb was weak—too weak to do anything but take orders like some damned slave.

Sim saw his hesitation. He saw everything. When they were young, Caleb had taken comfort in knowing someone in the world understood him. But later, not long before Josie betrayed them to Hannity's gang, he'd started to feel those gray eyes looking at him with judgment and contempt....

His fingers slackened. In a blinding motion Sim grabbed for the gun. Caleb stumbled back toward the window, banging into the half-open pane. He whistled sharply.

"Nice try, *compañero*," he said. His laughter came out like a donkey's bray. "You won't be doing that again. I got friends who'll be showing up just about any minute now."

Sim cocked his head as if in amusement. "You always did need help, didn't you? You couldn't stand up to your enemies on your own two feet. Never found the guts to confront your father when he beat your mama and spent all his money on them pretty ladies. Couldn't even face your ma with all her talk of hellfire and sin."

"Shut up."

Sim strolled toward him. "You and me, Caleb. We fight for the girl. If I win, you let her go and I show you the treasure. You win, and you can do whatever you want with us. I won't put up a fight."

"I have you anyway. Why should I agree?"

"To prove to both of us that you're not so scared of me that you're about to piss your pants."

Caleb leveled his gun at Sim's forehead. "Scared of you? What the hell are you talking about?"

"You weren't afraid of me in the beginning. What changed, Caleb?"

"You lying bastard."

"Maybe it was after that job in Crockett, when you killed that kid who couldn't even hold his gun straight. Or up in Lincoln Juntas, where we lost two men because you wanted to make yourself look like a fearless outlaw from one of them dime novels. That's when I started asking myself questions about the way you worked things."

Caleb glanced at Beth, who was pretending not to listen. But she heard, all right. She heard.

"You made sure you were never the one who got hurt," Sim went on, relentless. "People had a way of listening to you even when you didn't have much to say, so you got away with it. You hated your daddy, but you ended up just like him, fooling everyone with your smile and big talk."

"*Sim—*"

"You had dreams, and I didn't. That's why we stayed together so long, because you had a purpose, and that was what I needed."

"That's right," Caleb snarled. "I was the one who made all the plans. You would have let yourself be killed a hundred times if I hadn't given you a reason to live."

"That was true once, Caleb. We both hated the world, only I hated myself more. Then I started to doubt our friendship, and I guess you saw it. You wondered what I'd do if I ever stopped being your friend. I had to be willing to follow your orders or I might start getting dangerous. You'd double-cross your men if it suited you. You figured I'd do the same to my partner, sooner or later. I just didn't understand until you left me to die how often I did the hard work so you wouldn't have to risk your neck."

"I was as close to kin as you ever had in this world. You needed me, but I never needed you."

"The difference between us, amigo, is that you couldn't stand being alone. You wouldn't have stolen your first beef if you didn't have me or someone else to protect your back and take any bullet coming your way." He smiled. "You've always been a coward, Caleb. You still are."

"I'll kill you for that, Sim. I swear I will. And then I'll make the girl suffer—"

The door burst open. Two men came in, probably the toughest hombres in Caleb's current gang. They took up positions to either side of Sim, weapons ready.

Caleb grinned. "Now, *cabrón.* I'll tell you how it's going to be. You tell me everything you heard from André, draw me the map and translate them words, right here in this room. And then you can decide whether you or the girl dies today."

Sim's smile widened, exposing his white teeth. "The girl leaves first, out of this room and this saloon."

Caleb signaled to one of the men, who crossed to the bed and pressed the muzzle of his pistol to Beth's temple. The girl gasped and squeezed her eyes shut.

"You start talking now, or you'll get a real pretty look at the insides of the lady's head."

Silence sucked all the air out of the room. Caleb knew he'd won. Sim had frozen, his face expressionless. Defeated.

"Get down on your knees," Caleb ordered.

Sim stared at him. Slowly he knelt, hands out at his sides. Caleb circled him, twirling the gun around and around his finger.

"Me scared? Of *you?*" Caleb asked. "You were fast and strong and good with a gun, like you said. You had the book-learning from the whores, but I was smarter. I started to doubt you when I saw that softness you could never get rid of. I knew it would betray me someday. Now it's betrayed *you.* I'll still have the girl, and we'll find out who's the coward."

"Yes," Sim said without emotion. "I think we will."

Caleb aimed a kick at Sim's belly with the full weight of his body behind it. The blow never landed. Sim caught Caleb's boot, twisted, and flung Caleb against the wall. Flashes of light dazzled Caleb's eyes, and he suffered a wave of dizziness that made him think he saw Sim knock the two men aside with one swipe of his hand.

But it wasn't an illusion. His men were down, and Sim was stripping off his clothes like a madman. Black smoke filled the room. A few seconds later Sim was gone and a wolf crouched in the dissipating cloud. Beth whimpered from the bed.

Caleb looked into the wolf's eyes and saw that peculiar tone of icy gray he'd observed in only a single face. Gray eyes filled with hate. He dared to glance in Beth's direction. Her blatant terror told him what his mind didn't want to believe.

One of the men on the floor swore in foul Spanish and scrambled crabwise toward the door. He managed to pull it open and ran. The wolf didn't stop him. It advanced on Caleb, lips drawn back from white teeth.

"Sim," Caleb whispered.

The wolf laughed without a sound. *You had reason to be afraid of me,* the laugh said. *I am your death.*

Hot liquid soaked the seat of Caleb's britches. That minor shock did what the greater one could not. He shot at the wolf. Sim leaped straight up above the bullet, turned in midair and fell on Caleb. Powerful jaws seized the gun and crushed it, along with two of Caleb's fingers. Caleb screamed.

Black smoke. The stench of urine. Hot skin pressed on Caleb's throat. He choked and opened his eyes. Sim had become human again, and he held Caleb pinned to the wall like a rabbit ripe for butchering.

"Do you know what I am?" Sim asked.

Caleb could barely breathe, but he knew he must answer. "A demon," he said. "A demon from hell."

"That's right. I sold my soul, and I got this in return." He laughed, and his breath smelled like sulphur. "Your ma was right, Caleb. You're damned. I could have killed you any time since you came to Cold Creek, but I didn't. I gave you your chance for old times' sake. You threw it away."

Tears ran down Caleb's face, and he heard childlike sobs coming from his own chest. "Don't hurt me," he begged. "I don't want to die."

Sim squeezed, and Caleb's vision began to go dark.

"No," a faraway voice called. "No, please!"

The pressure on Caleb neck eased just enough for him to fill his lungs with precious air. Sim's face wavered before his eyes. Images of hellfire spun frantically through his head.

I don't want to die. God, I don't want to die....

"Don't kill him," Beth pleaded. "Not because of me."

Sim growled. He turned his head toward the door. Caleb found that he could still speak.

"I'll go away," he said hoarsely. "You'll never...see me again."

Abruptly Sim released him and got to his feet. He dressed swiftly, not even bothering to keep an eye on Caleb. When he'd finished, he took Beth by the arm and led her to the door. She looked back, tears streaking the paint on her face.

Then Caleb was alone except for the other man Sim had dispatched so easily. He groaned. Still alive. Caleb felt his throat, too weak to stand. After a while something heavy thumped against the door.

They were locking him in. It wasn't a reprieve; that monster from hell would be back to finish what he'd started.

Caleb felt his way up the wall. Light and dark whirled around inside his skull. He half walked, half crawled to the window. It was open just enough. Using all his strength, he pushed his body through the narrow opening, hung suspended two stories above the street and let himself fall.

SIM SHOVED THE DRESSER against Caleb's door and returned to the unoccupied room where he'd left Beth. She crouched in the farthest corner, weeping quietly. Sim ground his teeth and kept his distance.

"I know it's been hard," he said. "What Caleb did, and now

me—" He ran his hands through his hair in helpless frustration. "Tally's here in town. I'll go fetch her."

"No!" Beth looked up, smudging the black stuff around her eyes with the palms of her hands. "Please don't leave me alone."

It was a miracle that she wanted him to stick around after what she'd seen. He didn't know whether to be grateful or exasperated.

"Caleb won't hurt you again," he said. "He *is* a coward, and he's stuck in that room thinking about how close he came to dying."

She stared at him with wide, tearstained eyes. "You really did…turn into a wolf, didn't you?"

Hell, she was a tough one. Almost as tough as Tally. "Are you scared of me?"

"I don't know." She shook her head, tossing disheveled hair. "No," she said slowly, as if she surprised herself. "I don't believe you're any kind of demon. You wouldn't hurt me. It's just a little…hard to believe."

Sim admired Beth and hated Caleb more with every word the girl spoke. "There was a time when I had just as much trouble believing it as you."

Curiosity replaced the remnants of fear on Beth's face. "Have you always been this way?"

"I think I was born to it." He sighed. "Can you keep a secret?"

She thrust her fingers in the folds of her skirt. "A lot of people wouldn't understand, would they?"

"Not too many know what I am. Right now it's you, Tally and Caleb, and pretty soon it'll only be you and Tally."

"You're going to kill Caleb."

"Ain't that what he deserves?"

She crept away from the wall. "I heard what you said to him. If he's so bad, the sheriff will take him. I just don't want—" She took a deep, shuddering breath. "It was my fault. I should never have gone with him."

Sim cursed, bit back a stream of profanity and took the girl in his arms. She clung to him and buried her face into his shoulder. She was trembling so violently that it seemed she would break right apart if he didn't hold her together.

"You listen," he said, stroking her hair. "No one is ever going to find out what happened to you. I promise. The men in this place will keep their mouths shut. It'll be like it never happened."

She clamped her fingers around the front of his coat. "I just want to go home. Father will be furious. And Mother—"

"They just want you back," he said. "You'll be all right, Beth." He stepped away, tore off a piece of sheet from the bed and gave it to her. "Clean yourself up. Tally's coming."

She sniffled and pressed the cloth to her face. "How can you—"

Sim walked to the door and opened it. Tally stood staring at the dresser blocking the hall several rooms down. She turned and saw Sim.

"She's in here," Sim said.

"Where have you been?" Tally demanded. "I've been looking everywhere for—"

"I found Caleb," he said. "Beth was with him. I got to her in time."

Tally blanched. "Where is Caleb now?"

"In that room. You need to see to the girl. I'll take care of the rest."

She rushed by him, squeezing his arm as she passed. The door closed. Sim paused for a moment, listening to the soothing murmur of Tally's voice, and then dragged the dresser away from Caleb's temporary prison.

Caleb wasn't there. His *compañero* had regained consciousness and cowered against the bedstead, babbling incoherently.

Sim glanced at the half-open window and knew what Caleb had done. He looked out at the street below. No Caleb. He had probably broken something in a fall like that, so it wasn't likely he'd gone far.

Caleb's man was crawling toward the door, trying for escape. Sim planted his boot in front of the hombre's face.

"No," the man whimpered. "No, no, no…"

"I won't kill you," Sim said. "If you do something for me. But if you don't, I'll hunt you down and tear out your throat."

The man collapsed to the soiled carpet. "Anything. Anything you say."

"Good. I want you to ride back to Caleb's band and tell them what you saw here today. Some of 'em won't believe you. I don't care. But you make sure every man knows that Caleb's my blood enemy, and if he survives this day, anyone who rides with him will share his fate."

The man nodded wildly. Sim hauled him to his feet. "Now go," he said. "Caleb Smith is cursed, and so is any man who rides with him."

Apparently the man believed in curses. He fled at a limping run, nearly falling down the stairs. Sim followed at a more leisurely pace. Half the customers who'd been in the saloon when Sim arrived had left, figuring the ungodly ruckus from the second floor meant trouble. The stubborn remnant stared at Sim as he approached the bar.

"What…what do you want?" the bartender asked in a faint voice.

Sim dropped a handful of coins on the bar. "For the room and damages." He smiled. "What did you hear?"

"Nothing. I ain't heard nothing."

"You didn't happen to call the law?"

"No, mister. We don't want no trouble."

"I took care of your trouble for you." Sim turned and leaned his back against the counter. "What about you boys? You the curious types?"

A couple of the men opened their mouths. None spoke. The rest returned to their cards and drinks with alacrity.

"That's what I like about this town," Sim said. "Everyone minds their own business. Folks know how to be discreet." He tossed another coin on the bar. "Drinks for the room, bartender. You have a back door to this establishment?"

"Yessir."

"You take some decent female clothes—I said decent—up to the room at the top of the stairs. You do it personally, and you knock first. Then you escort the lady and the gentleman in the room to that back door and forget you ever saw them."

"Whatever you want."

Sim nodded and strolled out the saloon doors. The alley was empty except for a couple of cowboys, who took one look at Sim's face and beat a hasty retreat.

Allen Street held its usual crowd of miners, shopkeepers and cowmen. Sim walked around the corner to the stretch of dust where Caleb would have fallen. His scent was strong, but others overlaid it—men who'd stopped in the same place and lingered for several minutes.

Sim tracked the mingled spoor to a doctor's storefront. The doctor willingly reported that a man had been brought to him—a young man who'd fallen from a saloon window—but when the physician had stepped out of the room, the young man had disappeared. His injuries had included two severed fingers, which the doctor had bandaged, severe bruising around his neck and arms, and an ankle either broken or badly sprained.

A little more tracking and asking around told Sim what he needed to know. Someone had stolen a horse from a popular livery stable and apparently lit out of town like the devil was hard at his heels. A posse was gathering to hunt him down, but Sim doubted they would find the thief. Caleb wanted too badly to survive. He would ride for the border, killing his horse if he had to, and he wouldn't be back.

Sim went back to the saloon, weary and foul-tempered. The bartender was no longer behind his counter. The whores Sim passed on the stairs shrank from him, and one of them crossed herself as if she thought she still had a shot at heaven.

TALLY ANSWERED THE KNOCK on the door at the first rap, hoping that Sim had returned. She quickly concealed her disappointment from the woman who stood before her.

"Can I help you, ma'am?" she said, touching the brim of her hat.

The woman laughed, her voice grating with cynical humor. Her profession was obvious by the clothes she wore, but she still retained a measure of beauty, even though no amount of paint could conceal the lines and creases of encroaching middle age. Her figure was lush and firm for an experienced prostitute, and she obviously took pains to show it off.

"Ma'am," the woman repeated. "I haven't heard that in dogs' years. I'm Lisa, and Frank sent me up with these." She thrust a bundle of fabric at Tally. "Decent clothes for the *lady.*"

Tally took the bundle and hugged it to her chest. Sim must have arranged for the clothing; she blessed him for thinking of the simple necessities. She hadn't been able to leave Beth long enough to find out what else he'd been doing, but she hadn't heard gunshots or the sounds of violence from the room down the hall.

She hated Caleb Smith as much as she'd ever hated any man, but if Sim killed him and the law got involved…

Lisa leaned sideways, trying to see into the room. Tally

blocked her view. "Thank you, Lisa," she said, pulling a coin from her waistcoat pocket.

"Ain't you the gentleman," Lisa said with a sly smile, dropping the coin down the cleavage of her bodice. She reached out and rubbed his arm. "We don't get your kind very often. Sure you don't need any help in there?"

Tally tried to close the door. Lisa wedged her high-heeled boot in the crack. The lines in her face deepened in a frown.

"I don't know what's been going on up here," she said, "but this is my place as much as it is Frank's. If he let some new girl come in without my say-so…"

"It was a mistake," Tally said. "The girl was kidnapped."

"Damn that man." Lisa chewed her lower lip. Something in the gesture caught Tally's attention, but she was too distracted to follow the nagging thought. She had to get Beth safely out of this place without anyone else seeing her.

"Tally?"

Beth's voice still held a quiver of uncertainty. Lisa stared into the dimness beyond Tally's shoulder. Her seductive expression hardened into calculation just before she met Tally's gaze with a simpering smile.

"Well," she said, "I wish you the best of luck, Mr.—"

"Same to you, ma'am." Tally tipped her hat again and closed the door in Lisa's face.

"Is everything all right?" Beth asked.

Tally shook out the dress Lisa had delivered. "We have some fresh clothing for you," she said, putting the aging prostitute from her mind. "We'll leave as soon as Sim comes back."

"What do you think he's going to do to Caleb?"

"I don't know. After what Caleb has done—"

"It's my fault," Beth whispered.

"Never say that." Tally took the girl's shoulders and gave her a little shake. "You made a mistake, but Caleb is a cheat, a liar and a murderer." She looked away. "I hope Sim leaves him to the law."

"I didn't love him," Beth said, shamefaced. "I just fooled myself enough to go with him when he came for me."

Tally knew there was much more to the story of how Caleb Smith and Beth Bryson had become acquainted, but that could wait. A board creaked on the landing outside, and Tally prepared to fend off another visitor.

"It's me," Sim said through the flimsy wood.

"Just a moment." Tally offered up a brief prayer and helped Beth out of her ugly costume and into the plain dress. The fancy half boots Caleb had given her would have to suffice as shoes for the time being. Tally pinned up Beth's hair, untied the kerchief from around her own neck and arranged it over the girl's head in place of a hat.

She opened the door. Her gaze locked with Sim's.

"The girl all right?" he asked.

"As well as can be expected. What about Caleb?"

"He's alive." He clenched his fists as if he hated admitting what he regarded as a failure. "I showed him what I can do, what I'll do to him if he ever comes back. He jumped out of the window rather than face me again. He stole a horse and has a posse on his tail."

The knots in Tally's muscles gave way. "You did the right thing, Sim."

Sim pressed his lips into a grim, narrow line. "You ready to go home?"

"Oh, yes." She took his fists in her hands and uncurled each of his fingers one by one. "Let's go home."

CHAPTER EIGHTEEN

THE SECOND REUNION of father and daughter was even more joyful than the first. Beth was flushed with embarrassment, but when she saw that her papa was eager to forgive her, she fell into his arms and became his little girl again.

Tally gave the Brysons the privacy of her room while she, Eli, Miriam and Sim held council in the parlor. Between the two of them, Tally and Sim filled in the important details of their visit to Tombstone—all save those involving Sim's unique abilities and anything that might further humiliate Beth.

"It's a pity the Brysons won't likely be so hospitable to strangers after this," Miriam commented. "He's a wicked man, that Caleb Smith."

"You sure he's gone for good?" Eli asked Sim.

"He's a coward," Sim said, leaning back in his chair until it protested the abuse. "He used the girl because he was mad at me for driving him away from Cold Creek. He knows I'll kill him next time we meet."

Eli shook his head. "You're right about his cowardice. Still, if it'd been me—"

"You wouldn't have done any different," Miriam said, laying a hand on Eli's rigid arm. "Leave Caleb's judgment to God." She smiled at Sim. "I'm right proud of you, Simeon Kavanagh."

"That's a mighty heady reward, Miss Miriam."

"Best you not forget it," Eli said. But Tally noticed that he regarded Sim with more approval than dislike, and that was enough to make the victory complete.

Beth and her father joined the folk of Cold Creek for a hearty supper, though Beth kept her eyes on her plate. Tally found a chance to speak to Bryson alone, reassuring him that Beth had escaped the kind of ruin parents feared. Bryson was absurdly grateful. Tally had never felt so much a fraud as she did then.

That night, lying in her bed waiting for Sim, she came to a decision. It was time to end the deception. Oh, not all at once; she wasn't ready to announce to Sim, let alone the world, what she'd done in New Orleans. That would come eventually. But tomorrow morning she would tell Bryson what Beth already knew—Tal Bernard was a woman. Her secret would be a secret no more.

There was a second part to her resolve, one she hardly dared to think about. If she was to stop living in hiding, in fear of the past, she had to face the future. She and Sim had no future as they were now, sharing a bed without commitment or thought of the children that might come of their loving.

Sim had been prepared to marry Esperanza in order to make a new beginning. Maybe he needed time to get over her. But he'd called Cold Creek home, and that meant more to Tally than a hundred declarations of love. As soon as she found the courage to admit the mistakes she'd made—to come clean with Sim as he had to her—she would bring up the subject that terrified them both. And she wouldn't back down until she had a firm answer.

She didn't hear Sim enter the room. Her face was pressed to the pillow to muffle her weeping, but she felt Sim's touch on her hair and turned into his arms. For a long time he simply held her the way she wanted to be held, his big hands rubbing her back in a ceaseless, soothing motion.

"I'm sorry," she said, patting at his chest. "I got your shirt all wet."

He chuckled. Sim had never done that before; he laughed mockingly at himself or others, but this warm, indulgent sound was something new.

"This shirt has seen worse," he said. He wiped tears from her cheeks with his thumbs and lifted her chin. "What is it, Tally? What's bothering you?"

"Nothing. I'm just relieved about Beth." She sniffed, and Sim magically produced a worn but clean handkerchief. She noticed the threadbare embroidery before she used it.

"S.W.K." she read. "Your initials." She smoothed the handkerchief flat on the bed. "Who made this for you, Sim?"

"My mother."

His voice was flat, discouraging further questions. But Tally had one more. "What does the *W* stand for? Surely not *wolf*."

He snorted. "That would be better than the original."

"Which is?"

"Wartrace." He gave her a warning glance. "Name of a small town in Tennessee, where…where my ma lived for a while."

Tally ran her thumb over the uneven stitches. "You never talk about your mother."

"I don't aim to start now." When she tried to return the handkerchief, he folded her fingers around it. "You keep it."

"But, Sim—"

"Keep it for me."

She opened her fingers, uncrumpled the cloth and folded it again. "I'll keep it, Sim. But you'll want it back someday."

"I doubt it." He rose to leave.

"Wait. I've made a decision, Sim. I'm going to tell Bryson who I really am."

"That's fine. When are you going to tell me?"

She shivered. *Too soon.* "We women have to keep some secrets," she said lightly. She pulled him down onto the bed beside her, and they didn't do any more talking.

TALLY WAS UP before dawn. Sim had already left, but she'd heard wolves howling in the night and thought she knew where he'd gone. She had so much to learn about him, but she would have plenty of time to do it. She was going to make sure of that.

For breakfast she put on the gown she'd worn for Beth at her first visit. Bryson stared, flushed, and then hastily moved to pull back her chair. Sim looked thoughtful and amused. Eli raised a brow. The others got over their surprise quickly and dug into Miriam's offering with their usual enthusiasm.

"I'm sorry I deceived you," Beth said to Bryson when he and she were alone in the parlor. "I had my reasons for disguising myself, but I'll understand if you prefer I don't see Beth again."

Bryson shifted awkwardly in the too-small parlor chair. "Please, Miss Bernard. I'm the last man to judge you after what you did for my girl. This can be rough country for a woman." He twisted his hands together between his knees. "'Course I'll have to break it to Ida gently—she'll be upset that she didn't figure it out for herself."

"Beth did. That was why she came to Cold Creek before."

"She wanted to be like you."

Tally nodded, grateful for Bryson's discernment and tolerance. "It was never my intention to influence her in any way. I tried to explain the need for patience, but she envied what she saw as my freedom."

"Don't blame yourself, Miss Bernard. I just didn't see how lonely she was."

"Beth is an exceptional girl." Tally hesitated, aware that she might venture too far. "She's very young and has a great deal to learn. But she's faced a difficult situation and survived it. She may never be completely happy in the kind of life most women accept as natural. Still, as long as she feels she has some say in her future, I think she'll be more sensible from now on."

"I guess I need to talk to her more often. And listen."

"You're a very good man, Mr. Bryson. Beth is lucky to have you."

Miriam appeared in the doorway. "Coffee, Mr. Bryson? Miss Tally?"

"Thank you, Miriam," Tally said. She rose, and Bryson rose with her. "I wanted to tell you about myself, Mr. Bryson, because I won't be masquerading any longer. It appears that my brother may never recover, but I'll be homesteading Cold Creek under my own name. I have very good help here, men I trust with my life. And I hope I also have your friendship."

"You do, Miss Bernard."

She held out her hand. Bryson took it, tempering his hearty grip with a limp touch appropriate for a lady. Tally squeezed his hand. He grinned.

Beth and her father left Cold Creek in remarkably high spirits. Beth rode a borrowed horse, talking shyly to her father, while he listened with real attention. Tally and Miriam waved until the Brysons were out of sight beyond the *bosque*.

"Well," Miriam said. "Maybe some good has come out of this after all."

"I think you're right." Tally smiled to herself and turned back toward the house, looking forward to removing the gown and putting on her comfortable work clothes. The men had finished up the branding, and she had to consult with Eli about paying Don Miguel's vaqueros and gathering provisions enough for their return to Sonora.

Miriam caught up with her. "I didn't get a chance to tell you until now, but a rider came by yesterday from Los Granates up the Valley."

Los Granates was one of the biggest outfits in Sulphur Spring Valley, established some years earlier and situated on Antelope Creek, northwest of Willcox along the Winchester Mountains. The Garnetts, who'd named their property to reflect the family name, had been successful well before serious ranchers had settled in the south Valley. They had both wealth and a reputation for fine hospitality.

"Why did he come, Miriam?" Tally asked.

"Read for yourself." She fished in her apron pocket and withdrew an envelope.

Tally opened it and pulled out the beautifully printed card inside. "It's an invitation," she said. "The Garnetts are giving a party to celebrate their son's return from back East with his new wife."

"Then they must be inviting just about everyone in Cochise and Graham counties. The rider said he had a lot of stops to make before he headed home."

Tally tapped the card on her fingertips. "They invited us to a party last year, but André declined. I'd do the same this time, except—"

"Except you're ready to become Miss Chantal Bernard again," Miriam finished.

The sound of her own name gave Tally pause. "I thought I was. But I haven't ridden much outside the boundaries of Cold Creek, even as a man. If there'll be so many guests... I'm not accustomed to... Oh, Miriam, I don't know what it's like to be a normal woman among ordinary people."

"You'll learn."

"What if they guess what I've been?"

"You're a lady, Tally, no matter what you think. That's what they'll see."

"If they knew, these honorable and upright citizens, they wouldn't want me within a thousand miles of their wives and daughters."

"Then they aren't worthy of you." Miriam cupped Tally's cheek. "There's not a one among them who hasn't made mistakes. You repented. You have a different life now."

"What about Sim? Aren't he and I living in sin?"

Miriam met Tally's gaze with compassion and utter certainty. "Not for long, *ma chérie*."

Tally looked away. "This invitation is addressed to André and Tal Bernard. I'll have to make up some story about Chantal and her sudden appearance.... More lies."

"You could go as Mrs. Meeker."

"That would be the worst lie of all. I was never that person, Miriam."

"And you were never Mademoiselle Champagne, either. You won't have to be anyone but yourself from now on."

Tally gave Miriam a quick, hard hug. "I love you, Miriam."

"There's a lot of that going round." Miriam returned her hug and grinned. "Who are you going to ask to escort you?"

Tally thought of André lying in his bed and tried not to dwell on the guilt that always hovered in the back of her mind like a buzzard waiting for something to die.

"I don't know if Sim will agree," she said. "He's not the most sociable type. And he—"

He also has a past he might not want discovered.

"Just ask him," Miriam said.

Tally took Miriam's advice. After a day of satisfying work getting the branded cattle settled in their new home, she prepared her speech and sat on the edge of the bed until full dark brought Sim to her room. She approached the subject directly, rushing ahead without letting him get a word in edgewise.

Even when she was finished, he didn't speak. He simply took off his clothes, joined her on the bed, and loved her tenderly and fiercely, almost making her forget that he hadn't given an answer. But the next morning, as she stretched herself awake, Sim walked into the room dressed in a gentleman's coat and trousers, silk waistcoat, white shirt with cravat and polished black boots.

She shot up in bed. "Sim! Where did you—"

He pulled at the tight stand collar and shuffled his feet like a little boy. "I thought I might need it for the wedding."

Tally's mouth went dry. "The wedding?"

"Miriam's wedding."

"Of course." Tally clapped her hands. "You're perfect, Sim—*très élégant.*"

"I never felt like such a fool." He rubbed his jaw. "I guess I'll need a shave, too. And a haircut."

"Federico cuts the children's hair beautifully."

Sim scowled at his feet. "When do we have to leave?"

"It will take two days in the spring wagon to get to Los Granates, so we'd go the day after tomorrow." She gazed at him, bursting with pride and love. "I know you might not find the party entirely comfortable, Sim. You've spent so much time alone—"

"Not so much lately," he said with a wry smile.

"—but if you feel there's any danger that…someone might know you from your earlier days…"

"You're asking if I'm a wanted man?" He ran his finger under his collar again. "I reckon I am, but not in this Territory. The local law has its own homegrown varmints to keep 'em busy. If they had anything on me, they would've picked me up in Tombstone. Or tried to."

She heard the slyness in his tone and shook her head. "You won't be giving them any cause to trouble you from now on, Mr. Kavanagh."

"You trust me to escort you like a real gentleman would," he said quietly. "I won't make you ashamed."

"I'm nervous, too," she said with a laugh. "It's been a long time since I've been to any sort of gathering like this."

"Then we'll just have to face the enemy together."

"Thank you," she whispered.

He shrugged out of the coat and draped it over the back of the chair. "Can't have you thinking I'm a coward, can I?"

If you only knew how cowardly I've been. But not much longer, Sim, that I promise. When we return, you'll know everything.

But there was something she could tell him right now, in a language he could understand.

"I love you, Sim."

His body came to perfect stillness. "Don't say that, Tally."

"I have to, because it's true."

He crushed the wool of his coat against the chair back. "What do you want me to say?"

"Nothing." She smiled as if his response were the most natural thing in the world. "I've never said that to any other man. I just wanted you to know."

"Tally—"

She put her finger to her lips. "I'll see you at breakfast."

He left, nearly colliding with the wall on his way out. Tally wasn't surprised when he didn't appear for the morning meal, but he showed up at supper and came to her room that night. He loved her with no regard to his own pleasure, giving her a response more eloquent than the words he couldn't speak.

Two days later, they left at dawn, Tally wearing an older dress appropriate for dusty travel and Sim in his regular clothes. Miriam had helped Tally bake a pair of rhubarb pies, carefully wrapped in a basket and tucked in the boot of the wagon along with Tally's good gown, her men's clothes and Sim's suit. Alongside the wagon rode Bart, who had cheerfully offered to act as chaperone and visit with the Los Granates cowhands during the party.

After some discussion, Tally and Sim had agreed that Tally should introduce Sim as an old friend of André's who had come from Texas to help run the ranch when André was hurt. She had recently arrived in the Territory to care for André, and her twin brother Tal—Talbot—had left on an extended trip to handle family business in the East.

Halfway to Los Granates, near Three Sisters Buttes southeast of Willcox, Tally and the men made camp for the night. When the sun rose, Tally combed and repinned her hair into an easy but very proper style that required little fuss. Sometime in the afternoon she would change into her good gown; she expected that they would reach Los Granates in the early evening just as the party was officially to begin, though the Garnetts would be expecting guests to arrive both early and late, according to the lengths of their journeys.

On the last leg of the trip she and the men began to encounter others on the way to the party, some in fancy carriages and others on horseback. Garnett land stretched as far as the eye could see. Tally threw a cloak over her head and shoulders to protect her gown from the rising dust. Sim sat self-consciously erect as they drove through the pillared gateway that marked the boundary of Los Granates.

Soon they came within sight of the first of many huge corrals holding specimens of the Garnetts' prize imported cattle and horses. Stables and outbuildings lined the road. Tally could hardly imagine running such a huge outfit, but at the moment, nothing seemed impossible.

The facade of Los Granates' big house was plain enough, though several times as large as Tally's house at Cold Creek. The adobe structure was built around a huge courtyard, its outer walls strung with paper flowers. Torches burned to light the way through the dusk. Music floated on the pleasant breeze.

Cowhands in their best attire came to take the spring wagon, and Bart joined them. Sim took the basket of pies in one hand and offered his other elbow to Tally. She curtsied, bringing a charming blush to his face, and accepted his escort to the courtyard entrance.

A Mexican girl in festive dress greeted them, indicating that they should follow her. The November evening was unusually warm, permitting an outdoor gathering. The courtyard was already filled with guests sipping wine or punch from crystal glasses; lamps lit the space as bright as day, and a pair of glass-paned French doors stood open from a main room of the house. A small band of musicians played chamber music as a background to light conversation. Some of the women were dressed in elaborate gowns more suited to a night at the opera in a city like New York, but others wore gowns much simpler than Tally's. Few men were even half as elegant as Sim.

Tally lifted her chin and smiled to her fellow guests as if she had every right to be among them, respectable and equal. She received a number of smiles in return, along with appreciative glances from the men. Sim's muscles tightened beneath his sleeve.

The salon behind the French doors was well furnished, though not extravagant. Tally thought that the Garnetts showed their good taste in recognizing that many of their guests were neither as rich nor well established as they were.

Serving men stood behind trestle tables laid out with silver platters of thin-sliced meats, cheeses and finger foods, while other servants dispensed drinks. Like the courtyard, the room swarmed with guests. The maid gestured Tally toward a beautifully carved Spanish-style table, heaped high with cakes, pies and other baked goods. Tally set her pies among the others and tucked the basket under the table.

She turned to see how Sim was dealing with the crowd, but she had no time to speak with him. A tall, cultured woman with graying hair advanced on Tally, her orchid-colored gown complete with a many-flounced train that swept the tiled floor behind her.

"Good evening," she said. "I am sorry to be so tardy in greeting you." She smiled at Sim, who removed his hat and clutched it to his chest. "I am Mrs. Garnett. Welcome to Los Granates."

"Good evening," Tally said. "I am Chantal Bernard of Cold Creek, and this is my escort, Simeon Kavanagh, a good friend of our family."

"Cold Creek. Of course—from the south of the Valley." Her cool green eyes took Tally's measure. "The long journey clearly hasn't harmed you, my dear."

Tally smiled and lowered her gaze. "I have a confession to make, Mrs. Garnett. I hope you'll forgive my impertinence. Your kind invitation was addressed to my brothers Talbot and André, but neither could be here tonight. I've come in their stead to represent the Bernards of Cold Creek."

"But how delightful. I had no idea the Bernards had a sister residing there, or we surely would have invited you, as well."

"I have only recently arrived in the Territory, Mrs. Garnett."

"Then you have come to our Valley at an excellent time. And Mr. Kavanagh, I am so glad you could join us."

Sim mumbled some response, and a gleam of speculation lit Mrs. Garnett's eyes. Tally hugged his arm. "I hope you don't mind that I brought one of our hands as an additional escort. He's gone to the bunkhouse, but I assure you he won't be any trouble."

"No trouble at all. Some of our more distant guests have brought men, as well. They'll be made welcome by our boys."

"Thank you, Mrs. Garnett."

The older woman gave a stately nod. "Please, help yourself to refreshments. As you can see, we're quite informal here. When you've had a chance to rest, I hope I may introduce you to my son, Jim, and his new wife, Georgiana."

"I shall look forward to it," Tally said.

Mrs. Garnett excused herself and sailed away. Tally released her breath.

"If that's the hen," Sim said, "I wonder about the rooster."

Tally shushed him. "Mr. Garnett was a pioneer in the Territory, but he has always maintained a civilized way of life. Mrs. Garnett is a woman of good family from Boston. I'm sure she's had a great deal of inconvenience to put up with in Arizona. I understand she spends most of her time at the Garnett residence in Willcox and visits the ranch only occasionally."

"You don't have to talk so fancy with me," Sim grumbled. "Are you all right?"

"Except for the itch between my shoulders."

"I think I'll get myself a glass of wine. What about you?"

"Tonight I think I need a drink."

They approached the table that served as a bar, where Sim ordered a shot of whiskey and Tally a glass of red wine. Sim made the whiskey last for three swallows. The bartender poured him another.

"Feel better?" Tally whispered.

"I need air. Let's go back outside."

They went through the French doors into the courtyard. The band had struck up a waltz, and several couples had taken advantage of it. Tally's hands grew damp within her gloves.

She hadn't danced in so long, and those rare occasions had been with men she had no reason to respect. But Sim was beside her, watching couples spin around the courtyard, and she wanted to know what it would be like to waltz with the man she loved.

Sim cleared his throat. "Do you know how to dance like that?" he asked.

"Yes."

"I only done it once. A…woman I knew…taught me the steps."

"Do you think we might try it?"

"What if I step on your feet like a clumsy fool?"

"You won't, Sim. You're the most graceful man I've ever known."

He snorted. "What the hell." He studied the dancers a moment longer, took Tally's right hand in his and positioned his other hand at her waist. He began so suddenly that Tally was literally swept off her feet. They settled into the rhythm naturally, in perfect accord, as if they'd been practicing together since childhood.

"How many times did you say you'd done this?" she asked.

He grinned. "Any complaints?"

"None whatsoever." She closed her eyes and let him carry her around and around until she was sure they'd whirled straight up to heaven.

HELL WAS WAITING for him.

Caleb knew there was no escape. His mother had told him from the earliest time he could remember; the preacher in Hat Rock had screamed about damnation; and Caleb had gone right out and made sure everything they said about him came true.

Until he'd looked into Sim's demon eyes, he'd stayed

ahead of the devil. He'd cheated death again and again. But now he knew there were things on earth as bad as hellfire, and he had nothing left to lose. His men had deserted him. He was alone, completely alone, and Sim had called him a coward.

Sim the monster. Sim the freak. Caleb kicked his mount, the third he'd stolen after the first two had died under him, and tasted blood on his tongue. His swollen ankle hurt like it had been dipped in pure brimstone, and his maimed hand was near useless, but the pain was easy to endure compared to the blackness of humiliation.

Sim thought he would run away. That was what a coward would do. Sim assumed he understood everything about his boyhood friend.

But Sim wasn't a *man.* He couldn't understand what he'd never been. And the more Caleb thought about it, running from the posse into Mexico, the more he was sure that Sim was a liar. He'd lied about the treasure. He'd lied about not wanting it and giving it up to Caleb. And he'd lied about what he was.

If Sim had once been human and sold himself to Satan, he would have used his power to become rich and live in luxury. No creature from hell would care about a slut like Beth, or Tally Bernard. Servants of the devil relished pain and suffering, and they had no souls to lose.

If Sim was truly damned, he would have killed Caleb in that room and taken his prey to hell with him. He'd saved Beth instead.

Whatever Sim was, he had to be mortal. Flawed. He had weaknesses. And if Sim could be hurt, Caleb intended to hurt him as cruelly as he knew how.

Coward...coward...coward, his mount's pounding hooves beat out in the earth. Caleb spurred the animal until blood mingled with the horse's sweat. He forced the mare through the pass, careening down the other side with his arms held wide like wings.

I am an angel, he thought. *Sim's personal angel of death.*

The mare staggered as they reached the bottom of the pass, where a thick tangle of shrubs and small trees marked the edge of the Cold Creek *bosque.* Caleb tumbled from her back the instant before she fell. He balanced on his good foot, unbuckled his saddle, bags and bedroll from the horse's heaving barrel, and left her where she lay.

Under cover of darkness, he approached the homestead. It was after suppertime, so the men would have returned to the bunkhouse. The women should be in the main house, but Sim could be anywhere.

Caleb was ready. His gun hand wasn't much good now, but he could shoot well enough with his left. He would cripple Sim first if he could, let him live long enough to see who'd killed him. But if that wasn't possible, so be it.

Caleb left his gear hidden under some brush and half crawled his way toward the house. Lantern light shone from the kitchen window. A horse nickered from the corral, and Caleb froze.

He waited for a long time, just watching. The moon rose. The light in the house went out. Caleb crossed the open yard at a limping run and crouched beside the porch.

No Sim. Maybe he wasn't here at all. Maybe he'd taken Beth back to Castillo Canyon and lingered there a while. Encouraged, Caleb crept up the low stairs and opened the door.

The kitchen was silent, and so was the hall. The first bedroom door stood open. No one slept in the polished brass bedstead. But the second room was occupied.

The man in the bed didn't stir even when Caleb got close enough to see his face. Caleb wasn't disappointed. He poked the muzzle of his gun into the sleeping man's neck.

"André," he whispered.

André opened his eyes. He stared, and some emotion flickered in his eyes. His mouth stretched in a gaunt, slack face. He looked about a hundred years old.

"Remember me, André?" Caleb said. "You have something that belongs to me."

André blinked. Spittle dribbled from his lower lip.

"Sim said you was touched in the head," Caleb said. "He told the truth about that one thing. But he got you to talk, and you're still alive. Now you're going to tell me." He hauled André upright by the collar of his nightshirt. "You got a minute to start talking."

André smiled, the drool forming a long strand that hung from his chin. Caleb shook him. André's head rolled like a doll's. Caleb struck him across the face. "Talk!"

The only sound André made was a low groan. He felt pain. That was something. Caleb hit him again and again, spattering blood on the sheets and coverlet. He was drawing back his fist when a hard object hit him on the side of his head. He dodged the broom handle in its second swing and knocked it from its wielder's hands.

Miriam stood panting in the doorway, hands raised as if she had some hope of defending herself. Her nightgown gleamed white against her dark skin.

"You devil!" she cried. "Leave Mr. André alone!"

Caleb laughed. Sim would have been here by now if he was anywhere on the premises.

"Why, Miriam," he said, "I didn't know you were so dangerous."

Miriam's dark eyes blazed. "You get out of here before Mr. Kavanagh comes for you."

"Mr. Kavanagh?" He pretended to shiver in fear. "I'm surprised at you, consorting with an unnatural creature like him."

"I don't know what you're talking about."

"You don't, do you? Did he keep it a secret from everyone, even your mistress?"

"Get out," Miriam said hoarsely. "I've already sent for the men."

Caleb clucked his tongue. "You're lying. And even if you ain't, the next man who steps through that door is dead. I might spare you and Tally—"

"Tally's gone," Miriam said.

"With Sim? That's a real pity. I'll just have to hunt them down later. But you can tell me where they are after we've had a little fun."

Miriam held his stare. "I'm not afraid of you, Caleb Smith."

"Sure you are. But I'll give you a chance to defend your honor—if your kind ever had any—so no one can say you didn't fight for it." He kicked the broom toward her. "Course you could save Mr. André a lot more discomfort if you just lie down like a good girl and lift up them skirts…."

Caleb caught movement behind Miriam's left shoulder and lunged forward, grabbing her by the wrist with the remaining fingers and thumb of his right hand. He pulled her with him back to the bed and locked his arm around her throat as he jammed his gun to André's temple. Eli stepped into the room, his shotgun aimed at Caleb.

"Eli," Caleb said. "I was wondering when you'd turn up. Now you just put down that scattergun like a good boy."

Eli's grip didn't waver, nor did his stare. "You all right, Miriam?"

"Yes," she gasped, clinging to Caleb's arm as if she could keep him from strangling her.

"Let her go," Eli said.

"Why should I do that? You'll have to shoot through her

to get me, and of course poor ol' André—" He sighed with mock regret. "Well, he's near dead anyway, ain't he?"

Eli glanced at André. "What do you want here, Smith?"

"I want what's owed me. But I don't figure André ever told you about the map, did he?"

"As a matter of fact, he did. I have the map, Smith, and I'll give it to you just as soon as you release your hostages."

CHAPTER NINETEEN

CALEB LAUGHED. The sound was high pitched and strange, matching the irrational glaze in his blue eyes. He was clearly injured, favoring his left leg and missing two fingers on his right hand.

But that wasn't all. It took less than a second for Eli to realize that Caleb had gone crazy. He'd been dangerous enough before, and now he was unpredictable, as well.

Except in one thing. Eli had known Smith would be coming back to Cold Creek—known from the moment Sim admitted he hadn't killed his old friend. And Eli was ready.

"*You* have the map?" Smith said, half choking on his own amusement. "Did Sim give it to you for safekeeping while he was lying to me in Tombstone?"

Eli considered how best to answer. He wasn't shocked that Sim knew about the treasure; clearly Smith and Kavanagh had been in league from the beginning. Caleb knew that André had stolen the map. No surprise that he would send someone to steal the map back again. Except he hadn't counted on André's accident, or the map disappearing. And he hadn't counted on Sim falling in love with André's sister.

But he'd talked about Sim having the map, and the only way that could happen was if André had confessed to Sim or kept a copy that Sim had found.

"I have the original," Eli said. "The one André took from you."

Caleb's arm tightened around Miriam's throat. "Then you have the treasure."

"No." Eli lowered his gun slowly. "I never looked for it."

"Why not? You crazy?"

Eli sought a distraction. "What did Sim tell you in Tombstone?"

"That he'd give me the treasure. All of it. He'd lead me to it if…" Smith's eyes narrowed. "You didn't look because you knew Sim already found it. It's gone."

"I was never fool enough to trust Sim Kavanagh. I didn't know he had a copy of the map, but he can't have had it very long. He's only been working at Cold Creek since May. I would have noticed if he'd gone into the mountains and come down with sacks of Mexican silver and gold."

"You would've known?" Caleb tapped André's head with the muzzle of his gun. "Like you knew what kind of thing's been courting your boss-lady?"

Eli tried to make sense of Caleb's question. "I know he's a liar and an outlaw. He betrayed you, didn't he? You just want what belongs to you."

"That's right. Let me see the map."

"Not while you're holding Miriam."

"You think you can bargain with me, boy? I got no reason to believe anything you say."

Eli shrugged. "You can kill André if you want—"

"Eli!" Miriam gasped.

"—and I won't try to stop you. But hurt Miriam, and you'll never see the map. Unless you think you can take the copy from Sim when he returns."

Caleb seethed. "I'll kill him."

"That's none of my concern. I don't give a damn what happens to these white folks. I came to Cold Creek because I couldn't find work in Texas after André left, and because

Miriam went with Miss Bernard." He smiled. "You want to know why André's lying in that bed and I have his map? I saw that map in Texas, when he was trying to hide it. He admitted he stole it from you when you were out rustling—he was drunk, and he boasted about it, figuring I wouldn't dare say a word. But I told him we were going to be partners and share whatever we found, or I'd go straight to you."

Miriam closed her eyes. "Oh, Eli—"

Eli struggled to ignore her despair and rushed ahead. "André betrayed me. After we came to Arizona, he took off to find the treasure alone, claiming he was buying stock for the ranch. I followed him into the Chiricahuas and faced him down. We fought over the map, and he fell into an arroyo— been the way you see him there ever since. But I got the map. I didn't want anyone thinking I was involved with André's accident, so I didn't go back to the mountains to look for the treasure. And then you came when I was gone, and I knew you'd never let it alone until you got what you came for."

"You're a coward," Caleb snapped. "I know you deserted from the Tenth Cavalry because you turned yellow—as if every one of your kind isn't yellow at the core."

Eli's fingers cramped on the shotgun. "Right about now you're figuring you could kill me," he said to Caleb. "But the map is hidden where you'll never find it. You let Miriam go and you get the map with no trouble. Miriam and I will leave Cold Creek, and what you do after that is your own business."

Caleb spat on the floor beside the bed. "You're lucky I'm feeling generous today. I'm letting your bitch go, but if you turn on me, I'll shoot you both, and to hell with the map."

Eli nodded. Caleb released Miriam and immediately trained his gun on Eli. Eli threw the shotgun into the hall behind him. "Run," he told Miriam. She dashed past him. He knew exactly where she would go, but he couldn't tell if she despised him for what she'd heard or if she still trusted him in spite of it.

"You never told her about the cavalry, did you?" Caleb asked. "So much for the brave soldier. Now you take me to the map."

Eli backed away and walked through the house to the front door, pausing to light a lantern in the kitchen. There was still a good chance that Caleb would kill him, but the outlaw's insanity had become Eli's ally. He took his time getting to the barn, giving Miriam a chance to save the children and warn Federico to stay clear.

In the barn, Pablo had scratched out a hole in the packed earth floor where he kept a small wooden box stuffed with "treasures" he'd gathered since he was old enough to walk—feathers, colorful stones, bits of metal and coins. He'd covered the box with loose earth, straw and half a rusted plow in a corner where no one was likely to find it, but one day he'd boasted to Eli about his hidden place. Eli had dug a similar hole just large enough for an oiled leather pouch and the map inside.

Very much aware of Caleb's position behind him, Eli set down the lantern, leaned the plow against the wall and kicked the straw away. He crouched, half facing Caleb, and brushed the dirt from the brown leather. He could feel Caleb straining on his tether, barely controlling himself from leaping on the pouch.

"Throw it to me," Caleb ordered. Eli tossed it wide, forcing Caleb to back up and kneel to retrieve it with his maimed hand. In those few seconds, Eli moved to stand in front of the plow.

Caleb fumbled with the pouch and opened the tie with his teeth. His face split in a grin as he pulled out the map.

"So you didn't lie after all." He turned the map, trying to smooth the torn and fragile paper. Slowly his smile faded. "Now you're going to read it to me."

"Is that why you didn't look for the treasure as soon as you got the map? Because you couldn't read it and didn't trust anyone else to do it for you?"

"Shut up," Caleb snarled. "For your sake, you'd better know that Mexican lingo."

"I know what it says." Without waiting for more threats, Eli translated the Spanish text he'd memorized. Caleb peered at the map, lips moving as if he could confirm Eli's information.

"That's all?" the outlaw asked. "There ain't nothing else?"

"It's all the original owner wrote," Eli said. "The details match the country up near Castillo Canyon."

Caleb slipped the map in the pouch and tucked it in his belt. "There's one way of being sure. You're coming with me."

"So that you can kill me when you find the place?"

"I can kill you now."

Eli let his shoulders drop in feigned despair. "I kept my side of the bargain. Let me and Miriam go."

Caleb snickered, enjoying his power like bullying cowards everywhere. Eli slumped even more. He felt behind his back with his left hand and closed his fingers around the handle of the broken plow. Splinters speared into his palm. He turned to the side and swung the handle out toward Caleb in a single motion.

Pain blossomed in his left shoulder, and the sound of the gunshot deafened him. He fell to the straw. Roaring filled his ears. He lay still and waited for the next, fatal, shot. He didn't know how long Caleb stood over him; seconds slowed to hours. Then the thin lantern light vanished, leaving him in darkness.

An eternity passed before he dared to move. Nothing impeded him as he crawled toward the barn door, dragging his body with his right hand and pushing with his feet. A light burned in the house. Eli struggled to stand, gathering his legs beneath him.

The sound of the shot was muffled by the walls of the house. Eli reached out as if he could prevent what had already happened, knowing who had suffered the full weight of Caleb's wrath and hatred.

Caleb walked out of the house, holstering his gun. Eli ducked back inside the barn as the outlaw strode toward the *bosque* and then returned, carrying a saddle, bridle and packs over his shoulders.

Eli worked his way back to where he'd been shot and lay down again, feeling the lifeblood drain from his body. The last thing he heard was galloping hoofbeats headed north up the valley.

TALLY COULDN'T STOP laughing. The man with whom she danced, an older gentleman from a ranch on the other side of the Galiuro Mountains, was vigorous and enthusiastic, but not particularly graceful. He jogged Tally through the French doors and back again, wrenching her about as if she were a frisky heifer due to be roped and branded.

She didn't mind. She threw Sim a grin, and he saluted her with his fifth glass of whiskey. He didn't seem even slightly drunk, but the alcohol had relaxed him, and Tally would have sworn he was actually enjoying himself. He'd even deigned to speak with a few of the other male guests, and no one showed any sign of questioning his assumed identity.

He and Tally had done the right thing in accepting the Garnetts' invitation. The family had been more than gracious. Georgiana Garnett, its newest addition, had spent the better part of an hour with Tally, discussing the latest fashions as if she recognized a fellow devotee of sophisticated and modern tastes.

The situation had been highly ironic, to say the least. Tally was hardly familiar with the latest styles, having left such interests behind in Texas, but she had been trained to speak gracefully and well on almost any topic. Beauty had been her stock in trade. And though she had remained tense and alert to any hint of suspicion, Georgiana Garnett listened attentively to Tally's opinions and expressed relief that at least one woman in this wilderness had some understanding of culture.

After Georgiana's new husband had come to lead her off for a dance, Tally found herself at the center of an admiring retinue of men and women. She'd flirted with the men—subtly, to be sure—and gossiped with the ladies just like any woman who'd grown up learning to cook and sew and anticipate a future as a wife and mother. She could almost believe she was one of them.

Sim hovered nearby wherever she went, a silent and faithful shadow. Part of Tally's joy lay in knowing he would be beside her when the party came to an end and the weary guests tumbled into borrowed beds or set out for home.

The current dance ended, and the enthusiastic but clumsy gentleman released Tally with obvious reluctance. He had a smitten look in his eyes. Tally kissed him on the cheek, and he stumbled away toward the bar, grinning like a mooncalf.

Sim strolled up to join her. "A new conquest," he said with a lazy smile. "How many hearts you plan to break tonight?"

"None, if I can help it," she said, gazing into his eyes. "Do you think you can manage another waltz?"

"It might be arranged." He looked her over as if he would much rather scoop her up and carry her to the nearest unoccupied bedroom. "It's getting chilly. You want your wrap?"

"You're much better than any wrap." She held out her

hand. He took it, and the band played the opening notes of a Strauss waltz.

"Chantal!"

The voice was hoarse and slurred with drink, but Tally recognized her name. Sudden inexplicable dread clutched her throat.

"Chantal Bernard?"

A man Tally didn't know blundered his way into one of the couples and charged blindly past them. Sim saw him coming and pulled Tally to the wall of the courtyard. He set himself in front of her.

Tally watched the stranger's approach with bewilderment and growing alarm. He wore reasonably well-made clothing, but it was stained with food and drink, and his face was florid and soaked with sweat. He could be a fairly successful miner or a rancher or a merchant, but she couldn't remember meeting or seeing him before.

The man puffed to a halt a few feet from Sim and stared into Tally's face. "It *is* you," he said. "I'll be damned."

"Watch your language when you speak to a lady," Sim growled.

"A lady?" The florid man laughed. "That's not what Lisa called her."

Lisa. Tally's thoughts flew back to the saloon and the time-worn prostitute who had delivered Beth's dress. The woman had behaved strangely, though Tally had been too preoccupied to pay attention at the time. Or to notice then how Lisa had stared, as if she knew…

Sim thrust out his arms to hold the man away. "You'd better make yourself scarce, hombre."

The man didn't seem to hear. "Lisa's a friend of mine. I'm her favorite. She tells me everything, like about them good ol' days in New Orleans." He stretched the words out as if he relished them. "I saw you at the Red Garter. You fooled me, but not Lisa." He smacked his lips. "She was hurt you didn't remember her."

Mon Dieu. Tally's legs turned to jelly, and she leaned against the cool adobe wall. There had been an Elise at La Belle Hélène. Tally hadn't known her well, but she'd seemed young and in her prime. Lisa was neither. But the work was hard, and some women aged ten years in five.

What were the chances that two girls from a single high-class bordello in New Orleans should turn up in Tombstone at the same time?

"Who is this Lisa?" Sim asked over his shoulder.

How was she to answer in this public place? People were beginning to notice the man, whose intrusion had stopped the dancing. Whispers splashed about the courtyard like waves striking the shore.

"You never been to the Red Garter?" the man asked Sim, bending forward with a conspiratorial grin. "Lisa's the best girl there. Course, she's not a girl anymore, but she knows all the tricks. Reliable, that's Lisa. And she used to be the best at Belle Hélène's, right up with Miss Chantal." He winked at Tally. "Only you had another name there, didn't you?"

The whispers grew louder, and more people came out of the house. Women hid speculation behind spread fans. A handsome gentleman took a step forward as if he intended to interfere, but his wife pulled him back.

"Ma'am-zell Champagne," the drunkard chortled. "You still got your sparkle, pretty thing? Lookin' for new customers? Well, you come with me right now, and I'll—"

Sim's fist slammed into the man's bulbous nose. A woman screamed. The band scattered. A flock of females rushed into the house, and the men formed a ring around Sim and his victim.

"There's no need for violence," a tall, bespectacled gentleman said, pushing through the crowd. He eyed Sim warily and bent to examine the fallen man. "Are you all right, Mr. Collins?"

Collins rose to his elbows and clutched his streaming nose. "He…he hit me!"

"That's clear enough. What were you thinking, talking like that?"

"It's all true!" Collins spat a mouthful of blood at Sim's feet. "She's…she's a whore!"

Sim raised his foot, and Collins shrank into a ball. The tall man with the glasses stood between the antagonists, glancing from Sim to Tally.

"Miss Bernard," he said, "I don't believe we've been introduced. My name is Dr. Faraday." He pushed his spectacles farther up the bridge of his nose. "Do you know this man?"

"I have never…" Tally heard her voice shake and controlled it with an effort. "I have never seen him before."

"I'm afraid Collins is the worse for drink. I'll see that he finds a place to sleep it off. You'd best stay away from him, Mr. Kavanagh."

Sim didn't answer. He stared at nothing, fists clenched, jaw tight.

Georgiana Garnett emerged from the house, the flock of ladies around her. Her mother-in-law and her husband, Jim, joined her in the courtyard. They stared from Collins to Sim and Tally.

"What's going on here, Doc?" Jim Garnett asked.

"A misunderstanding." The doctor pulled Collins to his feet. "If you've a spare room where I can treat Mr. Collins—"

"I'm tellin' the truth!" Collins said, belligerent with humiliation. "You know me, Doc….Garnett! You invited a whore to your wife's party!"

Georgiana blanched, and her gaze met Tally's across the

courtyard—questioning, begging for denial, but on the edge
of belief. Tally's stomach heaved. Fragments of conversation
drifted though the air like poisonous gases.

"…such language, and in front of the women! Get him out
of here, before he…"

"What if it's true? I've never known Collins to lie, even
when he's…"

"…ever seen her before. No one really knows these Bernards. She could have been anything…"

"…heard some of those women in New Orleans can almost
pass as respectable…"

A collective shudder rippled through the crowd. Women
Tally had spoken with only minutes before—stolid ranchers'
wives, merchants' daughters, churchgoing ladies from Willcox and Tombstone—moved away as if they might be tainted
by Tally's mere presence. Tally could feel the speculative,
hungry stares of men who'd asked her to dance, men whose
company she had enjoyed.

Jim Garnett touched his young wife's arm and approached
Dr. Faraday. "You'd better take Collins out of here, Doc.
When you're done with him, I think my wife and mother
might need your attention. They're a little upset." His gaze settled on Tally, and she could already hear the questions he
wanted to ask, imagine him weighing the dangers of offend-
ing two of his guests against allowing his womenfolk to suffer the horror of having a soiled dove in their midst.

Sim's eyes focused on Garnett. He smiled.

"Anything you want to say to Miss Bernard?" he asked
softly.

Garnett flushed. "This is unfortunate, Mr. Kavanagh, Miss
Bernard." He glanced over his shoulder to make sure that Dr.
Faraday had removed the offensive Mr. Collins. "I would
apologize for any insult that may have been given—"

"I don't hear no apology," Sim interrupted. "I think you believe that lying son of a bitch."

The younger man straightened. "I'll ask you not to swear in front of the ladies."

"They survived your Mr. Collins's foulmouthed hogwash." He raked the onlookers with a scornful gaze. "Some of 'em look downright fascinated."

"You've created an unnecessary disturbance. This is not a barroom, Mr. Kavanagh."

"Or a whorehouse?" Sim added.

Women gasped. Georgiana Garnett grew even whiter. Her mother-in-law supported her and glared with aristocratic fury at Tally.

Jim Garnett curled his fingers at his sides. "You were invited in good faith, Mr. Kavanagh. I think…I think it might be best if you and Miss Bernard—"

Halfway through his sentence, Sim tensed to strike. Tally anticipated his motion and grabbed his arm, holding it down with all her weight.

"No!" she cried. "No. This has gone far enough." She pushed past Sim and faced Garnett. "Mr. Kavanagh and I have no desire to remain where we're not welcome. If you'll kindly send someone to fetch Bart and our rig, we'll be on our way."

"Is it true?" Georgiana's voice rang surprisingly strong in the shocked silence. "Did you…did you sell yourself for money?"

The elder Mrs. Garnett wrapped her arms around her daughter-in-law's shoulders and propelled her toward the French doors. Tally turned for the courtyard entrance. Sim seized her elbow in an almost painful grip and half carried her out the arched portal.

Whispers rose to a buzz of startled reaction behind them. Sim dragged Tally into the darkness, moving with the unerr-

ing accuracy of a nocturnal animal. He stopped beside a wall
and let Tally go.

She rubbed her arm, not because it hurt but because the
mindless, repetitive motion brought comfort when her world
was crashing down about her ears. Sim waited. She raised her
eyes to his.

"Is it true?" he asked, his voice hoarse to the point of
breaking. "Are you a whore, Chantal Bernard?"

THE WORDS CUT LIKE BLADES as they came out of Sim's mouth,
but he couldn't halt them. He could hardly feel his hands or
his feet, let alone his heart. It had gone stone-cold.

Tally held his stare, her face expressionless. He made himself study every line and plane and curve of it, committing her
features to memory as if this were the last time he would see
her in his life. He drew his fingers from her brow to her chin,
and she closed her eyes.

"Does it matter so much?" she asked. "Why did you defend me against those men if you had any doubts?"

He thought of all the times he had avoided speculating
about her past, accepting that she'd had a husband and shared
his bed. She wasn't a virgin. He'd never expected her to be.
But what she'd done before that marriage…he hadn't wanted
to know. Now he was paying the price for his willful ignorance—and for daring to accept a new dream.

"Tell me that Collins was lying," he begged, "and no one
will ever say anything about you again."

She didn't so much as twitch an eyelash. "He wasn't
lying, Sim."

His stone heart plummeted to his boots and shattered.

"I was going to tell you," she said, her eyes still tightly
closed. "I was afraid for a long time. But when I decided to
accept this invitation, I'd already planned to explain—"

"Explain?" Sim backed away, but he couldn't escape the sight of her, the smell of her, the searing memory of how it felt to hold her soiled body in his arms. "Explain how you spread your legs for any man who could pay?"

She flinched. "I only told you a small part of my past. It isn't what you—"

"You want to know about my past, Mamzelle Champagne?" he snarled. "I was born in Hat Rock, Texas, to a whore—a mighty fine whore who made a good living until she shriveled up and died of some whores' disease."

Tally's eyes snapped open. "*Mon Dieu.* Sim—"

"She was drunk most of the time. She had some use for me until I turned about three, and then I was just too much trouble. I got in the way. Them fancy patrons of hers didn't want no kid around. Sometimes, when she was feeling a little down, she took a belt to me. I got tired of that when I was eight, and I learned how to get by on what I could find in the street." He laughed. "Oh, some of her 'sisters' took pity and gave me things, like books and candy and cigarettes. Even taught me to read and write. And when I was thirteen, they showed me what it was to be a man."

Tally hugged her arms against her chest. "I didn't know. Sim, how could I know?"

"When Ma died, I went looking for my pa. He was rich, and he was powerful, but he didn't want no part of some whore's son. He sent my own half brother to kill me, but I survived. My only friend was Caleb Smith. When we rode out of Hat Rock, we swore we'd take what we wanted, that no one would get in our way and live to tell the tale."

"I believe that of Caleb Smith," Tally whispered, "but not of you. I...I see that you have had reason to distrust women, even hate them—"

"I didn't waste no time hating them. I used them, just like

my pa used Ma. Never had to take a single one unwilling. But then I found a female who seemed better than the rest. She led me to you."

"Esperanza." Tally's voice softened with compassion. "You learned to love her."

Sim despised her gentleness as much as he despised his own gullibility. "Do you know why I came to Cold Creek, Tally-girl? It wasn't to get work as a hand. It wasn't no coincidence that we met in Tombstone. I was sent by my good friend Caleb Smith. We split up years ago, but I went looking for him when I needed money to take to Esperanza. I figured he'd let me in on any 'business' he had going at the time."

He could see that she hadn't yet grasped what he was telling her. "I found Caleb in Texas," he continued. "He was in jail—framed, he said, by André Bernard. He told me all about a map to some lost Mexican treasure—a map your brother stole from him."

Tally stared at him without comprehension. "A map? I know nothing of this."

"André never saw fit to tell you. He came to the Territory so he could be closer to the place where the treasure was buried. Then he got himself in trouble looking for it in the Chiricahuas. Took a bad fall and lost the map to some thief I never did find."

"*Bien sûr,*" Tally murmured. "This explains so much. Ever since we arrived in Arizona…his strange behavior, as if he was keeping a secret from all of us, as if the ranch was unimportant."

"Because he never cared about Cold Creek." Sim leaned against the wall, trapping Tally's head between his arms. "It was pure luck for me that you needed extra help at the ranch, because I planned to stick around until André recovered enough to tell me what was on that map."

The dazed look in her eyes began to clear. "You were in with Caleb all along, because of this map?"

"That's right. But André didn't get better. Caleb got impatient and rode in to Cold Creek. I had to talk him out of rushing things."

She tried to turn her head away, but he caught her chin and forced her to look at him. "Do you see, Tally? Eli was right not to trust me. He suspected all along. Tell me…does he know what you are?"

"Yes. And so does Miriam."

Anger. She disguised it well, but she was finally starting to realize what he'd done. How skillfully they'd lied to one another.

"You should have listened to Eli's warnings, just like I should have known you were too good to be real. Too good in bed for a woman who hated her marriage."

Tally might have struck him if she could have moved fast enough, but she was too smart to try. "You were good, too, Sim. Better than most. Is that what you learned when you were thirteen?"

Her question took him back to that day of terror and triumph, just as if he were a boy again. He smiled. "Lottie was good, but you're better. You'll never starve, Tally-girl."

"I'm never going back." She wrenched her chin from his hold. "I was tricked into the profession when I was fourteen, and I didn't know how to get out. But I gave it up of my own free will. You said you were changing your life for Esperanza, but all the time you were still a thief!"

"André was the thief," he said. "He took his cut of the rustlers' profits in Texas, stole Caleb's map, and then turned on his partners so he could be free to find the treasure. But he made a couple of mistakes, and only one of them was getting himself crippled before he found the treasure. He made a copy of the map. I found it in the hem of your wedding dress."

"You…you went through my mother's things?"

"Did your ma know what you did for a living, Tally-girl?"

"No. I made sure of that."

She almost made him feel ashamed, but his anger had slipped its leash and couldn't be recalled. "I'll bet your husband didn't know what he was getting when he gave you his vows."

"I made a mistake," she whispered. "I shouldn't have married Nathan, but I wanted a real home—"

"And where was André when all this happened?"

"He was with *Maman,* taking care of her, and then I didn't hear from him for many years. I told him the truth. He accepted it."

"And that makes him a better man than me?"

"You want me to believe you hate me, Sim," she said, searching his face, "and you have reason to be angry. But we shared too much…too much caring to pretend it never happened."

"So you'd forgive me for lying to you all along? That's right noble of you, especially since everything I did and said was just part of the plan."

"All of it, Sim?"

Her calm infuriated him. He wanted her to hate him, despise him as much as he despised her. He wouldn't tell her how he'd changed his mind about the treasure and Caleb, or that—somewhere along the way—he'd switched his loyalties to Cold Creek and Tally. He wanted her to believe the worst, to hurt, to feel the rage he felt at being deceived.

"Any feelings I had were for a woman who never existed."

"Strange. I still see the man I came to care for, even now."

"You said you loved me. I can see why you were the main attraction at this fancy bordello in New Orleans. You made every man feel important with that fancy talk and those big eyes and soft lips…." He stopped himself before he could linger on memories he wanted to forget. "You and me have one thing in common, *querida.* Whores can't love, and neither can their sons."

Tally fixed her gaze at some point on his chest. "Yet you cared for Esperanza."

"She was different." He faltered. "She was innocent. Pure."

"Pure enough to save you from yourself. You were looking for a way out of your old life, a way to become a better man."

"It's too late to change."

"Then why did you stand up to Caleb and save Beth?"

"Caleb made the mistake of thinking he could double-cross me. He was using the girl to make sure I gave him what he wanted. I got her away from him just to prove what a coward he was."

"And to keep her from ending up like your mother."

Scorching heat raced up his arm and exploded into his fist, urging him to strike. He slammed his hand into the wall.

Tally blinked and shivered. "You won't hurt me, Sim. I've always known that. You wouldn't hit a woman unless she was trying to kill you, and maybe not even then." She took a deep breath. "You protected Beth, and you drove Caleb away. If you have this map, why haven't you gone to find the treasure yourself?"

"I was a little distracted. But I ain't no more." He stepped back. "I was going to give my half to Esperanza, but she don't need it. Caleb's gone. But I figure I owe you…for services rendered."

CHAPTER TWENTY

TALLY LEANED HER HEAD against the wall. Inside, she was falling apart, shattered into a thousand pieces, but she wouldn't let Sim see an instant of weakness.

"I won't accept it, Sim," she said. "Even if you find this treasure and it's enough to pay for a spread as big as Los Granates, I wouldn't take a plugged nickel from you."

He shrugged. "I don't give a damn what you do with it. Send it to your old friends in New Orleans. But once I'm through with the treasure, I'll be through with you. All debts paid."

He moved farther away into the darkness, becoming a vague shape she could no longer recognize. She heard the tearing of cloth and realized that Sim was removing his clothing in order to change. No farewells, no regrets. He would leave her as a wolf, denying her the chance to see his face one last time. And then she would never see him again.

A swell of revoltingly cheerful music burst from the Garnett house. No one had come to look for the errant guests. Perhaps the Garnetts preferred to pretend the incident had never happened and were willing to overlook the possibility that they had invited a prostitute to their party. Once the rumors spread, however, someone would confirm them, and Tally's reputation in the Territory would be established once and for all.

She didn't give a damn.

"Sim?"

Silence. She left the wall and found the pile of clothes he'd abandoned—fine suit, hat, boots and all. Huge paw prints pointed south down the Valley for the short distance Tally could see. Dawn rimmed the hills to the west. Soon there would be enough light to ride by.

"Miss Tally?"

Bart. She'd forgotten about him and her instructions about the wagon.

"Here, Bart."

He came to meet her. "Are you all right?" he asked.

"There's been an…incident at the party. Sim is gone."

"I heard somethin'," Bart mumbled. He turned his hat around in his hands. "You want me to hitch up the wagon?"

"Yes. Then I want you to lend me your horse and go home."

He squinted in confusion. "You ain't comin' with me?"

"No. Is there a quiet place near the stables where I can change my clothes?"

"Sure. I can show you. But, Miss Tally—"

"This is something I have to do, Bart. You'll hear some ugly stories about me—I won't blame you if you decide to leave Cold Creek. Eli will see to your pay."

"Hell…I mean, I wouldn't leave you, Miss Tally. Not for nothin'."

She touched his arm. "Thank you, Bart."

He ducked his head and turned quickly, leading her toward the stables. Though the local and visiting cowhands were still holding their own party at the bunkhouse, the other outbuildings were relatively quiet. Tally took the bundle of men's garments and a rifle from the wagon, grateful that she'd had the foresight to bring clothes suitable for riding. She changed in an empty stall, put on her coat and emerged to find Bart's horse, a mare named Bruja, saddled and ready for her.

"You sure you don't want me to come with you, Miss Tally?" Bart asked.

"Not this time." She swung into the saddle and offered her hand. "Take care, Bart."

"And you." He saluted her as she reined south, and for a moment she felt as if she were leaving her only friend in the world.

She knew she wasn't thinking straight. Anger at herself, at Sim, at the whole world, was driving her to an act of sheer and utter foolishness. She had no right to be so angry when harsh experience had taught her that she should never have expected a lasting relationship with any man, acceptance by decent folk, or a life free of her past.

But angry she was, and so she would stay until the cruel revelations of this night were somehow resolved. Sim had accused André of theft when her brother wasn't capable of defending himself; he'd admitted he was in league with Caleb from the beginning. He'd betrayed her, and what she found most unforgivable was that she hadn't been ready for it. He'd stolen not only her body but her heart.

At the root of all this pain and treachery was a treasure she hadn't even known existed. Whatever it might be, whatever its source, it must be evil indeed. The treasure was a thing she could hate, because she couldn't hate Sim.

She didn't have the map. But she remembered where she and Sim had found André, and that must be close to where her brother had been searching before his accident. She had no hope of reaching the place as quickly as Sim, but if he truly intended to collect the treasure, he wouldn't be able to manage it in wolf shape. She had a few advantages left.

Measuring her pace to spare her mount, Tally reached Willcox by noon. Heedless of her wild appearance, she watered Bruja and stopped in a store to buy jerky and freshly made bread. An hour later she was on her way again. She headed southeast, following the road to the mines near Dos Cabezas. Dusk found her and Bruja at the mouth of Castillo Canyon.

Tally knew that the Brysons would gladly put her up without asking awkward questions, but she rode past their homestead and as far into the canyon as she could before full darkness made travel too dangerous. She all but fell off Bruja's back and unsaddled the mare with shaking hands. Bruja drank from the trickle of water in the creek and munched on the grain Tally poured into her feed bag. Once the horse was settled, Tally sank down on a patch of rocky ground and chewed on bread and jerky while the stars wheeled overhead.

The air was chill, almost raw, but Tally scarcely noticed. *I've lost him,* her mind wailed. *I've lost him. I've lost him.*

You never had him, the hard part of her taunted. *It was all illusion. Your whole life has been a lie since you left New Orleans.*

But her love hadn't been a lie. Whatever Sim had done to her, she kept on loving him.

She untied her bedroll and took the saddle for a pillow. It didn't seem likely that she would sleep, but her body knew better than her head. She woke to faint light and the howling of wolves.

Instantly she remembered the pack that had accompanied her and Sim on their first visit to the Canyon. These could be the same animals. Their presence might have nothing to do with Sim. Her instincts told her otherwise. She got quickly to her feet and comforted a nervous Bruja.

The canyon was still in shadow. The wolves came closer. Tally saddled and bridled the mare, and made ready to move. The only way to run was back down the canyon, but unless the wolves attacked, she had no intention of retreating.

It seemed she wouldn't be given a choice. Bruja snorted and tossed her head in belated warning as the first wolf crept from the cover of bushes clinging to the canyon slope. The animal was slender and gray, only half Sim's size, but it had plenty of company. One by one its pack mates joined it, each gazing at Tally with luminous golden eyes.

They were trying to communicate, Tally was certain. *I don't understand you,* she said silently, not daring to break the quiet. But the first wolf waved its tail and gave a sharp yip. The other wolves worked their way around Bruja, wary of her hind legs, and formed a loose circle.

Then they did something for which Tally was entirely unprepared. They advanced on Bruja from behind, herding her higher up into the canyon. The horse rolled her eyes and bolted forward, only to be stopped by the wolves ahead. Tally laid her hand on the mare's quivering muzzle and did her best to obey the wolves' unspoken instructions.

The wolves knew where they were going. They were taking her to Sim.

An hour passed, and then another. Travel was slow, because of the wolves' deliberate pace and Bruja's fear. Tally recognized landmarks from her first climb into the canyon. At a level spot shaded by pines, the lead wolf paused and seemed to consult with its companions. It came to meet Tally, sat on its haunches and yipped at her again. Then it turned and raced up a slope that would daunt even the most sure-footed mule.

Tally understood that it wanted her to follow. She grasped Bruja's cheek-piece and looked the mare in the eye.

"I don't want to leave you," she said, "but I don't think the wolves will do you harm."

Bruja shuddered. Tally released the horse, pulled the rifle from its scabbard and backed away. Bruja took a step after her and was blocked by a wolf, which seemed uninterested in doing anything but keeping the horse in place.

Tally had no choice but to trust. She scrambled after the

lead wolf, who was waiting for her. She slipped on loose rock, trying to keep her balance with the rifle in one hand, but her guide was patient and picked out the least difficult path up the grade. When they reached the top of the incline, Tally felt a sense of familiarity and realized that the wolf had led her by a different route to the ledge where André had fallen.

The wolf allowed her a chance to rest and then indicated its impatience with a twitch of its expressive ears. It led her through a grove of trees, around several large boulders and into a clearing. At the other end of the open space stood a wall of the pinnacles for which Castillo Canyon was named. The joints between the pillars were black and deep.

The wolf urged her toward one such crevice. It seemed impossibly narrow, but as Tally drew closer, she saw heaps of rock and rubble suggesting that human hands had recently been at work clearing some obstruction from the opening of the cleft. The tracks of huge paws, human feet—shod and bare—and hooves crisscrossed the ground along the base of the pinnacles.

The prints were recent. Unless he'd stolen clothing along the way, Sim would be barefoot. Tally readied the rifle and advanced cautiously toward the cleft. It was so deep that no sunlight reached the bottom. But though it remained narrow past the opening, even a large man might make his way through if he walked sideways and didn't mind a few scrapes.

Scrapes were the least of Tally's concerns. This was a perfect trap, and Sim might already be inside it with whoever had ridden the horse and worn the boots. Tally slowed to a near-crawl. A few more steps and the cleft opened into a wide, sunlit space surrounded by more pinnacles, some rounded and others flat at their crowns.

Tally stopped short of the cleft's exit and let her eyes adjust to the brightness. Gradually she made out the shape in the center of the natural arena—a naked man, half crouched and ready to spring. He spun about to face her, shouting a warning. A gunshot cracked and the bullet sprayed dirt at Sim's feet.

"Won't do no good to run now," Caleb Smith said. He jumped down from his perch on one of the lower rocks surrounding the arena, favoring his right foot. He pointed his gun at Sim's stomach. "I know you're in there, Tally Bernard, so you'd best come out before I shoot your lover dead where he stands."

"Go back the way you came, Tally," Sim said in a tone of flat indifference. "He's going to shoot me anyway."

Sim listened intently for the sounds of movement from the cleft. Tally had no reason to believe anything he said now; she might even think this was another trick he and Caleb had cooked up between them.

Sim knew the wolves had led her to him, and to the treasure. If he got out of this alive, he and the pack leader would need to have a little conversation. But the wolves weren't really to blame. They must have traveled north when he and Tally had ridden for Los Granates; they'd been waiting for him in Castillo Canyon, almost as if they'd known he was coming. He'd spent hours mindlessly running with the pack because he didn't want to have to think, let alone look for the treasure. He'd reckoned that Tally would try to follow and he would see or hear her long before she caught up to him.

The wolves had found her first. Could be they sensed that she was his mate and belonged at his side. Could be they knew Sim was in danger and meant to help. They might have been of some use against Caleb if they'd stuck around, but Sim couldn't smell or hear them. In the end, the laws of nature drove them to protect their own survival.

God knew Sim didn't deserve to live after his stupidity in letting Caleb leave Tombstone. And then he'd walked right into this natural trap without once realizing Caleb was there. All his instincts, wolf and human, had been clouded by grief and rage.

Maybe some part of him wanted to die rather than face up to what Tally had told him and what he'd done to her. But he wasn't going to let her pay for his mistakes.

"You figured I really was too scared to come back," Caleb said, severing his thoughts. "You thought after what I'd seen, I'd run for the border and keep on running for the rest of my life. You was wrong."

Sim looked from the gun to Caleb's triumphant face. The blue eyes were alight with madness. "I guess I was, Caleb. I guess I underestimated you."

"You *have* gone soft. Not just Sim Kavanagh the man, but whatever the hell it is you are. Some demon." He peered over Sim's shoulder into the cleft. "Do you know what he is, bitch?"

"She knows," Sim said. "She couldn't accept it."

Caleb snickered. "That true, Tally? What's that they say— 'lie down with dogs and get up with fleas'?"

Tally remained silent, and Sim nursed a forlorn hope that she'd had the sense to escape while she could.

"Your pretty little Miriam told me you was out with Sim," Caleb continued. "Yet here I find him hunting for the treasure and you turning up after, like he left you behind. Didn't he want to share the prize with you once he thought he got rid of me?"

"You were at Cold Creek?" Tally asked, her voice echoing in the cleft.

"I figured either I'd get Sim or find something else he cared about. Well, I finally talked to André, and he was just as useless as Sim said. Sim wasn't lying about that."

"And Miriam?" Tally demanded. "If you hurt her—"

"Oh, *she's* alive." Caleb let his gun hand drop as if to prove how little he feared Sim. "How long've you known about the treasure?"

"She didn't know until yesterday," Sim cut in. "But that ain't why she's here. She found out I was working with you all along, using her—"

"And so she tracked you down to kill you? That story is just plain pitiful." Caleb shook his head with mock sorrow. "You can think up something better than that, can't you, Tally?"

"What did you do at my ranch?"

"I got the map. The real, original map your brother stole from me."

Sim tried not to show surprise, but Caleb had known him too long. "That was something you didn't reckon on, wasn't it?" Caleb said. "You said you got a copy of the map from André, but the original was lost. Well, Eli had it all along—took it right out of André's hands when he lay dying in that arroyo."

"You're lying," Tally said.

"Why should I? Seems Eli and your brother had a deal of their own, and André backed out of it. He paid the price for turning on his partner, and now Eli's paid, as well."

"No." Tally's protest broke on a sob. "You bastard—"

"That would be Sim." Caleb chuckled. "You can take comfort in the fact that Eli gave up the map to save his woman." He stared at Sim, and suddenly the smile was gone. "What'll you do to save yours?"

"My woman?" Sim shifted his weight, gauging the swiftness of Caleb's reactions. He had to buy Tally another chance to get away. "You want to know about my woman, Caleb? She's a whore. A lousy whore, just like my ma."

"Right now you'd say anything just to—"

"She worked at a high-class cathouse in New Orleans and then married some sap who didn't know about her past. She hid it from everyone, until a *puta* in Tombstone recognized her."

Caleb searched Sim's face through narrowed eyes and then began to laugh. "If that don't beat all," he said. "You never saw it. You rode her and never knew you was getting used goods—Sim Kavanagh, the man who despises any female who reminds him of his dear ma." He slapped his thigh in high good humor. "Couldn't you smell all them other men on her body?"

Sim let a little of his anger show, knowing Caleb would take pleasure in his former partner's humiliation. "I broke my own rule," he said. "I trusted a woman."

"Stupid of you, all right," Sim said. "But I'm curious…did she lie with you in both your shapes? Some females'll do anything for money."

Sim banked his rage to a single flickering ember. He prayed—to who or what, he didn't know—that Tally would give up on him and leave while she could. He needed more time.

"You can threaten her all you like, Caleb," he said. "I don't care what happens to her."

"It's too late, Sim. You showed your hand in Tombstone." He aimed his gun at Sim's foot. "You come on out of there, Tally, or I'll blow him to pieces bit by bit."

No sound from the crevice. Sim's senses told him she wasn't there, though Caleb didn't know it yet.

"This ain't her fight," Sim said. "Start shooting."

"Not her fight?" Caleb asked. "I killed her brother."

Sim stiffened. Tally would have reacted to such news if she'd been within earshot.

"She's gone," he said.

Caleb shrugged. "Don't matter. Once I take care of you, I can get her anytime."

"There's a problem with that plan, Caleb. Did you hear the wolves last night?"

His words had the desired effect. Caleb twitched and almost looked away. "I didn't hear no wolves," he said.

"They're there, all right. All around us."

"So?"

Sim couldn't afford to let Caleb sense the slightest uncertainty. "I talk to them, Caleb. They understand me, and I understand them. I can make them do whatever I want."

Caleb jabbed the muzzle of his gun into Sim's chest. "Not if you're dead."

"If I'm dead, they'll come after you."

"Let 'em come." He pushed with the gun, forcing Sim toward the pinnacle wall. "Your problem is that I ain't scared of you no more, Sim," Caleb said. "I'm betting you'll do anything to save your harlot. And if you do what I say, maybe I'll let her live." He pointed his chin toward one of the many joints dividing the pinnacles. "You know where the treasure is. Eli said he didn't think you'd ever taken it. He'd better not be wrong. You're going to go in and send it out to me."

Sim eyed the crevice. He was beginning to understand why Caleb had kept him alive so long. Caleb wanted to think he'd won, hands down—that he was Sim's equal, even his superior. He wanted Sim to witness every last moment of his triumph and acknowledge Caleb's victory.

"You get on your hands and knees," Caleb said, "and you crawl like the whipped dog you are. But you stay a man, or I'll go straight after Tally Bernard."

Sim dropped to his knees. He crawled toward the fissure, while Caleb stood over him and laughed. The joint between the pinnacles was shaped almost like a triangular cave, low and deep, just big enough for a man to enter on his belly. Sim flattened himself to the ground and slid inside the cleft. His eyes adjusted quickly to the darkness.

He didn't know what he'd expected. The fissure wasn't large, certainly not big enough to hold bag upon bag of silver and gold. But Sim was able to stand, half-crouched, and observe everything in the chamber with a single glance.

"Push it out!" Caleb called. "Hurry up!"

Sim laughed under his breath. "I can't."

"I'm warning you—" Caleb's voice took on an hysterical edge. "Sim!"

Sim stretched out on the red earth and crawled from the crevice, half expecting Caleb to blow his head off.

"Where is it?" Caleb shouted. "What have you done with it?"

"Nothing." Sim got up. "Go look for yourself."

Caleb's eyes were wild, and Sim braced for the bullet. If Caleb had any brains, he'd put it dead center in Sim's skull.

Gunfire cracked. Caleb cursed. Sim staggered, blinded by pain as Caleb's bullet struck his leg. Through a red haze he saw Tally perched on the lowest pinnacle, aiming a second shot at Caleb. Caleb spun and trained his gun on Tally.

Sim leaped at Caleb, his injured leg buckling under him. Two more shots boomed among the spires, and Tally fell as she dodged Caleb's wild shots. She landed hard, losing the breath in her lungs. The rifle flew out of her reach. She fought a wave of dizziness and rolled to her feet, trying to make sense of the scene before her.

Sim was on his knees, blood pouring from a wound in his leg. Caleb's gun had been shot out of his hand by an expert marksman. And Eli stood precariously balanced between two flat-topped pinnacles, his shoulder and upper chest bound in red-stained rags, his Colt ready to blast a hole in Caleb's chest.

Tally found her rifle, dented but intact, wedged in a joint between two pinnacles. She ran to Sim's side, trusting Eli to keep

Caleb still. The flow of blood from Sim's wound had already slowed to a trickle. The bullet had missed shattering his leg, but the wound looked severe enough to cripple a man for life.

"How bad is it?" she asked.

"Ain't nothing," he said through his teeth.

"My horse is back down the canyon. There must be something in the saddlebags I can use to bandage and splint it until we can get you to a doctor."

"No need. It'll heal on its own."

She could tell he wasn't lying for her benefit. She had to trust his judgment where his unusual abilities were concerned.

"Can you walk?" she asked.

"In a bit." He frowned and touched a scrape down the side of her cheek. "You could've got yourself killed, climbing them rocks."

"Caleb said he'd blow you to pieces. I believed him."

He sighed and closed his eyes. "Tally…"

They both knew this wasn't a time for conversation, no matter how much they still had to say to each other. Tally helped Sim move as far from Caleb as possible and propped him against the rock wall. She trained her rifle on Caleb.

"Eli?"

"I hear you, Miss Tally."

"Caleb said… I thought you were—"

"Dead?" Eli barked a laugh. "He thought so, too."

Tally risked a glance up at her friend. The bindings around his shoulder were rapidly filling up with fresh blood. "Is Miriam all right? The children?"

"Yes."

"I don't know how you made it from Cold Creek, Eli, but you need help."

"Not while Caleb Smith is alive."

Tally looked at Caleb. He was ashen faced, seemingly oblivious to the talk passing over his head. "I know that André is dead," she said. Her voice broke, and she forced the words past the grief she'd just begun to feel. "Caleb will hang for murder."

"Not only of your brother," Eli said. "Isn't that so, Sim Kavanagh?" His dark eyes dismissed Sim's nakedness as if it were just another sign of his natural depravity. "How many men have the two of you put in their graves?"

Sim stared up at Eli, his face blank even of pain. "I know what I've been," he said, "and what I am. So does Tally. I told her about the treasure."

"You admit you've been working with Caleb all along?"

"Not anymore," Tally said. She met Sim's gaze. "I believe their partnership ended before we went to Sonora. Sim has saved my life more than once. He—" She swallowed. "Did you know about the map, Eli?"

"Why don't you tell her what you told me, buffalo boy?" Caleb said, startling everyone. "How you was in league with André after he stole the map from me in Texas, and how you turned him into that thing I put out of its misery?"

Tally tightened her grip on the rifle. "No one believes your lies, Caleb."

"But Caleb believed mine," Eli said. "And not all of them were lies." He swayed and caught himself. "When Caleb showed up at Cold Creek yesterday, I told him I found out that André had stolen the map from him, and so I made your brother accept me as his partner to find the treasure. That part was the lie. I didn't even see the map until we got to Arizona." He stared at Caleb. "That map never belonged to Caleb or André. It was my father's. Caleb killed him for it, and I've been tracking the bastard ever since I left the cavalry."

Caleb laughed. "That worn-out old cuss was your pa?"

Sim started to get up and sank down again with a grunt. "Shut your mouth, Caleb."

"Don't you want to hear the whole story, Sim? It's a good one."

Tally resisted the urge to close her eyes in despair. Sim had told her that André had stolen the map, and now Eli confirmed it. She'd known André had faults and weaknesses, that he'd made most of his money from his partnership with the rustlers in Texas. But she'd believed he was trying to go straight, just as she was. Instead, he'd lied and risked his men's lives for wealth that might be no more than an illusion.

Sim ignored Caleb and addressed Eli. "You tracked Caleb to André's ranch in Texas," he said, "and you got yourself a job there. You worked at Peñasco Rojo for a couple of years. Caleb didn't know who you were, or he'd have took care of you long ago." He braced his hands against the rock wall at his back and pushed to his feet. "You earned Tally's trust, which ain't lightly given. Then you threw it away. Why did you bring your business to Cold Creek? If you wanted revenge for your pa, why didn't you kill Caleb in Texas?"

"It would seem that simple to a man of your nature," Eli said. He gazed down at Tally, limitless sorrow in his dark eyes. "I want you to understand. I deceived you, but only because I didn't want you or Miriam or anyone else to be hurt. After the things André had already done to you, I considered him as bad as Caleb. But you seemed to need—"

"As bad as Caleb?" Tally interrupted. "André took me in when I had nowhere else to go. He…he may have lied to me, but…"

Sim cast Eli a glance she couldn't interpret. He limped to Tally's side and steadied her with a hand at her back. "Finish your story, Patterson. How did André find out about the map?"

Eli released a short, sharp breath, but when he spoke, it was to Tally. "I don't know. Your brother and Caleb both liked to drink, and they talked. You know that André had Caleb and his men at the house on more than one occasion." He gave Caleb a look full of contempt. "Maybe he got drunk enough to show it to André and didn't remember afterward."

"You son of a bitch," Caleb swore. "I never showed it to no one."

Eli shrugged. "A few months before he sold his share of the ranch, André remarked to me about a new scheme that would make him rich without any work. I'd been watching Caleb closely, and I knew he was furious over losing some prized possession. One night while you and André were gone to town, I observed Caleb sneaking into the big house. He searched André's rooms. He didn't find what he was looking for. I figured then that André had the map."

Caleb twitched, and Tally lifted the rifle to her shoulder. "Stay where you are," she ordered.

"I'd listen to her if I was you," Sim said.

Caleb glared at Eli. Tally loosened her grip on the rifle very carefully. If she shot Caleb, it wouldn't be by accident. "Go on, Eli," she said.

"Your brother must have known how much of a risk he'd taken," Eli said, as if he hadn't been interrupted. "Not long afterward, Caleb was arrested by the Rangers. I had no reason to stay in Texas. Two of the three things I wanted were here in Arizona: the map and Miriam. The third could wait."

"The map meant more to you than revenge," Sim said.

"You and Smith are cut from the same cloth. Did he tell you how he got the map?"

"No."

"And you wouldn't have given a damn if you knew."

"I'm sorry about your father," Tally said, blinking to clear the blur of moisture from her eyes. "But Sim didn't kill him, Eli."

"It could just as easily have been Kavanagh…or any no-good scum like him." Eli's face twisted into an expression

Tally had never seen before, as if the terrible feelings he'd kept to himself were pulling him apart inside his skin. "My father worked all his life to build his shipping business in Delaware, make a good life for his family. But when the war started, anti-abolitionists set fire to his warehouses. My family lost everything. I was old enough to join the Union army, and my folks went to live with kin in Pennsylvania. I didn't hear from them for a long time. Eventually I learned that my mother had died and my father had gone west to get away from the war and the old life."

"I didn't know," Tally whispered.

"I never told anyone, not even in the army. When the war ended, I signed up with the Tenth Cavalry, figuring I'd have a decent chance of finding my father. But he'd disappeared. Then one day in Fort Concho a letter found its way to me from Mexico. My father had been working a mine there, but it didn't pan out. He'd bought a map from some old man in Sonora—a map he said would lead him to a lost treasure in Arizona Territory. It was the only dream he had left."

"Caleb's dream, too," Sim said. "He was always talking about finding some buried mine or Spanish gold."

"Patterson's father was just a stupid old man," Caleb said, "but he got to the map first. It should have been mine. I took it."

Eli swallowed, every muscle in his body straining for control. "You left witnesses to your crimes. When I found my father's grave in that little village, I swore to hunt you down."

"But you didn't even try to kill me," Caleb said. "You're a stinking yellow coward like all your breed. Worse—you're a deserter. A wanted criminal." He laughed. "André talked, all right."

Eli held rigidly still. "I won't justify myself to you, Smith," he said. He turned again to Tally, silently asking for her trust. "The map was my father's last will and testament, all I had left of him."

"André was an easier mark, so you went after him instead of me," Caleb taunted gleefully.

"No," Tally said. "Eli—"

"I did go after André eventually," Eli said. "When he left to buy the cattle in spring, I suspected he had something else in mind."

"Why did André wait so long to look for the treasure?" Sim asked.

"I don't know. Maybe he wanted to be sure Caleb was out of the way for good, hanged for his crimes. I'm sure that André didn't do anything with the map until this past spring. When Miss Tally sent me after him, I learned in Tombstone that he'd bought mules and gone on to the Chiricahuas. I tracked him, even caught him looking at an old piece of paper I knew had to be the map. That was the first time I'd ever seen it."

"André didn't know you were after him," Sim said.

"No, but he must have feared he might be followed, because he often doubled back or tried to hide his tracks. I left my horse behind when I reached the mountains and tracked him on foot. I'd hoped once he found the treasure that I could persuade him to behave honorably." Regret thickened his words. "You were my friend, Tally. For your sake, and Miriam's…I wouldn't have hurt him. But when I tried to explain about Caleb and my father, he turned on me. He said he didn't care what had happened to my father. I got very angry. We struggled. I grabbed the map, and he lost his balance. He fell."

"He left your brother to die," Caleb said to Tally.

"I told you to shut up," Sim growled.

Eli nodded to Sim and breathed deeply. "I saw André hit his head. He wasn't bleeding much, but the way he was lying—" He focused reddened eyes on Caleb's sneering face. "I know what you'd say. I wanted him to die so he couldn't tell anyone what I'd done. Maybe you're right. I waited too long, hoping he'd wake up."

"You were limping when Tally and me brought André back to Cold Creek," Sim said.

"That happened in the fight," Eli said. "My leg wasn't broken, but I couldn't climb down into the arroyo. In the cavalry we learned not to move a man in that condition without a stretcher. I told myself that if I left him alone, some animal would finish him off. Once or twice he showed signs of consciousness, but I could see he wasn't getting better." Tears mingled with the perspiration gleaming on his face. "God forgive me, I thought about running. Then I saw you and Sim coming up from the valley, and I assumed you'd find him. I went back to Cold Creek."

It was all Tally could do not to drop the rifle and let the tragedy of Eli's story overwhelm her. Sim's firm, gentle touch became the only reality, the only truth in this madness of murder and shame and greed.

"I should have known Eli was there," Sim said so only she could hear. "The rain washed away his scent, but I should have sensed it once I met him."

And what would she have done if she'd known? She wouldn't have believed Sim if he'd made such a claim. It wouldn't have seemed possible to her that Eli could act less than honorably.

She shook her head, unable to speak. Eli shifted on the rocks above. "You have every right to hate me, Tally," he said. "I couldn't admit the part I played in André's accident. I didn't want to lose what I had at Cold Creek. But I despised the map, just like I despised myself. And when I read it—" He made a sound, half sob and half laugh. "I knew why my father had died, why that map brought so much pain.

"It was cursed."

CHAPTER TWENTY-ONE

"YES," TALLY WHISPERED. "It's done nothing but destroy."

But Sim met Eli's bitter gaze and understood the Buffalo Soldier's true meaning. "Someone put a curse on the treasure," he said.

"The man who drew this map also wrote a warning," Eli said. "He was a monk, a servant of God, and it was God's curse he called down. Anyone who sought this treasure in greed or anger would suffer a terrible fate." Eli wiped at his face with his free hand, wincing as his saturated bandage slipped on his shoulder. "My father died for it, André was crippled, and I...I knew I'd never be able to forget what I'd done."

"Cursed," Caleb repeated. "That's why you wanted me to take the map." His eyes widened, and Sim almost expected him to froth at the mouth like a mad dog. "You wanted the curse to fall on me."

"It already has," Sim said. "I reckon you won't leave this canyon alive."

"That's right," Eli said. His face and voice were those of a man who had nothing left to lose. Or to live for. "When Sim said he'd let you leave Tombstone, I knew you'd be back. Nothing short of death would stop you. That was part of the curse. I hid the map and waited. I saved the treasure just for you, Caleb."

Caleb moaned low in his throat. "*You* saw it," he snarled at Sim. "You're the one who's cursed."

"I reckon so. But I'll be the last." He withdrew his hand from Tally's back. She didn't need him to hold her anymore; she was strong, stronger than anyone else in this little corner of hell. "Tally's free of it, and pretty soon she'll be free of us."

Tally glanced at him. Tendrils of blond hair, turned dark with perspiration, clung to her forehead, and her eyes were red with grief. Sim didn't dare look into them too long.

"Free?" she echoed. "What was in that crevice, Sim?"

In all this time, none of them had asked. Now they stared at him as if he held the secrets of the universe.

Caleb forgot his predicament, forgot the weapons pointed at him, forgot about curses. "What is it, Sim?" he begged. "Silver? Gold? Jeweled crosses?"

Sim smiled. "I'll tell you," he said, "and it won't do you no good, Caleb. It's something you wouldn't understand. Truth is in that cave."

Profound silence fell among the pinnacles, so complete that a distant bird call rang like gunfire.

"Truth?" Caleb began to tremble, shaking with soundless laughter. "You think that's funny? You think you can do this to me, Kavanagh?"

"Go look for yourself," Sim said.

"Kavanagh…" Eli warned.

"Let him see what he worked so hard to get. What he killed for."

Caleb's glance flew from Eli to Tally. "Swear," he demanded. "Swear you won't shoot me."

"I won't let them," Sim said. He pushed down the barrel of Tally's rifle. He looked at Eli, who reluctantly lowered his own weapon.

Eli wouldn't kill Caleb. Sim had known that from the start, just like he knew Tally didn't have it in her to take that kind of revenge, even on a man who had hurt her. If Eli meant to kill his enemies, he would have done it long since. Something held him back. Something good that didn't deserve to be destroyed.

But Sim wasn't like Eli. Caleb must never leave this place.

Caleb backed away toward the crevice, shuffling his feet, one kind of fear replaced by another. He squatted near the entrance, hesitated, then poked his arm behind him. Twisting his head to watch his enemies, he wriggled backward into the joint until he was swallowed up in the shadows.

Sim felt Tally's gaze and turned to meet it. Her eyes were bright and beautiful in joy or in suffering, generous and warm and brave. She questioned his motives, his sanity, everything but her own foolish attempts to save his life. His life, and his soul.

No point in getting maudlin now. He'd been a rogue wolf long before he learned how to Change, heedless of the carnage he left behind him, no better than Caleb. Nothing in Tally's past could match the least of his sins. When he'd raged at her, he'd raged at himself for daring to believe he had a chance of salvation. Even Esperanza couldn't save him, not with all the blessings in heaven.

"Eli? You hear me?" he said.

"I hear you, Kavanagh."

"You're about to keel over from that wound of yours. Take Tally back to the Brysons' and get it looked after. I—"

"Eli needs to see a doctor," Tally said, "but we're all going together."

The desperation in her voice gave her away. She *knew*.

"Eli has first claim on Caleb," Sim said, avoiding her eyes. "You want him, Patterson?"

The big man bent his chin to his chest. "No," he said. "Oh, I've waited for this moment. I've dreamed of it. But Miriam would never forgive me, even if she can... *No*." He sobbed the last word, racked by shudders from the depths of his body. "I'm done with killing."

"And you, Tally?" Sim asked, merciless. "He shot your brother. He would have killed Eli, Federico, Bart and the kids without thinking twice."

Tally closed her eyes. A tear glittered on her dirty cheek. "No. He goes to the law. He'll hang, Sim. That is justice."

He'd never admired her more than he did then. "Caleb might get what's coming to him," Sim admitted quietly, "but he might go free again. How will you protect your people if that happens?"

"I won't be driven away," she said. "I won't become what he is, no matter what I have been."

His heart was too full to let him answer. Sim lifted his head, hearing a subtle yet unmistakable cry from the surrounding hills. The first howl came from less than half a mile away.

"Wolves," Eli said.

"The ones who brought me here," Tally added.

"Brought you here?" Eli asked. "How—"

A shriek burst from the treasure cave, followed by hideous laughter. Eli gingerly climbed down from his perch, cradling his wounded shoulder, and edged toward the crevice.

"I think Caleb has found his treasure," Sim said.

Eli asked a question with his eyes but didn't speak it. "It seems his curse is to be madness."

Another howl floated down from the hill, and Caleb's laughter ceased.

"You two had better go," Sim said.

Tally set her jaw and planted herself between Sim and the cave. "I won't let you kill him," she said. "He was your friend."

"Men like me and Caleb don't have friends."

"But you and Caleb aren't the same." Her eyes sparked with challenge. "You're more than a man, Sim. You have a choice."

Yes, he had a choice. And the wolves reminded him that he could choose the path of complete forgetfulness. They would accept him as one of them. He could leave the human world behind him forever. Humanity, friendship…love…all would become dreams of a past life, discarded along with shame and guilt and conscience.

He turned to Eli. "I have to do this, Patterson. Get her out of here." The words rasped his throat. "You and Miriam…take care of her."

"This is madness," Tally said. "You act as if there is no other way. As if—" She broke off and stared at the trampled earth between them. "I won't let you protect Cold Creek at the cost of your soul."

"I don't need Cold Creek or you or anyone to give me reason to kill Caleb," Sim said. "He's done me harm enough."

"You said you came back here to find the treasure for me. Whatever it is, I don't want it. You've…more than paid for services rendered. You don't have to see me ever again."

Services rendered. Tally threw his cruel words back in his face. Hadn't she figured out that he regretted his accusations at Los Granates, that he wanted to make it right?

He had only one way of doing that, whether or not she understood. Only one woman had ever loved him, and he intended to leave her safe and free.

"Listen to me, Sim," she said, driven to pleading by his silence. "All I ask is that you leave Caleb's punishment for the law. Take my horse and ride out of this canyon. Don't look back."

"Are you sending *me* away?" he asked with a mocking smile.

Suddenly she raised the rifle and pointed it at him. "Yes. All those things you said at Los Granates—you were right. When I spoke of my feelings for you, I lied to both of us. Love was driven out of me long ago. But Cold Creek is still mine, and I want you gone before you can ruin what I have left. I'll send your wages wherever you—"

"Hang my wages," Sim said. She was talking too fast, trying too hard to make him think she had turned on him as completely as he'd betrayed her at the party. But she hadn't. She'd forgiven him somewhere between Los Granates and Castillo Canyon. He just couldn't forgive himself.

"Eli, give me your gun," he said.

"Hell, man, you're naked as the day you were born. You need more than a gun, and this one—" He holstered it firmly. "It isn't going to kill again."

With a swift, easy motion Sim snatched the rifle from Tally's hold. "This'll do as well."

Eli let his hand fall. "Tally was right," he said gravely. "You have a choice now, Kavanagh. Maybe there's hope for you, but this is your last chance to take it."

The wolves howled, even closer than before. They called for Sim to join them, now and forever.

"You hear them?" he asked Eli. "That's my choice."

Gray-furred shapes appeared on the ledge where Eli had stood and on every other surface that could hold them. Three more wolves ran through the arena entrance, crouching behind Sim like triple shadows. Eli went for his gun.

"No," Tally said. "These wolves belong to Sim."

"They don't belong to no one," Sim said. "But I reckon they consider me one of them."

"What are you?" Eli whispered.

Sim Changed. He felt his wounded leg heal as his shape altered. Eli watched with fascination and horror.

"Don't pull your gun, no matter what you see," Tally warned, her voice clear and yet strangely distant to Sim's lupine ears.

Head and tail high, Sim stood before the trio of wolves.

One of them was the pack leader. He had chosen loyalty to Sim over raw instinct and offered no challenge. He obeyed Sim's unspoken command, drawing his mate and the third wolf into a circle around Tally. Two more wolves jumped down from the ledge and advanced on Eli, holding him at bay.

"Tally—" Eli said.

"It's all right." The three wolves began to herd Tally toward the arena entrance. She didn't resist, perhaps fearing that Eli would try to defend her if she struggled. Tears ran down her cheeks. She tried to look back over her shoulder, but the wolves pressed at her legs until she had entered the cleft.

Sim Changed back and faced Eli. "Now you know," he said. "Tally's known for some time. She was always safe with me." The half-truth, one of the last he would ever have to speak, slipped off his tongue with ease. "You won't have to be afraid for her any more."

Eli supported his injured shoulder, staining his hands with blood. "What do you want of me?"

"Only what I said before. You stay alive and see that Tally gets back to Cold Creek. She still trusts you."

"If she does, it's more than I deserve." Eli gave a strangled laugh. "I don't know what's real anymore."

"You have Miriam. She's real enough."

He didn't mean for the bitterness to show, but Eli heard it. "God knows why," he said, "but Tally's heart hasn't changed. She wants you to stay."

"That ain't possible. But I have one question before you go. You said that André hurt Tally, but you didn't explain what you meant."

Eli's expression closed up like a fist. "He lied to her. He—"

"I don't mean about the map. Did André have something to do with her time in New Orleans?"

"How do you know about that?"

"Tally told me about New Orleans when we were at the party. Someone at Los Granates recognized her."

Eli turned away, hunching under his burden of pain and sorrow. "She worked so hard to leave the past behind." He glared at Sim. "You judge her for that—you, of all earthly creatures?"

"I don't judge her. I only want to know how it happened...how she got to be what she was."

"I might ask the same of you," Eli muttered. "She didn't talk about André?"

"No."

"Then I don't understand. When I said that about André hurting her, I thought she knew."

"Knew what?"

"That it was André who arranged to sell her to that man who came to her farm when she was just a child. Sold her just like they sold my Miriam."

The rest of the story poured out of Eli as if he knew his strength wouldn't last much longer. When he was finished, his legs crumpled beneath him, and Sim half carried him to the arena entrance.

"You're done here," Sim said. "Go to Tally."

Eli nodded, too weak to have summoned an argument even if he'd wanted to. He didn't notice when Sim took his gun. Once Sim was sure Eli had reached the other side of the crevice, he returned to the treasure cave. Half a dozen wolves gathered behind him.

"Come on out, Caleb," he said. "The game is over."

"YOU HAVE TO LET ME go to him."

Tally's voice was hoarse from pleading, but the wolves were implacable guardians. They could not be reasoned with, nor did they budge one step from Tally's side. When Eli stumbled from the crevice, they simply edged out of his path and closed ranks behind him.

Eli was in a bad way. Tally took as much of his weight as she could handle and eased him down on a flat rock. His bandages were all but useless now. Soon he would begin to lose more blood than even the best care could hope to restore.

She sat beside Eli, holding him upright. "Sim?"

"I…can't stop him," Eli said. "I'm sorry, Tally."

Tally shook her head. It wasn't his fault. It was no one's fault but her own. She'd already lost André. Eli would die, too, if she didn't get him to someone who could properly treat his wounds.

Sim had made his choice. She'd dared to believe she could hold a being so powerful and wild, hold him and make him change. She'd failed him in so many ways, but the greatest failure was letting him lose himself.

She used all her strength to pull Eli to his feet and started back down the canyon. The wolves stayed at the foot of the pinnacles. Waiting. Listening, as she did, for the sound of a fatal gunshot. But the world remained eerily silent except for the harsh sawing of Eli's breath and the uneven thump of her own heartbeat.

Bart's mare was waiting where Tally had left her, guarded by a single wolf. Bruja pricked up her ears and nickered in equine joy as Tally approached. The wolf loped away. Its job was done.

Tally pushed and cajoled Eli into the saddle. By the time she saw the smoke from the Bryson chimney, Eli was slumped over the saddle horn and barely conscious. Tally took a hand-kerchief from her pocket, wiped the tears and grime from her face, and urged Bruja to a faster pace.

Beth was working in the corral near the house, pouring grain into a trough for a pair of spotted cows. She caught sight of Tally and dropped the sack. A moment later she was running for the house.

She came out again, followed by both her parents. Mrs. Bryson took one look at Eli and returned to the house. Beth dashed up to Tally, wide-eyed and breathless.

"What's happened?" she asked. "How did Mr. Patterson get hurt?"

"I'll tell you as soon as we get Eli inside," Tally said. "We'll need fresh bandages and hot water—"

"Ida is preparing them now," Miles Bryson said, joining his daughter. "Let's get him down."

Tally and Bryson wrestled Eli from the saddle and carried him to the house, while Beth looked after Bruja. Mrs. Bryson led the way to the guest room. She'd already turned back the covers and had a stack of wide cotton strips piled on the bedside table. She helped her husband and Tally lay Eli on the bed, then pulled up a chair, examining the injured man with a detachment born of experience.

"It's a bullet wound," Tally said, "but I don't know if the bullet is still inside. Eli rode all the way here from Cold Creek in that condition."

"He's lost a lot of blood," Bryson said, "but I reckon he'd be dead if the bullet hit anything important."

Ida Bryson stared at Tally for a moment, and Tally realized that this was the first time they'd met since she had revealed her female identity to Miles. It was even possible that a rumor of the events at Los Granates had reached Castillo Canyon.

"I know something of tending such wounds," Mrs. Bryson said, returning her attention to Eli. She began to pry the blood-soaked bandages from his shoulder. "I'll clean him up as best I can, but he'll need a doctor right quick."

Bryson met Tally's gaze. "How did it happen?"

"Caleb Smith came back to Cold Creek while Sim and I

were away. He…shot Eli and left him for dead, but Eli followed him."

"Was Smith coming for Beth?" Bryson asked grimly.

"No. He wanted something else in Castillo Canyon, and he would have killed anyone to get it." She closed her eyes. "He killed André."

"I'm sorry, Miss Bernard."

"Caleb won't be troubling anyone again."

"Is he dead?"

"Sim went after him."

Everyone fell silent, Mrs. Bryson concentrating on her work as Miles considered what Tally had told him. He must have suspected that there was a great deal more to the story than she'd admitted.

"You're afraid for Sim," he said at last.

"Not…not for his survival."

Beth walked into the room, gingerly holding a tub of steaming water in both hands. She set it down on the table. Mrs. Bryson dropped the soiled bandages into a wooden bucket and peered at the exposed wound.

"It looks as though the bullet went clean through," she said. "Whoever took care of him the first time did good work. But he still needs a doctor."

"I can go," Beth volunteered.

Mrs. Bryson dipped a clean cloth into the hot water, oblivious to the steam that scalded her work-chapped hands. "No. I won't have you leaving this farm."

Beth bowed her head. "I wouldn't go anywhere else," she said in a small voice. "Only to the doctor—"

"Haven't you learned anything?" Mrs. Bryson began to blot at the dried and fresh blood on Eli's shoulder. He groaned. "You'd best get some whiskey in case he wakes up," she said to her husband. "Then you can ride to Willcox."

"Not until I see Caleb Smith's body," Bryson said.

Tally thought of André lying dead at Cold Creek. "If you'll lend me a fresh horse, I'll go myself," she said.

"From the look of you, you're in no state to ride anywhere," Bryson said. He left the room. Beth followed him. Tally heard low voices, and then Bryson returned with a glass and a bottle of whiskey. "Go to the kitchen and get something to eat. We'll do what we can for your friend."

Tally murmured her thanks and half stumbled from the room. Beth had filled a plate with biscuits and beans and set it on the kitchen table. Tally sank down into the chair and stared at the food, scarcely able to remember how to lift the fork to her mouth.

"I'm sorry about your brother," Beth said, sitting opposite Tally. She drew a pattern on the tabletop with a bitten fingernail. "Eli will be all right, won't he?"

"He's a strong man. He has a good reason to go on living."

"Miriam?"

Tally nodded and picked up the fork.

"You said Sim went after Caleb," Beth said.

"Yes."

"You love Sim."

Tally pushed the plate away. "Yes."

"If you aren't afraid Caleb will hurt him, why are you crying?"

Tally looked up, meeting Beth's worried eyes. "I don't think he's coming back."

"Why not?" Beth demanded. "He loves you, too."

He never said it, Tally wanted to shout. *He never told me. But he lived it, every day. He made me believe.*

"Sometimes love isn't enough," she said. "Other things get in the way."

Beth got up and paced around the table. "It's…it's not because of what happened in Tombstone? Because of me?"

"No, Beth." Tally stood and pulled Beth into a hard embrace. "It has nothing to do with you." She stroked Beth's dark hair. "Sim and I are...very different. I just didn't know how much."

Beth returned her hug fiercely and sniffed. "Sim is stupid if he leaves you."

But it wasn't only Tally he was leaving. That she could have borne. She could find peace in her own heart if she knew he would keep looking for the redemption that had eluded him, searching until he found a love strong enough to make him whole. But she knew he didn't care enough about himself to try.

"We're all stupid sometimes," she said. "But if we're lucky, we learn. And we go on as best we can." She let Beth go. "I should get ready to ride to Willcox. If you can lend me your fastest horse—"

"You'll get your horse, but not the fastest," Bryson said as he walked into the kitchen. "Beth will need Roadrunner. You can take Honcho to return to Cold Creek."

Beth stared at her father. "You'll let me go?"

Bryson sighed. "I reckon you have a debt to pay, and this is your chance." He looked at Tally. "It can't have been long since you lost your brother. You have business to attend to at home. We'll see that Eli gets cured and send him back to Cold Creek when he's ready."

Tally scrubbed at her face. "Mrs. Bryson—"

"Don't worry about Ida. She understands better than she lets on."

"Thank you, Miles." Tally squeezed Beth's hand. "You do exactly as your father tells you. Don't take any chances—Eli would never forgive himself if you were hurt, and neither would I."

Beth lifted her chin. "I'll be careful."

"Go change and pack your bedroll," Bryson said to his daughter. "I'll saddle the horses." He nodded to Tally and went out the front door. Beth hurried to her room. Tally returned to Eli.

He had come back to consciousness, his gaze fixed on the ceiling as Mrs. Bryson finished tying off the fresh bandages. The whiskey bottle stood untouched on the bedside table.

"Tally?" he said, hoarse with pain.

"I'm here." She crouched beside the bed and took Eli's hand. "You'll be all right, Eli." She smiled at Mrs. Bryson. "Thank you."

Mrs. Bryson rose, gathering the unused cloth and bucket of soiled bandages. "You're welcome," she said brusquely. "Don't tire him too much—he needs rest. I'll be in the kitchen."

"She's a…good woman," Eli said as Mrs. Bryson closed the door behind her.

"Yes, she is. Just like her daughter."

"Like you. You all right?"

"I'll be fine. Beth is riding for a doctor, and I'm returning to Cold Creek. I need to see André."

"Miriam…she talked it over with Federico before I left. They sent Pablo for the law and…someone to look after—"

"Hush. I only came to say goodbye. You rest, Eli. Get well, for Miriam's sake."

His eyes drifted shut. "I have to…tell Miriam about the army. About my father. She doesn't know the truth. I have to…"

"You can tell her when you're home." Tally bent to kiss Eli's cheek. "I'll tell her what's most important."

"I love her. Ask her to…forgive…." He breathed deeply and sank into exhausted sleep. Tally slid her hand from his.

"I will, my friend." *I'll ask her to pray for us all.*

CHAPTER TWENTY-TWO

TALLY SAT ON THE PORCH, listening to the happy laughter of Pablo and Dolores playing in the yard. The November day was cool with the promise of frost, but for the children it might as well have been midsummer. For them, the world hadn't changed at all.

A week ago André had died. Yesterday the folk of Cold Creek had buried him under a spreading, golden-leaved cottonwood, attended by the preacher who'd ridden from Tombstone with a deputy sheriff.

Since then, Tally had felt nothing. She knew that under the emptiness lay festering guilt over André's death, aching loneliness and grief for the loss of lives that could have been. Hers, André's, Sim's…they were all one now, blended together in a crucible of unvoiced sorrow.

Miriam had told her to cry. "You won't be right until you let it out," she'd said. "You got to mourn, child. That's the only way to healing."

But Miriam didn't understand. She had heard the whole story of what had happened in Castillo Canyon, except for the few facts Tally hadn't the right or desire to reveal. Miriam knew Sim wasn't coming back, and she'd wept for Tally's sake. She had prayed for Sim's soul as she'd prayed for Eli's recovery.

God had answered at least one of her prayers; Eli had come

home today, bundled up in the back of the Bryson wagon. Miriam took comfort in her faith and found continual proof of its power. Tally knew that she didn't have Miriam's strength, or her hope. What she did have was this ranch, days of hard work, and time. Perhaps even time enough to forget.

The front door opened, releasing the smell of baking bread. Miriam sat down beside Tally, tucking her skirts about her legs. A few moments later the deputy sheriff came out the door, tipped his hat to Tally and walked to the bunkhouse.

"Is he finished?" Tally asked.

"He wants to speak to Eli," Miriam said. "I asked him to wait until evening. He seems to like my cooking, so he didn't argue."

Tally nodded. The deputy didn't have much to do except take testimony about what had happened the day Caleb came to Cold Creek; there was little chance Caleb's body would ever be recovered. No one at the ranch had found it necessary to tell Deputy Osborn the whole truth about Sim Kavanagh, André and the map, and as long as he ate well, the deputy wasn't inclined to ask probing questions.

"Speaking of cooking," Miriam said, "you haven't eaten since yesterday morning. Am I going to have to feed you like a babe in arms?"

Tally reached for Miriam's hand. "I'll eat tonight at supper. I promise."

"Good. Between that deputy and Eli, I've been afraid you wouldn't get anything unless I fought those gluttons off with my frying pan."

Eli, Miriam had reported, was eating like a horse, giving his body the sustenance it needed to heal. According to Bryson, the doctor had been impressed with Eli's recuperative abilities and predicted a swift recovery. Beth was home in Castillo Canyon. Everyone was safe.

Tally was grateful. Eventually her heart would know it.

"Eli asked me a strange question today," Miriam said softly. "He asked if I still wanted to marry him."

Tally felt a twinge of concern. "What did you say?"

Miriam twisted the ring on her slender finger. "When he told Caleb that story about being in cahoots with André to find the treasure, I didn't know what to think. I was sick to hear that he'd fought with André and caused his accident. I couldn't believe that was my Eli talking. I've never been so…so—" She broke off, breathing deeply. "Then Eli was shot, and I didn't care what he'd done. I tried to stop him from going after Caleb, but he wouldn't listen."

"You couldn't have stopped him, Miriam."

"Because he wanted revenge for his father. If he'd told me the story before, I could have helped him, asked God to take the desire for vengeance out of his heart." She shivered. "Even though he believed in the curse of the treasure, he had to make sure that Caleb suffered his just punishment."

"He also helped me and Sim," Tally said. "I don't know what would have happened if he hadn't come. And he didn't…he didn't kill Caleb."

"Praise the Lord," Miriam murmured. "He couldn't. That was what he told me today. He begged my forgiveness for putting me and the folk here at risk, just because he couldn't kill Caleb long ago."

"He was a soldier, Miriam. Not a murderer."

"I knew he was a brave man, doing what he thought was right, protecting folk from danger. The army was his life. But he had to kill too many times. He got to where he couldn't kill any more. He was just waiting until he could take his leave honorably, so he could find peace. But when he found out that Caleb murdered his father, he broke the army law. He deserted."

Tally hugged her knees to her chest. Caleb had called Eli a "wanted criminal," but had never had the chance to explain.

"André knew," Miriam continued in a whisper. "Men came looking for Eli at Peñasco Rojo, but André didn't tell them Eli was working there. He let Eli know how he'd kept his secret. Eli felt beholden to him for that, even when he found out—" She wiped at her eyes. "Both André and Eli had too many secrets."

"Eli was afraid of losing you," Tally said.

"I know." Miriam sniffed and tried to smile. "Fool man, he thought I'd despise him more for deserting than if he'd killed Caleb. He didn't think I'd understand."

"Do you, Miriam?"

"Yes. Do you think I don't know what it is to hate? I have hated enough in my time. But it's no use, Tally. It wins us nothing. Eli realized that just in time." She gripped Tally's hand. "Can you forgive Eli for deceiving you and letting your brother be hurt?"

"I never hated him for that," Tally said. "He made mistakes, like André, like all of us. But he's a good man." She laid her head against Miriam's. "If he weren't, I wouldn't let you marry him."

Miriam hugged Tally close and let her go. "All wounds heal in God's good time," she said. She got up abruptly and went back into the house.

Tally didn't move. The sun descended over the western mountains, and she thought about chores that needed to be done by day's end. Winter was around the corner. Longer nights left plenty of hours for sitting in silence and imagining what might have been.

Imagining wolves howling in the hills....

She sat up straight, cocking her head. It wasn't imagination. The wolves were coming from the northeast, a whole pack of them.

Tally grabbed the porch railing and pulled herself to her feet, unable to trust the steadiness of her legs. Her heart banged inside her ribs. She stood absolutely still, afraid that if she moved again she would break the spell of hope.

Just as the wolves came near enough to alert everyone at Cold Creek, they grew quiet.

"No," Tally whispered. She took a step away from the porch. "No..."

A man stumbled out of the twilight. His clothes were ragged and stained, his face dark with many days' growth of beard, and his feet were bare. Tally could see the whites of his mad, rolling eyes.

It was Caleb Smith.

Tally turned, ready to run for the rifle she kept inside the front door. She paused as Caleb fell to his knees. His mouth opened and closed, but no sound emerged. The wolves circled around him—the same animals she remembered from Castillo Canyon, eyes burning red as they reflected the waning light.

A wolf nearly twice as large as the others broke from their ranks and stalked Caleb with stiff tail and lowered head. Caleb shrank to the ground, gibbering in terror.

"Sim," Tally said. "Sim!"

The wolf nudged Caleb with his muzzle and looked directly at Tally. He grinned in a lupine laugh. Then someone shouted from the bunkhouse, and he bounded away with the lesser wolves, headed back for the hills. Caleb remained on the ground, his arms crossed over his head.

Tally's legs buckled. Miriam rushed out of the house and helped her to her feet.

"I heard wolves," Miriam said. She peered into the yard and saw Caleb. "My Lord. It can't be."

Before Tally could respond, Bart and Deputy Osborn ran

into the yard. Federico came from the barn, Pablo and Dolores at his heels. He took one look at Caleb, stopped his children with outstretched arms and ordered them back to their cabin.

Osborn, his gun aimed at Caleb, edged close to Tally. "Is that who I think it is?" he asked.

She tried to measure her breaths, one by one. "Caleb Smith."

"I thought you said he'd been mortally wounded in the fight with your foreman and ran off into the mountains. He don't look dead to me. And why in hell would he come back here…beggin' your pardon, Miss Bernard?"

Tally almost smiled, remembering how often Sim swore and how seldom he apologized for it. "I don't think he came willingly, Mr. Osborn."

"Then how—" A wolf wailed less than a quarter mile away. "Did I hear wolves near the house?"

"You did." Tally clasped her hands and swallowed the laughter that threatened to make her look as crazy as Caleb. "I think you had better take your prisoner into custody, Deputy."

Osborn nodded and approached Caleb as if he still expected a battle. Caleb offered no resistance. He let the deputy handcuff him and drag him to his feet. His eyes stared at nothing; a thin line of spittle dripped from his half-open mouth.

"He don't seem to need medical attention," Osborn called, keeping Caleb at a safe distance from the womenfolk. "Just scratched and bruised, a few older injuries. No bullet wounds. You sure you saw him shot?"

"I'm not sure of anything now, Deputy," Tally said, feigning confusion. "I am…I am shocked to see him here. I'm afraid I—" She pretended to swoon. Miriam caught one of her arms, and Federico hurried to support her as she went limp.

"Please take that man away," Miriam said in her firmest voice. "Miss Tally has been through enough."

"I expect she has," Osborn said. "I'll just secure him in the bunkhouse and talk to Miss Bernard in the morning."

"Thank you, sir. I'll bring you a nice supper just as soon as it's ready."

Osborn grinned at his good fortune and hauled Caleb to the bunkhouse. Bart followed Miriam, Tally and Federico into the kitchen.

"I ain't never seen Miss Tally swoon," Bart remarked in a worried tone.

"And you haven't yet," Tally said. She straightened and patted Federico's arm. "I didn't want Deputy Osborn to ask any more questions tonight."

"The wolves brought Caleb here?" Federico asked, on the verge of crossing himself.

Miriam, Bart and Federico stared at Tally. She took a seat at the kitchen table, suddenly weak again.

"I saw it with my own eyes," she said.

"Mr. Kavanagh didn't kill Caleb," Miriam said.

Tally folded her hands on the table and rested her forehead against them. No, Sim hadn't killed his treacherous friend. Perhaps he'd done something almost as bad, driving Caleb to complete insanity, not that he'd had far to go. But there was a certain justice in reducing Caleb to what André had become before he'd died.

And Sim had chosen not to take another life. It didn't matter why.

"Is Sim coming back?" Bart asked.

"I don't think so, Bart," Tally said. "It's over." She raised her head and gratefully accepted the mug of coffee Miriam pressed into her hands. "Caleb Smith won't hurt anyone ever again."

No one spoke for a long while. Bart chewed on the ends of his mustache. Miriam finished preparing supper, and Federico went to fetch the children. True to her promise, Tally ate what she could, barely tasting the food. Perilous emotion waited at the edge of her thoughts, ready to sweep her away if she let down her guard for an instant.

She was grateful when the men returned to their bunks and Miriam took trays to Eli and Osborn. She sat at the table long after Miriam had gone to bed and the house had taken on the chill of night. She heard no more wolves.

Her bed was cold and empty. She removed her clothes in the dark and put on her nightshirt by rote, staring at the wall with unseeing eyes.

"You ain't been getting enough sleep," a deep voice said behind her.

She sat down hard on the edge of the bed. "Sim?"

He was all in shadow save for the square of moonlight that splashed his bare shoulder. "You're too thin," he accused. "Damn it, Tally, ain't you been eating?"

Tally pressed her hands to her face. "Why are you here?"

His feet made barely any sound as he paced from one end of the room to the other. "I couldn't stay away. I tried. I couldn't—" He spun to face her. "I couldn't go without telling you."

Dieu. Tally let her hands fall to her lap. There were so many thousands of things they could say to each other, but only a few words mattered now.

Stay with me. Love me.

"I'm sorry, Sim," she said. "I'm sorry for deceiving you about my past. I never got a chance to say that."

"I didn't give you one." He cleared his throat. "I was wrong, Tally. Everything I said to you... I had no right."

Tally tried to make out his features, but Sim stayed out of the light. "Thank you," she said simply.

"Damnation. I don't deserve no thanks."

"But I'm grateful to you, Sim. For saving my life, and Eli's. For stopping Caleb. And for not killing him."

Sim strode to the far wall and leaned against it, hand spread above his head. "He deserved it," he muttered. "But when it came time, I…" He slapped the wall. "Something's different in me, Tally. I don't know myself anymore. You…changed me."

"You changed me, too."

"I just about ruined your life."

"No, Sim. Before you came, I…didn't want to trust any man. Oh, there were a few I relied on, like Eli and Federico, and I loved my brother. But I wanted to hide from the world so I wouldn't have to deal with men except on my own terms. You came to Cold Creek like a whirlwind and made me realize I couldn't hide any longer."

"Because you *trusted* me?" He laughed. "I should have made you hate men even more."

"It didn't happen that way. It would have been easier, but…" She couldn't finish. There were no words to describe what she wanted to say. Words were like shadows, hiding the truth. "There are some things more powerful than trust."

"You loved André," he said.

"Yes."

"Even though he betrayed you?"

"He was my brother."

"Just because someone's kin don't make him worth hurting over."

"Did you hate your mother, Sim?"

She asked the question half in anger, half with a genuine need to understand. She regretted it instantly. He'd already given her the answer.

But he sighed, a harsh and ragged breath that in anyone else would have portended tears. "I hated her," he said. "And…I loved her."

Tally almost went to him then, but she knew it would be a mistake. He was too vulnerable now, when he'd just admitted he was capable of love—love for a woman who had neglected and despised him.

"She was my mother," he said, as if he had to explain. "I should have been able to save her."

"Save her?" Tally pounded the mattress with her fist. "When you were three years old? Or five?"

"I knew more at eight than most boys do at eighteen," he said. "If I'd taken her away…"

"You couldn't, Sim. She'd been in the life too long. I know. If I hadn't gotten out when I did…"

She heard Sim move closer to the bed. "You said you were tricked into it. Do you still blame yourself?"

"No."

"You're lying, Tally. You tried to defend yourself when I said them bad things about you, but in the end you let me go."

"I knew I couldn't hold you—"

"You tried to stop me from killing Caleb, but not because you thought I'd come back. You didn't think you were good enough. Good enough for *me*. Just like you didn't think you were ever good enough for André." He hesitated, and Tally felt the wind of his passing as he paced the room. "There's something I got to tell you, something Eli told me. Don't blame him…. He thought you already knew. I made him explain what he meant when he said André had hurt you enough."

"He—"

"When you were still a kid and he wasn't much older, André got himself into bad gambling debt with some dangerous men in New Orleans. But your family was poor, and he couldn't repay what he owed even after he stole what little your ma'd put aside for his education."

Tally shook her head in bewilderment. She remembered how sick *Maman* had been the year before she left for New Orleans, how there never seemed to be enough money for food or medicine.

"André was supposed to have a job on the Beaudry farm," she said. "I tried to get work, but they wouldn't hire a girl."

"André didn't pay them gamblers back by working at a farm. They threatened to kill him."

"Eli told you this?"

"He told me what André said to him in Texas, during one of his drunks. I guess even André couldn't live with his guilt. He had to tell someone—anyone—as long as it wasn't you." Sim growled in his chest. "André made a bargain to save his own skin. He brought a man to meet you—a man who said he'd take you away and marry you so you'd have money to send back home."

A man. A man whose name Tally couldn't remember now. But she could still see his bright blue eyes and his white smile, hear his smooth voice making wonderful promises of a life she could scarcely imagine. He had seemed such a perfect gentleman.

"André convinced you that you'd never get any better than what the man offered, and you wanted to help your ma. So you went away with the man. But he didn't marry you. And André knew he never would."

CHAPTER TWENTY-THREE

No. The man hadn't married her. He'd taken her away just as he'd promised—to New Orleans, where the elegant ladies and fancy shops had dazzled her ignorant country sensibilities. He'd brought her to a place filled with velvet furnishings and laughter and the smell of perfume. Tally had watched the girls in their lacy underthings, while the man had talked to a round-faced woman with red paint on her cheeks.

She hadn't guessed anything was wrong when the woman had told her she was to spend the night in her own room while the man attended other business. He would come for her later. But that night she would be given a pretty gown and have her hair done, and see what it was like to be an important lady.

Tally grabbed handfuls of the bed quilt and felt the fabric tear under her fingers. The memories hadn't been so vivid in years. It was as if she had to speak them aloud to dispel them once and for all, even though Sim might be the last man in the world to understand.

"The man never came back for me," she whispered. "He left me in that place. The next night the madam told me La Belle Hélène would be my new home, and I had to earn my keep or my *maman* would find out I wasn't married after all. So I listened to the things she told me. But I didn't understand until the other man came to my room."

Sim made a terrible, wrenching sound. "Do you remember his name?"

"No. It hurt so much. I only wanted it to be over. But it wasn't over. Not the next night, or the next. And Madame Lucy kept telling me that I mustn't let *Maman* find out, or she would die of shame. But I could help her with the money I earned. So I stayed."

"It wasn't your fault."

She hardly heard him. "I hated all the men who came to see me, but I learned to pretend. Madame Lucy and some of the other women taught me how to speak like the rich folk from the Garden District and write with a beautiful hand. I had the finest gowns. I was given books to read, because some men liked women who could talk to them in a way their wives could not. And I wrote to André from a false address, asking him to tell *Maman* I was happy. He said that my money was making her well."

"He didn't give your ma a red cent."

"I never knew. She died the next year. But by then I was used to La Belle Hélène. I was never hungry. I had friends... like Miriam, who worked as a maid there. So I kept sending the money for André's education, until he stopped writing."

"He used your money to buy into Peñasco Rojo."

"I didn't know where he had gone. I learned to live from day to day, and 'Mademoiselle Champagne' became a great success. I laughed, I flirted, I played my part so well that the richest and most successful men flocked to me."

Sim was quiet a long time. "You hated those men."

"But I convinced myself that I had power over them, that I used them as they used me. Until a...one of my clients made me do something...something I couldn't bear. I fought him. I had never resisted before, but I felt clean for the first time in years. While he was shouting at Madame Lucy, I realized how I'd deceived myself. I had nothing—no power, no pride. Miriam gave me the courage to leave La Belle Hélène."

"No one had to give you that."

Tally shook her head. "We went to live in a respectable part of town. Somehow Miriam and I scraped by, but the money I had saved finally ran out. That was when I met Nathan Meeker, at one of the finer shops on Rue Royale. He was older and rich and looking for a young wife. He assumed I was lady, a true lady, and I let him believe it. I didn't love him. I thought I could learn to respect him, finally have a real home of my own."

"You didn't have nowhere else to go."

"I married him because I was used to pretty things and good food, and I didn't want to be poor and alone again. But marriage to Nathan was no different than being a whore. He used me…in bed, as a pretty ornament on his arm. I was his mistress, not his wife. But when he discovered what I had been in New Orleans, he became so enraged that he suffered an apoplexy and never recovered."

"He got what he deserved."

It didn't seem possible that Sim was saying such things, or that André had done what he claimed. Nothing was real anymore, nothing certain.

"Nathan didn't have a chance to change his will before he died," she said. "He left me little enough—a bit of cash, some jewelry, my clothing. But André had found me and written from his ranch in Texas. I told him…what I'd been, and he didn't turn me away. I was grateful. He treated me like family. Except for Miriam, he was all I had."

"He thought he could ease his guilt just by letting you live with him."

"I…I could see he had made mistakes while we were apart. I thought if we'd stayed a family, if I hadn't let that man fool me, I could have helped André be stronger. I didn't want him to be stained forever, as I was. I was so happy when he decided to break away from the men who were taking advantage of him. We could both leave our old lives behind."

"He only left Texas because of the map," Sim said harshly. "Everything that happened to you came from his greed."

Tally's eyes were dry and aching, bereft of tears. "He knew I loved Cold Creek from the moment I saw it. There were times when we barely had enough to keep it going. When André went to find the treasure…maybe he meant to make up for what he'd done."

"Do you believe that, Tally?"

"I want to." Her voice cracked. "I have to, Sim. He was family, and I never really knew him. He died with that guilt tearing at his heart. If I'd only known…"

"Stop it." Sim banged into the bedstead, rattling the brass posts as if they were prison bars. "Stop blaming yourself."

"But I am exactly like my brother," she whispered. "I deceived you, Nathan and the people of this Territory. If I don't…if I can't forgive André, how can I ever forgive—"

"How can you forgive me?" His weight pressed down the mattress beside her, and she smelled the heady masculine scent of his body and felt the warmth of his breath. "I thought I knew all about Caleb and what he could do. I figured I could control him when we went after his treasure. I reckoned he was my friend, because he was the only one I had for the first twenty years of my life."

She didn't dare touch his hand where it rested between them on the quilt. "I understand."

"No. You were wrong about André, and you're wrong about me. Caring about me. I was born into wickedness, and that's how I've lived."

"You didn't kill Caleb."

"I wanted to. The urge was in me, strong as ever. I'll do

more bad things—to you, to other good people—as long as I walk this earth as a man."

She drew her arms across her chest and jumped up from the bed. "So you'll go to live with the wolves, where you'll never face temptation again?"

"Wolves don't know right and wrong. They can't do evil. They only understand survival."

"And with them, you can forget. You won't have to feel guilt for what you've done."

He rolled off the bed on the other side, keeping it between them. "That's right. No guilt. No responsibility. No shame."

"No hope. No joy. No…no love."

She felt rather than saw his shrug. "I've done without them things most of my life."

Her heart tripped over itself. "You loved your mother, in spite of what she was. You loved Esperanza. You had dreams. You must have known joy."

Sim backed into the wall and closed his eyes. Oh, he'd felt joy…when he'd held Tally in his arms, when he'd known Beth was safe from Caleb…other times, too, since he'd come to Cold Creek. More than he'd felt in all the years before.

But he found contentment in running as a wolf, and in forgetfulness. In knowing he couldn't hurt Tally or Miriam or anyone else, because they were human and far beyond the scope of his animal existence.

"Can you be happy here, after Los Granates?" he asked hoarsely.

He could see Tally in darkness as she couldn't see him— all her beauty and grace and strength shining like starlight from her skin and eyes and hair. She turned toward him, searching.

"I will be," she said. "I'm not giving up on my dreams, Sim. Maybe the people in Sulphur Spring Valley won't accept me when they learn the rumors are true. But I'll prove to them that I am worthy of their respect and trust, even if it takes the rest of my life. I won't run. I still have my family—Miriam and Eli, Bart, Federico, the children. We believe in each other. We…know how to love."

Sim strode to the window and stared out the thick glass pane. The moon painted a path that seemed to lead straight up into the hills, where the pack waited for him.

"It's easier to give up," Tally said softly behind him. "If it weren't for André—no matter what else he did—I never would have found Cold Creek. If not for you and Beth, I might have gone on pretending to be a man just so I would never have to face being a woman. I don't know what I would have done if I could have changed into a wolf and run away forever." She moved closer, her bare feet brushing the floor. "But can you ever be truly one of them, Sim? Can you be only a wolf, when you're so much more?"

"They accept me. They don't care what I've been."

"Neither do I. I care about what you are now, what you *can* be."

He swung on her, fingers curled. "Don't."

Her sigh stirred the sensitive hair on his chest and sent shivers racing up his spine. "I can't change my feelings any more than I can change my past. I still love you, Sim."

"No."

"What did Esperanza say to you in the church in Dos Ríos?"

Startled by the sudden change of subject, Sim struggled for composure. "She blessed me."

"She absolved you of your sins?"

"Only priests can do that," he said bitterly.

"But you believed for a while that Esperanza had the power to save you."

"I was wrong."

"Even an angel couldn't absolve you, Sim. You know it can't be done until you face the darkness in yourself and ask forgiveness of the people you've hurt, even the ones who deserved to be punished. Even the boy you were and the man you became."

Sim saw Esperanza's face as clearly as if she were standing beside Tally, the two of them beating at him with their cursed compassion. He knew now that he should never have come back to Tally, not for a moment. She hadn't needed him to break the chains of André's treacherous legacy. She was already free.

He started for the door. Tally caught up with him. She touched his arm. He froze.

"There is one more thing I must know before you go to your wolves," she said. "You saw the treasure."

"I saw it," he said. "I buried it again."

"Good. I want no part of an evil that caused so much tragedy."

Sim wanted to laugh. It was right that she should realize how little she'd lost, but then she would also know that André had died for nothing.

"There wasn't any treasure," he said. "There used to be, a long time ago. But all I found in the crevice was a rock with a story scratched into it, some bones and a wooden cross."

Tally's fingers dug into his arm and slowly relaxed. "What was the story?"

He could remember every word, though he hadn't let it affect him then or any time since. "It was written in Spanish," he said, "by one of the men who stole the treasure. He was the one who made the curse."

"He must have been an evil man."

"He didn't die evil."

"Tell me."

He pulled his arm from her grip and bowed his head. "A hundred years ago, a great hacendado, grateful for the blessings given to him by God, sent a caravan carrying gold and silver and holy relics as an offering to a new church in Guaymas. The treasure was guarded by a priest and soldiers, but *bandidos* waylaid the caravan and killed all the men, including the priest. The bandits ran north into the mountains we call the Chirica-huas. Five men started out with mules and the panniers of gold and silver. One was killed by Apaches, one by the bite of a snake, and two more by a bitter fight over division of the spoils."

"The curse was already at work," Tally murmured.

"One man survived, and he hid the treasure in the place the last three men had chosen. He made a map to remind him how to find it, so he could pass the treasure on to his children if he didn't get back to the mountains. He returned to Sonora to find his family dead of disease.

"Every day after that he had only bad luck. He could trust no one to help him take the treasure. Finally he recognized that his evil deed had condemned him. He became a monk, devoting himself to holy works. But he kept the map, unable to part with it. He went to live in a small village where he could be at peace. Eventually he told the bishop how to re-cover the treasure and return it to the Church."

"And they found it."

"They found it, but no one else knew, not even the monk. A man in the village discovered the map among the monk's few possessions when the monk was away. Soon after that the monk fell ill, and he saw the villager putting poison in his food. So the monk called a curse down on the map and wrote a warning, hoping the village man would heed it and save his own soul. He left the map and the village, and spent the last of his strength returning to the mountains, where he carved out his story."

Tally released her breath. "He cursed the map. He wasn't able to forgive."

"But he did. Just before he died, he wrote that he regretted the curse—that it wasn't his business to judge the sins of men. That such a right belonged only to God. He believed someone would find the hiding place someday, and he left a message that he hoped would make up for the evil he'd done."

Sim remembered brushing his fingers across those last sentences, laughing bitterly to himself. The joke was on him, on Caleb, on André. On all of them, all the men who thought they could take the short and easy road.

"The message," Tally urged. "What was the message?"

"Ye who enter here," Sim recited, "if you have come so far and survived the curse of greed and avarice, then you may hope to find the world's true treasures. Love, forgiveness, and life itself."

"*Mon Dieu.*" Tally leaned against the door frame, trembling as if with fever. "He understood…he saw the best and worst that people can be. Just like you and me."

"It was a story," Sim said. "Maybe it was all a lie. The dreams of a dying man."

"When Caleb asked you what the treasure was, you told him it was truth. You knew what it meant, Sim. You knew."

Sim flung open the door and ran, from the room and from the house. The wolves howled. The way to the hills was swift and sure. Inevitable.

"Sim!"

Tally's voice tugged at him like a chain on a half-wild dog. He stopped halfway across the yard.

"I know you hear me, Sim. I won't try to hold you. I never could. But please…don't give up on life. Go wherever you must, but don't give up. Keep searching. Search for the truth until you recognize it and make it your own." She retreated, fading from his senses. "I'll never forget you. *Adieu, mon seul amour.*"

She vanished—from sight and scent and hearing, from every sense so vastly superior to any human's. She had set him free. He need never look back.

A howl bubbled up in his chest and died there.

He saw the best and worst that people can be. Just like you and me.

The best and the worst. Tally and Sim. Sim and Tally.

Sim fell to his knees and began to laugh. He knew the truth. He'd known it from the day he first saw Tally dressed like a boy and staring him straight in the eye like the orneriest son of a bitch in the Territory.

That damn fool monk was right.

Weak as a day-old pup, Sim climbed to his feet. Miriam stood in the doorway, clutching a wrapper to her chest with one hand and holding a lantern in the other. Her mouth opened as she took in his state of undress. Then she grinned.

"Well, I never! Simeon Kavanagh, you no-account, scoundrelly, wicked—"

He bounded past her, down the hall and to the door of Tally's room. It was shut. He didn't knock. He pushed the door open with his shoulder. Tally stood by the window, but not for long. He lifted her off her feet and kissed her as earnestly as any man had ever kissed the woman he loved.

"Sim!" she gasped between kisses. "You—"

"Miriam already told me. I'm a no-account—" he nuzzled her neck "—scoundrelly—" he nipped her shoulder "—wicked—"

She silenced him with a kiss of such vehemence that they both fell back onto the bed. He raised himself up and gazed down at her bewildered, beloved face.

"There was something else I forgot to tell you," he said.

"What could that be, *mon loup?*"

"I can't go looking somewhere else for truth and hope and all those other things that make life worth living. It's right here." He kissed her again. "I love you." He laughed like a drunk. "I love you, Chantal Bernard. I lo—"

She took the words from his lips and gave them back again. "I love you, Simeon Wartrace Kavanagh. With all my heart."

He touched his forehead to hers. "Then it ain't too late to find that forgiveness you mentioned? Make up for all the evil I've done?"

"You were never evil, Sim," she whispered. "Only human."

A strange sensation gathered in the pit of Sim's belly and worked its way up into his throat. After a moment he realized that his face was wet and he couldn't catch his breath for the sobs coming out of his chest.

He was weeping like a baby. Like a woman. Weeping for his mother, for Caleb, for all the people he'd hurt, even the ones who'd done worse things than he could imagine. Weeping for the innocent boy he'd been so long ago.

"I'm sorry," he croaked. "I'm sorry."

Tally's eyes were glossed with tears like his own, spilling over her cheeks to soak the pillows and the golden strands of her hair. Sim felt worn, soft cloth against his face and recognized the handkerchief his mother had made for him so long ago. In some strange way, his mother was finally trying to comfort him.

"You aren't alone anymore, my dearest one," Tally said. "We have started the journey together, and we will find our own treasure. We'll make it right. Together."

"You'd best make it right," Miriam said. "And as soon as possible."

Lantern light beamed through the open doorway. Sim stiffened and dragged his arm across his face. "Can't a man get no privacy in this house?" he demanded.

Miriam clucked like a mother hen. "Not a man who runs around naked as a robin and accosts ladies in their bedrooms. My Lord, what is this world coming to? If you intend on staying, Sim Kavanagh, I expect you to make an honest woman of my Tally."

Sim grinned. "I wouldn't take her any other way."

"Then you put on some clothes like a decent person and get out of Miss Tally's boudoir this instant!"

He almost obeyed. He sat back instead, turning his head so that Miriam could see his weakness. His humanity. His hope of salvation. And his love.

"Do you know of a preacher around these parts, Miriam?" he asked.

Miriam studied his face. Her stern features softened, and in them he saw the deep affection she felt for Tally and Eli, the strength and compassion that had been Tally's support during the hard times.

"It just so happens," Miriam said, "that a preacher man left Cold Creek this very morning."

Sim glanced at Tally, looking for the pain of André's death. But her face was at peace. He kissed her brow and jumped off the bed. Miriam's eyes widened in understanding just as he grabbed her and kissed her soundly on the mouth.

She pushed him away with arms made strong from kneading bread and scrubbing laundry. "If you don't put on some clothes this instant, I'm going to scream, and Eli will get right out of his bed and tear off his bandages, and you'll be to blame if he sickens all over again!"

Sim covered his parts in pretended shame. "Eli has to save his strength for you. He's going to need it."

"Miriam!" Tally said from the bed. "This is only the second time I've seen you blush."

Miriam put her hands to her face and rolled her eyes heav-

enward. "Lord give me strength." She addressed Tally, stead-
fastly ignoring Sim. "Eli and I were thinking…if it wouldn't
disappoint you too much…we were thinking of not waiting
for January to be married. We don't need a fancy wedding,
and after all that's happened…"

Tally leaped out of bed. "That's wonderful, Miriam. But will
Eli—" She mirrored Miriam's flush. "Will Eli be able to—"

"Don't you worry about him, missy. You got your own
problems." She glared at Sim and suddenly smiled, opening
her arms in an embrace that took in the whole wide world. "I
think if we send Pablo on our fastest horse soon as dawn
breaks, we might even catch that preacher before he reaches
Tombstone."

Sim whooped loud enough to wake the dead. Tally
laughed. The wolves howled, mournful and sweet, and faded
into the hills.

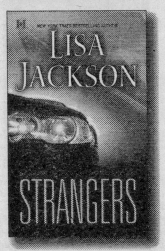

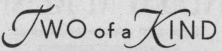